RUNES

To Tori
Enjoy another adventure

RUNES

ALEX WALKER

Alex Walker

DEEDS PUBLISHING | ATLANTA

Published by Deeds Publishing in Athens, GA
www.deedspublishing.com

Printed in The United States of America

Cover design by Matt King

Library of Congress Cataloging-in-Publications data is available upon request.

ISBN 978-1-947309-25-8

Books are available in quantity for promotional or premium use. For information, email info@deedspublishing.com.

First Edition, 2018

10 9 8 7 6 5 4 3 2 1

This book is dedicated to my old friend George Scott, an early mentor to me and my novels, a book seller, and Director of the charitable organization Books for Heroes that distributes books all over the world to our men and women in the military. George is one of the main characters in this and two other books as the inscrutable Professor George Scott.

PROLOGUE

The Caribbean Sea, 1632 AD

The Nuestra Señora de la Merida, a graceful looking Spanish galleon, slipped through the rolling swells like a wounded whale. With a 39-foot beam and 112-foot hull, the helmsman manipulated the wheel as best he could to take advantage of the favorable westerly wind pushing against her billowing three masted sails. There was a reason for the ship's sluggishness. She was a *Nave real del Tesoro*—Royal Treasure ship. The holds were filled with gold bullion, ingots, gold and silver coins, precious gemstones, and rare artifacts from the new world—a treasure weighing no less than ten tons. Her destination was the port city of Seville and the royal treasuries of reigning King Phillip III.

The ingots, coins, and bullion had been minted at the LaCasa de Monede de Mexico located in Mexico City. This was the first mint built in the new world and established in 1535. Like many other treasure laden ships before her, the cache had been transported from Mexico City to the port city of Veracruz and then loaded on the Spanish galleon for transport across the Atlantic. The galleon would have normally followed the usual northeast trade route through the Gulf of Mexico with a brief stop in Havana. The route would have continued past the Bahamas through the Northeast Providence Channel and then into the Atlantic Ocean with a stop in the Azores and then on to Spain. This voyage would be different and would not follow the normal trade route. The Nuestra Señora de la Merida would deviate from the usual northeasterly passage and sail southeast through the Caribbean Sea to the Isla de Margarita, located just off the coast of Venezuela. Prior to departure, Captain Fernando de Pontillo had received his new orders to pick up a Spanish general and contingency of soldiers stationed at the Santa Rosa Fort in the easternmost town of La Asunción. He did not like this severe deviation to the southeast and knew it would add over two and a half weeks to the journey, but he kept his displeasure to himself— orders were orders.

Pontillo left his position on the forecastle and slowly made his way back to the quarterdeck where his helmsman held tightly to the wheel. The galleon had slipped by the eastern most point of the Mexican Yucatan Peninsula and now through the Yucatan channel into the Caribbean Sea. The weather seemed to be holding well enough so Pontillo estimated he could make port at La Asunción in less than a week, providing the favorable wind would hold steady. "Ahoy Helmsman," the captain shouted as he approached the rear deck. "How is she holding?"

"A bit sluggish, sir. We are heavy in the hull with all the weighty cargo we are carrying, but with this favorable wind I am managing to stay on course."

"Well, let's hope she holds steady," Captain Pontillo replied. "I want to make Margarita and La Asunción within five or six days."

= = = = =

Nearly six thousand miles to the southeast, off the west coast of Africa, a hurricane was born in the Gulf of Guinea. Aided by the warm waters of the south Atlantic and favorable winds, the disturbance slowly increased its rotation to 40 miles per hour and managed to pick up an amazing speed of 35 miles per hour steadily to the northeast. At this speed, it would take approximately six days to reach the South American continent and the Caribbean Sea, provided it maintained its current course.

Four days had passed since the galleon had entered the Caribbean, and thanks to prevailing winds and relative calm seas, the Merida had reached a midway point of deeper water just north of Columbia, known as the Columbian Basin. Pontillo was making one of his frequent rounds when he was approached by his first mate, Alonso Navarro. His disheveled appearance indicated he had been in an unpleasant confrontation. "What's the problem with you, Alonso? The captain shouted. "You look like you just jumped aboard a British man-o-war and took on the entire crew single handed."

"Just as bad sir," the first mate replied angrily. "I caught one of our crew below deck filling up some bags with gold coins. He was going to stash them away and steal them when we reached port."

"Who was it?" Pontillo asked angrily.

"One of our gunners…a man named Sanchez."

"Where is the man? You realize that stealing from King Phillip's treasure is a capital offence that has to be dealt with in the harshest terms."

"I have him contained below deck."

"When we reach La Asunción you can assemble the crew and bring him to me," the captain ordered. "An example has to be made to show our complement that it is a very serious crime to steal from our king."

"Yes, sir," Navarro answered as he turned to check on the prisoner and resume his duties.

= = = = = =

The next two days were uneventful as the Merida passed the 66-degree latitude mark and the Isla La Orchila. The helmsman, showing a hint of concern, dispatched a seaman to fetch the captain to the aft deck. When Pontillo arrived, the helmsman expressed his apprehension which was clearly evident by the tone of his voice. "Sir the wind is increasing steadily and those dark clouds coming in from the east look very bad. I have turned the ship to the southeast and by our map we just passed the Isla La Tortuga. I am estimating we should reach our destination by late this evening, provided this headwind doesn't get worse."

"Good, Helmsman, keep her steady. We have to beat that damn storm."

In the distance, they could barely see the western tip of Isla de Margarita off their starboard side, but the visibility was diminishing by the minute as the outer edge of the hurricane overtook them. Within minutes, the crushing wind slammed into the ship with a fury, ripping the sails into shreds and tearing the top yard arms from the foremast and main mast. The helmsman felt the wheel become non-responsive as the Merida was pushed toward the island. Pontillo screamed, "Turn her toward the northeast…toward the wind."

"I can't," the helmsman shouted in despair, "I have no rudder. I've lost control." One of the rudder cables had snapped.

The searing gale hit the windward port side of Merida's hull and pushed her sideways and closer to the rocks protruding along the shoreline. The unnoticed danger lurked just below the surface as the ship slammed against the jagged reef with an incredible force. The keel and hull planks were ripped apart like thin sticks and the bottom of the ship collapsed, allowing the king's cargo to spill out of the holds. The heavy treasure chests quickly settled to the sandy floor below. "Abandon ship," Captain Pontillo screamed, not realizing his command was unheard above the howling wind. Crew members had already begun jumping over the railings in a hopeless effort to swim to shore. Lifeboats were unheard of during this early period of sailing ships. A heavy riptide overwhelmed the hapless swimmers and pushed them further away. The once proud Spanish galleon started to break apart and tons of seawater flooded through what was left of her shattered hull. Her bow filled quickly as she began to nosedive into the sea. Within minutes, the Nuestra Señora de la Merida was gone. There were no survivors.

= = = = = =

Escaping the hurricane and sheltered safely in a cave overlooking the tiny coastal village of Punta Arenas, Araujo Toro silently watched with anxious fascination as the tri-masted vessel struggling in the sea below was torn apart by the howling wind and hurled into the formable reef located just beyond the shoreline. Seeing the hurricane approaching, Toro had swiftly pushed his small boat ashore and sought shelter in the remote cave he had visited several times before.

A local fisherman from the nearby village of Boca de Rio, Toro knew these waters well. His livelihood depended on the abundant fish that swam along the reefs surrounding Isla de Margarita. On occasion, he had seen these ships before and immediately knew it was a Spanish Galleon en route to Spain, most likely loaded with the sacred metal bars and coins confiscated and minted from the gold and silver ornaments that once belonged to the Mayans, Aztecs, and other native tribes of Mexico. He was a bit confused as to why the ship was this far south from the usual trade routes—they normally took the more direct northern route around Cuba and the Azores.

Toro continued to stare at the spectacle below as the wind slammed the ship into the reef with such force the masts and rigging broke apart and fell across the decks. The ship floundered for a few moments longer and was quickly shoved forward by the wind for several hundred feet before suddenly plunging beneath the waves. He looked for signs of any crewmen emerging from the water seeking safety on the beach but there were none. The fisherman made a mental note of the location where the ship had struck the reef and vowed to later return with his sons to dive the spot and hopefully find the precious metals that had most likely fallen from the keel of the ship to the sandy bottom. As the storm began to diminish, he thought this cave would be a most likely safe place to hide and cache any treasure they might find.

1

Washington, DC – April 1878

President Rutherford B. Hayes was in a foul mood as he sat at his desk discussing the recent events from Congress with his Secretary of the Treasury, John Sherman. Hayes was especially upset about the passage of the Bland-Allison Act of 1878 that had been passed by Congress, despite his veto which had been overruled by the legislators just less than one week before. In 1873, Congress had passed a law called the "Coinage Act" that removed usage of silver dollars from the list of authorized coins. The five-year depression that followed led to a "free silver movement" that advocated the unlimited coinage of silver. The 1878 Bland-Allison Act required the Treasury Department to purchase a certain amount of silver each month from western mining companies and put it into circulation as silver dollars. This created a bimetallism silver and gold standard that would no doubt lead to an unstable monetary situation affecting banking, investments, manufacturing, and the overall circulation of money throughout the country.

"Those idiots in Congress don't realize what a destabilizing effect that damn act will cause with our monetary policies,"

Hayes fumed. "All that new silver they're bringing in from mines in Nevada and other western states will certainly drop the price of silver to a fraction of that of gold. There is no way the value of both metals will remain stable, especially silver. What do you think, John?"

Sherman pondered the question for a few seconds and then answered. "Everyone knows that William Bland has strong ties to silver-producing interests and he and Senator Allison of Iowa did a real selling job on the other congressmen. It will be virtually impossible to maintain a bi-metal standard with that much silver required to be purchased…$2-4 million dollars' worth each month by my Treasury Department. The relative price between the two metals cannot possibly hold up."

President Hayes, displaying his anxiety added, "That outrageous act will certainly create an inflationary monetary panic in the country that will eventually lead to another depression. Our only hope is to shore up our supply of gold in the Treasury and revert back to a total gold standard."

"And how do you suggest we do that, Mr. President?"

"Find us some gold. We need to fill our vaults with gold… lots of gold."

2

Iceland – May 1878

Professor George Scott felt that he was close to an amazing discovery. An accomplished archeologist, he was in charge of the procurement of artifacts for the Washington National Museum and was following a solid lead he had discreetly received about some priceless Viking runestones said to be hidden in a cavern beneath a former ice cap. His journey had carried him by ship from Washington to the town of Reykjavik, Iceland, situated on the southwestern coast of the island. He was accompanied by three associates who had helped him on previous missions to acquire antiquities for the museum's vast displays. His accomplices would be paid a handsome commission by the museum and a bonus if their mission was successful.

It was well known within scientific circles that Iceland had been discovered and settled by the Norsemen in the late ninth century and occupied by the Vikings until around 930AD. Runestones were slabs of rock inscribed by the Vikings with runes, or inscriptions, engravings, and symbols, depicting various bits of history, key directions, and other important information. They were also commonly used by the Vikings to mark the graves of significant individuals and heroic warriors who fell in battle. The runestones Scott was seeking were said to be smaller slabs in the form of tablets that contained lines of inscriptions describing the Vikings discovery of the North American continent and contacts with various native tribes and other events they had experienced. Legend also stated that these runestones contained clues of a vast treasure cache of gold, precious gems, and other ancient priceless artifacts the Vikings had confiscated from various towns and villages they had conquered throughout northern Europe. It appeared that much of this treasure had been transported to the remote and uninhabited land of ice and snow now called Iceland and cached in a remote secret cavern for safe keeping. The lure of such a vast treasure was too much for the Washington National Museum to ignore, so Professor Scott was dispatched to try and find it.

This early in the spring, the land was still covered in snow and ice as the guide and transportation they had hired, a horse drawn sleigh, carried them in a southeastern direction along the coastline. Their objective was the Seljalandsfoss Waterfall, located on the southern coast of Iceland. The falls was a majestic flow of water that tumbled 200 feet from the plateau and over the sheer cliff above. Behind the falls was supposedly a large cavern and somewhere within this cavity a hidden tunnel leading to another cavern deep under the plateau. It was here where the runestones and other ancient Viking artifacts were said to be cached.

Although cold, the weather cooperated with clear skies and the two-day journey carried them to the base of the cliff where the breathtaking panorama before them offered a spectacular view of the magnificent waterfall cascading over the cliff far above and collecting into a clear blue pool at the base of the precipice. The first thing Professor Scott noticed were the wide spaces on either side of the falls, depicting a relatively shallow depression directly behind the mass of falling water. *The tunnel had to be hidden somewhere along the base, most likely behind a false wall of stone,* he thought.

When the hire was consummated in Reykjavik, the guide was informed of the importance and secrecy of this mission and he would be handsomely paid for his discretion. He was also instructed to wait at the base of the falls until the men returned from their mission and transport them back to Reykjavik and to the chartered ship that awaited them at the docks.

The men had purchased several tools at a shop in Reykjavik which included a pickaxe and two shovels. Scott also had benefit of the mirrored oil lamp that had served him so well on his two previous expeditions to the Peruvian Andes and Amazon Basin in Brazil. He remembered fondly the dangers he had faced and incredible discoveries they had found during these expeditions with his two former companions, Simon Murphy and Elijah Walker. He thought of them often and wondered if he would ever see them again.

The group approached the cliff and made their way behind the falls to search for signs of a concealed entrance to a tunnel. They explored every inch of the wall surface, but most of the cavity's face was either solid rock or piles of stone that had been eroded away by ice and the falling water. They poked along the rock face with the pick, trying to chip away loose stone or listen to any hollow sound that might reveal a space hidden behind it and hopefully access to a passageway. The professor was getting annoyed that nothing resembling a false wall was detected. He turned to his associates, "That entrance has to be somewhere along the base of this cliff...someplace that would give the Vikings and their booty easy access. Jonah, you and I will search along the base of the cliff more to our right of the falls and you other two men fan out and search further to the left. Look for anything suspicious...a depression, cavity, loose boulder, or a pile of rocks that might conceal a wall or opening into the rock face."

Scott and Jonah Steele moved to their right while the other men moved in the opposite direction, exploring every square inch along the rock wall along the way.

With the field of mineral mining becoming more prevalent, Steele had a keen interest in the newly established fields of mineralogy and geology and had achieved a degree in the subjects at the Columbia University School of Mines that had been established in 1870. He had a keen eye for various rock formations and liked to analyze their geological origins. He especially enjoyed examining rock strata and the fact that layers of different types of rock had been formed over an unimaginable time of millions of years. He also recognized that many of the formations and land features in Iceland had been carved from glaciers that were prevalent during the ice age or the Pleistocene Epoch that began nearly 1.8 million years ago and lasted until roughly 12,000 years ago.

He turned to Scott. "Professor, the rock strata along this cliff is too uniform and doesn't show any signs that it has been disturbed, except from normal erosion from water and freezing ice. I'm going to search further away from the falls while you keep checking along the base. I have a gut feeling that the opening to a tunnel or shaft will be further away from the falls where the access would have been easier for the Vikings."

There was no argument from Scott who was aware of Steele's keen knowledge of rock formations.

The young geologist moved along the base of the cliff until he came to another significant recess in the rock that extended nearly fifteen feet deep. They had not seen the cavity earlier because it had been partially hidden by a slight curve in the cliff face and obscured by a prominent overhang. Below him, in front of the recess, he noticed the rock had been eroded and worn into the shape of a shallow trough indicating that water had once flowed through the face of the cliff and down through the depression carved below him. This could only mean that a small underground river or stream had once flowed from the rock, most likely several thousand years earlier. He turned and observed the strata carefully. Something was out of place.

Steele turned to Scott and shouted, "Professor, over here, I've found something. Grab the other two men and get over here with the pickaxe and shovels."

Within minutes, Scott and the others were standing next to Steele staring at the blank wall within the recess. "What do you see?" Scott asked.

"I see nothing but a blank rock wall," one of their colleagues responded.

"That's all I see, too," the other man added.

Scott, who stared at the blank wall quizzically, added his thoughts. "I see some slight irregularities in the horizontal lines in the rock. Some of them don't match evenly."

"Good observations, Professor," Steele complimented. "If

you'll follow this line," he said, tracing his finger vertically up the wall, "you can see there is an uneven rock strata pattern extending about five feet up from the base and the same irregular pattern about four feet across coming back down to the floor. The strata lines don't quite meet and appear to be off about a quarter of an inch. The outline pattern appears to be in the shape of a single rectangular slab of rock...perhaps a covering to an entryway. If this is a false wall, then you must admit that someone did a very fine job of fitting it tightly back into place. It's hardly noticeable to an untrained eye. Hand me that pick and I'll see if I can chip it loose at the edges. The rock appears to be limestone, so it shouldn't be too hard to break through."

Steele stood back and started chipping away at the irregular vertical lines of the suspect panel. The strikes of the pick against the rock were different. An unnatural hollow sound resonated from the irregular lines, indicating the center panel was thinner and certainly not solid like the rock surrounding it. One of the other men, named Paul, turned to his associate. "Let me take over, Jonah."

He began striking the sharp point against the rock panel. More stone chips fell to the ground and then the point finally crashed through, leaving a suspicious black hole staring at them through the vertical surface.

"We've broken through," Steele shouted. "I knew that panel was a false wall."

With a few more well-placed blows, the slab shattered and fell to the ground, exposing a mass of total darkness...a passageway.

Professor Scott was ecstatic. "Amazing," he said. "My information and the legend were correct after all. Now let's climb through that opening and see what we can find from the world of the Vikings."

3

Seljalandsfoss Waterfall, Iceland

The passageway was relatively wide, allowing easy passage for the group to walk single file, but the five-and-a-half-foot ceiling height made it necessary for the men to stoop slightly. Professor Scott had made sure to supply the team with some small mirrored oil lanterns like the one he had used on his prior two expeditions. Developed by a friend, they were quite effective. The canisters of refined oil, combined with the small reflective mirrors, provided very sufficient illumination, especially in dark confined spaces like the tunnel they were facing. Each man was furnished with a lantern with two extras in reserve and spare canisters of oil.

The young geologist, Steele, was the first to make the observation. "Look closely at the walls, floor and ceiling. Do you notice anything unusual?" he asked.

Paul answered quickly. "The rock sure seems awfully smooth. Sure doesn't look like human hands could have carved out anything this smooth, especially a thousand years ago."

"Correct," Steele answered, a tinge of excitement in his tone. "This tunnel was carved by flowing water that dissolved and eroded the limestone. It is the bed of an ancient stream that flowed through here most likely hundreds of thousands of years ago. The water carved out a perfect tunnel that leads well under the hill above us. No telling how deep it is. This damn thing could go for several miles. It's going to be interesting to see where this passageway will take us. I'll lead the way with my lantern," he added.

For security, the men carried an assortment of arms provided by the museum. Professor Scott, a crack shot with firearms, had exchanged his beloved Model 73' Winchester carbine for a newer Model 1876. The newer model was basically a similar design but was chambered for the newer .45-70 Centennial cartridges. Instead of the new cartridge, the professor selected the .40-60 caliber as it was a bit lighter and more functional for his use. He also carried the brand-new Colt 1878 double action Frontier 6 shot revolver that chambered the standard .40-44 cartridges. This replaced his faithful Model 1872 Remington single action revolver he had carried on his Amazon expedition. Scott was very meticulous about his guns and always wanted the latest in design and performance. He regularly practiced at the local range to keep his shooting skills at the highest level.

His three companions each carried later production 1875 Remington single action revolvers and two of the three accomplices carried 1873 Winchesters. The third man, Joseph, decided his revolver was enough. Sufficiently armed, they thought they had enough firepower to take on any unforeseen danger that might confront them.

The tunnel continued for nearly a half mile when they passed a small vertical opening cut into the rock, barely large enough for a man to pass through. Chisel marks on the rock revealed that this passage was definitely manmade. Their curiosity soared as they eased through the opening into a small chamber. The oil lamps illuminated the space to reveal several six-foot-wide shelves carved into the walls and spaced three high. A closer view revealed human remains occupying each recess. The chamber was a crypt.

"This place is nothing but a burial chamber," the fourth man, Joseph, shouted. "I don't see anything stacked around the walls."

"Let's take a closer look at those remains," Scott remarked elatedly.

The giveaway was the assorted weapons lying on top of the remains…they were definitely Viking. The remains had been interred in cloth wrappings that had long since rotted away, leaving skeletal parts and bits of hair and sinew. Three of the skeletons bore half dome shaped helmets over the skull and two had more elaborate helmets with winged shaped extensions pointed upward and metal face and neck guards projecting downward on each side. This confirmed the identification of the remains. Several skeletons had Viking broad swords lying on top and others had a combination of battle axe heads and spear points lying about, the wooden handles and shafts long ago disappeared.

Steele noticed something different. "Look at this guy," he said. "He seems much shorter than the others." The remains were different. Bits of hardened animal hide lay scattered over the bones and there were two carved stone spear points lying on top on him."

"Who do suppose this fellow was?" Paul commented.

"Well he certainly doesn't resemble any of the other Vikings in the crypt," Steele answered. "He might have been an Eskimo who served as a guide. He would have had to be special to be buried with honor with these Viking warriors. My guess is that he might have been a big chief of some kind who helped the Vikings accomplish something important, or died fighting alongside them."

Scott was exuberant. "These Viking helmets, swords, and axes are every museum's dream. We'll have to grab some of these things on the way back. Now, let's move on and see if we can find those runestones."

The group proceeded through the tunnel, hoping to find another side room, but there was only the smooth walls and ceiling that stared back at them. It was an eerie feeling in the confined space, knowing they were hundreds of feet underground. One of the lanterns starting flickering indicating it was time to replace the oil can. They knew the other one would give out soon and would also have to be refueled. Joseph was getting a bit claustrophobic and uneasy with the feeling that the walls were closing in on him…he was ready to get out of this stinking hole. "What if this shaft goes all the way across the whole island?" he grumbled.

"Then I guess we'll have a good view of the Greenland Sea at the other end," Scott answered irritably. "Just calm down, Joseph, we should be hitting a larger cavern soon. The Vikings had to have a place to store their things and it can't be too much further."

Scott was right, because in another hundred yards the tunnel suddenly widened and the space just ahead suddenly became a huge black void. They were entering a large grotto. It was interesting that the ground before them started gradually descending into a uniform depression and continued to a depth of nearly four feet. Steele picked up on this and announced, "What we see here is the bed of an ancient underground lake. The passage we just came from was apparently the river channel that drained the lake. I'll bet at the other end we'll find another similar passage that fed the lake."

"Wonder where the Vikings stored the runestones?" Paul questioned.

Scott responded, "We know the Vikings occupied this cavern by the fact that they buried their dead in that crypt back there in the tunnel. They would have certainly discovered this large chamber, so I think we need to spread out and search every inch of this place. There must be a hidden cavity or vault somewhere adjoining this room. Look for something that will trigger a doorway or move a slab to an opening."

The men dropped their packs and rifles to the ground and spread out toward the edges of the depression. Something embedded in the walls would hold the key to any hidden rooms. Professor Scott spotted a few small depressions in the rock but they were only areas that had been eroded by water. Steele noticed the same thing but nothing was evident to trigger any opening. Slowly the four men moved around the perimeter of the cavern searching for anything suspicious. Joseph was examining the far wall when he spotted a deeper fissure positioned waist high in the wall. The crack was about six inches wide and continued vertically to nearly two feet. He noticed something very peculiar protruding from the rock...the handle of a sword. He turned and shouted to the others. "Over here... quickly... I found something really strange...the handle of a sword sticking out of the wall."

In his exuberance, he grabbed the handle and pulled with all his strength. A sleek Viking broad sword withdrew from the slot. Scott, who saw Joseph tugging the object yelled, "Stop... don't touch anything...might be a trap."

His warning was too late. The sound of two loud clicks reverberated across the room, followed by a slight grinding noise, indicating something within the wall was moving. Suddenly the stone threshold panel Joseph was standing on pivoted downward, revealing a huge dark void beneath. Still holding the sword in hand, he dropped like a rock and, without a sound, disappeared through the opening into the empty space below. The others rushed to the wall and peered into the darkness... Joseph was gone.

"I tried to stop him," Scott said, "but my warning was too late. I've seen these traps before in similar caverns. We experienced these during our expedition to the Andes and again during our search for the lost city of El Dorado in the Amazon. The ancients devised some very devious ways to protect their treasures and kill a man. Apparently, the Vikings had some of those skills. The lesson here is simple. Do not touch anything until you examine it carefully and consider all the options."

The slight grinding noise continued inside the wall and then a well concealed panel before them began to slide to their left and into a hidden recess in the rock. The dark hole before them revealed a hidden passage or possible room on the other side. "I think we have found what we are looking for," Scott said excitedly.

"But how do we plan on getting past that big hole in the floor without ending up down there with Joseph," Paul asked with concern. "We sure can't jump over the damn thing."

Professor Scott had learned a few things about traps during his previous expeditions. "We have to reverse the process that caused it to open. We need to put the sword back onto the slot."

"I think the sword disappeared with Joseph when he fell," Steele remarked with concern. "He was holding on to it."

"There were several more swords back there in the crypt we passed that were buried with the Viking skeletons," Scott reminded him. "We'll have go back and grab a couple of those. They are most likely similar swords as the one that Joseph pulled out of this slot."

Paul volunteered. "The crypt is only a short distance back so I'll go and grab a couple." He turned and walked back into the tunnel.

Steele walked to the rim of the opening and peered over the edge. "This void looks like a bottomless pit," he remarked. "No telling how deep it is and poor Joseph's lifeless broken body is laying down there somewhere on the bottom. It happened so fast."

"Isn't it unusual that a huge cavern could be located just below this room we're standing in?" Scott questioned. "We have one cavern on top of another."

"Not really," the young geologists answered. "These two caverns were apparently carved out by two different ancient river systems at different times in their geological history. The one below us would be the older of the two and the river that carved this cavern we're standing in would have dried up before the rock that formed this floor was dissolved or eroded away. That's why this floor we're standing on is still here. It also forms the ceiling for the cavern we see below us. It is a very unusual formation though," he admitted.

Paul soon returned with three swords in hand. "I don't think the former owners would mind if we borrowed these," he said grinning. "Don't think they'll need them in Valhalla or wherever they might be."

Scott took one of the swords and hefted it in the air. "Good balance," he commented. "The Vikings knew how to forge good steel and make strong weapons. Now, let's try this one out in the slot."

"What is it supposed to do by sticking it back in the slot?" Paul questioned.

"I learned in the caverns in Peru that there are internal mechanisms within the walls that make the panels move. They can be very tricky. You have to reverse the sequence of movement to restore the panels back to their original positions. Sometimes you have to move the triggering device more than once to initiate the process. Let's see what happens when I reinsert the sword."

He placed the blade into the slot and firmly pushed it into the recess. They heard a click then a soft rumbling noise. The floor panel began to pivot upward and snapped firmly back in place. A loud click indicated that it had locked. It was obvious the panel was suspended by a strong spindle operated by a spring assembly. He pulled the sword back from the slot and then reinserted it. This triggered the door panel that slid back into place, resealing the passage. "Now I see how this thing works," he announced proudly, as he pulled the sword back out of the wall to watch the floor threshold panel spring open again. Scott then reinserted the sword to close and lock the floor panel and then repeated the process to open the wall panel. Now they could safely enter the room.

"Ingenious," Paul commented with obvious respect for the designer's ingenuity. "How did the Vikings figure that out?"

"Many of the ancient civilizations were pretty ingenious," Scott answered. "Just look at the Egyptians, Greeks, and even some of the pre-Columbian Indians of the Americas like the Toltecs, Mayans, and Aztecs and the magnificent pyramids and structures they built. Their engineering skills were way ahead of their time."

With the oil lantern held to his front, Scott entered the passageway, with the other two men following. They found the space to be a small room. At the far end were stacked an assortment of weapons and armor once worn by the proud Vikings. The artifacts were in remarkably good shape, thanks to the lack of destructive moisture and air over the centuries that helped to preserve them. Stacked against the right wall lay the objects of their search…two stone tablets with carved inscriptions and strange markings engraved on one side…the Viking runestones. Scott was ecstatic as he lifted one to test the weight. *Not bad,* he thought. *About fifteen pounds each. We can carry these easily and some weapons and other artifacts.*

Steele was also enthralled by the discovery. "How on earth do you plan to interpret all those inscriptions and symbols on those stones?" he asked.

"The source we had for the location of these stones is a Georgetown University professor of ancient history with a special interest in early Scandinavian and especially Viking civilizations. He is considered an expert historian on ancient Nordic cultures. His name is Aavik Johansen and he is originally from Norway. He is also a friend of our Washington National Museum curator, Robert Drake. Johansen has seen and studied many of the Viking runestones throughout the Scandinavian countries and knows quite a bit about the ancient languages. He has agreed to help us interpret the inscriptions."

"I can't wait to learn what these stones will say," Steele confessed.

"I feel the same way," Scott said, "but first we have to get them back to Washington and start our research."

Paul, who was at the far wall sorting through the stacks of weapons and armor, pulled something different from the stack. It resembled a small thin rectangular shield. It was most unusual. "I found something strange," he announced, carrying the object over and handing it to Scott.

It was a thin rigid metallic tablet filled with strange glyphs and symbols. Scott examined it carefully and turned it in his hands. Then he stopped with a complete expression of shock and astonishment. "I have seen these inscriptions before," he stammered, "both in Peru and in the lost city of El Dorado. They resemble the *Toltec* logbooks Elijah found on the ship."

"What are you talking about?" Paul asked suspiciously.

"I'll have to explain later," Scott answered. "Let's grab some of those swords and helmets and get back to the sled quickly. It's very important that we get these to the museum as soon as possible."

The three men took the tablets, two helmets, and gathered as many of the Viking weapons as they could carry and then headed for the cavern to retrieve their packs and rifles.

As they left the room, Scott pulled the sword from the slot and then reinserted it to reseal the door panel. The men then turned toward the tunnel to make their way back to the outside.

4

Washington Arsenal, Washington, D.C.

Major General Caleb Kirby sat behind his desk shuffling through some routine papers and getting quite restless with the boredom. His job of heading up procurement and equipment development for the Army was starting to wear on his nerves, especially during peacetime. He often thought back to the exciting journey he had experienced in 1865 when he was dispatched to the Yucatan to capture the two Union and Confederate officers who had vacated their post at the closing of the war to search for the lost Toltec city of Xepocotec and the vast treasure that was said to be hidden there. He recalled their names...Simon Murphy and Elijah Walker, who surprisingly turned out to be blood cousins. They also turned out to be good friends and companions to Kirby during that journey.

He recalled working with them in their preparations for their later expeditions to Peru in 1870 and the Amazon River journey in 1873. He fondly remembered their companion Professor George Scott, the eccentric archaeologist who had accompanied them on their last two ventures. He knew Scott still worked for the Washington National Museum and had kept up with him through some periodic scientific journals Kirby enjoyed reading. Scott's greatest exploits were the work he did deciphering the Atlantean scrolls the group had recovered from the sunken island of Atlantis. From this, Scott had proved that Atlantis had existed and the writings of the Greek philosopher Plato were true.

The general had lost track of Murphy and Walker but he had heard Murphy was now a married man with a son and lived somewhere around the Washington area, most likely in Maryland. He recalled hearing someone tell him that Walker was living somewhere on a ranch in southern California and had moved there to be with that beautiful little Mexican girl he had met during the Yucatan affair. He had no idea whether they had married. His reverie was interrupted by a knock on the door.

"Come in," he responded annoyingly.

His aide, First Lieutenant Charles Maxwell entered and gave Kirby a customary salute. "Sir, with your permission, I have an incredible story to tell you…something that may turn out to be of national interest."

"Have a seat, Lieutenant," Kirby answered with interest.

"Thank you, Sir. As you are aware, the president is very upset with the Bland-Allison Act that was passed a few weeks ago by Congress and the fact the legislators overturned his veto. The new law is trying to promote a multi-metal standard between gold and silver. The word is going around that President Hayes and Secretary Sherman have a big push on to fill up our treasury with enough gold to force a reverse of the new law and support a strong fiscal gold standard."

"Yes, I am aware of that, Lieutenant, but what's that got to do with us?"

"Sir, you are the top procurement officer for the army so what if I told you we have a sergeant that might be able to help us obtain a fortune in gold from a sunken Spanish treasure ship, a galleon that was lost in the Caribbean Sea back in the early 1600s. I think the president and treasury secretary would love to have that large amount of gold added to our treasury department's vaults. Perhaps it would help shore up support for a gold standard, and I'm sure the president would appreciate it if you were the one procuring a large cache of gold for his vaults. Who knows, Sir, it might produce another star for you."

The general's curiosity was aroused, and the thought of a third star certainly stirred his interest. "Who is this man?" Kirby questioned. "What does he know about a sunken treasure?"

"His name is Javier Peña and his parents were from Venezuela somewhere in the mountain region near the Caribbean coast."

"Why would a man from Venezuela want to give us any information like that?"

"Sir, his parents moved to the United States about twenty-five years ago and he was born here...I believe in Florida. He is an American born citizen and currently serving in the army. He would have to share with you the details of the information himself."

"You said he was a sergeant."

"Yes sir, I did some checking and found that Peña enlisted three years ago and was initially assigned to the 8th Maryland Infantry Regiment stationed near Baltimore, but he is now with our 14th Field Artillery unit here at the Washington Arsenal. Based on the story he told his lieutenant, his ancestors were the ones who recovered the Spanish treasure from the bottom of the sea and hid it in a cave on an island called Isla de Margarita, just off the coast of what is now Venezuela. He said some of the family later moved the treasure from the island cave and hid it somewhere inland in the mountains on the mainland near the coast. His lieutenant is a friend of mine and told me this story."

"Very interesting," Kirby confessed. "Perhaps we should have a talk with Mr. Peña and hear what he has to say. Why don't you bring him to my office in the morning…say about 10:00 A.M.?"

"Yes, sir. I'll see to it."

= = = = = =

The next morning at ten sharp, Maxwell showed up with the young sergeant, Javier Peña. After a brief introduction, Kirby asked Peña, "Sergeant, I understand you have a fascinating story to tell us about a buried treasure from a sunken Spanish treasure ship."

"Yes, sir, it is a story that has been kept within our family for four or five generations."

"Then, Sergeant, tell me why you are willing to divulge this information to us after so many years of secrecy."

"Well, Sir," the man hesitated for a moment to collect his thoughts; "I am an American born citizen and have a great fondness for this country. My father is gone and now I have an aging mother to care for. Also, I have a girlfriend and soon would like to marry her and start a family. I do not have the means or resources to go down to Venezuela and recover such a treasure, but I know our government does and could bring it back to the States. All I would ask is to have a modest portion of the money to purchase a house to support my mother and get married and raise a family. The government could have the rest."

The general smiled and replied, "I'm sure I could arrange to get our government to allow you some of the rewards, provided we recovered the treasure. Now, why don't you tell us your story and the location of this treasure?"

Peña felt more at ease now with Kirby's response. He reached back into his memory to recall the story that had been handed down through his family for over two hundred-fifty years. He began his recollection as it was told to him by his father. "Well, Sir, it started back when Spain ruled Mexico and much of Central and South America. As you know, the Spanish Conquistadors conquered the Aztecs of Mexico, Incas of Peru, and other Central American tribes and then confiscated their gold and other wealth the Indians had accumulated. They melted a lot of this gold into bars and coins and sent it back to Spain on their galleons or treasure ships. The story was told that sometime in the very early 1600s, one of their ships was caught in a hurricane off the Isle de Margarita located near the coast of Venezuela. The ship hit a reef and sunk, spilling all its treasure to the bottom of the sea, but in an area shallow enough to dive. It was witnessed by my distant relative, a great-great grandfather who was a fisherman on the island. During the hurricane, he was apparently sheltered in a cave overlooking the area and saw the ship when it hit the reef and sunk. Later, when the storm passed, he and his sons dove over the spot and recovered the treasure chests from the bottom. They then hid them in the island cave where it sat undisturbed for many years. It must have taken them several weeks or months to bring it up from the bottom."

"How did all that treasure end up in Venezuela on the mainland?" Kirby asked.

"My ancestor was part Cumanagoto Indian who lived near the coastal town of Cumana. The town was a small village named Barbacoas, just to the south. He was a fisherman and familiar with the Isle de Margarita, because he had fished those waters around the island many times. He kept his boat moored in a small fishing village called Mochima in the inlet to the west of Cumana. It is most likely that he visited the island cave on several occasions. Sometime around the late 1600s, he and his two sons decided to locate and move the treasure from Isle de Margarita over to the mainland. It must have been a long process, but they were finally able to move it secretly by boat, and then by burro or cart to its present location. There is a small range of mountain just to the north of Barbacoas that offers many great places to hide such a treasure and we believe it was cached deep inside a hidden cavern under one of those mountains and has been sitting there for over two hundred years.

"Do you know where that cavern is located?" Kirby questioned.

"No, but there is a map I am told."

"And, where is it?"

"It is actually hidden in in the port city of Cumana. I understand it was hidden by my great grandfather."

"So, all we have to do is go there and find the map…it could be hidden anywhere."

"That might not be so easy," Peña added. "The Venezuela army unit stationed in Cumana does not like outsiders in their area, especially Americanos. The garrison is commanded by a very bad hombre named Colonel Manuel Gallegos. He has been in the region for many years and I have heard he enjoys using very cruel and painful methods of torture before he slits his victim's throats."

"Interesting fellow," Kirby mused.

"But there is one thing that might be helpful," Peña added.

"And what might that be?"

"My father had a diary that listed a clue for the location and description of the map's hiding place, and it is in my mother's possession."

5

Washington National Museum, Washington, D.C.

Professor Scott sat at a table with his associate Jonah Steele, the young geologist who had accompanied him to Iceland. They were examining the two stone tablets lying on the table in a secluded room located in the basement. The room was furnished with specialized tools dedicated to the examination and refurbishing of artifacts destined for the museum's extensive exhibits. The three Viking swords and two helmets they had brought back had already found a prominent spot with various other tenth century displays. "What do you make of these tablets?" Steele asked Scott.

"I really don't know. These runes and the various inscriptions are completely new to me. Our curator, Robert Drake, is currently meeting upstairs with that Harvard Scandinavian artifacts history expert, Aavik Johansen, and should be coming down here shortly. He wants to personally examine the tablets."

"What about this other one we found…the metallic looking one?" Steele asked. "The inscriptions look totally different to me than the ones on those runestones."

Professor Scott's expression confessed a hint of recognition.

"They are different," he offered. "I've seen these engravings before and think I have a good idea where they came from. This tablet is made from a type of metal compound unlike anything anyone has ever seen. The fact it was even there in that Viking cave confirms that the Vikings were visited by some very unusual visitors many years ago."

"You've totally lost me, George. I don't understand what you're saying," his young companion responded with a bewildered expression on his face.

"It's a long story, Jonah. I'll explain it to you soon. But first I want you to hide that metallic tablet. We don't want Mr. Drake and Johansen to see it right now. They should be here any minute and I want them to concentrate on the Viking runestones."

Steele carried the metallic tablet from the room, secured it in a concealed storage compartment, and then returned just as the two newcomers entered the room where Scott was waiting.

Drake made the introductions and Johansen walked over to the table and looked down at the stone tablets. "Well, Mr. Scott," he said enthusiastically, "it appears you have discovered some very interesting artifacts from the Viking era. Mr. Drake showed me the Viking swords and helmets you brought back from Iceland—very fine and well preserved specimens I might add. Now let's examine these stone tablets you have here. You found them in a cave, I understand."

"That is correct, sir. We found them in a cave near the Seljalandsfoss Waterfall located on the southern coast of Iceland. It is not far from the town Reykjavik. We also found a room that was used as a crypt with the remains of several Vikings identified by the swords, helmets, and axe heads that lay over their bones. These two stone tablets were stored in another room that was hidden behind a false wall in a larger cavern. It was there along with several stacks of well-preserved weapons."

Johansen turned his attention to the tablets. "I have seen runestones in various locations throughout northern Europe in areas that the Vikings conquered and where they lived. These tablets are quite unusual however...primarily because of the smaller size. Most of the runestones you see are much larger and were used to mark certain events or recognize important Viking individuals like chiefs or special warriors. You might say similar to grave markers. I must admit that these are some of the smallest runestones I've seen throughout my many travels in Scandinavia. It appears they served as transportable instruments used to register and store records or significant information... quite advanced for the Vikings."

"Can you interpret the inscriptions?" Scott asked.

"Yes, but it will take some time. With your permission, I'll make a charcoal overlay impression on paper and carry it back to the university where I have the archives and files to examine and research the runes. Hopefully, I will be able to convert the inscriptions to English so you'll understand what they say. I would bet there is some very fascinating information concerning the Vikings discoveries of the new world inscribed on these tablets."

"That sounds reasonable," Drake consented.

Professor Scott pursued the conversation a little farther. "I was under the impression that the tablets might contain information about a map that might lead to a large Viking treasure made up of contraband and loot they confiscated from areas they conquered in Northern Europe and transported to the new world."

Johansen chuckled. "That's an interesting thought, Mr. Scott, but I would rather doubt that the Vikings had possession of any large quantities of gold, gems, and other precious metals. Back in the ninth and tenth centuries, except for the royalty and ruling class, most of the population that occupied the towns and villages were mere peasants who derived their subsistence from farming. These people didn't possess anything of value such as gold or gemstones. Except for several castles that fell into their hands, most of the lands the Vikings conquered were occupied by the poorer classes. On the other hand, there are many things we don't know about the Vikings, so it is not impossible that they might have brought some treasures to the new world with them. I will examine the runes and perhaps they will tell us more."

From his pack, Johansen pulled out a roll of special thin paper and placed a sheet over the face of a tablet. He then took a slender charcoal block and methodically began rubbing it over the paper. The inscriptions began to appear on the paper as if he were copying each symbol by hand. When finished with both, he carefully rolled up the sheet and placed it into a slender cylinder. Robert Drake led him from the room after thanking Scott and Steele for their time and a promise that he would furnish a report as soon as possible.

The two men were alone again when Steele turned to Scott. "Professor, you told me you would explain to me what you know about the metallic tablet we found. You said it was made of a metallic compound no one had seen before and you were familiar with the inscriptions. Could you please explain?"

Scott nodded. "Bring the tablet back in here and I'll explain it to you."

With the unusual looking panel lying before them, Scott began his incredible story. "Back in '65 in the Yucatan jungle, while on our expedition in search of the lost Toltec Indian city of Xepocotec, two of my associates, Simon Murphy and Elijah Walker, made a remarkable and startling discovery. Deep within a cavern beneath the lost city's pyramid, they found a strange device that led them to an ancient flying ship that had been hibernating there for nearly nine hundred years. Incredibly, it had been kept alive by an inexhaustible fuel source called tracx. The device turned out to be a communication module that allowed them to communicate with the ship's mechanical intelligence. It was a spaceship from another galaxy and it had lain there all these years in need of repairs. The original travelers had long since died out, leaving the ship dormant in the cavern. Using the talking device, or *Zenox*, they later learned, Simon could communicate with the strange machine and awaken it from its state of hibernation. With instructions from the ship's mechanical intelligence, they could find and use parts stored on the ship to make the necessary repairs to enable it to fly again. The ship's intelligence we later learned was a device they called an information storage bank. It appointed Simon as the new ship's commander and, through his voice commands he could fly the craft out of the cavern, barely escaping hordes of vengeful Indians who were nearly upon them. They now joined up with a general named Caleb Kirby and our curator, Robert Drake, and flew the craft to Washington where they scared hundreds of people who observed it soaring across the sky.

"After realizing they were not being invaded by an unknown alien enemy, President Andrew Johnson and General Grant welcomed the former deserters back to civilization and re-commissioned them back into service to command the strange new craft. Named the *TOLTEC* by Simon and Elijah, President Johnson and top cabinet members decided to press this new machine, with its deadly weapons called laser guns, with incredible unknown power, into service under the direction and command of the Navy. Some of the cabinet and top military officials suggested some very aggressive intentions for the ship, not realizing the potential dangers it could impose upon mankind. Voicing their strong objections, Simon and Elijah were relieved of command and ordered back into civilian life. Prior to departing the *Toltec*, Elijah took the ship's logbook and hid it from the authorities. I examined the book and observed that the metallic pages in the log were very similar to the metal composition of this tablet and many of the inscriptions look the same.

"Simon and Elijah sensed the potential dangers and destructive power of the alien ship and the cataclysmic damage it could inflict on the earth's populations. So, while departing Washington, Simon ordered the craft to fly over the Atlantic Ocean and self-destruct. Distraught over the loss of their newly acquired powerful weapon, the president and other officials believed the ship had been ordered back to its own world by an unknown source. Prior to its departure, the *Toltec* planted a strange capsule into the ground, only to be found by a construction worker two years later. The device, called a Zenox, was used by Simon and Elijah to communicate with another hibernating ship hidden in the Andes, leading to their harrowing expedition to Peru five years later. I accompanied them on that expedition.

"A third ship, designated the X326, was buried under the

ice pack in the Arctic, and awakened by a signal from the dying ship in the Andes. With its inexhaustible fuel element tracx, the ship became re-energized and broke through the tomb of ice where it had been hibernating for several centuries. It then traveled through the air to the Andes and allowed us to board it. Incredibly, through some voice commands from Murphy, the flying ship rose into the sky and flew us from Peru to Washington. While on the flight, Simon named this new ship CUZCO after the ancient Inca capital and dedicated the ship to their harrowing expedition in Peru. President Grant suggested that we make a test run to learn more about the machine, so Simon commanded it to fly us over the ocean. A strange signal took over command of the machine and we were confronted with a frightening experience when we found ourselves plunging under the sea and ending up in an airtight bubble on the sunken continent of Atlantis. This is where I got the Atlantean scrolls that I could interpret. There we would meet an alien commander named Ahular and another alien named Nezar who would befriend us and help save our planet by thwarting a devastating underwater earthquake and cataclysmic split in the Eurasian and African tectonic plates. The earth was saved from blowing apart by a coordinated concentration of laser power from the alien craft to weld the splitting plates together.

"Five years ago, in 1873, I accompanied Murphy and Walker on another expedition to Brazil where we found ourselves traveling up the Amazon River in search of the fabled city of gold, El Dorado. We found the city in southern Peru along with an underground base occupied by our old friends Ahular and Nezar. Also, parked in the cavern was the spacecraft *Cuzco*. We accompanied them into space where the ship could destroy a huge asteroid hurling toward our sun. This saved our sun and certain destruction of our solar system and our own earth."

Jonah Steele stood there in shock and disbelief. "You've got to be kidding," he mumbled.

Scott laughed. "I told you it was an incredibly unbelievable story but nonetheless true. You see why I'm so anxious to get this tablet deciphered, but to do so we need to get the logbook from my old friend Elijah Walker."

"How do we do that?"

"First we have to look up his cousin Simon Murphy and find out where Walker is."

6

Washington, D.C., Office of the Treasury Secretary

Secretary John Sherman was sitting at his desk sorting through some routine papers when his assistant entered his office. "What is it, Sara," he said, his thoughts momentarily interrupted.

"Sir, there is a General Caleb Kirby here to see you. He is the officer in charge of weapons procurement and development for the Army at Washington Arsenal. He says he has some important information he thinks you would be interested in hearing."

"Well, please show the good general in," Sherman responded, his curiosity aroused.

Kirby entered the room and made his introduction. "Please have a seat, General," Sherman offered. "What possible news could our Army Procurement officer have for my Treasury Department?" he asked curiously.

"Mr. Secretary, I am aware of the recent Bland-Allison Act and the concerns you and the president have on its effect to our monetary system. I also believe you have a desire to add more gold to our vaults to help establish a firm gold standard."

"That is quite correct, General Kirby. The dual metal standard of both gold and silver is devaluating both metals and will certainly create another depression unless we can revise a single gold standard. But I must ask you, sir, what does all of this have to do with the army?"

Kirby hesitated for a moment to further pique Sherman's interest. "What if I told you we have solid information about a huge cache of gold that was recovered from a Spanish galleon that sunk in the Caribbean sometime in the early 1600s?"

Sherman's interest suddenly soared. "I would be most interested, General Kirby. Do you know where such a treasure is located?"

"We know it is hidden in a cave near a small town in Venezuela...somewhere near the Caribbean coast. We suspect the cave is in a small mountain range just west of the town of Cumana and close to the coast."

"How reliable is this information?" Sherman asked inquiringly.

"We have a sergeant at the arsenal whose parents came from that area of Venezuela and it was his ancestor that recovered the treasure from the sunken ship and hid it. The story has been handed down in his family for several generations and has been guarded in strict secrecy with the family. He told me that there is a map that will lead us to the site."

"Why would this sergeant divulge such a family secret to us?" Sherman asked.

"He was born in the United States and is a citizen. His father is deceased and he has an aging mother to care for and a girlfriend he plans to marry and start a family. I also believe most of his relatives in Venezuela are now deceased, but he thinks he might have a cousin or two left in Cumana. The man lacks the resources to go retrieve the treasure himself, so for a modest reward he is willing to help us recover it for our government."

Sherman nodded and replied enthusiastically. "General, I believe you and I need to pay a quick visit to the White House. President Hayes will be very anxious to hear your story."

= = = = = =

The president was sitting in his office conversing with Secretary of the Navy, Richard Thompson.

An aide knocked on the door and entered. "Sir, Secretary Sherman is here to see you, along with a general named Kirby. He says he has some very important information to share with you."

"Please show Mr. Sherman in," Hayes responded curiously.

"Mr. President," the secretary announced, "This is Major General Caleb Kirby. He is the weapons procurement and development officer for the army and he is stationed at Washington Arsenal. I believe he has a very fascinating story to tell you."

Secretary Thompson stood up and said, "Perhaps I should leave."

"No, Richard, why don't you stay and hear this. I have a feeling the navy might be somehow involved."

Thompson sat back down. *Wonder what the army has that is so important to interrupt our meeting?* he thought. *This might be interesting.*

"General Kirby, please tell us what must be so important to have Mr. Sherman bring you here?"

Kirby spent the next thirty minutes telling President Hayes his incredible story about the lost Spanish treasure, especially alluding to the vast amount of gold bars and coins involved.

Like Sherman before them, both Hayes and Thompson were enthralled with the story. Kirby continued, "You see, Sir, Sergeant Peña is willing to help us locate the treasure and give it to the government provided he gets a small reward to help care for his mother and future family."

The president smiled, "I believe you can tell Mr. Peña I'm sure we can work something out in compensation and certainly an increased pay grade for the man. We could sure use that gold in our treasury to help bolster gold prices and return our monetary system to the gold standard. That damn silver act will surely hurt our growing economy. Tell me, General Kirby, how do you suggest we proceed?"

"I would suggest we mount a secret expedition to go down there and recover the treasure." Turning to Secretary Thompson he continued, "This is where your navy can help us. The group will need transportation to the northern coast of Venezuela, near the port town of Cumana, and transport back with the treasure." Thompson nodded his understanding, pleased that the navy would be involved.

"And who do you recommend we send down there to retrieve this bounty?" Hayes asked.

Kirby answered confidently. "I have three men in mind. They were involved in finding the Toltec treasure in the Yucatan in '65, they were the ones who found the golden Inca statue in '70, and in 1873 they were the men who went to the Amazon and discovered the lost city of gold, El Dorado, in Peru. They also recovered the hidden Confederate cache of gold in North Carolina that same year. When it comes to treasure hunting, these men are the best we've got. And if you will remember, they are the ones who contacted the strange visitors from space and were with them when they saved our planet by welding the tectonic plates together in the Atlantic Ocean. While on the Amazon expedition, they also helped destroy a giant asteroid that was on a collision course with our sun."

"Yes, I remember hearing about that absurd story. And what were their names?" the president asked.

"Simon Murphy, Elijah Walker, and Professor George Scott," Kirby answered.

"Well, General, I suggest you round up these treasure hunters, assemble the expedition team, and then bring them to me as soon as you can for a briefing. Secretary Thompson will coordinate the transportation for your team with the navy."

"Yes sir, Mr. President, I will get right on it," Kirby answered as he saluted and left the office.

General Kirby sat at his desk discussing the names of the expedition members with his aide, First Lieutenant Charles Maxwell. Although Kirby would not be participating in the mission, it was his duty to assemble the best group possible and act as coordinator for the mission. On a pad of paper, he began to jot down some names. Heading the list was Simon Murphy followed by Elijah Walker, Professor George Scott, and of course Sergeant Javier Peña who had informed him about the treasure. He knew the sergeant spoke fluent Spanish and knew the area from prior visits to relatives there. He was hoping Peña could enlist the help of any remaining relatives to arrange the secret movement of the treasure from the cave to the American ship that would be waiting in the harbor, that is if any of them were still alive and living there. Due to the size of the treasure to be recovered, he knew he would need two or three more members—he would leave those choices up to Murphy and Walker.

"How do we find Murphy and Walker?" Maxwell asked, glancing down at the list.

"I know Murphy lives somewhere close to the Washington area but I've heard Walker lives on a ranch somewhere in California," Kirby answered. "I think the best place to start is with Professor Scott. Why don't you pay him a visit at the Washington museum and bring him back here? We'll discuss the mission with him and I'm sure he can tell us where Murphy and Walker can be found."

= = = = = =

Professor Scott was surprised when he was summoned into the curator's office to meet with an army officer. Lieutenant Maxwell introduced himself and told Scott he was to accompany him back to the Washington Arsenal to meet with General Caleb Kirby. He stressed the importance of the meeting. Scott remembered Kirby well and was pleased that he would see the general once again. They left the museum and climbed aboard the carriage that would take them to the arsenal.

Kirby was in a jovial mood when Maxwell ushered the professor into his office. "Great to see you again, Professor Scott," he said as he exchanged a firm handshake. "We have a lot to talk about so please have a seat and I'll explain why I summoned you here."

The general spent the next few minutes explaining about the hidden Spanish treasure, the conversation with Sergeant Javier Peña, and the president's desire to recover the cache for the U.S. treasury. They talked briefly about the need for a gold standard and how it would help to stabilize the disparity between gold and silver by allowing the free market to control the prices of both metals. Kirby knew he had the professor's attention so he continued with his intended formation of the expedition team. "The president asked me my suggestions for members of the expedition and my immediate thought included three of the best treasure hunters I know of.

"And who might they be, General?" Scott responded, already suspecting the answer.

"Our old friends Simon Murphy, Elijah Walker, and you, of course."

Scott laughed, "Well, I have to admit we have all searched for and found some interesting lost treasures before. Our travels turned out to be wild adventures and we certainly met some very interesting 'people'…that is, if you can actually call them people."

Kirby grinned, acknowledging the inference. "Do you happen to know the whereabouts of Murphy and Walker?" Kirby asked.

"Murphy lives just across the Anacostia River in Maryland…a town called Bladensburg and I heard Walker moved out to southern California on a ranch near Capistrano. Simon keeps up with him and should know his exact location."

"Do you have any other recommendations of anyone with special qualifications that should accompany the group?"

"Yes sir, I do have an associate at the museum that would qualify. He is a young geologist named Jonah Steele. He specializes in a new field called geology which involves the study and analysis of minerals, rock strata, and rock formations useful in mining operations. He is quite an expert on caves and has been very helpful on some of my architectural digs. Jonah might come in handy to help us searching for a cave."

"Is he married?" Kirby asked.

"No sir, he is not."

"Very well, Professor. You can explain our mission to Mr. Steele and bring him to the meeting when we round up Murphy and Walker. Tell him the mission is classified and top secret. I will probably send my aide, Lieutenant Charles Maxwell, along as my advisor and contact man. He will be a handy addition since he speaks, reads, and understands enough Spanish to converse with the locals. We understand the Venezuela military stationed in Cumana are not too friendly toward Americans so you might need his special skills with firearms. I also happen to know you are a pretty good shot with a rifle. Your group will be furnished with the newest weapons available. Winchester's newest Model 1876 carbine replaced the old '72 model and a brand-new model 1878 Colt double action revolver was just released that will provide the group some formidable firepower if needed."

"Ironically, General, I happen to have both of those guns in my possession and can confirm their effectiveness. They are very excellent weapons."

Kirby was a little surprised but didn't say anything.

Scott did not want to divulge any information about the Iceland runestones discovery or the fact he had carried these specific weapons on that project. He especially did not want anyone to know about the strange metallic tablet they had found. He needed Walker's logbook to help him decipher the strange inscriptions and symbols and only Elijah and Simon could offer any help since they were aboard the *Toltec* and had seen these engravings before. He was anxious to physically compare the two objects. Anyway, there was really nothing to disclose about the Iceland affair until Professor Johansen could interpret the rune tablets.

Kirby continued, "I would like for you to personally ride up to Bladensburg and fetch Murphy. Tell him the army will handle the bill for his stay at the Burlington House. When we determine Walker's exact location, I'll send a wire to our Fort Guijarros installation in San Diego and detail a couple of men to gather him up and stick him on a train."

"What if he doesn't want to come all the way to Washington?" Scott questioned.

"Oh, he'll come. Aside from making this a presidential order, I know that Walker won't turn down an opportunity for some excitement and adventure. It's in his blood."

7

Bladensburg, Maryland

Simon Murphy had dropped out of the Navy soon after the Peruvian affair, mainly because he hated routine paperwork and didn't particularly like traveling around the ocean on ships. Like his cousin Elijah, he tended to get seasick in rough weather and had spent his prior Civil War service on a horse. Elijah had also spent his military service on a horse and could just look at the ocean waves and get nauseous.

Simon and his wife Maggie had purchased a modest home just north of Washington in Bladensburg. He liked being away from the Washington political chaos and enjoyed the open air and bird hunting in the lush Maryland fields and fishing in the Anacostia River only a short walk from his house. Simon had tried several unfulfilling jobs but ended up doing something he swore he would never do again…selling hardware. Established in 1843, the Stanley Rule and Level Company had just acquired the Leonard Bailey Company with their extensive line of wood and metal rulers, hand drills, hammers, and levels. This 1878 merger was the beginning of Stanley Tools and Simon found himself selling these products to hardware stores in Washington and surrounding rural towns in Maryland. *What the hell*, he thought, *it's a living and puts food on my table.*

He was in his front yard playing with his five-year-old son Thomas when he noticed a horse and rider trotting up his drive-way. As he came closer and dismounted, Simon recognized the man. "Good Grief!" he shouted, "It's Professor George Scott." Simon couldn't believe his eyes. The eccentric professor was the last person on earth he would expect to see riding up to his house.

"Good grief, George, I can't believe it's you," he shouted.

"It's me in person," Scott laughed. "I was sent all the way up here by our old friend General Caleb Kirby to find you."

"Well, you found me and it's getting late, so you better plan on spending the night and having dinner with us and then we'll discuss whatever you came up here for over some great Kentucky Whiskey I happen to have in the cabinet. Maggie will be glad to see you…I hope," he added suspiciously.

After getting his horse settled in the barn, a big hug from Maggie, and settling himself into the guest room, Professor Scott and his two hosts sat down to one of her scrumptious dinners. Maggie had prepared an excellent chicken and vegetable stew served over rice, accompanied by yeast rolls and with the meal topped off with fresh apple pie. It was one of the best meals Scott had eaten in a long time.

"Now Professor," Simon declared, "let us adjourn to the study and have us a whiskey while you tell me why the unexpected visit."

"Very smooth," Scott pronounced as he took a sip of the amber colored liquor. "This whiskey has an excellent taste, I might add, and an interesting name too...Buckhorn Creek. That must be the location where it is distilled."

Simon nodded. "I have a good friend that brings me a few bottles up from Kentucky now and then. Now tell me, George, what's up?"

"General Kirby, on instructions from the president, asked that I bring you back to Washington for a high-level meeting with President Hayes and Treasury Secretary Sherman. It has something to do about recovering a huge treasure to help shore up our treasury to help them revert to the gold standard. They also want Elijah Walker to attend, but they need to know where to find him."

"Elijah lives with Rosita on the Rio del Viejo Ranch in California, near the town of Capistrano," Simon reminded him. "That's a hell of a long way from Washington."

Scott continued. "Kirby will send a wire to Fort Guijarros in San Diego and have a detail pick him up and put him on the nearest Union Pacific train. Kirby thought he was somewhere living on a ranch in southern California. He told me this is the closest army installation to Capistrano and the ranch."

Scott hesitated momentarily to put his thoughts together. He wanted to tell Simon about the Iceland exhibition. The professor explained how they found the cave and secret room where the Vikings runestone tablets were stored. He told him about Professor Johansen and the fact that he was in the process of deciphering the runes. "There is one more thing you need to know, Simon, something perhaps more important than the Spanish treasure in Venezuela. When we discovered the Viking runestones, we found something in that cave that was totally out of place. We found a thin metallic tablet inscribed with strange markings and symbols. The inscriptions and color of the metal document look very much like those pages in the logbook Elijah took from that spacecraft you found in the Yucatan...the one you named the *Toltec*. If it is the same, it would mean that the Vikings were visited by Commander Ahular's and Vice-Commander Nezar's ancestors around eight hundred years ago."

Simon was speechless. "What an incredible coincidence that would be," he admitted. "I'll send Elijah a wire and tell him to be sure and bring the logbook with him. We'll compare the two documents. That could prove quite interesting. I have some duties to tie up around here before I leave. The hardest part will be to tell Maggie I'll be gone for a few weeks. Her parents still live in Washington so she'll probably want to stay with them while I'm gone. I'll meet you at the Burlington House in four days. It will take Elijah a week or so to travel here from California."

Simon felt a tinge of excitement with the thoughts of embarking on a new treasure hunt. Like Elijah, the thrill of an adventure was also in his blood.

Rio del Viejo Ranch, California

After the Amazon affair, Elijah had left Washington and caught a Baltimore and Potomac train heading west. His connection with the Union Pacific in Salt Lake carried him to California. He would follow up on his promise to visit Rosita, the beautiful Mexican girl he had met during their Yucatan exhibition in 1865.

She had confessed her love for him and he reciprocated with the same feelings. Rosita had inherited the huge Rio del Viejo ranch when her husband died from an accident in '73. Although they had not yet married, Elijah lived with her and helped manage the ranch and the large herds of cattle and horses owned by Rio del Viejo. Elijah's former companion, Santos, who had accompanied him on the three prior expeditions, was Rosita's brother and lived on the ranch. He helped his sister manage the many duties associated with running a large cattle ranch.

Elijah was sitting on his horse overlooking the cattle grazing the north pasture when he saw a rider galloping toward him. It was Santos. "You sure are in a big hurry," Elijah shouted.

Santos reined up beside him. "There are two visitors down at the house that want to see you. They are soldiers from Fort Guijarros in San Diego. One is a lieutenant."

"What do they want?"

"I don't know but they said it was very important."

Elijah rolled his eyes and responded, "Two soldiers…sounds like big trouble to me."

As Elijah approached the house, two men in uniform were standing on the front porch talking to Rosita. He approached the men suspiciously. "I'm Elijah Walker…I understand you are looking for me."

"Yes, we are, Mr. Walker. I am Lieutenant John Portman and this is Sergeant Roberts. We were dispatched all the way from San Diego to get you. You have been summoned to Washington D.C. by a General Caleb Kirby for a meeting with the president. The wire also said your cousin Simon Murphy and a Professor George Scott were also summoned."

Oh, good grief, Elijah thought. *I know this is trouble.* "Any idea what this is all about, Lieutenant?" he asked.

"No, sir, only that it is a very urgent meeting. We are to escort you to the train station in Los Angeles where tickets are waiting for you on the Southern Railroad to San Francisco. From there you will transfer to the Central Pacific to Salt Lake, the Union Pacific to St. Louis, and finally the Baltimore and Ohio to Washington." This is the quickest and most direct route. I have been assigned to accompany you."

Elijah knew something big was in the works, most likely another expedition and wild goose chase to Lord only knows where. "Okay, Lieutenant Portman, let me pack a few things and I'll be with you shortly."

"It's about a 70-mile ride from here to Los Angeles so we need to get going very shortly," Portman replied.

Rosita was distraught as she followed him in into the house. "You can't leave me here by myself," she said, tears streaming down her face. "We were talking about getting married. I can't stand the thought of you going off on another wild goose chase and getting yourself killed in some godforsaken place."

He took her into his arms. "This meeting might not be as bad as you think and take long at all. I'll be back as soon as I can…I promise. This is a direct summons from the president and you know I can't refuse that. If I refused to go I might find myself sitting in a prison somewhere and you don't want that, do you? You and Santos can handle things here while I'm gone."

Elijah was getting restless with the everyday mundane duties of ranch life and deep down inside the thoughts of another adventure with his cousin Simon brought him a slight feeling of exhilaration. There is no way he could miss out on this. General Kirby was right…adventure was in his bones.

Elijah threw a few clothes into a bag and grabbed his model 1872 Remington revolver from the shelf, the same gun he had carried into the Amazon. There was one more thing he remembered. Although he had not yet received the wire from Simon, he went to a drawer and pulled out the old logbook he had taken from the *Toltec* in '65. *I might need this,* he thought and shoved it into his pack. Based on his prior journeys, he knew the logbook might come in handy. He then walked out to meet the soldiers waiting for him. They had brought an extra mount along so he could accompany them. Giving Rosita a last hug, he mounted his horse, gave her a parting wave and departed the ranch. In his mind, he knew another exciting but perilous journey was about to begin.

8

The three riders made it to Capistrano where they veered north to follow the coastal route. The plan was to stop in the town of Costa Mesa and transfer to a carriage that would carry them to the train station in Los Angeles. The relay had apparently been well planned because when they arrived the cart was waiting for them. The lieutenant turned to Elijah. "Here is where we part with Sergeant Roberts. I believe I told you that I am to accompany you all the way to Washington where I am to be reassigned to a post somewhere in the east. Hope you don't mind." That explained the extra bag loaded in the cart.

Elijah chuckled. "Of course, I don't mind, Lieutenant Portman. At least I'll have someone to talk to and pass the time away."

"Since we're going to be traveling companions and since you are a civilian, please call me John."

"Okay, John, and you can dispense with Mr. Walker and call me Elijah."

A new friendship was born.

"Are you armed?" Portman asked.

"Yes, I am," Elijah responded. "I have a model '72 Remington single action revolver, .40-44 caliber."

Portman replied, "Just before we rode out to your ranch, I

was issued a brand new '78 Model Colt double action revolver, same caliber as your Remington. This gun was just released to the army and I was lucky enough to get one. I haven't even fired the damn thing yet. I honestly think it was issued to me because of my assignment to accompany you to Washington. It's a long way across country and I hope we don't have to use them, but it's good to have this protection just in case."

= = = = = =

The short trip to San Francisco took only part of a day when they arrived early evening and then transferred to the Central Pacific bound for Salt Lake City. This leg of the journey was uneventful and the time passed quickly, aided by the casual conversation between the two men. Portman was curious why Elijah would be summoned all the way across the country to meet with the President of the United States. He bluntly asked his new friend, "Do have any idea why they have called you to Washington for such a high-level meeting with the president?"

Elijah grinned, "I have my suspicions. It probably pertains to some of the prior missions I participated in, searching for lost treasures in some of the craziest places."

Portman's interest was now stimulated. "You are a treasure hunter?"

"Perhaps I had better tell you a few stories, John, but I'm sure you are going to have a hard time believing them and will probably think I'm half crazy. I trust you will keep this to yourself."

"Try me," he said, his curiosity soaring. "No problem with the security…I have an official military security clearance."

Looking around to make sure he would not be overheard, Elijah spent the next two hours telling Portman about their journey into the Yucatan and the vast treasure they found in the lost Toltec city of Xepocotec. The story of their expedition to Peru was equally gripping, but the explanation of their last trip into the Amazon in search of El Dorado left his new friend speechless. Elijah held the story of their discoveries of the alien ships and contact with the alien commanders Ahular and Nezar to the very last. The part of Elijah's near death experience on the asteroid was the final blow. Portman was just shaking his head when he said, "You're kidding me of course."

"No, I'm not kidding you…it is all true. That's why I think they're calling me and a couple of other of my former associates to the Washington meeting. I have a feeling that the president wants us to mount another expedition to look for another lost treasure somewhere. Our politicians are always looking for more damn money to spend."

"Wow! Portman declared, "That sounds exciting. Wonder how I could be a part of your expedition. Searching for lost treasure would really be interesting and maybe they would let me go along as added security…I'm pretty good with a gun."

Elijah was beginning to really like his new friend. He turned to Portman and said, "I would like to have you along, so let's see what we can do. Based on our last experiences, I have a feeling we're going to need all the able bodies and guns we can muster."

At Salt Lake, the two men transferred to a Union Pacific

train going to St. Louis. The short stop between transfers enabled the men to grab a quick lunch before parting.

Elijah noticed a gruffly looking man boarding from the next platform. He was swaying slightly and glaring at the passengers around him...he obviously had too much to drink. "Looks like we have some trouble," Elijah muttered.

The route would take the train on a southeasterly direction across southern Wyoming into the grassland plains country of southern Nebraska and then dip down to the large cattle stockyards located in Kansas City. From there it was a straight shot across Missouri into St. Louis where they would transfer to the B&O and on to Washington. In Kansas City, Elijah planned to send a telegram to General Kirby and advise him of his progress and estimated arrival time. The trouble started soon after the train pulled out of Omaha.

John Portman was asleep in the window seat while Elijah sat next to him on the aisle reading a copy of the Tribune he had purchased in Salt Lake. It was a two-day old newspaper but Elijah didn't mind...news was news and it was something to occupy his time. He glanced up from the paper when he heard distracting noises in front of him. It was the intoxicated man he had seen boarding from the next platform and it appeared he had been deeply engaged into the whiskey bottle again. Old gruffly was in a foul mood and cursing with every swaying step. The drunk stopped and stared at a male passenger then knocked the hat off the man as he yelled, "Quit starring at me."

Seated across the aisle from Elijah were a young mother and her three-year-old son sitting next to her. The man staggered up to her seat and stammered, "Hey, cutie, I want to sit next to you."

The terrified lady answered, "I'm sorry, sir, but this seat is occupied by my child."

The brute bellowed a loud curse and then roared, "So move the damned kid!" He then swiped his hand and slapped the top of the boy's head, causing him to start crying.

Elijah had enough of this punk so he drew his leg back and slammed his heel as hard as he could into the drunk's knee. The passengers around heard the noise as bone, tissue, and ligaments shattered and the man's leg caved inward. He slammed to the floor, screaming in pain. The thug turned to see Elijah glaring at him. This infuriated him further as he reached into his belt and pulled out a 7" Bowie knife. "I'll cut your head off," he shrieked.

The man froze as he felt something cool pressing against his temple. "Drop the knife you drunk bastard or I'll blow your brains out."

Lieutenant Portman, with arm extended, was holding the muzzle of his Colt .40-44 against the drunk's head. The man dropped the knife. "Why don't we throw the animal off the train?" Portman suggested as he gave Elijah a wink.

"Good idea," Elijah agreed as he and his companion grabbed the man by each arm and started dragging him down the aisle toward the passageway. He started screaming again, "You can't do that…my leg is broken. I can't walk and I'll just lie in the dirt until some wolf eats me."

"That's the idea," Elijah yelled back.

The brute screamed again.

A voice from behind said, "We'll take over from here, Gentlemen." Elijah and Portman turned to see two serious looking men standing behind them. "We are Pinkerton agents and one of the passengers told us about the trouble you were having. I would say you two gentlemen did a darned good job handling the problem. The Union Pacific thanks you."

Elijah nodded and released the man. "He is all yours."

As they headed back to their seats, a passenger asked, "Would you really have thrown that man off the train?"

"Elijah chuckled, "Well, he certainly deserved it but probably not. We just wanted to scare the devil out of the drunken brute."

The remark was met with a loud round of applause and laughter from some very appreciative passengers. The young woman with her little boy was especially grateful. She softly took his hand and said, "I can't thank you enough, sir. He scared my son and me half to death."

"You are most welcome, ma'am," he responded appreciatively. The warmth of her soft hand was gratitude enough.

Seated once again, Elijah leaned over to his new companion. "John, it looks like you and I will make a good team.

Portman grinned and responded, "It sure looks that way, partner."

= = = = = =

Before they changed trains in St. Louis, Elijah checked with the B&O office to find out when they were scheduled to reach Washington. He learned the remaining trip would take two and a half days and their train was scheduled to arrive about 3:00 PM on Sunday. He then stopped by the Western Union Telegraph office close by and penned out a wire to General Kirby at the Washington Arsenal, advising him of his estimated time of arrival. While he was looking forward to seeing his cousin Simon and Professor Scott, he could hardly wait to sit down to one of Fanny Whittington's famous meals at the Burlington House. He could already taste her succulent roast beef, fresh field peas, mashed potatoes, and hot biscuits slathered in gravy. His mouth watered at the thoughts of her hot apple pie. Elijah was known for his ravishing culinary habits and he knew in addition to a summons from his president he felt that Fanny's meals were well worth traveling all the way across the country for.

9

Washington, D.C.

The train pulled into the B&O station at 3:35 PM with General Kirby waiting at the platform. Elijah and Lieutenant Portman exited the train and immediately recognized Kirby. Glancing to his left, he also saw the wounded drunk being escorted from the train in handcuffs by the two Pinkerton agents. He had to be half carried due to his shattered knee. Elijah saw he was in obvious pain. "Old gruffly" grimaced when he saw Elijah who nodded back to him and said, "Good riddance, you drunken bastard."

Kirby spotted Elijah and walked over to him, hand extended. "Elijah Walker, how good to see you again."

"Thank you, General. It's great to see you as well. It's been a long time."

Portman, now back in uniform, came to attention and offered the general a stiff salute. He smartly said, "Lieutenant John Portman reporting for duty as ordered, sir."

"Kirby returned the salute and replied, "You may stand down, Lieutenant. If you two gentlemen will follow me, I have a carriage waiting in the front that will take us over to the Burlington House. Elijah, I believe you have two old friends anxiously waiting to see you."

= = = = = =

The ride from the train station took about forty minutes, which gave General Kirby and Elijah some time to talk. "Do you know why you have been summoned?" Kirby asked.

"I have a good idea it means another expedition to look for hidden treasure somewhere."

Kirby laughed. "You are quite perceptive."

"Have you assembled your team yet?" Elijah asked.

"I'm the process of doing that now…definitely you, Simon, and Professor Scott. Do you have any thoughts?"

"Yes, sir, I have one individual in mind," Elijah said, glancing at his new friend. "Lieutenant Portman here would make a fine addition to the team, plus he has quick reactions and is very good with a gun. He can help us with security. He saved me from getting stabbed by a drunk on the train. Having been stationed in southern California, he also speaks and understands the Spanish language, which could be helpful, depending on where we are going."

Portman commented, "When you are assigned to San Diego like I've been for the past four years, you have to learn to speak Spanish to communicate and get along with many of the locals."

Kirby turned to Portman. "You were assigned the duty of escorting Mr. Walker back here to Washington and since you are unmarried I was going to reassign you to a unit at the arsenal. Would you be interested in accompanying the team on this special assignment?"

Lieutenant Portman smiled and eagerly replied, "Yes, sir, General, I would love to be included with the group. Elijah told me some of the stories about his past journeys and incredible adventures and I would definitely like to be a part of this assignment, whatever it is."

"Well, Lieutenant Portman, I will see that you are included. I'll explain more in detail when we get to the Burlington House where we will arrange a room there for you as well."

= = = = = =

The Burlington House Proprietor, Fanny Whittington, met them at the door and gave Elijah a big hug. She remembered him for the great appreciation he had shown for her excellent cooking. "Why Mr. Walker, how nice to see you again…it's been at least four or five years. Mr. Murphy told me you would be here today. He is waiting for you in the parlor."

"Thank you, Fanny, nice to see you as well." She ushered the newcomers back to a secluded room where Simon and Professor Scott were waiting.

When the newcomers entered the room, Simon jumped up to greet his cousin with a big bear hug. "I knew you wouldn't miss out on this undertaking," he said to Elijah. "You always love it when trouble knocks on the door."

Elijah laughed, "You like to have me around to help keep your ass out of trouble. Beside ranch life is too much work."

Professor Scott also joined in with his greetings. "Good to see you old chap. It's been a long time."

"Yes, it has, Professor. I'm glad to see you are back with us."

General Kirby interrupted the greetings when he said, "Gentlemen, you can catch up with each other later, but first let's get down to business and talk about why you are here. We have a meeting in the morning at ten o'clock with President Hayes and the secretaries of the Treasury and Navy. I need to brief you before the meeting. But first I want to introduce you to the newest member of the team who will be accompanying you on the mission. This is First Lieutenant John Portman who escorted Elijah from California. I understand he is very good with firearms."

Simon and Scott nodded their approval. "Glad to have you on board," Simon acknowledged.

Kirby continued, "There is another addition to the group. I am adding my aide as my liaison officer...First Lieutenant Charles Maxwell. Also, per Professor Scott's request, we are adding an associate of his, a young geologist named Jonah Steele."

Kirby noticed the confusion on Portman's face and knew it involved the question of rank authority between the two equal ranking officers. "Mr. Portman, to clear up any confusion, you and Mr. Maxwell will be traveling as temporary civilians so all military rankings will be lifted for the mission. Technically, Mr. Maxwell will be in charge, but all of you will work as a team to make decisions as situations arise. This has worked very well with our last three missions and that's why Mr. Murphy, Walker, and Scott are still alive and with us."

Portman nodded his understanding and obvious relief.

"Another man will also be included. His name is Sergeant Javier Peña. He is the man who told us about the treasure story. His parents were from Venezuela and he said that he has visited there several times."

Kirby spent the next hour relating the story of how Peña's ancestor witnessed the sinking of the Spanish galleon, recovered the gold from the sea, and hid it in a cave on the Island of Margarita, just off the coast of Venezuela. He further explained how his great, great grandfather had relocated the treasure to a remote location in Venezuela, not far from the coastal town of Cumana, most likely hidden deep inside a cave. He told them about an alleged treasure map and the fact that Peña thinks he can locate it.

"He indicated he might have a relative who lives somewhere around Cumana and can help him find it," Kirby continued. "The mission will be fully explained at the meeting, so I'll meet you in the morning at 9:15 for our walk over to the White House."

He turned to his two officers, discontinuing any references to any military rankings. "Mr. Portman, since Spanish is the language of Venezuela, your knowledge of the language will come in handy. And Professor Scott, I suggest you go fetch your geologist friend Jonah Steele and bring him back to the inn. He will need to attend the meeting in the morning. I'll arrange a room for him before I leave…and Professor, tell him the government is picking up the charges." The general left the room.

As Elijah had hoped, Mrs. Whittington had prepared a special feast for her new guests. Like her mother before her, she reveled in the compliments she received for her culinary excellence.

Her kitchen was her domain and she treated it like a shrine with its assortment of pots, pans, and succulent recipes handed down from her mother and grandmother before her. Tonight would be a meal her guests would long remember. Elijah thought he was in food heaven and he would not be disappointed with the feast of roast duck, crispy sea bass, beef pot roast, mashed potatoes, fresh green beans cooked with ham hock, corn pudding, freshly baked yeast rolls, and a big pot of rich brown roast beef gravy. The meal was topped off with fresh apple and cherry pies. She had obviously gone out of her way for her *distinguished guests*.

As with her previous meals he had relished, Elijah piled his plate and topped everything with a lake of gravy. Three refills conveyed his pleasure, which Mrs. Whittington noticed and appreciated. Simon just rolled his eyes in resignation and quietly muttered, "How the hell can he find his food under all that gravy? The man is an animal."

Early the next morning, the five men accompanied the general on the short walk to the White House. Simon and Elijah had time to engage in some quiet conversation. "How about you and Rosita?" Simon asked. "I remember after the Amazon affair you were sure anxious to jump on that train to California. Did you two ever get married?"

"No, not yet, but we might get married when I get back from this mission," Elijah responded. "She sure wants to bad enough."

"What has held you back then?"

"I don't know exactly. I love Rosita but sometimes I wonder if I'm cut out for being so confined to married life. I'm just too damn restless I guess. But you seem to be doing pretty well being tied down to Maggie."

"Yeah…I have a great woman there and a great son I enjoy a lot. I have no problem with married life, but it's that ridiculous and boring job I have that bothers me. You won't believe it but I'm back in the hardware business."

"You're kidding…after all that mess you went through with the Fox brothers at your hardware store in Michigan."

"This time I'm working for a large company that sells tools and all sorts of things for hardware stores. The pay isn't bad but I sure get tired of doing the same old thing day after day. This is one reason I'm a little excited about us going on another treasure hunting expedition. I'm sure we won't get bored."

Elijah laughed. "I know what you mean. After watching cattle graze all day, I could use a little excitement myself…that is if we don't get ourselves killed first. What's Maggie going to say about you leaving again on another treasure hunting expedition?"

"She is not going to like it, but she knows the system and understands that a request from the president takes precedence. Her parents still live in Washington so she'll either go stay with them or her mother will come to our house to be with her and Thomas while I'm gone. Now let's go see what this important meeting is all about."

10

The White House

A member of the White House staff ushered General Kirby and his seven-man team into a meeting room in the North Portico. President Hayes was already waiting with Treasury Secretary Sherman, Secretary of the Navy Thompson, and Secretary of State William Evarts. Kirby introduced each man and described his qualifications. The former exploits of Simon, Elijah, and Professor Scott in the Yucatan, Peruvian, and Amazon affairs were well known to the Washington insiders and Hayes had been well briefed. The president came right to the point.

"Gentlemen, General Kirby has given each of you a briefing of the mission so I won't bother you by repeating what he told you. As you know, our country is in a very precarious situation due to that damnable Bland-Allison Act that was passed a few weeks ago by Congress. It made our monetary system very unstable with the dual gold and silver standard. We need to revert to a total gold standard. The only way we can do that is to increase our supply of gold to our treasury, and quickly. By keeping the dual standard, we could easily slip into a deep depression which would be catastrophic to our citizens, our economy, and our government. Mr. Kirby told you about the Spanish treasure hidden in Venezuela. I want you to secure that treasure and bring it back to Washington. Each of you will be generously rewarded for your effort. You have all the details, so I'll let the general help you set the plan in motion."

"Mr. President," Kirby said, "I will move the team to the Washington Arsenal where we will issue them new weapons and finalize the details of the mission. Of course, we will need transportation by the navy both to and from Venezuela to transport the gold."

Hayes turned to Secretary Thompson. "Richard, I want you to assign one of your fastest ships to this mission, one that is well armed and large enough to transport the heavy weight of the gold."

"Yes, sir. I will handle it."

President Hayes stood up and made his final statements. "Gentlemen, I know I can count on you to complete this mission successfully. Our country is counting on it."

He then addressed his final remarks to Simon, Elijah, and Professor Scott. "I was fully briefed on your extraordinary successes in your prior missions. Some of the things you accomplished are incredible, especially those where you and your... hmmm...strange new friends helped save our planet."

The president hesitated for a moment, trying to reflect on what he had just said. He had not been involved in Simon or Elijah's previous missions and the information about the extraordinary visitors had been told to him by his predecessor. The information had been difficult to believe.

"I am confident your success in this mission will prove equally successful." He then turned and left the room, signaling the meeting was over.

General Kirby had the seven team members transported to the arsenal where weapons would be issued and final details would be concluded. The date of departure was in four days.

Each man was issued a new 1878 model Colt double action revolver .40-44 caliber and a Model 1876 Winchester rifle. These were the same weapons procured by the museum and given to Professor Scott for his runestone excursion into Iceland a few weeks before. He was now very familiar with the weapons and had participated in several practices at a local range. His personal guns were securely locked up in the museum so he was supplied new similar replacement weapons to save him a trip back to retrieve them.

The combined firepower amounted to a small army, considering most of the soldiers in the Venezuelan army still carried an assortment of muskets purchased from Germany or Bulgaria.

The group spent several hours at the arsenal's range familiarizing themselves with the new weapons. Elijah was proud that he beat his cousin with thirteen of fifteen bull's eyes with the Winchester. As usual, Scott bested all of them with his fifteen of fifteen bulls.

= = = = = =

The day before departure, General Kirby assembled the group to finalize some details. This had to be a clandestine operation, he explained, especially the actual search for and extraction of the gold out of Venezuela. A map of the Venezuelan coast was posted on the board with some suggested entry and extraction points marked with pins. This would take close coordination with the Navy to pull it off. The group of six of the seven team members was assembled in a room for the briefing, but there was a slight delay because Javier Peña was a bit late. He had to ride over to his mother's house to retrieve his father's diary. They would need the code so they could find the map.

When Peña arrived, Kirby stood up and addressed the group. "Gentlemen, from this point on we will formally dispense with rank and I'll address you by your civilian name. You are about to embark on a long and perhaps dangerous journey to retrieve the Spanish treasure in Venezuela. This mission will have to be coordinated with the Navy to make your rendezvous with the ship and take the treasure out. Simon, Elijah, and Javier Peña will have to be secretly taken to Cumana to find the map while the rest of you will be put ashore through an inlet near Mochima." He pointed to a pin on the map.

"You must choose a safe place somewhere along the coast and link up with Simon and Elijah with the map. You can select a designated place near the town of Barbacoas, the home place of Mr. Peña's parents. He knows the area and can pick a secure spot. From there you're on your own to find the treasure and transport it to a designated spot in the inlet near Mochima where our ship will pick you up with the treasure. You will coordinate the spot with the ship's captain. I believe you will need to hire at least three wagons locally to transport the gold."

The general hesitated a few moments to allow his remarks to sink in. Then he continued, "I am sure each of you will want to know more about the captain and ship that will take you to Venezuela. Mr. Murphy and Walker know him well. Your old friend Captain John Whitmore and the USS Halifax will be assigned to your mission. Captain Whitmore gladly volunteered his ship when he learned you two were involved. Since he was unable to complete his mission with you in Brazil, he wanted to finish it with you in Venezuela. The Halifax has been refitted with new guns and is well equipped to help you complete your mission."

Elijah glanced at Simon and shrugged his shoulders. "We'll be glad to see Captain Whitmore again. This time we will make sure he completes his mission," Simon responded humorously, remembering how they had abandoned Whitmore and his ship to take the journey up the Amazon River in their search for the lost city of gold…El Dorado.

General Kirby, not very amused, picked up the inference and continued, "Thursday morning a skiff will be waiting at our docks near the arsenal to transport you down the Potomac River to the Chesapeake Bay. You will rendezvous at a place called Smith Point where you will transfer to the Halifax that will carry you to the Caribbean and Venezuela. Any questions?"

"Yes," Simon answered. "How are we supposed to find the map to the treasure?"

"Mr. Peña has his father's diary that supposedly has a clue to the location to the map."

He turned to the sergeant, "Mr. Peña, would you please look at the diary and tell us the clue?"

"Yes, sir," he answered as he pulled a small weathered leather

bound book from his coat pocket. "The map is hidden somewhere in Cumana. When I was a boy, my father told me the
story about the sinking of the Spanish galleon and the treasure
that was recovered and removed from the island to the mainland
by my ancestors. I remember my father telling me the code for
the map was handed down by his grandfather to his father. I am
not sure when he recorded this in the diary, but here is the clue
and my father's last entry in the diary…CSM- SE-CS-8."

"Any idea what that means, Mr. Peña?" Kirby asked.

"Not exactly, sir, but I do know that there is an old fort in in
the center of Cumana called Castillo Santa Maria de la Cabeza
that was built by the Spanish in the late1600s. The CSM in the
code may refer to that fort. That would be a good place to start."

"Very well…I'm sure you will figure it out. You men will depart early in the morning and I wish you Godspeed." The meeting was concluded.

= = = = = =

The next morning, the team was transported to a small dock
that occupied a spot where the Anacostia River and Potomac
joined. The men boarded a small screw propelled steamer commanded by a captain named Palmer. He had been briefed and
knew the group was headed up by Simon Murphy and Charles
Maxwell. He ushered them to his small cabin where he gave
them a short briefing of the trip downriver to the Chesapeake
Bay. He informed them that the linkup with the Halifax would

be sometime late afternoon. Simon and Maxwell then joined
the others on deck and settled in for the ride. The cruise brought
back many memories to Simon and Elijah. They had taken this
same shuttle in '73 en route to Brazil. Elijah well remembered
passing by Mt. Vernon and Fort Belvoir and listening to Professor's Scott's historical lectures about the sites. He was thankful
he didn't have to listen to the same orations all over again. The
professor stayed at the bow engaged in conversation with his associate, Jonah Steele, and Sergeant Peña. He was no doubt giving them the same historical sermons about the different sites
along the way.

Rounding Smith Point, Simon recognized the spot by the
old dilapidated lighthouse that overlooked the mouth of the
Chesapeake Bay. This is the location where the Halifax had
met them to embark on their previous journey to Brazil and the
Amazon expedition in '73. Moored at the dock, the USS Halifax was waiting for them. The group gathered their equipment,
said their goodbyes to Captain Palmer, and then walked over
and stood at the bottom of the Halifax gangway. Captain John
Whitmore and his first mate were waiting for them at the railing above. Maxwell shouted, "Permission to come aboard, sir."

"Permission granted," Whitmore shouted back.

With Simon leading the way, the seven team members
climbed the plank and gathered on deck. Captain Whitmore
smiled and walked over to Simon for the first hand shake. "Well,
Mr. Murphy, it appears that you and Mr. Walker have decided to
take another spin to South America with me. Perhaps this time
I can return you back to Washington safely."

Simon shook his hand and replied, "Captain, I wish to apologize for causing any problems for you and your ship, but the trip up the Amazon was necessary, plus we made some amazing discoveries."

"Yes, I was briefed thoroughly about your Amazon adventure…I believe you actually discovered the legionary city of El Dorado and the lost Inca gold treasure."

"Yes, sir, we did and I'm sure you have been briefed about this mission."

"Yes, I have…this time searching for more treasure from a sunken Spanish galleon I understand."

After all the introductions were made, Whitmore directed some remarks to Lieutenants Maxwell and Portman. "I understand all military ranks between you two have been suspended for this mission. I don't quite understand but I'm sure there was a good reason so I'll address you men by names only. Now, if you will follow my first mate, Mr. Andrews here, he will show you and your men to their quarters. We have a long trip to the Venezuelan coast so I had better get the Halifax underway."

11

Aboard the USS Halifax

Simon and Elijah occupied one cabin, Professor Scott and Jonah Steele another, and Lieutenants Maxwell and Portman the third. Javier Peña was assigned a bunk in the crew's quarters located in the forecastle or forward section of the ship. The Halifax was well into the Atlantic Ocean and cruising due south parallel to the North Carolina shoreline. Simon and Elijah were relaxing on their bunks, trying to get a bit of rest while quietly discussing what they would say at the upcoming meeting scheduled the next morning with Captain Whitmore. The conversation was interrupted by a rap on the door...it was Professor Scott holding an unusual object under his arm. Simon looked up. "Well, come in Professor. I sure didn't expect to see you until dinner. What's up?"

"I have something very strange to show you. We found it in an ancient cave in Iceland along with some Viking weapons and runestones." He held up the metallic tablet. "No one knows about this but Jonah and me."

This really piqued Simon and Elijah's curiosity. The tablet looked familiar.

"It was hidden in an adjoining room that had been carved into a rock wall connected to the main cavern. This tablet was in the same room as the weapons and runestones. You can see the texture of the surface, and the inscriptions and symbols look very familiar. I wanted to compare it to that logbook Elijah found on the *Toltec*."

"You did bring the logbook, didn't you?" Simon asked with a hint of concern. "I sent you a wire reminding you to bring it."

"I must have left before your telegram was delivered, but I did bring the log," Elijah replied, turning to retrieve it from his pack.

"Let's lay them on the table and take a look," Simon said. The curiosity was building.

The men examined each of the documents as they lay side by side. The similarities were startling. Scott offered the first observation. "Even though my tablet is thicker, the feel and texture seem very similar to the pages in this logbook—they seem to be made of the same metallic material. I also notice that several of the glyphs and symbols are identical. You told me that logbook came from the spacecraft, *Toltec*…the one you discovered in the cavern in the Yucatan. Do you suppose…?"

Elijah finished the sentence. "Do you suppose the Vikings were visited by the ancestors of Commanders Ahular and Nezar eight hundred years ago?"

"It would sure appear that way," Simon answered. "I really would like to know what those inscriptions mean on the tablet…I hope we get a chance to find out. Who knows, maybe we'll get an opportunity to have our old friends interpret the tablet."

"What's that supposed to mean?" Scott asked suspiciously.

"You remember what Ahular told us back in '73 just before they took off from Washington. He left the Zenox with me and told me that it might come in handy sometime. I have a feeling we haven't seen the last of Ahular and Nezar."

The professor chose not to pursue the matter so he left the tablet with Simon and left the cabin with weird thoughts reeling through his head.

= = = = = =

The meeting the next morning was held in the small conference room next to Whitmore's cabin.

The captain was there with first mate Alan Andrews and the seven men assigned to the mission. "Gentlemen," Whitmore began, "I have been thoroughly briefed on the mission and aware of the story Mr. Peña related to General Kirby. I believe the first phase will be to get Simon, Elijah, and Peña ashore in Cumana so they can recover a map. We will have to use one of our dinghies and row you in late at night. Hopefully, we can deposit you ashore undetected. We have some special clothes for you to wear so you will blend in with the locals."

Simon and Elijah nodded their understanding. Turning to Peña, Whitmore asked, "I believe you said you had visited your parents several times in the past but they are now deceased. Do you have any relatives left in Cumana or the surrounding area?"

Peña said, "I believe I may have a cousin still in Cumana,

named Fabio. He is the son of my father's brother. I have not seen him in several years though, and not even sure where he might live."

"Do you think he would be of any help to us?"

"The more I thought about it, I really don't think Fabio would be of very much help. I don't know if he has any connections to the military there, but I believe we would be more secure if we leave him out of it. I think we can find the map without him."

Whitmore concurred. "I understand the military unit stationed in the town of Cumana and the surrounding Sucre district is commanded by a very sadistic and cruel military man named Colonel Manuel Gallegos. We hear this guy is a cruel son-of-a-bitch, so you don't want to fall into his hands. I'm sure he would be most interested in forcing information out of some unknown American visitors poking around his town. You'll need to find the map as quickly as possible and travel the coastal road west to a small fishing village called Playa Cautarito where you will rendezvous with the others in your party. It should be about a four or five-mile trek. If you can grab some horses, it won't take you very long to meet up with the rest of the group. Then it will be up to you to secure the wagons and go find the treasure."

Professor Scott couldn't resist injecting some of his historical knowledge to the conversation. "Gentlemen," he politely interrupted, "Cumana has quite a historical significance. The town was founded by the Spanish in 1521 and was the first city built on the American continent. Cumana derived its name from the Cumanagoto Indians who then occupied the area. To the Indians, the name means the union between the sea and the river.

The Spanish built a large fort there in the 17th century that was to protect the city from pirate raiders."

Captain Whitmore chuckled and said, "Thank you, Professor Scott, for your interesting history lesson. I see you have done your homework."

Simon saw Elijah glancing at him with that *oh no, not again* look. He grinned when he saw him shrug and roll his eyes.

Whitmore then turned and pointed to some topographies on the large map spread out on the table. "We will be anchored off this point just north of the mouth of this inlet…not far from Playa Cautarito. Here the Halifax will wait for you to complete the mission, then rendezvous with us at Playa Cautarito. There is a good stretch of beach here, so it shouldn't take long to transfer the treasure containers to the ship. You will have to stay concealed until dusk so you won't be spotted. We will toss anchor here in exactly four days from now at 1900 hours or 7:00 PM," he added, pointing to a spot on the map. "This should give you plenty of time to secure the map, secure the treasure, and then meet us at the designated rendezvous point. Any questions?"

There were none.

That evening the Halifax slipped past the Isla de Margarita, past the tip of the Araya Peninsula, and into the mouth of the narrow inlet bordering the town of Cumana. Captain Whitmore waited until dark and then ordered a small rowboat to be lowered over the side. Accompanied by two oarsmen, Simon, Elijah, and Peña dropped into the boat. Simon turned to his cousin. "I hope you didn't forget your new Colt revolver."

Elijah grinned and patted his side. "Wouldn't leave home without it."

The two oarsmen hesitated just off shore to make sure there was no one about and then silently pushed the small craft to the beach where the three men disembarked near a small dock. As the rowboat turned back for the return to the ship, the men crouched behind nearby bushes to make sure they were undetected. The area was deserted.

Simon turned to Peña. "You said you were born and raised in a town nearby. You must know your way around Cumana, don't you?"

"Yes," the sergeant replied, "I have been here several times but it has been a few years."

"The first thing we need to do is to interpret that code. Any ideas?" Simon asked.

Peña reached into his pack and pulled out his dad's old log book with the code. He examined it for a few seconds and then repeated it aloud, "CSM-SE-CS-8."

"What the devil could all of that mean?" Elijah asked.

"I've been studying this book and looking at some of the notes my father wrote down. He had a real obsession with the old Spanish forts. There are two notable old fortresses in Cumana. As the professor mentioned in the meeting, one is the Castillo de San Antonio de la Eminencia and the other is the Castillo de Santa Maria de la Cabeza. They were built in the late 1600s. The Santa Maria was damaged by an earthquake in 1799 and again a few years ago, in 1853. This last quake reduced it to ruins, but some of the walls still stand today. I am almost certain the CSM means Castillo de Santa Maria. The map is most likely buried somewhere in the old walls if they're still standing."

"We've got to be more specific," Simon noted. "Wonder what the SE stands for."

Elijah picked up on this. "How about a direction…like southeast for example. Maybe it's hidden in the southeast section of the fort, or perhaps the southeastern part of the wall."

"Okay, that sounds plausible," Simon agreed. "Probably a good place to start."

"What about the letters CS and the number 8? I think those letters seem to be the real keys to the map's location."

"I guess we'll have to get to the fort to figure that out," Simon replied. "Meanwhile, let's move over to those trees and try to get a couple of hours' sleep. How far to the fort, Javier?"

Peña answered, "I would say we have about a two-mile walk. Santa Maria is close to the St. Agnes Church on Sucre Road. I can find it easily. We need to leave very early so we can get there before sunrise."

"One thing we know for certain," Simon said with a hint of concern, "we've got to find that map and get out of Cumana as quick as possible. The last thing we want is to get caught by that murdering swine, Colonel Gallegos. I do have a fondness for my head."

Elijah emitted a nervous laugh as he unconsciously rubbed his neck.

12

Cumana, Venezuela

With Peña's good memory and sense of direction, the three men arrived at the base of Fort Santa Maria just as the morning light began to appear dimly in the east. The streets were empty. They walked around the fort trying to get their bearings and familiarize themselves with the surroundings. The men arrived at the southeast corner of the fort and examined the walls. They had to move fast. "Let's concentrate on solving the last two parts of the clue. What are your thoughts, Javier?" Simon pressed.

"There is one entry in his log that says, "The turret stares at me like a sentinel and makes my blood run cold. I grasp my chisel like a sword."

Simon glanced at the top of the wall and saw a small circular tower with small slits as windows. "That's interesting," Simon pondered while glancing at the wall. "So, he must have been holding a chisel. That means he was chipping away at some rock or mortar and maybe that was the same turret that was looking down on him."

"Let's look at that clue again," Elijah suggested. "CSM-SE-CS-8. We're here at the southeast corner of Castillo Santa Maria so we need to figure out what the CS and 8 mean."

All three were trying to connect the 'CS' to a specific location. "*Center section,*" Peña offered.

"Not specific enough," Elijah countered.

"How about *circular stairs*?" Simon suggested.

"I know of no circular stairs in the fort," Peña informed them.

Simon looked up again. "We'd better figure something out quickly because I just heard some voices on top of the wall."

"I've got it," Elijah whispered. "How about *corner stone*?"

The three glanced up the wall and saw heavy stones embedded in the corner of the wall, extending all the way to the top. Elijah continued. "Maybe the number eight refers to the eighth stone from the base. It looks reachable from the ground."

Mentally, the men counted eight stones up and fixed their eyes on a heavy rectangular coral block protruding slightly from the wall. The mortar between the joints appeared to be inconsistent, indicating that the joints may have been once chiseled out and replaced with a grout-like filling. Something was definitely different.

Their thoughts were broken by a demanding shout from above. They had been spotted.

"Cuál es usted hombres que hacen abajo allí?"

"What is he saying, Peña?" Simon asked.

"He wants to know what we are doing down here."

"Tell him we are just admiring the fort and the old construction methods the Spanish builders used."

"Somos justos admirando los viejos métodos de la construcción que los constructores españoles utilizaron," Peña shouted back.

"La fortaleza es cerrada y visitantes no permitida. Licencia ahora," the voice boomed out.

"He says the fort is closed and visitors are not allowed. We must leave now."

Simon assessed the situation and whispered, "Let's nod our understanding and wave to whoever it is shouting at us and casually walk off like we are just curious visitors. We'll come back soon when it looks clear."

The men waved to the top of the wall and casually moved toward the church located close by. They found a partially concealed spot in a small stand of trees behind the church, overlooking a tidy graveyard that gave them a clear sight of the southeast corner of the fort. Simon knew their time was short and they had to move quickly. He also knew if they were spotted removing the corner stone, they could be arrested and the entire mission would have to be aborted, not to mention most likely their lives wasted. The voice above had to be from one of Colonel Gallegos' soldiers guarding the old fort.

"What do we do now?" Peña asked apprehensively. "I didn't think those old ruins would be guarded."

Simon answered, "I wish we had some more darkness to cover us, but unfortunately we don't have time to wait until tonight. We have to do this now. What we need is a slight diversion in the front of the fort...something to draw the guard's attention. I doubt if there are more than a couple of men stationed here."

He thought for a moment. "Javier, since you speak Spanish, why don't you walk around to the front and engage one of the guards in some conversation while Elijah and I remove the corner stone and look for the map. You can ask him a couple of questions about its history and construction. Tell him you live in a town nearby and was just visiting some kinfolks and have a fascination for old forts. You can meet us back at this spot and we can get out of here fast. It shouldn't take us but a few minutes."

Peña nodded. "I can do that." He then turned and headed toward Sucre Street and the front entrance to the fort.

"How long do we wait?" Elijah asked his cousin.

"Let's give him fifteen minutes and then we'll move out."

The minutes passed quickly as Simon and Elijah slipped out toward the fort. They kept wary eyes toward the top of the wall, hoping not to spot any movement...it appeared empty. Quickly they reached the southeast corner and stared at the eighth block, forming a section of the corner of the building. Reaching up, Simon could touch the block. He pushed it with one hand, hoping to feel movement...nothing. "Elijah, the damn thing is too high. I can't get any leverage to put any pressure on it. I need something to stand on."

There was nothing in sight to allow that. Elijah knelt on one knee. "Try this...stand on my leg. That'll give you a couple of extra feet."

Simon grabbed the wall with one hand and stood on Elijah's leg. The block was now at eye level. He grasped the block with both hands and tried rotating it to the left then right. It wouldn't budge. "Maybe we misinterpreted the code," he grumbled.

Elijah pulled his Bowie knife from his belt. "Here, take my knife and pry some of the mortar out of the joints."

The knife point dug into the soft mortar and it easily crumbled and fell to the ground. He handed Elijah his knife back and again grasped the block. He pushed it to his left and felt slight movement. He pushed harder and finally moved the block to expose a space with a narrow dark opening.

"Hurry up, Simon. I can't hold you much longer. You weigh a ton."

"I'm hurrying fast as I can," he snorted back.

The opening was now large enough to stick his hand in. He groped the space for a few moments and felt something. His fingers grasped a firm slender object which he withdrew from the cavity—a small cylinder he dropped to the ground. Simon then gripped the stone block again, pushed it back into place, and then hopped down. "About time…thought my leg was going to break in half," Elijah moaned.

Grabbing the cylinder, Simon whispered, "Let's get outa here…back to the trees and fast."

No sooner than they reached the thicket, they spotted Peña rounding the corner of the church. He made it to the trees and motioned for his companions to conceal themselves as best as possible. "What happened?" Elijah asked.

"I did find a guard at the entrance and another soldier climbing down some steps toward me. He looked suspicious and could have been the same guy that was yelling at us from the top of the wall. They wanted to know what I was doing there. I think they accepted the story about my fascination with old forts."

Simon motioned them to silence. "I hate to say it but look over at the fort…the top of the wall."

A figure was plainly visible peering over the wall at the spot where they had been previously standing. The men cautiously moved further back into the grove.

"Did you get the map?" Peña asked.

"I haven't looked at it yet, but I did retrieve a cylinder hidden behind the cornerstone." He opened the tube and pulled out a roll of parchment.

The paper was in remarkably good shape, considering it had been stored in the wall for over a hundred years. The sturdy leather tube had protected the document well. Simon carefully unrolled the scroll and gazed at the roughly drawn map. "That's it," Peña whispered excitedly. "I see Playa Cautarito marked on the map and also Barbacoas to the south. The treasure spot is marked by that X you see in those mountains. There is a small village nearby called Antenas and I have been there when I was a kid. The valley above it is where the spot is marked. The location is only about three or four miles from the coast and the village of Playa Cautarito. That's where the rest of our party will be waiting."

"So how do we get to Playa Cautarito and our companions?" Elijah asked uneasily.

"That's easy, Amigos," Peña injected with a big grin. "We steal three of the horses I saw corralled at the front of the fort. They must belong to the guards. There are four horses there, which mean the guards must have a couple of visitors or maybe a change of the guards is about to happen."

"Then what are we waiting for," Simon declared. "We're running out of time."

13

The three men left the grove of trees and made their way around the far side of the church to Sucre Street. The front entrance to the fort was only a few steps away. "Where do we go when we get the horses," Elijah asked Peña.

"We make our way toward the coast and travel southwest on the coastal road past the Los Patos lagoon, and then on to Playa Cautarito to meet up with the others. Luckily, the horses are saddled, which makes it much easier for us. The guards or their visitors must be close to departing. I have a feeling two of them are the replacement guards, which means the other guards will be leaving soon."

The four horses Peña had mentioned were easily visible in a small corral close to the wall of the ruins. The wall would provide them some temporary concealment as they silently made their way to the corral. They slipped around to the gate and entered the enclosure. Each man mounted a horse and walked the mounts into the street. "This way," Peña said as he veered away from the front of the fort and toward the church. Suddenly a thunderous voice boomed down from above. They had been spotted. "Alto! Ésos son nuestros caballos!"

"What did he say?" Simon yelled.

"He is telling us to halt. The horses belong to them."

"Let's move it before the whole damned garrison gets on our tail."

Following Peña, the men spurred the horses and veered off Sucre Street and on to another unpaved street that headed north toward the bay. They would pick up the coastal road and cut sharply southwest toward the lagoon and on toward Playa Cautarito. It was likely they were seen by bystanders who could point the direction they were headed. In a matter of minutes, mounted soldiers would surely pick up their trail. Soon the three riders reached the coastal road and spurred the horses to a steady gallop. The men turned southwest toward the Los Patos lagoon. Peña reminded them it was about a five or six-mile ride to Playa Cautarito so they had to move it. The three men would bypass a small coastal fishing village named Playa el Chivo where it was possible a few soldiers might be located. It was imperative they slip by the village undetected and make their way along the coast as quickly as possible. Their other concern was the thought there could be mounted patrols along the coastal road. They would do their best to avoid any contact.

Garrison Headquarters, Cumana

Colonel Manuel Gallegos was sitting at his desk rummaging through some papers when his aide burst into his office. "Sir," the lieutenant shouted, "We have a report that three men just stole some horses from the guards at the Castillo Santa Maria and were seen riding toward the docks. It was also reported that two of the men were thought to be gringos."

Gallegos jumped up so fast that he sent his chair crashing to the floor. "Assemble a mounted troop of twenty men and we will find those damnable horse thieves. I want to show them what justice means in my garrison. If those thieves turn out to be Americanos, they will receive a double and painful justice."

"Yes sir...Sergeant Garcia is attending to that right now." Gallegos ran into the courtyard to find the complement of men already mounted and ready to ride. Sergeant Garcia was mounted and a soldier was holding the reins of the colonel and lieutenant's horses. Both men mounted and commanded the troop to head for the docks with all haste.

Holding the mounts to a steady gallop, Simon, Elijah, and Peña passed the lagoon, maintaining a steady course along the coast. They kept the Caribbean constantly in sight and soon the small village of Playa el Chivo appeared just ahead. Simon turned to his companions. "There is a good chance by now the garrison knows we stole some military horses and most likely has a complement of soldiers chasing us. We need to throw them off track and head inland. First, we have to make sure some of the locals see us turn to the south so they will report our change of direction to our pursuers. Once out of sight of the village, we can swing back toward the coastal road and on to Playa Cautarito."

Peña spoke up. "As I remember, the main coastal road ends at Playa el Chico and turns toward a southerly direction. However, there is a small unpaved road that continues along the coast and runs along the top of mountains overlooking the sea. We should have no trouble traveling along this road with the horses."

Both men nodded their understanding and agreement.

As they approached the village of Playa el Chivo, they saw the road turning sharply to the south and the small road that headed out of the village toward a southerly direction and directly away from the coast. They knew that any observers that might see them would know this was the normal route travelers would take heading inland. Luck was on their side. Two men, a woman, and two children were walking along the coastal road toward the village and two more men were tending some crops in an adjacent field. They rode by the pedestrians and waved to catch their attention. One of the men waved back as the Americans veered their horses to continue on the intersected road. In about one half mile, and out of sight of their roadside observers, they would traverse across a field and back toward the unpaved coastal road, hoping their pursuers would move inland and continue the chase to the south on the main route.

Colonel Gallegos and his detachment reached the docks and coastal road but couldn't be sure which direction the thieves had taken. There were no bystanders in sight to ask so he had a decision to make. He looked in both directions, but no riders could be seen. The colonel felt that they most likely turned left toward the west, but he couldn't be totally sure. He turned to his aide. "Lieutenant Rojas, I want you to take seven of the men and head east along the coastal road to Guaracayal. I'll take Sergeant Garcia and the remaining men to the west toward Playa el Chivo. I want those thieves alive, but if you find them and are forced to kill them, then do so. Also, I want you to dispatch one man to assemble the remainder of the troops at the garrison. Have him direct a few of them to the east, but the rest along the coastal road to the west to follow me and my attachment."

"Yes, sir," Rojas replied as he cut the last seven soldiers from the column and moved out to the east with one of the men dispatched back to the garrison as ordered.

The Americans rode past a deserted overgrown pasture and spotted the dirt track bordering the field. They turned their mounts to the west with the intent of taking a circular route back to the coastal road and on to Playa Cautarito to rendezvous with the other members of the expedition. Simon was hoping Lieutenants Maxwell and Portman had been successful in securing at least two or three wagons and enough sturdy horses to move the treasure back to the coast and into holds on the USS Halifax. But first, they had to find the treasure and avoid the soldiers who were most likely in hot in pursuit. Elijah confirmed his thoughts when he shouted, "Hey, Simon, I'll bet every damn soldier in that Cumana garrison is scouring the countryside looking for us. From what we heard about that crazy murdering colonel, we'd better get to Playa Cautarito fast and find that treasure."

Simon nodded, "That's what I'm trying to do. The last thing we need now is to meet up with any mounted soldiers."

In forty-five minutes, they had made their way back on the coastal road and well past Playa el Chivo. No horsemen were in sight. "Playa Cautarito is the next town," Peña reminded them. "It's about four miles from here."

"Let's hope our comrades and Captain Whitmore haven't

given us up for dead and departed back to the U.S," Elijah added.

Simon gave him an anxious look. "Let's hope. It wouldn't be very healthy for us to get stuck here."

14

Village of Playa Cautarito

In the distance, Simon spotted the steeple of the Catholic Church located in Playa Cautarito. It was a relief to know that they would be meeting up with their comrades. With the additional firepower they would now have, it gave them a bit of comfort knowing they were most likely now being chased by Colonel Gallegos and the soldiers from the Cumana garrison.

"Where are we supposed to meet our group?" Elijah asked.

"Maxwell said they would meet us at the local tavern," Simon reminded him. "He thought there was only one tavern in town since the place was only a very small fishing village."

Actually, Playa Cautarito was a very tiny fishing village facing a small stretch of beach. There were only three worn looking buildings there and some nearby weathered cottages that housed the few fishing families that dwelled there. A small hand painted wooden sign hung over the door of one of the structures and labeled *Tiburón Hambrien—Hungry Shark*. This was the small saloon and cantina that served the local fishermen after a hard day at sea. Simon immediately recognized Professor Scott standing outside the front door talking to Maxwell, both holding a glass of beer. The two men looked up to see their companions riding up on their horses. "You made it!" Scott shouted.

Simon responded, "Yes, we made it but with the whole damn Venezuelan army chasing us."

The men dismounted and followed their companions into the bar. Portman and Steele were sitting at a nearby table but quickly rose to greet their associates who had just arrived from Cumana. More beer was served as the men related their story of finding the map at the fort and escaping on the horses stolen from the guards. "You mentioned the whole Venezuelan army was chasing you," Maxwell asked. "What is that supposed to mean?"

Simon explained. "We were spotted by the guards just as we were leaving the fort on their horses. There is no doubt the word got back to Colonel Gallegos and he now has the entire garrison scouring the countryside for us. There is only one main road leading out of Cumana and the road goes both east and west along the coast. By now he is turning every town upside down looking for us. It's just a matter of time until he gets to Playa Cautarito and some of the locals will surely tell him we were here. I suggest we get out of here pronto. Do you have the wagons?"

"I was only able to get two wagons and four mules to pull them," Maxwell answered disappointedly. "Most of the people around here travel by boats. Did the map give you the location where the treasure is buried?" he added.

"Yes, Mr. Peña is familiar with the area to the south of here. The cave is located a short distance in some mountains just north of a small town named Barbacoas. He has been there several times with his parents because they were raised in a small town just east of there. There is a main road that passes through Barbacoas to Cumana. I'm sure Gallegos also has a detachment searching along that road as we speak."

"Then it is best we leave immediately," Maxwell remarked. "Peña can drive the lead wagon and I'll ride with you and Elijah on the horses. "Mr. Portman," he added, "why don't you drive the second wagon with Professor Scott and Mr. Steele can ride with Peña. I assume you know the route we need to travel," he said, glancing at Peña who nodded affirmably.

"Yes Lieutenant, there is an old unused road that leads out of town and through the mountains. When we leave town, this road will cross the coastal road and the track beyond is seldom traveled. It winds through a valley and on to Barbacoas. According to the map, the cave lies along that route and between Barbacoas and where we are now. It's pretty well marked, so we shouldn't have too much trouble finding it. It should be a straight passage through the valley and, depending on the shape of the road, we should arrive at the cave location in two or three hours. The valley gets very steep so we will be looking for some rock cliffs and overhangs. We have to cross the coastal road so here is where we need to watch for any soldiers looking for us."

"We sure don't want to get into any fights right now," Maxwell replied. "We have a treasure to recover, so let's move out."

As several local residents curiously observed, the small convey of wagons departed Playa Cautarito and headed south. One observer in particular, a man named Gomez, made a mental note of the wagons and size of the party accompanying them. *This information might prove useful,* he thought.

The group halted the wagons shortly before they intersected with the coastal road while Simon and Elijah rode ahead to look for signs of any soldiers. The track was deserted, so within minutes the wagons crossed the intersection and continued toward the concealment of the narrow valley. As Peña had informed them, the road turned into a narrow dirt road. Luckily, the ground was dry and solid, firmly holding the weight of the wagons. Soon they had reached the valley protected on both sides by two formable mountain ranges. Peña stopped to look at the map. "The cave should be about a mile or two ahead and to our left. The entrance appears to be about half way up and just under an outcropping." The feature was clearly outlined on the map.

Jonah Steele, whose keen eye was trained to observe unusual geological features, was the first to spot it. "The outcropping…I can see it," he shouted excitedly, pointing upward.

It was plainly visible as everyone peered upward to observe a small clump of a jutted rock formation projecting out slightly from the face and the thick vegetation surrounding it. "If that map is correct, the cave entrance should be just below that," Steele added.

Parking the wagons, the seven men carefully made their way up the slope to find the cave entrance. With the aid of a narrow rocky path, the climb was relatively easy. Although the sides were steep and covered by a variety of wild bushes and patches of high weeds, there was very little concealment along the pathway. Especially worrisome was the fact there was no place in the narrow valley to conceal the wagons and horses. If the treasure was actually stashed in this cave, they would have to move quickly to recover the boxes and load and move the wagons before they were spotted by a patrol of soldiers that might pass by. The distance was about two hundred feet up to the outcropping and, precisely as the map indicated, the small entrance to the cave was there, partially concealed by some high bushes and scrub grass. So far, the map had proved accurate. The excitement was mounting as Maxwell spoke up, "Let's go in and check it out."

Professor Scott had given Simon one of the oil lamps he carried in his kit so Simon pulled a match from his pack and carefully lit the wick. He led the way through the entrance. Sergeant Peña was designated to stand by the entrance to look out for unwanted visitors. The cavern was much larger than expected. Steele made the first observations as he glanced at the walls and shape of the room. "There is no doubt this cave was formed by a prehistoric river, most likely long before the mountains were formed and uplifted by huge underground forces from nature. No telling how far back this passage goes through the mountain."

The men carefully made their way half way through the cavern and then spotted the irregular shapes stacked along a wall. There were numerous wood and metal boxes layered three to four feet high. Elijah rushed over to the first stack and hastily removed the lid. The light from the lantern struck the tightly packed stacks of gold coins and reflected streams of dazzling rays across the room. The men were euphoric as more boxes were opened, displaying the same glittering radiance.

"How about that?" Maxwell shouted. "Peña's story and map were correct. These are most likely the gold doubloons from the Spanish galleon Peña's ancestors recovered and cached here." He turned to the others. "I sure hope no one comes along and spots the wagons. That's the only way we can move this treasure back to the ship."

Elijah voiced a very unnerving comment. "Yeah, those wagons are an obvious give away. If they are discovered, we could be stuck up here in this hole with no place to go."

Professor Scott and Jonah Steele had separated from the group to explore the rest of the cavern. Steele was particularly interested to see how deep the cave was and find out if the ancient river bed continued further into the mountain. Scott held his lantern up to display the strata of the rock along the walls. "How old do you suppose this cave is?" Scott asked the young geologist.

"I would venture to say this cavern is very, very old. The different layers of rock represent many different geological time periods before the upheaval of these mountains. The river that carved out this cavern came much later in time, something like a couple of hundred thousand years ago."

As they arrived at what appeared to be the end of the cave, Scott's lantern reflected a most unusual and startling sight along the far left wall. Both men were totally stunned as they gazed at the bizarre scene before them. Steele broke the silence. "Well, I'll be darned, this is really incredible…unbelievable."

15

Village of Playa Cautarito

The occupants of the village were not surprised to see a small contingent of nine solders ride into town. It was obvious that they were there on a serious mission. Their first stop was the *Hungry Shark* to quench their thirst with a beer. A rough looking sergeant approached the barkeeper, ordered the beer then said, "I am Sergeant Estévez from the army garrison in Cumana and have been dispatched by Colonel Gallegos to search for some Americanos who we believe recently visited this village. Tell us what you know and there will be no trouble."

Most of the populace residing in the Sucre State of Venezuela was aware of the reputation of the garrison commander and the mere mention of his name struck fear into the hearts of everyone.

The earlier observer, Gomez, who had watched the American strangers leaving town, was sitting at a nearby table and spoke up. Thinking he might derive some benefits, perhaps money, by offering his earlier observations, said to the sergeant, "Sir, I believe I can give you the information you are looking for."

Estévez turned to him and barked, "Your name?"

"I am Manuel Gomez and there were some Americanos here earlier."

"How many and what were they doing here?"

"Four of them arrived here yesterday and seemed to be waiting for someone. They were joined by two or three others this morning. They left earlier today and were driving two wagons."

"Which way did they go?" the sergeant shouted gruffly.

Gomez answered, "They were headed south on our main road from town toward the coastal road. That is the last anyone saw of them."

"Anything else?" Estévez asked.

"I heard one of them mention the mountains."

The sergeant nodded to one of his men and they abruptly turned to leave the bar. "Don't I get something…a reward or something for giving you this information?" Gomez shouted sheepishly.

Sergeant Estévez turned and laughed, "Yes, you get to keep your head."

It was a short distance to the coastal road where Estévez halted the detachment. "There are three routes the Americans could have gone," he said. "The coastal road follows along the coast and away from the mountains. There is also a rough dirt track that extends from this road and heads toward that mountain range in front of us."

Turning to one of his men he issued an order. "Juan, take one man with you and scout the track ahead to see if you can spot signs of wagon wheel marks and fresh horse tracks. Look for fresh scuff marks in the dirt. We'll wait here for your report."

The two men spurred their horses forward to the dirt road leading toward the mountains. They were back within twenty minutes. "Sergeant, we found fresh signs of horses and wagon ruts. There is no doubt that someone traveled that road very recently."

Estévez turned to Corporal Mendez. "Corporal, I want you and Private Sanchez to ride back to our garrison at Playa el Chivo and get word to Colonel Gallegos that we think we have found where the Americanos are going. I believe they have one of those new telegraph machines there. Give him the directions and you two personally lead him to this road. Ask the colonel to please bring a large contingence of soldiers with him…we may need them. I know he will want to be here with his men when we find the Americanos. We will find those devils and we need a strong enough force to annihilate them. Another thing, corporal, if you and Sanchez run across any detachment of our troopers, make sure you give them the directions and tell them to get here as soon as possible to reinforce us. Now move it quickly."

"I understand," the young corporal acknowledged as he turned his horse. "We will get word to the Colonel."

With a steady gallop, it did not take Mendez and Juan long to reach the small garrison at Playa el Chivo. Reporting to the officer of the day, Mendez said, "Sir, it is urgent I send a wire to Colonel Gallegos in Cumana."

By 1871, the telegraph was just being introduced to Cuba and a few of the Central and South American countries, and by 1878 it was in use between Cumana, Caracas, and a few of the military garrisons along the Caribbean coast. With new lines installed, the post at Playa el Chivo had recently been connected to the army headquarters in Cumana by telegraph.

"What is so important that you need to communicate with Colonel Gallegos?" the lieutenant asked Mendez curiously.

"Sir, I need to get word to him that we found the Americanos he has been searching for."

"Then, why don't you tell him yourself," the officer said as he pointed toward the door.

Mendez turned with a total look of shock as he watched Gallegos walk through the door of the office, with an aide following him.

"What is it you wish to tell me, Corporal?" the colonel asked, having heard part of his previous remarks.

"Sir, I was sent here by Sergeant Estévez to tell you we believe we have found the Americanos. At least the route they took. I was going to send you a wire to your headquarters in Cumana."

"No need for a wire. I have been here since yesterday. Now where are the Americanos?"

Mendez explained, "I was part of Sergeant Estévez's detachment that was looking for them along the coastal road near Playa Cautarito. They were there yesterday but departed southward with two wagons."

Mendez further explained about the dirt road leading into the mountains toward Barbacoas and that his detachment was currently following them. "Sergeant Estévez sent me and Private Sanchez here to get word to you and request that you send more troops to reinforce him. I am to lead you to the location."

Colonel Gallegos turned to the post lieutenant, "How many men are stationed here?"

"Counting cooks and a few support people we have close to forty-five men."

Turning to his aide, Gallegos said, "Captain Morales, you and the lieutenant here assemble as many troops as you have available and prepare them to move out within thirty minutes. Forget the cooks...I need fighting men."

Morales saluted and left the office with the lieutenant in tow.

With his normal cruel expression, he said to Mendez, "Corporal, you and Private Sanchez will lead us to that road you were talking about. By tomorrow, I will have those American swine in chains."

16

Lieutenant Maxwell did not seem very impressed as he stood there staring at the wall. "Looks like some ordinary old Indian cave drawings to me."

Professor Scott was annoyed at Maxwell's indifference. "These are not just any old cave drawings. The drawings predate the Toltecs, Mayans, and Incas by thousands of years. It has been estimated that the Meso-Indian period dates as far back as 4,000 BC to 1,000 AD. I wonder if these drawings could possibly go back that far."

Jonah Steel offered his opinion. "Based on the good condition of the drawings, I would guess somewhere between 1,000 and 1,500 years old."

"The height of the Mayan civilization," Scott injected.

"I would say so. These were probably drawn by Mayans who at one time occupied much of Central and the northern parts of South America."

Simon noticed a peculiar drawing at the top right corner of the grouping. It looked vaguely familiar. It was oval shaped with a small dome projection on top. The object appeared to be resting on three post or stick-like objects…one positioned at the front and two at the rear. Pointing upward he said, "We've seen that drawing before…in the cave in Peru under the mountain where the Inca fortress Miccu Piccu is located."

"You're right," Elijah shouted. "It looks just like that drawing of the alien ship we found in that cavern under the Inca citadel. It was damaged and trapped under rock debris from a cave-in. It self-destructed right after we made it out of the cavern. Before it destroyed itself, the ship sent out a signal to another ship buried under the ice pack in the Arctic. This ship somehow broke through the ice and flew to Peru. We were able to escape and fly it back to Washington. We named that ship the *Cuzco* and this was the spacecraft we encountered again during the Amazon expedition in search of the lost city of El Dorado."

Lieutenant Maxwell, with a look of total shock, stared at Elijah as if he were a madman. Portman spoke up. "Elijah, does this relate to some of that wild alien stuff you were telling me about on the train from San Francisco to Washington?"

"Yes, it does."

Professor Scott admitted, "I related that same story to Jonah Steele at the museum…in strict confidence of course."

Steele nodded his head to signify confirmation.

Simon laughed. "Well, Mr. Maxwell, why don't you have a seat? We have an incredible story to tell you."

Maxwell shook his head suspiciously and sat down on a nearby rock formation. The other men did likewise.

Simon began his story, "Thirteen years ago, in the Yucatan jungle, while on an expedition in search of the lost Toltec Indian city of Xepocotec, Elijah and I made a remarkable and startling discovery. Deep within a cavern beneath the lost city, we found a strange device that led us to an ancient flying ship that had been hibernating there for nearly nine hundred years. Incredibly, it had been kept alive by an inexhaustible fuel source called tracx. The device turned out to be a communication module that allowed us to communicate with the ship's mechanical intelligence. It was a spaceship from another galaxy and it had remained there all these years in need of repairs. The original travelers had long since died out, leaving the ship dormant in the cavern. Through the use of a talking device or communication unit, we later learned, I was able to communicate with the strange machine and awaken it from its state of hibernation. With instructions from the ship's intelligence box or a computer, we later learned, we were able to use parts stored on the ship and make the necessary repairs to enable it to fly again. The ship's computer information storage bank appointed me as the new ship's commander and through my voice commands we were able to fly the craft out of the cavern, barely escaping hordes of vengeful Indians who were nearly upon us. Elijah and I then joined up with General Kirby, Professors Robert Drake and George Scott and flew the craft to Washington and scared hundreds of people who observed it soaring across the sky.

"After realizing the country was not being invaded by an unknown alien enemy, President Johnson and General Grant welcomed us back to civilization and re-commissioned Elijah and I back into service to command the strange new craft. We named the ship TOLTEC. President Andrew Johnson and top cabinet members decided to press this new machine, with its deadly laser guns and incredible unknown power, into the U.S. arsenal, under the direction and command of the Navy. Some of the cabinet and top military officials suggested some very aggressive intentions for the ship, not realizing the potential dangers it could impose upon the human race. Voicing their strong objections, Elijah and I were relieved of command and ordered back into civilian life.

"We both sensed the potential dangers and destructive power of the alien ship and the cataclysmic damage it could inflict on the earth's populations. So, while departing Washington, I ordered the Toltec to fly over the Atlantic Ocean and self-destruct. Distraught over the loss of their newly acquired powerful weapon, the president and other officials believed the ship had been ordered back to its own world by an unknown source. Prior to its departure, the Toltec planted a strange capsule into the ground, only to be found by a construction worker two years later. The device was a communication unit called a Zenox and was used by Elijah and me to communicate with another hibernating ship hidden in the Andes. This resulted in our expedition to Peru five years later. A third ship, designated the X326, buried under the ice pack in the Arctic, was awakened by a signal from the dying ship in the Andes. With its inexhaustible fuel element tracx, the ship re-energized its power systems, restarted the engines, and broke through the tomb of ice where it had been hibernating for several centuries. It took flight to the Andes, enabling us to board it and fly from Peru to Washington. I was appointed the new acting commander by its computerized command module. On a test flight from Washington, we lost all control of the ship and it was directed by an unknown source to dive into the Atlantic Ocean, somewhere just west of the Straits of Gibraltar. We were confronted with a frightening experience when we found ourselves under the sea in an airtight bubble on the sunken continent of Atlantis. It was here we met the alien senior commander named Ahular and his assistant Nezar. He explained to us that they were from a distant planet in a solar system millions of miles away and were sent here to study humans and our planet, Earth. He trusted and befriended us. We helped them save our planet by thwarting a devastating underwater earthquake and cataclysmic split in the Eurasian and African tectonic plates. The Earth was saved from blowing apart by a coordinated concentration of laser power from the alien craft to weld the splitting plates together with molten rock. Elijah was the one who suggested to Ahular that they combine all their laser guns to concentrate the power on the plates.

"Five years ago, we encountered the same ship on a third expedition into the Amazon in search of El Dorado. It was located in the alien command center deep within a cavern under the lost city. It was the same group of alien explorers commanded by the same officer named Ahular. Professor Scott, Elijah, and I accompanied Ahular and his crew on an incredible journey deep into space to destroy a huge meteorite that was hurling toward our sun. The meteorite was destroyed by the special weapons they called laser guns that saved the sun from blowing apart. It also saved all the planets in our solar system, including Earth and everything on it, from vaporizing."

The look on Maxwell's face betrayed his shock and disbelief. "You're kidding, of course?"

"No, I'm not kidding," Simon responded. "The story is true. Just ask Elijah and the professor. They were there with me and can confirm the story."

Maxwell glanced over at the two men to see them nodding

conformation. Elijah told him, "I can assure you all of it is true, Charles, every bit of it."

Professor Scott directed the attention back to the sketch on the wall. "You know what that drawing means, don't you?"

Simon was quick to answer. "Yes, it means that the Meso-Indians who carved that drawing were once visited here by the earlier alien explorers, just as they did with the pre-Columbian Mayans and Toltecs of Mexico."

The conversation was quickly interrupted by Peña who rushed in from the entrance. "You had better come quickly," he shouted. "We have visitors."

17

A quick glance through the cave entrance revealed a group of men milling around the wagons. Two of them were staring down at the ground, apparently looking for fresh tracks. These men were not local farmers or peasants that had accidentally stumbled upon the wagons. They were mounted soldiers, most likely a search party sent out to look for the Americans who had escaped from Cumana. After searching the wagons, they spread out to search for possible hiding places, most likely along the sides of the two slopes on either side.

"Did anyone notice how many men were out there?" Maxwell asked.

"I counted nine of them," Scott answered. "There could be more nearby."

"There are seven of us and we have five of these new Winchester repeaters," Elijah suggested. "We could take them all out easily."

"I glanced at the rifles they were carrying and they sure didn't look like muskets to me...more like bolt action. I heard that some of these South American countries have purchased newer guns from Germany and Switzerland. The damn things could be more modern than we think. The problem is, to get a decent shot, we would have to expose ourselves on the path while they have the protection of the wagons. I think we should wait a bit to see if they leave. Maybe they won't spot the entrance to this cave."

On the Coastal Road

To the north and fast approaching the intersection to Playa Cautarito, Corporal Mendez was guiding a large contingency of soldiers led by Colonel Gallegos and Captain Morales. The detachment consisted of fifty-four mounted and heavily armed soldiers, all part of a small group from the small garrison of Playa el Chivo and a larger contingency from Cumana that had joined them. They were all soldiers from the 8th Sucre Division of the National Venezuelan Army commanded by Colonel Manuel Gallegos, whose reputation included rarely taking prisoners. Finally reaching the intersection from Playa Cautarito, Corporal Mendez led the detachment southward into the valley.

Evening was fast approaching when Simon peeked out of the opening, only to see that the soldiers were still there. It looked as if they might be settling in for the night. His assumptions were right when he saw two campfires being lit. It now appeared that he and his group were stuck in the cave for the night. Elijah suggested they slip out under the cover of darkness, but was voted down as the attempt would be too risky. With the six Winchesters and superior firepower, he assumed they could escape, but Maxwell believed they would have a better chance fighting their way out during the daylight hours when they could see their targets. There was also the object of their mission to consider…the treasure chests. It was clear that in order to move the treasure, the group of soldiers would either have to leave voluntarily or be eliminated in order to regain access to the wagons. They would have to rotate shifts at the opening for guard duty and Peña was selected for the first two-hour shift. They did not need any surprise visits from curious soldiers. It would be a long and restless night.

Elijah was detailed to the last shift as the sun rose and cast the first shadows of early morning light into the valley below. He peered through the opening and could not believe his eyes. The road below was filled with soldiers milling around. Colonel Gallegos and his large detachment had arrived during the night. Elijah moved swiftly and shook Maxwell and Simon awake. "You won't believe the big mess we're in now," he said. "The whole damn Venezuelan army is sitting out there."

Instead of the eight men Professor Scott had counted earlier, the contingency of soldiers now facing the small group of Americans had risen to sixty-two men, led by a cruel and merciless colonel who would not hesitate to chop off their heads.

Simon and Elijah silently awakened the remaining men and informed them of the situation. When the group was assembled, Maxwell turned to Simon and said, "Any suggestions, Mr. Murphy?"

"We don't know for sure they have even spotted this cave and, if so, if we're even up here," Simon responded. His doubts were quickly answered by a loud and heavily accented voice shouting from below. "Americanos, we know you are up there. Our commander says for you to throw out your weapons and come down peacefully and we will spare your lives."

"That answers our questions," Elijah answered annoyingly. "That voice must be an interpreter speaking for their leader. I wonder if it's Colonel Gallegos down there."

The loud voice from below came booming back. "Our colonel says you have fifteen minutes to comply or we shall take your position by force…and he said there will be no prisoners taken. You will all die."

"It's Gallegos alright," Simon decided. "What do you think, Mr. Peña? Those men are some of your former countrymen down there."

Peña hesitated for a moment and then answered, "Colonel Gallegos is a madman. I believe if we surrender, he will most likely kill some of us on the spot. The others he will save for torture and a very painful death. Simon, Elijah, and I were the ones spotted at the fort stealing the horses, so we are probably the ones he'll save for torture. In any event, if we surrender we are all dead men anyway."

"What about all this treasure?" Portman asked. "I would hate to see that colonel get his hands on it."

"If we're all dead, I guess it won't make any difference to us, will it, Mr. Portman?" Simon reminded him.

"I see your point. So, it looks like we have a big fight on our hands."

Maxwell agreed. "It looks that way," he concluded. "No other options as I see it."

The configuration of the cavern did offer some protection

and a decent view of the valley below. Entering the opening, the nearest walls of the cave extended for several feet on each side, offering suitable protection from bullets entering through the entrance. The ricochet from the speeding projectiles did, however, create concerns. Hopefully they would be mostly spent and shattered upon impact with the softer limestone laden ceiling and walls. The oil lamp was extinguished by Scott, casting the rear of the cavern and treasure cache in darkness, however, light from the entrance did illuminate the forward section of the cavern. As a precaution, the Winchesters were cocked and ready.

Jonah Steele, who was watching the entrance, interrupted the discussion with a shout. "Here they come…soldiers sneaking up the path…a dozen or so."

18

Several of Gallegos' soldiers had been dispatched to feel out the Americans and test their strength and resistance. They made their way silently along the path, hoping to catch the Americans off guard with a sudden rush through the entrance of the cave. They were unaware they had been spotted by Steele. Professor Scott, the undisputed best marksman of the group, took his Winchester and carefully peeked around the opening in the wall. The leading man was approaching and only about fifty feet away. Quickly Scott pulled his rifle around the wall and in succession, pumped six rounds into the approaching column. The first man took two rounds into the chest and the second and third soldier took a bullet into their foreheads. The heavy impact from the .40-60 caliber bullets propelled each man off the path, hurling their lifeless bodies down the incline like sacks of wheat.

Scott was able to get one more shot into the column, which struck another soldier in the abdomen, again throwing his torso down the rocky incline. Scott quickly pulled back into the cave and motioned the others to press themselves against the front walls, expecting the dreadful onslaught to follow. As he expected, forty rifles erupted from below, hurling .52 caliber slugs through the opening and into the rear walls of the cavern.

Maxwell shouted out to Simon and Elijah, "Well, it looks like our fight has started. We're trapped in this hole like rats in a barrel."

Simon answered with a tone of concern in his voice, "I think we have the firepower to hold them off for a while, but that's not our biggest problem."

"What do you mean?" Elijah asked.

"The real problem is the fact we only have three canteens of water and no food with us. The food we brought is all down there in those lousy wagons. Gallegos can starve us out in two or three days."

"Against the wall!" Steele shouted as another hail of bullets tore through the entrance and shattered against the rear cavern wall.

The same booming English speaking voice broke the silence that followed the last fusillade. "Americanos, do you hear me?"

"I'll answer him," Maxwell responded as he moved near the opening. "What do you want?" he yelled back.

"My commander wants you to show yourself so we can talk a truce."

The lieutenant slowly walked through the opening and peered over the ledge. "Okay, let's talk," he shouted.

At that instant, several loud reports barked from the rifles below as Maxwell was peppered with numerous lead slugs slamming into his body. He was dead before his body recoiled and tumbled over the ledge.

"What happened?" Portman shouted to Steele.

"That same voice we heard earlier shouted that they wanted to talk to us about a truce and when Maxwell showed his head, those bastards shot and killed him. He should have known better than to expose himself."

Peña was incensed as he yelled out, "I told you that Gallegos was a murdering madman. He has no intention of calling any truce or taking any prisoners. The only thing that's going to satisfy that swine is our blood."

Simon, trying his best to maintain his composure, assessed the situation. It appeared that they were hopelessly trapped in the cave with no choice but to try and fight their way out. While Steele maintained his position guarding the entrance, Simon tried to come up with some viable options…they were very limited.

Elijah drew Simon aside and reminded him of a prior similar situation they had once been confronted with. He said to his cousin, "Do you remember we had this same dilemma five years ago when we were trying to recover the hidden Confederate gold in North Carolina. We were trapped in that cave with those renegade killers covering the entrance."

Simon nodded his recollection.

"Do you remember what you did to get us out of that stinking mess?"

"Yes, how can I forget that? I used the Zenox to communicate with Commander Ahular and his ship the *Cuzco*. Luckily, our alien friends were still up at the Arctic doing some research on our magnetic polar fields. I remember they flew down to help us and his assistant, Vice-Commander Nezar, brought that air powered vehicle up to the level of the cave where we were able to load up the treasure and escape. I believe he called that thing a dacidron. It had some kind of special covering or skin that shielded us from the bullets being fired at us."

Elijah responded, "They saved our ass that day so perhaps they can do it again. You did say you brought the Zenox along, didn't you?"

"Yes, it's in my pack."

"Then why don't you get that talking gadget out and let's try to communicate with Ahular. He and his crew might still be somewhere on earth doing more research. Before he left Washington, he did tell us they would be back someday. Do you remember the last thing he told us before he boarded his ship back to their galaxy?"

"Yes, how can I forget? He told me if I ever get into trouble again and need some help, trust the Zenox."

The conversation was interrupted by another shout from Steele, "We have some more visitors down there."

A quick glance revealed additional soldiers milling around below.

"Looks like Gallegos got more reinforcements during the night," Simon mumbled. "I would bet he now has at least a hundred men…maybe more. So much for fighting our way out of here," he added.

"Simon, grab the Zenox out of your pack. We have no other options but to try and reach Commander Ahular," Elijah whispered.

"Okay, we'll try it," he answered as he walked over to the wall to retrieve his backpack. He reached into his bag and retrieved the small device Ahular had given him. It fit snugly into the palm of his hand. He pressed a small button and was relieved to see the tiny green light appear, signifying the gadget was now active. He was a bit surprised because he had not used the Zenox since their Amazon expedition five years ago. He looked at Elijah. "I can't believe this thing is still working. I haven't tried to turn it on since '73."

Elijah was also intrigued. "It must use a similar power source like the fuel on that spaceship we discovered in the cave in Peru. The fuel they used keeps their ships active for hundreds of years. I remember Ahular and Nezar called the fuel *Trax*. Maybe some of that stuff powers the Zenox as well. Now let's see if you can contact our old friends."

Simon pressed a transmit button and spoke into the device. "Hello, this is Simon Murphy calling Commander Ahular. Come in, please." Dead silence greeted him.

"Does anybody hear me? This is Simon Murphy calling Commander Ahular or Vice-Commander Nezar. Come in, please." Still silence.

"I was afraid of this," he said, with a look of despair. "They must be back on their own planet or maybe exploring another galaxy millions of miles away and out of range."

"So, what do we do now?" Elijah asked, knowing there was not a hopeful answer.

"I guess we're all out of options. We'll have to take our chances and try to sneak out of here after dark."

"You know we don't have a chance against a hundred or so guns shooting at us."

Suddenly the expression on Simon's face displayed a look of total shock and surprise.

Elijah noticed it. "What is it?" he asked.

"This is strange. The Zenox is vibrating and some weird force is pulling on my hand. This Zenox is pulling my arm toward the rear of the cave…like it's trying to tell me something and guide me somewhere."

"Well, let's follow it," Elijah responded.

Professor Scott had noticed the disturbance and joined his companions. He heard Elijah's remarks and followed them toward the back of the cavern. Simon stopped, facing the drawings but the strange force kept pushing the Zenox upward and toward the figure of the oval shaped image they had seen earlier.

"What's it doing now?" Elijah asked.

"This is really strange. The Zenox is trying to tell me something about this drawing."

Scott interrupted, "Do you remember what Santos told us about his ancestors, the Mayans? They were master builders and their engineering skills were far advanced for pre-Columbian civilizations. They were known for using ingenious lock systems to open secret doors to hidden passages and chambers inside their pyramids and temples. I think the Zenox device is pulling you toward that drawing for a purpose. After all, it does resemble the spaceship we flew on in Peru with Ahular—the one that took us into space to destroy the meteor that was going to collide with our sun. Maybe there is a passageway that extends beyond this cavern—one hidden behind a wall concealing the opening."

The conversation was again interrupted by another shout from Steele, "We have more soldiers trying to sneak up the path."

Scott said to Simon and Elijah, "You two keep searching around that drawing to see if you can find any kind of triggering device that might open a doorway. I'll see if I can stop those guys outside from getting into the cave." He abruptly turned to retrieve his rifle.

19

Slightly protected by a small rock outcropping and a ledge protruding slightly from the cave entrance, Scott eased his head around to observe another column of soldiers trying to work their way up the narrow path to get to the cave opening. The intent was to amass enough men to rush through the entrance and engage the Americans in a fire fight. It was clear that Gallegos was ruthless and did not care how many men he sacrificed to get to the Americans. His lust for blood was stronger than his concern for his men.

Scott eased his Winchester through the entrance and squeezed off four rapid shots. He was satisfied to watch five bodies tumble over the ledge and roll down the hill. *Two men with one bullet…not bad,* he thought. Despite the loud screams from below, most likely from a very angry colonel, the remaining group of men withdrew. They knew that to try to force their way up the path any further was suicide.

Back at the cave drawings, Simon and Elijah were trying to find any kind of clue that might be a triggering device to open a doorway. With their past experiences, they knew the key to activating a door would be in the form of a small indentation, button, projection, or anything that would initiate mechanisms behind the wall to start the progression of movement to open a stone slab or panel. They knew the Mayan engineers would have used their incredible engineering knowledge of weights and balances to move progressively larger and larger objects…like stone levers and rods. The process would start very slightly and then progress with the release of sand or pebbles on heavier objects in succession that would complete the progression. They just needed to find the trigger to start the process.

Simon was sure there was an opening to a passage beyond the wall. The Zenox was telling him this. Jonah Steele had mentioned that this cavern was carved by an ancient stream or river and there had to be a continuation of the cave further into the mountain. He felt certain that the wall was created by a collapse of a section of the ceiling that blocked the extension of the passageway beyond.

The strange force generated by the Zenox was still directing Simon's hand toward the oval shaped drawing. He traced his fingers along the edges, trying to detect anything unusual. Simon then moved his hand to the etching and toward the small dome shaped outline on the top of the drawing. Something felt a bit unusual…a slight bulge. He glanced at Elijah with a grin. "I may have found something," he said, pushing forward on the small protrusion. Nothing moved.

"Push harder," Elijah told him.

Simon applied more pressure and felt some slight movement. He then used the heel of his hand and pushed harder. The small dome shape finally broke loose and depressed deeper into the wall. It then stopped. "Nothing is happening," Simon shouted in frustration.

"Give it time," Elijah replied. "Remember what happened in Peru. Those activation triggers take a few seconds to get things moving."

They listened intently and placed their ears against the side wall with the etchings. Soon a very low rumbling noise erupted from behind the wall, followed by a distinct scraping and grinding sound. "Something heavy is moving," Elijah mumbled.

Suddenly, a large stone slab began to move laterally and disappear into a deep vertical recess positioned in the wall. A large black void was revealed…another passage that extended beyond the cavern.

"We've found it," Simon yelled.

Portman, Scott, and Steele watching the scene moved quickly to the back of the cave while Peña kept his position at the entrance.

"I knew there had to be a passage beyond this wall," Steele shouted. "That ancient river didn't just flow from nowhere. How did you open it?" he asked.

Simon pointed to the Zenox in his hand. "This communications gadget told me where to look for the trigger and the weight and balance gears and levers on the other side did all the work."

"Amazing," he answered. "I'm wondering how far back the passage will take us."

"Simon shrugged his shoulders, "Well, Mr. Steele, I guess we're about to find out because we sure can't walk out of here by the front door."

Scott, assessing the situation, added his thoughts. "I have to think that this passage might lead us to another opening on the other side of the mountain. I don't think the Mayans would have gone to the trouble to build this entry if the other side was a dead end."

Simon replied, "I agree with you, Professor. Let's just hope there wasn't a major cave-in somewhere back there that's blocking the tunnel. In that case, we might be entering our graves."

Elijah spoke up, "What about all of this treasure? We sure can't leave all this stuff here for Colonel Gallegos to grab. You know very well he would keep it all for himself."

Simon had the answer. "We'll move all of the treasure boxes to the other side of the wall and store them there and hope the soldiers can't figure out how to open the wall. We can load our packs with all we can carry and close the door to seal off the passageway. I doubt if Gallegos or his men will be able to figure out the key to open the wall. But first we need to check out the other side and find the closing device."

Professor's oil lamp provided sufficient illumination to light up the passage. The small stone protuberance located to the top right of the doorway was easy to spot. It was a small round stone set into a slight depression that could be pushed into the wall. It would activate the reverse process that would close the panel.

Elijah wandered about a hundred feet into the corridor when he came across a decent sized cavity recessed in the wall, a perfect place to cache the treasure chests. He hurried back to the opening to tell the others.

"It will take two men to move a chest so let's get started. Discard anything you don't need in your backpack and we'll load them with all the gold coins we can carry. We have a long hike back to Playa Carcarito and might have to move quickly to rendezvous with Captain Whitmore and the Halifax. When things cool down here, we can always come back to this cave and recover the treasure."

After loading their packs with gold doubloons and gemstones, working in pairs they began to carry the chests through the new passageway and stack them against the wall of the cavity Elijah had discovered. Peña maintained his watch on the entrance. He noticed a great deal of activity in the area below. An officer was standing on the seat of a wagon shouting inaudible orders. Something big was about to happen. Simon was informed of the increased activity.

"Let's get those crates moved quickly," he shouted. "It looks like Gallegos is preparing his troops for an all-out assault on the cave. We've got to get the rest of those crates and ourselves on the other side now."

They were down to eight more boxes when Professor Scott swapped places with Peña. With rifle in hand he peered carefully over the ledge to find Colonel Gallegos standing on a wagon barking out instructions. Elijah walked over and asked him, "What are you doing?"

Scott replied, "I intend to delay things a bit and do a big favor for Mr. Peña's countrymen."

Simon understood and went back to the treasure boxes. *Three more boxes to carry*, he noticed.

On his stomach, Scott inched his way to the ledge to ease the barrel of his Winchester slowly over the shelf. He took careful aim. Noticing a slight breeze blowing from his left, he adjusted slightly to compensate. He estimated the distance at about seven hundred feet, so he elevated his sight just enough to allow for a nominal drop in the bullet trajectory. The front sights were placed just slightly to the left of Colonel Gallegos' neck. Scott took a deep breath and slowly squeezed the trigger. The .40-60 slug sped through the air and penetrated a spot in the center of the colonel's chest and the impact lifted him and hurled him from the wagon. He landed on his head with a heavy snap. With a large hole in his chest, the bullet cleanly did the job, but the way his head was sharply bent revealed that his neck was clearly broken. The ruthless murdering colonel was dead when he hit the ground.

Scott quickly withdrew and joined the others as the last treasure box was being lifted and carried into the passageway. "What happened, Professor?" Simon asked, already knowing the answer. Professor Scott rarely missed a target.

Scott's wide grin confirmed the answer. "Well, our friend, Colonel Gallegos, won't be bothering us anymore. He is now history and on his way to hell."

Simon nodded, "I'm sure his other officers are preparing their men for an immediate assault on the cave so I suggest we grab our packs, get through that door, and into the tunnel, and then we close the thing up tight."

20

The reset button was pressed inside the passageway to allow the stone door to slowly move back into place. It took several moments for the levers and other mechanisms to reverse the process. The grinding noise became more audible as the door panel started to emerge from its recess and slide back into its closed position to seal off the passage. The other side of the cave wall resumed its normal appearance, leaving no signs of a doorway. The soldiers entering the cave would find that the Americans had totally disappeared as if they had been swallowed up by an unknown demon from the underworld.

In the valley below the cave entrance, Captain Morales, who was now the ranking officer in charge of the soldiers, assembled his lieutenant and two sergeants to plan the attack on the cave. He had no remorse over the death of Colonel Gallegos. He was a tyrant and a ruthless murderer and would not be missed. There was a sense of relief by Morales and most of his men that Gallegos was gone.

He knew that the only way to gain access to the cave was along the pathway to the entrance. The slopes below were much too steep, and scaling from the top of the mountain would prove too difficult. The latter option was out of the question as they lacked sufficient ropes to rappel down anyway. His only choice was to send enough men along the path and try to gain entrance by sheer numbers while his troops below would provide enough firepower through the opening to keep the Americans from returning fire by keeping them away from the entrance. Morales issued the order to start the column of troops to move up the path. The leading man, a private name Sanchez, inched his way along the trail carefully. He pushed his back against the wall behind him, hoping for some protection. He was followed by a line of twenty-five men ready to rush into the opening. Sanchez was surprised that he had not yet seen any activity above and no gunfire had occurred. He reached the edge of the opening ready to rush through...still no sounds from the cave. With his rifle poised, he charged through the entrance with two soldiers following. He and the others were shocked to find the chamber empty.

Word was passed down to Morales, who made his way up the path to the empty cavern. The first thing he noticed was the blank walls and ceiling of a large empty room. There were no side passages anywhere to indicate that the Americans had access to another way out. He did notice the ancient etchings on the wall, but did not make any connections to any other exit. *Just some old Indian drawings,* he thought. Morales had seen similar pictures before and didn't place any significance to them. Being somewhat of a superstitious man, as far as he could tell, the mountain had just swallowed the Americans up.

One thing bothered Morales and he couldn't get it out of his mind. What were the Americans doing in this cave and why were they in Venezuela in the first place? What were they after and why did they need the use of two wagons? Whatever they were after, it had to be something very heavy for them to need the wagons. The questions kept spinning through his head and he couldn't let it go. Perhaps it was something very valuable. In any event, he had to find out. There was always that remote possibility that they were still alive and would somehow escape miraculously through an extension of the cave.

However, he did take comfort in the fact that Gallegos was dead and was content that life would be much easier and more pleasant in the future. He was pleased that he now had two more wagons and four horses to add to his stables.

He called his two lieutenants together. "Those Americanos came to our country for a reason. Why did they come to Cumana and what were they doing at the old fort where they stole the three horses? They were after something big and most likely learned it was stored in this cave. I want you to take a detail and search every square inch of this cave. Look for anything that might open a door to a passageway. We know they didn't just disappear into thin air. I want to know what they were after."

With torches lit, a detail of twelve men began their search.

Inside the newly discovered passageway, after carefully adjusting the heavily loaded backpacks, Simon and the five remaining men began their trek through the mountain with Peña leading the way. The corridor was relatively large and the well-worn path indicated that this route had been used many times by the ancient Indians...most likely Mayan warriors passing through to the other side of the mountain. The oil fed mirrored lamps Scott had brought along provided excellent illumination that highlighted the smoothly carved walls and ceilings. As Steele had mentioned, they were most likely formed by an ancient underground river or stream flowing from the other side and before underground forces caused the mountain to uplift.

The small column had walked about a quarter mile when Peña suddenly stopped. To his right there appeared to be a door like opening in the side of the wall, leading into a large side chamber. Simon's first thought was perhaps it was some type of storage room like they had experienced in the caves they had visited in the Yucatan and Peru. He was the one holding the lamp and decided to be the first to enter the room. His past experiences reminded him of the many deadly traps the Indians had devised to keep enemies from entering their sanctuaries. One such trap was a non-suspect panel that would suddenly drop out from under a person when pressure was applied and hurl him to the depths below. The traps were usually placed just beyond a threshold of a doorway or opening into a wall. The results were usually a ghastly death to the unlucky victim. Simon remembered one such trap where spikes had been set into the floor below, designed to impale a victim when he hit the bottom. He carefully poked around the floor with his right foot until he was satisfied the floor was solid. He remembered another deadly trap that propelled a spike studded frame from the wall, intended to impale an unsuspecting victim who happened to step on a release mechanism embedded in a floor panel. They had lost a man to one of these traps during one of their previous expeditions.

The shadows cast by the oil lantern danced across the cavern walls, revealing eerie apparitions and giving the feeling the room had been occupied by ancient evil spirits. The first thing Simon noticed was the stack of elongated figures stacked in one corner. A closer examination showed they were well preserved mummies, but of a much different appearance than the pre-Columbian natives of that period. There were seven figures in the group. The bodies were much taller and appeared to have a lighter skin tone. The most striking difference was the presence of well-preserved lighter colored hair hanging freely from mummified heads. These were definitely not Indian remains, but most likely those of European descent. On top of the stack were two swords, two battle axes, a shield bearing figures of a dragon head, and a metal helmet bearing two horns, one on each side.

Scott made a first identification. "Gentlemen, I know you won't believe this, but I think these mummies could be Viking warriors."

"You've got to be kidding," Portman countered in disbelief. "The Norsemen settled in the far north and never traveled this far south."

"How can you be so sure?" Scott asked. "They were incredible seamen and these are definitely Viking weapons. You can tell by the designs. We have some of these weapons in the Washington museum and those mummies are definitely not Indians."

Simon also expressed his skepticism. "Vikings in South America! Isn't that a bit farfetched, Professor?"

"Perhaps, but these are definitely Viking style weapons and the mummies do look to be early European in appearance with their increased height and light hair. They are certainly not Indian."

"Okay, I'll buy that, as incredible as it seems."

Scott continued, "Of special interest here are the swords and the helmet. Those particular weapons were usually carried by the higher-ranking Vikings and perhaps a couple of their leaders. The ordinary warriors mostly used axes and spears. No question in my mind that those mummies and weapons are Viking. The question is why and how did they get here? We know the Vikings settled in Iceland around 875 AD and Greenland about 985 AD. Some of our people think they may have ventured as far south to parts of our southern coastline, but who knows, they might have sailed into the Caribbean. In any event, the mere fact these mummies and relics are here really adds to the mystery of this place."

Scott picked up the swords. "We're taking these back to the museum," he said. "They won't believe this incredible story."

On the other side of the room, Elijah had been rummaging through an assortment of spears and stone axes left by Mayan warriors. The room apparently was a storage depot for weapons and supplies as the native warriors passed through the mountain. Two strange objects leaning against the wall caught his eye. They looked like plaques or tablets of some sort, with inscriptions engraved into the surfaces. There was a noticeable difference in each. One was made of stone and the other was constructed of a much thinner metallic like material. Inscribed on the face was a series of strange ciphers, glyphs and hieroglyphics. *Strange,* he thought, looking at the metallic panel. *I've seen these symbols before.* He picked up the two objects and carried them over to the spot where the rest of the group was standing. "Look at these strange things I found," he said.

Professor Scott was ecstatic as he gazed at the items in Elijah's hands. "Where did you find those?" he asked excitedly.

"On the other side of the room, stacked against the wall."

"The larger stone tablet you have is a Viking runestone and the other is made out of a very unique metal. They are exactly like the tablets Steele and I found in Iceland a few weeks ago. We have to take them back with us."

"How are you going to carry those tablets back with you in addition to the weight of the gold in your pack?" Simon asked. "You'll be too overloaded to walk."

"It looks like I'll have to leave some of the gold here," Scott answered. "These two tablets are much more valuable than all the gold in our packs. And if that metal tablet is what I think it is, then the ancient Indians in this region were also visited a long time ago by some very unusual visitors.

21

Aboard the Halifax

Captain Whitmore and the Halifax were moored in a small bay protected by a thin strip of a mountain range jutting down enough to offer good protection from any storms. Luckily, it was close to the small village of Playa Cautarito, their rendezvous point in two days. There was no way for him to know the Americans had been discovered and pursued by the Venezuelan army or if the group had even found the map or discovered the treasure. He was keenly aware of the relentless reputation of Simon Murphy and his treasure hunting companions and felt confident that they would meet the ship at the designated time. Whitmore wasn't expecting any trouble, but to be safe, he instructed his first mate to check all of the guns and ammunition to make sure everything was in good working order and fully prepared in the event of a confrontation by a Venezuelan navy vessel.

= = = = = =

Back in the cave, Simon led the group out of the room and continued along the passageway through the mountain. Professor

Scott was exuberant over the Viking swords they had discovered, but was especially overjoyed with the unlikely find of the Viking runestone and another metallic tablet. He couldn't wait to get back to the Washington museum and turn the runestone tablet over to that Scandinavian artifacts expert, Aavik Johansen, for his interpretation of the glyphs and symbols inscribed on the surface. Like his find in Iceland, Scott would hold onto the metal plaque in hopes to have it interpreted by another source. The information gathered on those particular artifacts might change history, he thought.

Carrying the heavy packs loaded with gold coins, the group pressed on with hopes of finding another way out. To Simon's satisfaction, the sound of splashing water could be heard up ahead. With very little food and water in two days, they were getting desperate as the last drop of rationed water was finished that morning and a deep thirst was building up in each of them. A short distance ahead, they came to a large cavity in the ceiling that disappeared into a dark cavity above. A small stream was trickling down from the fissure and collecting in a small pool. The water then slowly drained under a rock outcropping and disappeared into another underground tunnel.

"This water is a Godsend," Elijah shouted as the group rushed to the pool and took hearty drinks of water and filled up the canteens.

Jonah Steele took special interest in the fissure from where the water tumbled down. It appeared that instead of a vertical shaft burrowing straight up through the rock, this particular chute offered a steep slope which allowed the stream of water to moderately flow instead of a free fall from the top of the shaft.

I wonder if that shaft is passable for a man to climb through to the outside, he thought.

Simon assembled the men and continued the journey through the tunnel. Again, Peña took the lead position. After walking nearly another three hundred yards, the group was halted by an accumulation of huge boulders blocking the corridor. A massive cave-in had dropped tons of dirt and rock across the path, permanently sealing the passageway. Their worst fears were confirmed...they were hopelessly trapped inside the mountain.

"Looks like we're in a hell of a mess," Elijah grumbled to Simon. "There is no way we can break through that wall of boulders."

Simon's expression conveyed his disappointment. "Yeah, this cave could be solidly blocked for another mile or so and I didn't notice any side passages that might take us out of here. I guess there is only one option left. We turn back and take our chances with that army outside. We know that Professor Scott took out that Colonel Gallegos so maybe if we have to surrender we might be able to reason with the officers in charge if we show them how they can find the treasure."

"I wouldn't be too sure about that," Elijah replied. "His replacement might be just as bad and have us taken outside and executed."

Steele offered an idea. "When we passed the small pool back there, I took a look up at the fissure where the stream of water was flowing. Instead of a sheer vertical shaft, I noticed it was sloping upward at a relatively reasonable angle. When we get back to the pool, I want to try climbing up that shaft to see if it might give us another way out of here. If the fissure is passable, we can use our two ropes to make us some rigs to haul our backpacks up behind us. I think it's worth a try. That stream has to flow from somewhere, and I'm hoping it starts from outside this mountain."

"Okay, Jonah," Simon agreed. "Go for it. I guess it's worth checking out…anything is better than confronting all those soldiers out there."

Arriving at the pool, Simon pointed the lantern up toward the opening while Steele scaled the wall, using stone outcrops he was able to grasp. Through the tumbling water, he reached the top and slithered through the fissure. He was able to maneuver almost thirty feet higher until he came to an abrupt stop. The tiny stream was flowing through an opening under a rock ledge and the gap was just barely large enough to allow a man to squeeze through. Soaking wet, Steele worked his way back down to the passageway to report his findings. "I did find an opening big enough for us to wiggle through, but it won't be an easy climb."

Professor Scott offered a suggestion. "Do you suppose the soldiers gave up and left when they found the chamber empty? With Gallegos dead, maybe they decided to forget about us and return to Cumana. It sure would be easier to leave the way we came in rather than struggle our way up through that hole and get everything soaking wet. For all we know, that shaft could be a dead end. Maybe we should check out the cavern first and if the soldiers are still there we might be able to hear them through the wall."

A quick walk back to the wall panel confirmed their worst fears. The banging and heavy thudding sounds from the other side told them the soldiers were trying to break through the barrier. Now, there was only one option left…to try climbing through the fissure and follow the path of the stream.

Back to the pool, they fashioned short lengths of rope to be tied to the backpacks. In groups of two, the six men began climbing up the vertical wall. They soon realized dragging the heavy weighted packs was more difficult than they had thought, however, through sheer strength and determination, the climbers slowly worked their way up the slippery surface and squeezed through the fissured opening. With Steele leading the way, they clawed their way past the ledge where the water flowed from under the breach. As the young geologist had suggested, it did appear to be passable. Holding one of the oil lanterns and dragging his pack behind him, Steele wiggled and squirmed his way through the hole and found himself in a decent sized shaft that appeared to be relatively level. Although he had to stoop slightly, the passage was high enough to allow him to walk through the shallow stream bed. He shouted his discovery through the hole and told the men to come on through. With considerable effort and a lot of swearing, the other five climbers finally made it up the waterfall and through to the other side. Elijah took one look and jested, "Now I really know what rats feel like buried deep in their holes."

Simon laughed, "Well, think of the positive side. I don't think those soldiers would ever find us up in this shaft. If they manage to break through the wall, they'll find those treasure boxes and forget all about us."

"That's what bothers me," Elijah responded irritably. "Just the thought of them finding all of that gold sure makes this whole trip useless and a big waste of time."

"You will admit that keeping your head on your shoulders is better than having all that gold." Elijah nodded his head and just mumbled something to himself.

Sergeant Peña relieved Steele as point man, and now leading the group in single file, they followed the stream bed for several hundred yards when the shaft made an abrupt turn to the right. Just before the bend in the passageway, the stream disappeared into a small cavity under another ledge, leaving the path dry to walk on. There were no significant obstacles so their movement was relatively easy, except for the inconvenience of having to bend over to avoid scraping heads on the low ceiling. Peña made the turn toward the new direction when he noticed a faint glow of light well to his front. "I think I see an opening," he shouted.

With deep concentration while glancing toward the light, he failed to look down at the ground as he moved forward. Within ten steps, Peña let out a piercing scream as a floor panel disappeared and hurled him into a dark chasm below. Simon, who was directly behind Peña, was holding the lantern and noticed the deep fissure just in front of him. "What happened?" Steele shouted.

"Peña disappeared into that hole," Simon yelled back, holding the lantern over the opening and staring into the endless black cavity. "This is not a trap but just a wide crack in the floor."

"I wasn't expecting this," Steele confessed. "Somehow an underground disturbance has caused the walls to separate enough to allow this fissure to open up and the floor to collapse. I'm afraid Mr. Peña is gone."

Both men noticed the faint light in the distance. Steele continued, "It looks like we might have an opening ahead that distracted Peña's attention. He took his eyes off the floor when he saw the light. A fatal mistake, I'm afraid."

The other three men, hearing Peña's scream, rounded the curve and stood just behind Simon and Steele. One glance down at the fissure confirmed their fears about Sergeant Peña. "How far does that fracture drop?" Scott asked.

"No telling how deep it is…most likely all the way down to the bottom of this mountain," Steele answered.

Simon held the lantern high to his front again while Steele took a closer look. "The opening looks like it might be about eight or nine feet across and it's certainly too wide to jump over. The light ahead tells me we might have a way out of here so we need to find a way to bridge that gap. We certainly can't turn back."

22

Back in the cavern and with the use of a pick and sledge hammer, the soldiers broke through the rear wall to discover the cave continued beyond the obstruction. Captain Morales was now convinced the Americans had found a way to pass through the wall to the other side…perhaps through a secret door panel. He instructed his men to continue breaking up the rock to allow enough space to pass through. It did not take long to achieve a large enough opening to the other side and suitable for a file of his men to enter. With the use of pre-prepared torches, and in single file, Morales led his soldiers into the extending passageway. "Now we have you Gringos trapped," he whispered to himself.

It was only a short distance when Morales reached the cavity where the treasure boxes were stacked against the wall. He stopped the detachment long enough to pry off the lid of one of the crates, only to be shocked at the strong glitter of shimmering gold coins reflecting from the light of the torch. The captain was elated as he stared down at the piles of gold before him. "Now I know why the Americanos are here in our country and in this particular cave." he shouted. "They were here to grab all of this treasure and haul it away with the wagons."

He dug his hands into the box and held up a pile of gold doubloons. "To hell with the Gringos...we don't need them anymore," he yelled as he held his open hands up to watch the gold coins spill through his fingers and on to the floor.

"Wonder where all of this gold came from?" a young officer asked.

"Who cares," Morales shouted, "It doesn't make any difference. It all belongs to us now."

Jonah Steele knelt and closely examined the deep chasm immediately to his front. He was trying to figure how a man could manage to climb across the opening to the other side. He knew they had enough rope left to rig some type of a sling to pull the others over if he could just get across. Someone had to get to the other side to secure a rope. Being a trained geologist, Steele had a keen eye for unusual irregularities in stone formations and earth strata. He knelt and carefully examined the fissure before him.

He noticed something of interest along the foundation of the wall where the floor had broken loose. Along the base were a series of small irregular protrusions and narrow ledges of stone that projected out enough to offer a possible foothold. They needed to be solid enough to hold a man's weight. His concern was for the need of a small ledge or some protuberances about shoulder height that would enable him to hold on to while he positioned his feet. Although he was an experienced rock climber, he realized that one slight mistake would propel him into the dark hole. He shuttered to think that he might experience the same fate as Peña.

Another look revealed a slight horizontal cut in the stone

that might provide his handholds or to at least rest his fingers. He pondered his chances and then turned to the others. "I think I might be able to scale across to the other side using my hands and bare feet. It's risky, but it's our only chance if we are going to get out of this hole alive."

"Are you going to fly across?" Elijah said sarcastically.

"No, I'm going to try to inch along the wall barefooted and use those small protrusions in the rock wall to maintain a grip. I'll attach the rope to my waist and if I fall, you guys grab me and pull me up. We'll tie the two pieces of rope together with a square knot to have sufficient length."

Simon looked at him with a concerned look. "Jonah, if you think you can do it, it's worth a try. The only other alternative is for us to go back and face the soldiers or just sit here and starve to death. We have enough hands to hold on to the rope and catch your weight if you slip."

Steele secured the rope around his waist and grasped a small stone outcrop slightly above his head. He looked down and positioned his right foot against a narrow lip against the wall. He then eased himself over the dark void, allowing his one foot to support his weight. It held. With his free hand, he felt along the wall to find another spot to place his fingers. With a secure grip, he worked his toes along the base to find another protrusion.

Inch by inch, Steel worked his way along the wall, using his fingers to tightly grasp every depression he could feel. Clinging to the wall like a spider, he was almost to the other side when he placed his foot on another narrow ledge, only to feel smooth rock as he shifted his weight forward. With a feeling of horror, he realized his mistake as he lost his balance and grip and pitched forward into the cavity.

Simon and the others saw the mishap and held tightly to the rope around his waist and braced for the impact of his fall. The rope saved Steele's life as he instinctively grabbed the line with both hands and jerked to a sudden stop. He felt his body swing freely in midair and one glance below him revealed the huge dark space of nothingness.

"Are you okay?" Simon yelled.

"I'm still here," Steele shouted back. "Pull me up."

Four pair of hands pulled the rope until Simon saw him reach over the edge to grasp the floor. He and Elijah grabbed Steele's arms and pulled him up and over to rest on solid ground. Shaken but safe, he looked up at his companions and smiled. "Wow, that was close," he said. "Thanks."

"Now what?" Simon asked him.

"I was nearly there before I fell...only one more step and I would have made it. I've got to try again," he said confidently. "We have no other choice. First, let me catch my breath."

With the rope still attached to his waist and his companions holding the loose end tightly, Steele took his first step for the new attempt. His toes found the first foothold and fingers grasped the rock outcrop slightly above his head. As the others played out the rope, Steele slowly inched his way across the wall until he came to the spot where he had slipped. He hesitated and looked down to locate an indention or ledge to gain a foothold. All he needed was one last step and he could swing to the other side, but he could only see a smooth surface and no foothold. *I have to make that last three feet,* he thought, trying to weigh his options. "Feed me about five more feet of slack," he yelled.

Steele took a deep breath and planted his right foot next to his left and with all his strength and arms extended, he turned and leaped toward the edge of the opening. With the sheer power of his arms, he caught the ledge, pulled himself up and over, and on to the solid floor of the pathway. He was rewarded by robust cheering from the other side as he rolled over on his back and faced his companions with thumbs up. Simon responded by tossing his shoes to him over the fissure.

"We will toss you our rifles, but how do you plan to get us and the packs of gold across?" Simon shouted to him.

"Rather than try a sling rigging, I want you to secure the rope on your side to something against the wall. We will use the rope as a hand hold and safety line. If anyone slips or loses their footing, you can hold on to the rope to regain your foothold. Tie your end on a rock outcropping or something that projects out that can be looped several times. I'll do the same on this side. The last man will tie the rope to each pack and we'll haul them over one at a time. When the packs are secured, he can re-secure the rope and come over like the rest of us did."

Simon yelled back to Steele, "There is nothing to tie the rope to. This wall is as slick as glass, with only a few small cracks visible."

A quick glance at the wall confirmed what Simon had said. Steele did not see any rock protrusions to fasten a rope to, but he did remember something he had put into his pack. He called back to Simon, "Look in the right pocket in my backpack and you'll find two metal objects with a ring on one end and threads on the other end. Keep one and toss me the other."

Simon found them and held the objects up. "What are these?"

"They are called carabineers, used in rock climbing to tie off rope to rock walls. Now look for a small fissure in the rock and screw it into the wall. I'll do the same over here. This will give us something secure to tie down each end of the rope. I thought they might come in handy, so I stuck a couple in my pack."

"No one will be left over here to untie the rope so we can pull it back over," Lieutenant Portman reminded him.

"We'll just have to leave it. The opening is just ahead and we shouldn't need it anymore."

Professor Scott found a small fissure in the wall and, with Simon's help, screwed the object tightly into the crack. He tied the end of the rope through the carabineer's loop. "Make sure that rope is pulled tight because it might have to support a man's full weight," Simon reminded him.

"Don't worry," Scott replied, "this rope could hold an elephant, and to prove it I volunteer to go first."

Steele did the same on his side of the fracture.

Scott removed his shoes and tossed them over. Remembering the steps Steele had made, he secured his foot into the small ledge and felt for the first handhold. Holding tightly to the rope, Scott inched his way across and landed safely on the other side. Using the same sequence of steps, Simon made it over safely. Portman faltered in one instant but was able to steady himself with the hand rope and made it across. Elijah was last. Next, all the shoes and rifles were tossed over. The heavy gold laden backpacks were next. One pack at a time, he tied an end of the rope to each strap, and then pushed each one over the shelf. The men on the opposite side were then able to retrieve them by pulling each pack up and over the ledge.

Now it was Elijah's turn. He tied the rope back into the carabineer then tightly grasped it and lowered his foot in search of the foothold. He felt it and distributed his weight to one leg. He was halfway across when his right foot slipped and he lost his balance. He dropped off the wall like a stone. It was fortunate that he was holding the rope with both hands because it saved his life. The rope bent sharply from the sudden impact of Elijah's fall. The line held with Elijah holding on for dear life. Simon shouted, "The rope is tied down on both ends and we can't pull you so you will have to do it yourself…hand over hand. You can do this."

With the thought of falling to a certain death, the adrenalin kicked in, causing an added surge of strength to flow into his arms. He started moving slowly upward by placing one hand above the other and pulling with all his might. His head finally eased above the ledge when Simon and Portman grabbed his shoulders and hauled him out of the fissure. "I thought I was a goner," Elijah gasped.

Simon turned to Steele and said, "Great job, Mr. Steele. I'm not sure we could have made it without your ingenuity and rock climbing ability. Now I suggest we all get the hell out of this stinking rat hole."

23

The opening was large enough for the men to exit the cave and walk out into the sunlight. The fresh air was refreshing after the stale air they had breathed inside the shaft. The entrance was located about a hundred feet higher than the level of the valley floor below them, so with the heavy packs on their backs, the decent was difficult but manageable by grabbing some of the limbs on the small trees and bushes that covered the slope. In addition to the gold in their packs, Scott and Steele carried the two runestones, the stone tablet being the heaviest by about ten pounds.

Each man managed to work their way down to the valley floor unscathed. Professor Scott, who had been relatively quiet, spoke up. "Simon, how far would you estimate our hike would be to Playa Cautarito?"

"It was about a four-mile trip from the village to the cave, so I would guess we have about a five-mile walk ahead of us since we're on the other side of this mountain. We had better get moving if we're going to make our rendezvous with Whitmore and the Halifax."

With the heavy gold-laden backpacks, the hike was tiresome, requiring frequent rest breaks. It took longer than expected to finally reach the coastal road. Simon made an observation, "We need to get off this road and move over next to that tree line because I'm sure the army probably has scouting parties out looking for us. We've got to get to the beach tonight unobserved."

After another mile, the group was exhausted and took another break. Steele commented, "At this rate we'll never make it to the rendezvous in time. These heavy packs are sure slowing us down."

Following the concealment of trees, the group continued to move along parallel to the coastal road. Elijah was in the lead when he suddenly held up his hand, motioning a halt.

"What is it?" Simon asked.

"I see some saddled horses up ahead, but no sign of any riders."

Moving closer, they saw a group of eight horses with reins tied to several bushes. "Look over through the trees," Elijah whispered. "I see smoke from a fire...most likely a campfire. Those horses look like army mounts so I'll bet there is a detachment of soldiers over there cooking some dinner. I have an idea; we now have a much quicker way to get to Playa Cautarito."

"I get it," Simon said with a sly grin. "We steal us some horses."

The men carefully approached the horses, eased the reins from five of the mounts, and silently walked them over to the other side of the coastal road, just far enough away so they wouldn't be noticed. Attaching the backpacks behind the saddles, each man mounted and headed toward the village in a trot. Once out of sight, they picked up the pace. It was crucial that the group was not spotted by any observer that might divulge their whereabouts to the soldiers.

Once they reached the intersection to the village, Simon directed them well off the road and toward their rendezvous point at the eastern most section of the beach. They kept the mounts well into the trees where they would wait until dusk when the Halifax would pick them up with the rowboats.

Simon gathered the four remaining men for a brief discussion. "What do you think we should do with the gold coins we were able to load into our back packs?" he asked.

Elijah was the first to answer. "With all the trouble we went through to get here alive and in one piece, I think we should keep what little of the treasure we were able to grab from those boxes. That's a small payment for the risks we took."

"What about President Hayes and the U.S. Treasury? Isn't that why we were sent down here to this place," Steele remarked. "After all, the government did finance the expedition."

Portman added his comment, "I don't think we even need to mention anything about the coins. The amount of value we have in those packs is not enough to even make a dent with the treasury."

"I have a better idea," Scott suggested. "Why don't we give the Washington museum half of the coins and divide the other half among the five of us. They could display some of the coins in an exhibit, and it would provide them some funds to acquire other displays."

"I like that idea," Simon concurred. They all agreed with Scott's suggestion.

Professor Scott's mirrored lantern would transmit the prearranged signal to the ship, giving Whitmore the sign to send the boats ashore. It was very late in the day with only two hours before dark so now it was only a matter of waiting and staying out of sight. None of the men noticed a farmer walking on the other side of the road observing the small column of five riders passing his line of sight along the opposite tree line.

Back at their location near the coastal road, the soldiers finished their meal and packed up to retrieve the horses for their trek back to the military post in Playa el Chivo. Captain Morales had already pulled his command out of the valley and back toward Cumana with the wagons full of the treasure boxes. The small detachment observed by Simon and his companions was one of the few remaining scouting parties that had been left behind to search for the Americans, if by some slim chance they were able to escape from inside the mountain.

Like Morales, the soldiers were convinced the Americans had been buried alive and were most likely dead by now. Their vigil had been relaxed and their only interest now was to get back to the post and their own bunks. Sergeant Silvio was furious to discover five of his horses missing. "Private Tortola," he screamed, "you were supposed to keep an eye on the horses. What were you doing?"

The hapless private could only stammer and mumble, "Sorry, sir, I came in to get a plate of food. I didn't see anyone near the horses."

"That's no excuse," Silvio shouted to the man as he mounted one of the horses and selected two other soldiers to follow him. "If those thieves were the Americanos, then they most likely headed toward Playa Cautarito and the coast. We'll head that way and see if we can find anyone who might have seen them pass by. The rest of you will have to start walking back toward our post in Playa Cautarito."

At a rapid pace, Silvio soon came to the intersection and turned north toward the village and beach. It didn't take long before they spotted the farmer walking along the road toward Playa Cautarito. Silvio stopped and confronted the man. "Hola señor, usted ha visto paso de los jinetes cerca?" *"Hello mister, have you seen any riders pass by?"*

"Si señor, earlier I saw five men riding toward the village over along that tree line. They looked like gringos and they were in a big hurry."

"How long ago?"

"I would guess about an hour ago."

Silvio nodded his thanks and spurred his horse forward at a gallop with his two men following. Soon they reached the outskirts of the village and halted. He assessed the situation. "They would not have approached the village to be seen, so the only other way they could have gone is east along the beach. We'll head that way and try to spot them before it gets too dark."

Concealed in the trees, Simon and the group had dismounted and watched closely across the bay, hoping to see the Halifax. The sun was setting fast and darkness would descend in a matter of minutes. As arranged, Captain Whitmore and his ship had eased close enough to shore as possible to be able to anchor in water deep enough to avoid getting grounded. He wanted to be able to allow his two rowboats to get to shore, pick up the men, and get back to the ship as quickly as possible.

"See anything, First Mate?" Whitmore asked the seaman standing beside him.

"Nothing yet, sir,"

Professor Scott lit and handed Simon the mirrored lantern. He passed his hand over the mirror twice and delayed the light for three seconds and then passed his hand over twice again. Nothing came back from the water. He repeated the signal two more times. Suddenly, the same signal came back to them from out in the bay.

"They've seen us," Simon shouted with relief. "Turn the horses loose and let's head for the beach and wait for the boats."

Captain Whitmore had a keen sense for trouble and for some reason he had a gut feeling that he had better prepare for a possible confrontation, either from another vessel or from the shore. The Halifax was equipped with a new prototype Krupp 88mm rifled breach loading cannon that had not yet been used in battle, however, tests had proved the weapon to be quite effective if needed. He instructed his armaments officer to prepare the gun in the event of a problem.

The two rowboats had already beached when Simon and his group reached the water. Quickly, they loaded the heavy packs and boarded the boats for the return to the Halifax.

Sergeant Silvio and his two men passed the five horses racing up the beach and quickly spotted the Americans as the boats were launched from the shore. They dismounted and brought their rifles to bear and fired. The dinghys were halfway to the ship when shots rang out from the beach. Bullets splashed small plumes of water on either side of them. Luckily, no one was hit. Three more shots were heard as Portman took a slug through his upper shoulder…he let out a loud groan and slumped forward.

Captain Whitmore saw the gun flashes and turned to his gunnery officer. "Mr. Parker, one round from the Krupp against those gun flashes you see on the beach."

"Yes, sir," he answered as he passed the instructions on to his gunnery crew.

The blast from the cannon ripped through the air as the 88mm round sped to the beach and exploded with a ball of fire and shrapnel. Three bodies were hurled across the sand and lay still. The threat was over.

The rowboats bumped the hull of the Halifax and ladders were lowered to receive the boarders. "Permission to come aboard, Sir," Simon shouted to Whitmore. "We have a wounded man here."

"Permission granted, Mr. Murphy. We'll fetch the doctor immediately."

The Americans and their packs were loaded aboard, and with the small boats secured, the Halifax was turned to the north for the trip home. Professor Scott and Jonah Steel had been unable to carry the Viking sword and helmet, leaving them behind in the shaft, but somehow they had managed to secure the runestone tablets to their packs and get them safely to the ship. Lieutenant Portman was carried to the infirmary where it was determined that the bullet passed through the fleshy part of his upper arm with no damage to bone or an artery. He would recover with no severe damage.

Captain Whitmore turned to Simon and Elijah. "Well, gentlemen, I noticed you don't have any heavy boxes with you, so I assume you failed to complete your mission and acquire the treasure."

"Yes, sir, you are correct. Unfortunately, the Venezuelan National Army grabbed all the treasure when we were trying to escape through a hidden shaft. We were barely able to escape with our lives."

"I understand, gentlemen. I am just glad that you were able to get back to the ship without any further loss of life. The good news is that Lieutenant Portman only sustained a minor wound so he should be able to recover quickly."

Simon nodded a sigh of relief and politely suggested, "Now, sir, if you will be so kind to lead us to the officer's quarters, we would love a good stiff shot of whiskey because we have a very interesting story to tell you."

24

Washington D.C. — Office of the President

President Rutherford Hayes and Treasury Secretary John Sherman were very displeased to hear of the failure of the mission to retrieve the lost treasure from the Spanish galleon, but after hearing Simon, Elijah, and Professor Scott's story, he did display a little compassion and thankfulness that most of the group had survived a very harrowing confrontation with the Venezuelan Army. The explanation of their narrow escape through the tiny shaft in the mountain was compelling enough to exonerate them from their failure to acquire the treasure.

Most disturbing to the president was the news about the death of Captain Maxwell and the possibilities that the Venezuelan soldiers had broken through the wall to the inner chamber and confiscated the treasure. This information would exclude any future attempt to return to Venezuela. Although disappointed, President Hayes thanked the three men and dismissed them. The president turned and left the office with Secretary Sherman following him. The meeting was over.

Simon invited his cousin to accompany him to his home in

Bladensburg, Maryland where he would stay a few days before his return to California. He assured Elijah that Maggie would cook him meals that would satisfy his unusual culinary tastes and even include enough gravy to smother his plate. This Elijah couldn't resist.

Before Professor Scott returned to the museum, he explained to his two companions in more detail about the possibilities of the information inscribed on the Viking runestone they had found in Iceland. He told them about the Nordic culture expert, Professor Aavik Johansen, and the fact he was in the process of translating the Iceland runes and should have the translation completed by now.

When he informed them of the strong possibility the tablets could reveal the whereabouts of a lost Viking city and a vast treasure buried somewhere near the Arctic Circle, perhaps in Greenland or Iceland, this incredible information piqued their adventuresome spirit and interest enough to compel Elijah to stick around for a few more days. In addition, Scott assured them that Professor Johansen would be most anxious to translate the other runestone tablet they had found in the cave in Venezuela and perhaps help solve the speculation of Vikings sailing as far south as the Caribbean Sea and visiting some of the natives living along the northern coastal regions of South America. Also of special interest was the unusual drawing of the spaceship-like object they had found on the cave wall. There were a lot of unsolved questions to be answered and Elijah did not intend to be left out.

The professor was sure the museum's curator, Robert Drake, would be most pleased to receive the two packs of gold coins they carried with them for the museum. The curator would be advised to treat the gift with complete discretion as a confidential donation from private donors, fearing the Treasury Department would attempt to confiscate the coins if Hayes and Sherman found out about it. Most likely, if the government knew the treasure hunters had divided up some of the coins for themselves, they would assuredly grab them as well. Scott assured Simon that the secret would be safe with Drake.

Bladensburg, Maryland

Maggie was overjoyed to see her husband when he opened the door, accompanied by his cousin Elijah. She had learned he had returned to Washington and couldn't wait to see him. He swept her into his arms and gave her a lingering kiss. Especially exciting was when his five-year old son, Thomas, ran around the corner and jumped into his father's arms. Maggie was very glad to see them and promised Elijah a great dinner that she had been preparing for their return.

Aware of Elijah's enjoyment of good meals, she had put together a dinner that neither of the men would soon forget. She knew that the type of bland food that they must have consumed the past few days would make them ravenous and starving for a good home cooked meal. The two men were not disappointed with Maggie's scrumptious dinner, and for Elijah's enjoyment, the meal included plenty of rich brown gravy to smother over his plate. The roast beef, a heaping mound of potatoes, and two rolls on Elijah's plate formed tiny islands in the sea of gravy that covered everything else. *What an animal,* Simon thought as he rolled his eyes while gazing down at Elijah's plate. His southern cousin never ceased to amaze him. The dinner was delicious, as attested by Elijah's three helpings.

After dinner, the men retired to the study where Simon pulled out a special bottle of his eight-year old Buckhorn Creek Kentucky Bourbon. Suitably comfortable in easy chairs, the two men engaged in casual conversation.

"What are you going to do if that Nordic history professor translates the runestones and finds out that there is a Viking city and large treasure hidden somewhere up north?" Elijah asked. "If there is really something big up there, I can't just pack up and go back to California without being a part of the search team. That could be one of the biggest finds in North American history."

Simon glanced at the doorway to make sure they were not being overheard. "You've got to be kidding. You don't really expect me to let you and Professor Scott travel up there and discover a prize like that and get all the glory, do you? The discovery of a Viking city in North America would change history books."

Elijah laughed, "I didn't think so. You and I have the same adventurous blood."

Simon nodded and continued, "Professor Scott told me a meeting is scheduled at the Washington National Museum tomorrow afternoon and the translation by that expert should be complete. He mentioned that you and I should stop by the museum around two o'clock to learn of the results, plus it would be nice to see our old friend Robert Drake from the Toltec affair."

Elijah took another big sip of the bourbon. "Wow, this stuff is really smooth," he added with a nod of satisfaction. "We'll do that. I can't wait to find out what that Nordic expert found out."

"Elijah, don't mention anything to Maggie until we have more information from the meeting. The thought of me leaving her again on another wild treasure hunt wouldn't go well with her."

That night, Simon enjoyed a restful night with Maggie cuddled in his arms. Their passionate lovemaking in the next room kept Elijah awake for a while, but he soon fell asleep due to exhaustion from the last few days in Venezuela.

25

Washington National Museum

After profusely thanking them for the confidential gift of gold coins and assuring them the source of the donation would remain secret, Robert Drake escorted Professor Scott and Jonah Steele into a private room located near the rear of the museum. Scott had the Venezuelan runestone safely concealed in a leather satchel, which he placed under the table. He planned to reveal this new tablet after he learned what the Nordic expert found out from the runestone they had discovered in Iceland. The second tablet they found in Venezuela was considerably different than the stone tablet in the bag … it was lighter and had more of a metallic feel. They secured this plaque with the comparable one from Iceland and concealed them in a secret compartment Scott had constructed behind a wall. He and Steele made an agreement not to divulge the existence of these tablets to anyone but Simon and Elijah. Scott was convinced these thinner metallic tablets had no connection to the Viking runes, but more likely linked to another group of unlikely visitors. They would, however, show the new stone tablet to Aavik Johansen after he divulged the translation from the first runestone they had found in Iceland.

Scott conveyed to Robert Drake, "I invited our old friends Simon Murphy and Elijah Walker to attend the meeting. They should be here at 2:00 PM. I'll accompany you to the front to meet them and escort them to this room."

Drake acknowledged his approval. "It will be great to see them again. Johansen should also be arriving at any minute."

The two men walked to the front reception area to meet their new guests and found all three men waiting for them. Simon, Elijah, and Johansen were escorted into the meeting room and took seats around the table. After brief introductions and handshakes, Johansen said, "Gentlemen, let's get right to the point. The translation of this stone tablet revealed some incredible material…information that changes our concepts about the Vikings and their travels and settlements in North America.

"First of all, let me tell you about what we do know of the Vikings and their discoveries in North America. In the late ninth century, around 875 AD, Viking explorers sailed their ships westward across the Atlantic and discovered the island of Iceland where they established a few settlements. Later about 950 AD, a Viking chief named Erik the Red sailed from Norway and landed on the shores of Greenland. Viking settlers later established settlements there about 985. Although much of the island's interior was covered by ice, they found fertile lands around the fjords that were suitable for planting and pastures for their livestock. There was also a wealth of fish, seals, whales, and fowl.

"Around the year 1000 AD and 500 years before Christopher Columbus sailed to America, Erik the Red's son, Leif Eriksson, sailed several ships further westward and landed on the shores of Newfoundland. Several settlements were later established there. Traces of Viking dwellings have also been found on Baffin Island and Labrador. The Norsemen were very accomplished seamen with very seaworthy ships. Some scientists have even speculated that the Vikings might have traveled as far south well down the eastern seaboard of America and as far as Florida, but this is mere speculation. Nonetheless, the Viking presence in North America lasted nearly 500 years."

Professor Scott was getting impatient, "Mr. Johansen, what can you tell us about the Viking runestone we showed you…the one we found in Iceland? You made a sketch of the runes."

The man held up the tablet and began his explanation. "This tablet gives us some incredible information and clues of a lost Viking city and a vast treasure of gold and artifacts the Norsemen confiscated from the nobles of Europe during their conquests. Aside from the gold coins, many of the artifacts no doubt are made of solid gold. Of all places, the rune inscriptions point to a location on Baffin Island, inside one of the fjords that feed into the Labrador Sea. One of the clues mentions a barren piece of rock now called Kekertukdjuak Island, no doubt an Eskimo name. Our research indicates the fjord is located just south of a small Indian village called Pangnirtung. A discovery such as this would be an incredible find and provide us valuable new information about the Vikings and their presence in North America. I would also imagine the gold artifacts that might be found there would be priceless."

"How about a Viking presence in South America?" Scott asked, preparing to reveal the discovery from Venezuela.

Johansen's perplexed expression expressed his surprise at the question. "I'm afraid I don't understand what you mean, Mr. Scott."

Scott glanced at Simon and Elijah and then reached under the table and lifted the satchel from the floor. He opened the bag and pulled the tablet out and placed it in front of Johansen. "Here is a runestone very similar to the one you have in front of you from Iceland. A few days ago, we found this particular stone tablet hidden in a cave near the Venezuelan coast. We think it might be of Viking origin."

The Nordic historian was totally speechless as he gazed at the new stone tablet Scott had laid on the table. "Oh, my goodness," he gasped. "You found that tablet in Venezuela?"

"Yes, in a remote cave located near the Caribbean Sea. We also found a stack of light skinned mummies with traces of lighter hair. They were considerably taller than those of the local native ancient Indians of the period. Also, of special interest we found some Viking swords and a helmet with horns adorning either side of the crown. Unfortunately, we had to leave them behind in a very narrow escape from inside a mountain with the Venezuelan National Army after us."

Johansen replied, "If what you say is true, this will definitely shake up the history books and stir up archeologists and scientific circles all over Europe and the Americas." He turned to the new tablet Professor Scott had handed him. "I do see some familiar runes and inscriptions on this stone. Let's see if I can translate any of this."

Johansen reached into his bag and pulled out a large leather bound book. The worn appearance indicated it had been used frequently. Simon noticed long lines of inscriptions, glyphs, and symbols followed by multiple lines of text, most likely written in Norwegian. The historian began to scan the tablet and simultaneously open pages of the book to cross-reference the runes. This would allow him a translation corresponding to the runes carved into the stone. In the process, he made several notes. Periodically, he would glance up at the other occupants in the room with a surprised expression.

It was obvious that some of the information being revealed had a profound impact on the historian. Simon, Elijah, Scott, Steele, and Drake remained silent.

Finally, Johansen closed the book and looked down at his notes. "Gentlemen, this tablet is definitely of Viking origin. It appears four Viking ships commanded by one of Leif Erikson's captains, named Harold Gunnhild, sailed southward along the United States coast, past the tip of Florida as far as the Caribbean Sea, and beyond. They landed on a distant shore of an unknown coast line with a series of small sandy beaches and high cliffs. The Vikings encountered a large tribe of natives, most likely ancestors of the Chibcha. A fierce battle took place and the Vikings lost several warriors. They barely escaped in two of the longboats and the other two boats were captured and burned by the Indians. This runestone was carved by one of their scribes while they were there and apparently left behind and buried in the cave with the mummies you spoke of."

Johansen pulled out a map of the Americas and with his finger traced along their probable route. "Based on what I see, the Vikings apparently landed on that section of the Venezuela coast close to where you found this runestone. This tablet proves that the Vikings sailed well to the south of their northern settlements and as far as the northern coastline of South America. Since by custom the Vikings usually cremated their dead, those mummies you discovered must have been some of the fallen Viking warriors apparently mummified by the Indians as respect for their bravery and an appeasement so they wouldn't be haunted by their departed spirits. This information is truly an astounding revelation that will certainly shake up the Nordic history community and your American history books."

"Professor Johansen," Scott asked politely, "is there any way I could obtain a copy of that translation book you have with the Viking and Scandinavian inscriptions and symbols? There is a possibility I might find some other runestones, and it would be very convenient if I could interpret the tablets on site. I might be in a situation where I can't bring the stones back to the museum for you to translate."

Johansen emitted a light chuckle as he reached over and removed another notebook from his satchel and handed it to him. "Funny that you ask, Mr. Scott. I anticipated that possibility and had a copy made for you with the side notes translated into English. All I ask is that you keep this book very secure and secret. Also, promise me that you will show me any tablets that you might recover and share with me any interpretations you might make on any of the runestones you are unable to bring back from your travels."

Scott acknowledged the gift with a big nod. "Thank you, Professor Johansen. I will certainly comply with your requests and make sure you are kept informed on any further Viking discoveries we might encounter."

Robert Drake escorted Professor Aavik Johansen to the front door of the museum and thanked him for his help. He then returned to the meeting room.

26

Once seated again, Drake turned to Professor Scott and asked, "George, what do you think we should do?"

"I think we should mount up an expedition and go find that Viking city and all the treasure. The prestige of the museum would soar and visitors from all over the world would want to come and see the Viking exhibits."

"I agree," Drake concurred. "The four of you would make a strong team and if anyone could find the city, you experienced treasure hunters could."

Simon and Elijah glanced at one another for mutual reinforcement and in unison said, "Count us in." The temptation of such a discovery was too much to refuse.

Jonah Steele raised his hand. "I'm in, too."

"Great," Drake shouted. "What about informing someone with the U. S. Department of the Interior about this venture? This museum falls under their jurisdiction and the government does help sponsor and provide funds for the museum, you know."

Scott had a quick answer. "Robert, I think we should keep this venture very confidential for now. As you know, there are no secrets within the government and for safety reasons we should keep this mission to ourselves. If we find the treasure and return it safely to the museum, then we can release the news to the world. As Mr. Johansen said, this discovery will send ripples around the scientific circles and change the history books."

Simon added his thoughts, "I have to agree with the professor. If the word gets out about such a treasure, then all the crooks and pirates in North America will be after it. For safety's sake, we need to keep this very confidential."

Drake agreed that the mission should be kept a secret, but had issue with keeping it from the proper government officials. He countered the issue with his remarks. "The museum is subsidized by the United States government and any vessel we secure for this mission will need to have the approval of the Interior Department. The Navy has to be involved. I have certain friends with our naval command center who can supply us a suitable vessel to get you safely to Baffin Island. Besides, the government would turn over all the artifacts to the museum anyway for public display. I feel certain I can get proper government and military officials to designate this project as top secret and keep word of the expedition from getting out."

Simon and Elijah understood his dilemma and consented. Satisfied this would be the best course of action, Simon remarked, "I guess it would be comforting to know that the navy would have our backs."

Drake continued, "Go ahead and put together a list of provisions you'll need and we'll shoot for a possible departure date in a couple of days. You have the coordinates and general idea where to locate the target, so I suggest you gather your necessary supplies and prepare for the journey."

= = = = = =

Robert Drake acted swiftly in arranging a meeting for the group with a friend, Thomas Ross, at the Georgetown docks. He was accompanied by another man he introduced as Captain Barnaby Swift, a seasoned naval seaman who had experience with prior voyages as far as Greenland, Iceland, and Hudson Bay. He had sailed through the Davis Strait past Baffin Island a few times and was familiar with most of the northern sea routes. A good choice of captains, Simon thought.

The ship commissioned was the former USS Shannon, a sleek three masted steam driven vessel with a length of 161 feet and width of 28 feet. She was a sleek navy warship that had been overhauled and refitted with the latest armaments. Her oscillating cylinder compound engines provided her enough horsepower to easily negotiate the journey, provided weather conditions were reasonably favorable. The voyage along the coastline would carry them from the Atlantic Ocean, into the Labrador Sea, and on to Baffin Island and to their destination into the Cumberland Sound. Being early July, they anticipated the ice would be melted enough to allow easy access to the fjord leading to a cavern entrance they would have to search for.

After the introductions, Ross left the group with Captain Swift to prepare a briefing on the upcoming voyage. They later met with Simon and his three companions in the captain's quarters where Swift had a map displayed of Canada and the northern territories. Simon, Elijah, Scott, and Steele listened carefully as the captain explained the details of their journey. He then turned to the subject of their mission. "Well Gentlemen, I understand you will be searching for a lost Viking city and perhaps a large treasure of priceless artifacts the Vikings might have cached there."

"That is correct Captain," Simon acknowledged. "Hopefully, if we find it we'll transport it back to Washington on this ship."

"We can certainly accommodate that," Swift assured them. "Is it true that the location of this Viking city and treasure was revealed by a stone tablet you discovered in Iceland?"

Professor Scott answered, "That is correct. Mr. Steele and I found it stored in a hidden cave located behind a waterfall. The tablet is referred to as a runestone and was carved by Vikings and with inscriptions referred to as runes. It was translated by a history professor at Georgetown University. He is Norwegian and an expert of the early Norsemen civilization."

"Very interesting," the captain replied. "My concern is that someone outside this group besides your museum curator and Mr. Ross know about the treasure and the location. Our secretary of the navy, Richard Thompson, knows about the mission and will keep it top secret. But I have to wonder about your translator of the tablet. I understand he is of Scandinavian descent, so would he not mount a separate expedition to search for the treasure? I'm sure the Norwegian Government would love to get their hands on that Viking treasure for themselves since it originally came from Norway and other Scandinavian countries. Since the treasure belonged to their Viking ancestors, I'm sure they would not take kindly knowing those priceless artifacts were sitting in an American museum."

"You make an interesting point, Captain," Simon acknowledged.

"No telling what type of confrontations we might encounter on our journey. Will you be properly armed?" Swift asked.

"Yes sir, Captain, we still have our firearms from the Venezuelan affair...some very formidable weapons. We have five Winchester Model 1876 repeating rifles and three Colt Model '78 Frontier double action revolvers that take .40-44 caliber bullets. We should be prepared for most any unpleasant confrontation."

"I would say you will be well prepared," the captain agreed. "The USS Shannon has a total complement of six officers and twenty-one sailors aboard. She has an armament of ten deck guns, one Gatling gun in the bow, and a British made Nordenfelt four barrel one-inch rapid firing gun on the rear stern deck. This should give us adequate protection. The weather is holding well so I would like to depart by day after tomorrow, so prepare to be aboard ship by 7:00 AM Tuesday morning."

27

Bladensburg, Maryland

Maggie was furious when Simon informed her of the new expedition to Baffin Island in search for the lost Viking city and alleged treasure hidden there. "You just came back from one of your expeditions to Venezuela and here you want to go on another wild goose chase to some forsaken ice covered rock off the coast of Canada," she yelled. "You're my husband and a father and Thomas and I need you here."

"I know, Maggie, but this is an opportunity of a lifetime and I just have to go with Elijah and the others to find that treasure and bring it back to the museum. Besides, I will be very well paid for the job. I promise you this will be my very last expedition of this sort."

"That's what you told me last time," she vented.

"Maggie, you know how much I hate being a hardware salesman."

"You can always find another line of work and stay at home to be a good husband to me and father to your son."

"Okay, when I get back I'll look for another job and stay home with you and Thomas. Besides, you know from my prior expeditions that we have a substantial amount of gold coins locked away to provide for us for many years."

Maggie glared at Simon for a brief moment, then threw herself into his arms. "You crazy man, you had better come back to me alive and in one piece," she cried. "You and that senseless cousin of yours had better take good care of each other and not get yourselves hurt or killed."

"I promise we'll be very careful," Simon assured her.

= = = = = =

The early morning buggy ride provided by the museum to escort them to the docks gave Simon and his cousin time to talk about the journey ahead. Elijah couldn't resist asking the question. "I overheard some yelling from the kitchen last night. I take it you and Maggie talked about the expedition and she didn't take it very well."

"That's an understatement. She was as mad as a pissed off alligator chasing a rattlesnake. She made me promise this would be my last treasure hunting trip. I need to start concentrating on being a good husband and father. Besides, I'm probably getting too old for this treasure chasing business anyway, especially getting trapped in caves and dodging bullets from all the bad guys."

"Yeah, I know what you mean. When I get back to California, I may just have to marry Rosita if she hasn't already married someone else by now. But we would sure miss the excitement of the adventure, wouldn't we?"

Simon gave him an understanding nod.

They pulled up to the docks at 6:45 AM and the short walk to the pier placed them at the foot of the gangplank exactly two minutes before the requested departure time. Captain Swift was waiting at the top of the plank. "Permission to come aboard, Sir," Simon requested.

"Permission granted," the captain replied.

Swift greeted them on deck with a hardy handshake. "Welcome aboard," he said. He noticed the Winchester rifles the two men were carrying and nodded his approval. "Looks like you did come well prepared. Professor Scott and Mr. Steele are in the mess having coffee and a bit of breakfast. I'll have my men stow your gear in your staterooms and you can join them."

He then immediately turned to his first mate and gave orders to pull the gangplank and prepare the ship for sailing. At precisely 7:35 AM, the seamen from the USS Shannon hoisted her anchor and steamed toward the Chesapeake Bay where they would turn northward into the Atlantic Ocean and on toward Greenland. The search for a huge piece of Viking history was about to begin.

= = = = = =

Ever since his translation of the Viking runestone, Professor Aavik Johansen had fumed over the idea that an American museum would most likely embark on a secret mission to find the lost Viking city and perhaps the greatest Viking treasure cache of all times. After all, he reasoned, the priceless artifacts mentioned in the runes once belonged to his fellow Norse countrymen and rightfully now belonged to his native land of Norway.

Those priceless artifacts and relics should be displayed in the National Museum of Oslo and not in a museum in Washington. Perhaps he should do something about that.

= = = = = =

In 1814, Norway had been ceded to the King of Sweden by the Treaty of Kiel that established the country as a part of the Swedish empire. Toward the end of the 19th century, the population and ruling classes in Norway wanted to be liberated from the Swedish alliance. Through the help of some brief military actions against their neighbor, Norway declared the dissolution of the union with Sweden in June of 1905, enabling the country to finally achieve its independence. Although it would be twenty-seven years later before Norway would develop a Ministry of Foreign Affairs and formal diplomatic relations with the United States, the fledging Scandinavian country assigned a few discrete and unofficial individuals to Washington to make some connections with selected government officials in hopes for a future strong alliance with America. One such individual was Asbjørn Ulvestad who was also an acquaintance of the Georgetown University professor, Aavik Johansen. It was Ulvestad who Professor Johansen would seek out that day.

Through a bit of research, he found Ulvestad's home address to be a small bungalow located on a side street just off Connecticut Avenue and close to Farragut Square. Johansen approached the house and knocked on the door. An attractive middle aged woman opened it. "Good day, Mrs. Ulvestad, I am Professor Aavik Johansen from Georgetown University and I am looking for your husband. I am an acquaintance of Asbjørn and need to talk to him. Could you tell me where I might find him?"

"Well, yes, Professor Johansen, I've heard him mention your name before. I would imagine he is about to have lunch at Rasmuttens. He usually eats there on Thursdays because that's the day they serve smoked salmon, braised red cabbage, and pannekaken…Norwegian pancakes."

"Why yes, I know where that is. I've eaten there a few times myself. Thank you for your help, Mrs. Ulvestad." Johansen mounted his horse and turned toward the capital.

= = = = = =

Johansen spotted Ulvestad sitting at a small table at the rear of the restaurant. He was alone. The professor approached the table and said, "God ettermiddag Asbjørn, er det nove deg igjen." "Good afternoon, Asbjørn, it's good to see you again."

"Well, hello, Professor. It's been a long time and a pleasant coincidence meeting you here."

"Actually I wanted to talk to you and stopped by your house. Your wife told me where I could find you."

"In that case, have a seat. You should try the smoked salmon and red cabbage. That's the Thursday special here. Now what's on your mind that you wanted to see me about?"

After placing his order with the waiter, Johansen glanced

around the room to make sure they could talk in private. In quiet tones, he spent the next hour telling Ulvestad about the Viking runestones and his translation divulging the location of a lost Viking city and vast cache of priceless Nordic treasures and artifacts. Also of special interest was the second tablet the Americans had found in Venezuela. For a few moments, Asbjørn Ulvestad was speechless. "Do you have any idea what this means, Professor?"

"Yes, I certainly do. It means that our Viking ancestors discovered the Americas well before Columbus embarked on his voyage in 1492. It means history books will have to be drastically changed and our former countrymen will have to be credited with the discovery of both Americas. It also means that if such a treasure exists it would belong to its rightful owner... Norway."

"Do you know of the location of this city and treasure?" Ulvestad asked.

"Yes, I do and unfortunately so do the Americans. I imagine they are in the process of mounting an expedition to Baffin Island right now to find and recover the treasure for their museum. Perhaps they have a ship chartered and are already on their way."

"Then, I think we had better move fast, don't you agree, Aavik?"

"Absolutely," Asbjørn, "absolutely."

28

The USS Shannon was making good time as she sailed up the Virginia coast and passed by Hog Island. By nightfall, they anticipated reaching the small stretch of coastline belonging to the state of Maryland. The sea was relatively smooth, giving Elijah a sigh of relief and sparing him from his normal habit of getting violently seasick. He found Simon at the bow of the ship staring at the passing distant shore. "Hi Simon," he said, "I've been meaning to ask you, did you remember to bring that Zenox communication device with you?"

"Absolutely, I would never start out on one of these expeditions without it. Remember, it did save our hides in Venezuela by showing us the clues to opening the door to the other passageway where the treasure was stored. It has also saved us on a few other occasions as well, especially that mess we got into in North Carolina five years ago. Besides, I remember Commander Ahular telling me to always carry the Zenox with me and that it will keep us in constant touch with our alien friends."

"I wonder where Ahular and Nezar are located now. They did tell us we would most likely see them again sometime in the future," Elijah added.

"No telling where they might be. They could be sitting on

some distant planet in a way off galaxy or they could even be somewhere here on our planet. I remember Nezar telling me they had been assigned to study planet Earth since we were very similar to their own home planet Xeres. Nonetheless, I have a gut feeling we haven't seen the last of them."

Washington Docks

Asbjørn Ulvestad was standing with Professor Aavik Johansen gazing up at the sleek corvette moored before them. "What do you think?" Ulvestad asked. "Not bad for a very quick notice, is she?"

"A real beauty she is. I sure hope the ship is fast enough to beat the Americans to Baffin Island," Johansen responded.

"I think you'll find her speed is quite adequate. This vessel is privately owned and aptly named the Aberdeen. I was told she is a three masted steam powered ship with a gross tonnage of 4,600 tons. Her length is 198 feet and breadth is 27 feet. The ship was built in England by the Laird Brothers and her horsepower was rated at 3000." Looking at Johansen he added, "I see you are all packed and ready to go. I wasn't sure you were even going."

"I have to go because I'm the only one who knows the approximate location and I would never forgive myself if our homeland's possessions fell into the hands of the Americans."

Ulvestad remarked, "I agree. Let's hope you don't encounter any trouble, but if you do, I understand the Aberdeen has six 64-pound muzzle loading rifled guns and a light Paxton 20mm deck gun mounted fore and aft."

"How about the captain and crew?" the professor questioned.

"The captain is a German man named Karl Wolfe. He a well-seasoned seaman and has a particular fondness for money. The crew consists of eighteen deckhands and two cooks… all well trained in the use of personal firearms and the ship's armaments. I'm not sure of their nationalities, but Albert Larsson assures me they are trustworthy for the mission."

"How are we paying for all of this?"

"You'll be happy to know we have a very influential supporter who wants the Viking artifacts and treasure returned to Norway badly. He is our reigning King Oscar II of Norway.

"I'll say this for you Asbjørn, you certainly have the right connections."

The Norwegian laughed. "Now, let's meet Captain Wolfe so you can be on your way."

The captain was a tough and confident looking fellow who was used to the hardships of the sea. He had been briefed about the mission, so he quickly welcomed Johansen aboard and ordered one of the crew members to usher him to his quarters. He quickly turned to another deckhand and commanded him to cast off and immediately get the ship underway. It was obvious Wolfe was not a man to trifle with. Johansen noticed some of the crew had firearms strapped to their waist and two men had rifles slung over their shoulders. He also noticed their rough appearance, resembling the type of men who enjoyed heavy drinking and starting bar fights. He turned to the captain and said, "Captain Wolfe, I noticed that several of your crew members are carrying weapons. Is that really necessary?"

His harsh glare should have answered the question as he

coarsely replied, "My employers hired me take you up north to grab up all of that Viking loot and failure is out of the question. My crew is well trained to make sure the mission is a success."

Johansen nodded his understanding and turned to follow Ulvestad back to the gangplank. The diplomat turned to the professor and whispered, "King Oscar II wants that Viking treasure to be in Norway really bad, and he'll spare no expense of getting it by any means necessary. I would try to stay out of Wolfe's way…that man is a professional killer."

"Sounds like a real pleasant cruise ahead of me," he replied, wondering how the devil he got himself into this mess.

From the deck, Johansen waved farewell to his friend and the first thought that came to mind was, *maybe I should have kept my mouth shut and sided with the Americans.*

Aboard the USS Shannon

With favorable weather, the steamer traveled steadily north, rounding the spit of land called Cape Cod. Captain Swift informed his passengers that they would soon reach the coast of Maine where they would briefly stop at the town of Bar Harbor to take on water for the boilers. He informed Simon and his group that they would have time to disembark and stretch their legs on dry land. A beer at one of the local pubs and a quick meal of fresh lobster would be a welcome break. The steamer docked at 4:30 PM and the gangplank was lowered to allow the men to leave the ship. Swift instructed them to be back on the ship by 7:00 PM in time for departure.

Elijah was the first to spot the sign... *The Rusty Nail Bar and Grill*...a perfect place to refresh their hunger and thirst. The four men entered the building and selected a table close to the door.

A shapely blond waitress came to the table and asked for their order. "What do you suggest, ma'am?" Elijah asked.

"Our local *Periwinkle* beer is quite popular here," she said. "That is what most of the locals' order when they come here."

"I'm curious, what is a periwinkle?" Scott asked. "I've never heard of that name."

"Why, sir, a periwinkle is a small edible sea snail. Some of the folks love to eat them either raw or steamed. They are also used as a bait to catch fish."

"The beers won't taste like snails, will they?" Elijah joked.

The waitress laughed. "No, sir, you'll find the beer to be quite good."

"In that case, Miss, please bring us four *Periwinkles*."

The young lady turned to get their order when she passed by a table next to the bar. Two scruffy looking men were sitting at the table drinking straight shots of rye whiskey. It was obvious that the men were well into the libation because the bottle was three quarters empty. As the young waitress walked by, one of the drunks grabbed her arm and pulled her into his lap. She screamed, "Let me go, you drunken brute!"

"How about a big kiss, Sweetie?" he yelled, holding her thrashing body tightly. The other man at the table was roaring with laughter, encouraging his companion to apply more suggestive moves. Elijah was up like a flash with Steele close behind. In an instant, he grabbed the man's arm and jerked it hard over his shoulder, emitting a loud crack. His rotator was shattered. He dropped the woman to the floor and lunged at Elijah, who countered with a thrust of his boot heel into the man's knee that emitted another loud crack of a shattered knee cap. The man slammed to the floor, shrieking and yelling obscenities. He grabbed his knee with his good hand and started whimpering like a baby. He was finished.

The other drunk rose from his chair to attack Elijah but was confronted by Jonah Steele who moved in like a cat. The man charged Steele but was surprised when the young man grabbed his arm and twisted it violently downward and then upward behind his back. Using the drunk's own momentum, Steele performed a lighting quick maneuver with his shoulder to lift the man in midair and rotate his body downward to slam against the wooden floor. The force of the blow rendered him unconscious. The fight was over. The young waitress threw herself into Steele's arms with a big clinging hug. "Thank you, oh, thank you for saving me from those animals."

"You are most welcome, ma'am," he answered as he returned the hug and then released her with a big smile.

Simon and Scott grabbed their two companions and ushered them out of the door. "Let's get back to the ship before we run into any more trouble," Simon shouted. "Hey, Jonah, that was a nice move you made on the other punk in there. Where did you learn that?"

"I had a Japanese instructor in college who was an expert in Jujutsu. He taught me a few of his moves. You never know when they'll come in handy."

Professor Scott turned to his companions with a look of anguish. "It seems like every time we go into a bar we keep getting into fights. Why can't we just find a respectable bar somewhere and avoid trouble?"

Simon answered, "Because bars are places where misfits get drunk and somehow we always seem to pick the ones that have those drunks looking for a fight. If you had rather us go to a tea room, then pick one that serves beer."

Scott glared back at Simon with no comment.

Elijah had to add his remark, "Jonah, I have a question. How come that good looking blond waitress jumped into your arms instead of mine? I was the first one who saved her from being pawed by that drunken brute."

Simon was quick with a comeback. "That's easy to answer… because Steele is younger and much better looking than you."

Elijah just rolled his eyes as his other three cohorts erupted into a fit of laughter.

29

The stop at Bar Harbor, Maine cost some valuable time, allowing Captain Wolfe and the Aberdeen to make up considerable miles and close the distance to the USS Shannon and the Americans they were following. Professor Aavik Johansen had an uneasy feeling ever since he had boarded the steamer, met Captain Wolfe, and observed the dangerous looking crew aboard. Needing some fresh air, he left his cabin and walked through the passageway toward the officer's mess. He passed a cabin with the door slightly ajar and heard his name mentioned. The voice was from Wolfe, in a conversation with his first mate, a man named Schröder, most likely of German descent. He pressed close to the bulkhead were he could overhear the discussion.

"That fool Johansen thinks we are chasing the Americans to confiscate the Viking treasure and return it to the King of Norway. He and that Norwegian diplomat Ulvestad have some foolish idea that the treasure belongs to Norway since the Vikings once lived there."

"What are your plans, Captain?" Schröder asked.

"That treasure has been hidden for centuries on the North American continent, so whoever gets possession of it owns it. That's what I plan to do...grab all that gold and the priceless artifacts for ourselves and sell them on the open market to the highest bidder. I'm betting the Americans will pay a handsome price for some of it. We'll pay the crew a good wage and you and I will become rich men."

"And what do we do about the Americans and Johansen?"

"Johansen is the easy part. We will dispose of him and dump his body in the ocean for the sharks to enjoy. We can say he had an unfortunate accident and was lost at sea. As for the Americans, once we reach our destination, we will close on the American ship and sink it with all hands aboard. The Aberdeen is equipped with enough heavy guns to do it."

Schröder suggested, "We have a copy of the map Johansen gave us, so why don't we dispose of him now and be done with it?"

"No, we'll wait until we enter the Cumberland Sound and confront the American ship. We can dump his body into the Sound. We can always say he was killed by gunfire from their ship and we buried him at sea."

Aavik Johansen was aghast as he tiptoed past the door to make his way topside. He heard all he needed to know to confirm his worst suspicions. Wolfe and his crew of cutthroats were nothing more than a band of ruthless pirates. Somehow he had to figure out a way to escape this ship and warn the Americans. He realized the dilemma he faced. He couldn't jump overboard because he would freeze within minutes in the frigid water before he swam fifty yards. He couldn't steal one of their dinghys because it takes two men to detach and lower a boat into the sea. He could try to hide somewhere on the ship and attempt to make it to land when the Aberdeen eventually tossed anchor, but he knew that trying to survive in this harsh terrain would be impossible without the proper clothing and equipment.

His situation looked hopeless after considering all of his options, but he was determined to somehow stop Wolfe from stealing the priceless Viking artifacts. He would slip back to his cabin after dark to retrieve what belongings he might need and then try to locate a secure hiding place until the ship reached its destination. He knew in his mind, however, that no matter where he tried to hide, the crew would eventually find him.

Aboard the USS Shannon

The Shannon had finally reached the southernmost tip of Baffin Island and past a tiny chunk of rock called Resolution Island. The next maneuver would be their westward swing into the Cumberland Sound and the fjord that would hopefully take them to the cave entrance. Captain Swift was in the officer's mess having coffee with Simon and his other three guests when First Mate William Stinson rushed into the room. "Captain, we need you up on the stern deck immediately."

"What's up, William?" he asked.

"Our lookout spotted another ship following us…no identification flag visible."

The captain quickly followed his first mate topside and to the back of the ship with Simon and his three companions following close behind. At the stern railing, a young seaman was holding a spyglass staring to the rear at something on the distant horizon. He immediately turned and handed the glass to Captain Swift. "Sir, there is a three masted frigate following behind us and it has slowly been closing its position in the past hour as if the ship were trying to overtake us. She has full sails unfurled and the stream of smoke I see rising from a stack tells me she is steam powered."

The captain scanned the horizon and picked it up in the glass. "I see it," Swift confirmed. "It looks like she's steaming full ahead in an effort to catch us. I see no flags and find it hard to believe a ship like that would be sailing in these remote waters unless…unless it was trying to overtake and perhaps confront us." He turned to his first mate. "William, order the gunnery crews to their guns immediately. I want a crew on this stern deck gun now and a few more men with rifles."

"Yes sir," he said as the first mate turned to gather up and assemble the gunners.

Scott's intuition took over as he shouted out to no one in particular. "Johansen!"

"Who is Johansen?" Swift asked.

"He is the translator who interpreted the Viking runestones for us and found out about the existence and location of the lost Viking city and treasure. I'll bet he's behind this and most likely aboard that ship."

Elijah jumped in to add his opinion. "I'm sure he didn't want us to acquire the treasure for the Washington museum but wants to secure it for his native country of Norway…or perhaps even himself. The lack of an identification flag on the ship tells me that captain and crew might be a bunch of renegades who want to steal the treasure for themselves. My gut feeling tells me we could be in for a big fight when that ship catches up."

As they entered the Cumberland Sound, it was clear that the ship following them was rapidly closing the gap. Through the spyglass, Swift could see crewmen on deck manning and preparing the deck guns for action. It was now obvious that their intentions were hostile. He could make out a man peering at them through a spyglass, presumably the captain. As the ship drew nearer, he could clearly make out the man's distinct features…he recognized him. "Captain Karl Wolfe!" he shouted. "That ruthless murdering thief is nothing but a stinking pirate who wants the treasure for himself."

"You know him?" Simon asked.

"Yes, I met him once and know of his reputation. This guy is as bad as they come."

Swift turned to his first mate and yelled, "Mr. Stinson, get those guns ready to fire because a battle with that ship is imminent."

30

The Aberdeen had moved within fifteen hundred yards when Captain Wolfe gave the orders to open fire. The first shots were wide to starboard and splashed into the water, throwing large plumes of water into the air. The second shots ripped harmlessly through the sails on the rear mizzenmast with no apparent damage. Swift observed the Aberdeen starting to make its turn to deliver a broadside, which he knew would be devastating. "Full steam ahead," he ordered. "Make for the protection of that small island just to our starboard." He was referring to Kekertukdjuak Island which guarded the entrance to the fjord they were about to enter.

Swift then ordered his crew on the Nordenfelt stern gun to open fire. The four rapid fire barrels erupted and delivered one inch slugs across the forecastle of the Aberdeen, dropping two of Wolfe's gunners to the deck.

Simon, Elijah, Scott, and Steele stood by the stern railing with their Winchesters ready to engage the pirates, if and when they came within rifle range. Two more shots were fired from the Aberdeen's stern gun that shattered a portside railing and tore through the front of the Shannon's wheel house. Luckily no one was hurt and the navigation instruments and controls avoided any significant damage.

= = = = = =

In the forward lower hold of the Aberdeen, Professor Aavik Johansen hovered between some boxes as he heard the loud booms of the gunfire above. He was desperate and didn't know what to do. He looked toward the bow and saw what appeared to be two large tubes attached to the hull of the ship. They were connected to unusual brass connections that looked like valves with attached horizontal levers that could be turned to the opposite direction. The sign above said: WARNING—Do not open the valves on the seacocks unless scuttling the ship.

He was now convinced he would not escape the ship alive and unless he was willing to sacrifice himself by drowning, he would surely be shot and thrown overboard as soon as he was discovered. There was only one choice he had if he was to save the Viking treasure and the American's lives. Johansen made his choice and grabbed the handles and turned both valves. He watched in silence as a flow of cold seawater began to surge through openings in the hull and into the ship.

The Aberdeen was completing its turn for a broadside when Captain Wolfe and First Mate Schröder noticed something unusual. With a loud series of explosions, the first broadside of eight cannons was delivered to the Shannon but all of the shots went wide to the portside of the ship and landed in the water, throwing large plumes into the air. Turning to his captain, Schröder said, "Sir, our stern appears to be rapidly rising in the water, causing our shot to go wide. Something seems amiss."

Both men ran toward the center of the ship and noticed the Aberdeen was listing heavily toward the bow. "We're taking on water," Schröder shrieked. "And we haven't even been hit."

Wolfe shouted back, "Get below decks and find out what's going on."

From the stern of the Shannon, Captain Swift and his four American passengers also noticed the change taking place with the pirate's ship. Elijah was the first to speak. "That ship is dropping by the bow and I can see the underside of the stern rising out of the water. I believe the ship might be sinking."

"Captain Swift remarked, "I think it would be a wise thing to help it along and rid the world of those murdering swine." He turned to the Nordenfelt gun crew. "I want you to deliver several bursts into the bow of that ship…right along the waterline."

The four barrels fired five bursts of one inch slugs into the hull of the bow and shattered the wooden planks, resulting in a three foot wide opening. As the bow sunk further, the hole dipped below the waterline and more water surged through the hull. Swift and the Americans knew then that the pirate ship was doomed.

Schröder reached the second deck and started down the steps to the lower deck when he suddenly stopped. The lights were still burning so he could see the water lapping at his feet just below the lower deck ceiling. He peered under the deck toward the bow and spotted a figure submerged up to his neck in water.

The expressionless face staring back also saw Schröder at the same time. "Johansen!" the first mate screamed. "It was you who opened the seacock valves. You are trying to sink this ship."

The professor just smiled and said nothing. Schröder then pulled his revolver and raised it toward the floundering figure, but he was too late. Professor Aavik Johansen slipped well below the surface and inhaled his last deep breath. The icy water flowed into his lungs and a peaceful darkness engulfed him. Within seconds he was dead.

Schröder rushed topside and reported to Captain Wolfe. "It was Johansen. He was the one who opened the seacocks to flood the ship."

"I knew I should have killed him earlier."

"No need to worry about that now," Schröder replied. "Just as I was about to shoot him, he slid under water and drowned himself."

"Good riddance. Can the seacocks be reached to turn them off," Wolfe shouted.

"No, Captain, the water level has now flooded up into the second deck and it's only a matter of minutes before the ship goes under. The ship is lost."

Standing at the bow, Wolfe and Schröder noticed the ship was listing at a 45 degree angle and would soon begin its descent into the sea. "Do we have any boats?" Wolfe asked.

"Only one longboat but I was told it broke from its yoke and fell into the sea."

The requirement that private vessels carry a complement of life boats was not enforced and wouldn't be a maritime requirement for several years. Following the sinking of the French liner La Bourgogne in 1898 with the loss of more than 500 people and the Titanic in 1912 with losses of over 1500, it became apparent that new rules needed to be enacted to safeguard passengers with a specified number of lifeboats, depending on the size and type of ship and number of passengers aboard.

Wolfe hurried to the wheelhouse where he found the helmsman frantically trying to maneuver the ship. "Head for that spit of land over there to our starboard," he shouted. "We can beach the ship and save ourselves and the crew."

"I'm trying, sir, but I'm not getting any response from the rudder. We are listing too far to the bow and I'm afraid the rudder and screws are now out of the water."

"Then save yourself," Wolfe shouted as he turned to return to the main deck.

As he approached his first mate, he bellowed out, "Abandon ship!" It was a little too late as many of the crewmen had already jumped overboard with the hopes of swimming to the small island they had spotted in the distance. Within minutes however, the freezing waters of the Cumberland Sound numbed their limbs and engulfed them with hypothermia that caused the swimmers to lose consciousness and slip under the water. Captain Wolfe, First Mate Schröder, and the few remaining crew members still on board held tightly to the railing and stared in horror as the Aberdeen hesitated for a few moments and then began its plunge into the sea. Within seconds, the sleek frigate was gone and the ice cold waters insured that there were no survivors.

31

Aboard the USS Shannon

Captain Swift, First Mate Stinson, Simon, Elijah, Scott, Steele, and all the crew stood by the starboard railing and watched with fascination as the Aberdeen slipped bow first into the deep waters of the Cumberland Sound and settled to the bottom. Stinson remarked, "What do you think about that? That ship sunk without us engaging them and firing our cannons. We only fired our Nordenfelt stern gun after we saw her sinking. How the devil could that happen?"

Professor Scott was the first to offer his theory. "I think someone scuttled the ship and it was most likely our translator friend, Johansen."

"Please explain, Mr. Scott," Swift asked curiously.

Scott nodded and continued. "Johansen found out about the Viking city and treasure from the runestone Mr. Steele and I discovered in Iceland. He translated the tablet and identified the location on Baffin Island. He is a native Norwegian, so I believe he wanted to secure the treasure for his homeland and return it to the original lands of the Vikings, thinking the treasure rightfully belonged to Norway. Apparently, he had some interested benefactors who helped commission that ship to follow us and somehow acquire the treasure and Viking artifacts for Norway. Sometime during the voyage, he must have discovered the truth about the renegade Captain Wolfe and his band of pirates who wanted to steal the treasure for themselves. He knew they would have probably killed him when he led them to the cave."

"A very interesting story you have, Mr. Scott. Please go on."

"I would think Johansen somehow learned of his fate and realized there was no way he could escape the ship so he decided to sacrifice himself and flood it by opening the seacocks. He must have been desperate with his desire to keep the treasure from falling into the pirate's hands."

"You have a very plausible explanation so I would agree with your story," Swift confessed.

The others also concurred that Scott's story made perfect sense. Simon added his final thoughts. "It had to be Johansen aboard that ship because he was the only person, besides us four, that had the coordinates and knew the exact location of the Viking city and treasure. I don't believe Johansen would have willingly shared that information with anyone else. We may never know the real truth, but Professor Scott's story makes the most logical sense so I guess it would be fair to credit Mr. Johansen for sparing us to fight a very tough sea battle and probably saving a lot of our lives."

= = = = = =

The Shannon passed through a clump of bare rock islets jutting up on their portside and a narrow strip of barren land that extended to the right. They soon reached the large barren rock called Kekertukdjuak Island that loomed up on their starboard and the helmsman carefully maneuvered the ship around the islet and through a narrow passage into the Kingnait Fiord. To their surprise, they noticed that much of the shoreline and cliffs along the passage were still covered with thick sheets of glacial ice, proving it had been a very harsh and cold winter on Baffin Island.

Scott reached into a satchel and pulled out the map Johansen had provided them and then he and Steele meticulously studied it in an effort to match it with the surrounding land features. According to the map, their target was a narrow bay that was located on the west side of the fjord. Their objective was to look for an entrance to a large cavern along the shoreline. It did not take long for the ship to reach the access to the narrow bay marked on the map. The Shannon was slowly eased through the narrow slot leading into the bay and stopped when it came to an ice-covered cliff with a narrow fissure visible high up in the sheet of ice. The cove was barely wide enough to allow the ship to maneuver a 180 degree turn and position the bow to face the exit from the fiord and back into the bay. Simon and the expedition team assessed the situation and concluded this might be the opening to the cavern once occupied by the Vikings.

The problem facing them was that the small fissure in the thick slab of ice was inaccessible and too small to allow a human body to squeeze through. The other challenge was that it was possible that water from the bay receded well into the cavity and would require a small boat to get the group inside and deposited on to the cavern floor. Somehow, the ice had to be cleared from the entrance to allow one of the rowboats to transport the team and supplies to a stepping off point inside the cavern. Captain Swift recognized their dilemma and offered a suggestion. "Gentlemen, I think I can solve your problem." He then turned to his first mate. "William, please assemble the Nordenfelt gun team again and get them up here."

Within minutes, Stinson came back to the bow with three crew members following. Swift gave the orders. "I want you men to use the rapid-fire feature of the gun to break off that ice sheet you see around that split on the face of the ice. Place your pattern about ten feet from the top and fifteen feet to either side of the opening. The impact from the slugs should crack the ice enough to break it loose from the glacier."

The seamen took their positions and prepared the Nordenfelt for firing. Flames burst from the four reciprocating barrels with one inch bullets that ripped through the air and tore large chunks of ice from the surface. Once the sheet started to crack, the process accelerated as more slugs slammed into the ice. Suddenly, a loud ripping and crunching noise erupted as tons of ice sheared loose and tumbled into the water. The results revealed a large dark breach in the rock wall. Simon and his team members and the ship's crew cheered as they realized they had most likely discovered the doorway to a major historic link to the Vikings past...the first European explorers to visit and set foot on the North American continent.

Professor Scott was ecstatic. "Do you realize what this means?" he shouted. "We may have found solid evidence of the first European settlers to set foot and build structures on the American continent. If there really is a Viking city inside this cave, then history books will have to be rewritten. Now, I suggest we all go see what it was really like inside the world of the Vikings."

Simon pulled Scott aside. "I just wanted to be sure, but did you bring those two metallic tablets along…the ones you found in Iceland and Venezuela?"

"Yes, they are secured in my pack."

"From what you described, I think we have some old friends that might be able to translate the symbols on the tablets. As a matter of fact, I would suggest they were inscribed by some of their ancestors who visited our earth hundreds of years ago. Also, if you'll remember, as we found out on our exhibitions to Peru, we seem to have a strange way of running into Commanders Ahular and Nezar in some weird places. As I remember, they were doing a lot of exploration around our North Pole and Arctic Circle. When we enter the cavern, bring those two tablets along. I have a feeling they may come in handy."

"Yes, I think you could be correct," Scott conceded. "That Zenox Ahular gave you has been a little active lately and that could only mean it is receiving signals from somewhere close by."

Simon nodded his head in agreement. "Now, let's go find that Viking city and perhaps a treasure like the world has never seen before."

32

A Cavern on Baffin Island

The rowboat was readied and lowered into the water with two men assigned to paddle the boat into the cavern. The five men to make up the exploration team were Simon, Elijah, Scott, Steele, and First Mate Stinson. They were lowered and boarded into the boat by a special sling. Several packs filled with food, water, and other essential equipment and supplies followed. Professor Scott's three mirrored oil lanterns were some of the most valued of the supplies, but several torches were also prepared to be used to conserve the oil required by the lanterns. As commander of the USS Shannon, Captain Swift chose to stay with the ship to protect their only means of transportation back to Washington. He would have given anything to accompany the search team, but knew his primary duty was to safeguard the ship.

The two seamen propelled the boat forward and as they passed through the entrance, it was apparent the cavern was much larger than expected. It was nearly a fifty-yard drift through the interior bay toward a small spit of land. The first thing they saw was a huge object resting to one side of the cavern on a low rock embankment. It was one of the most astounding relics they had ever seen.

Lying before them was the fairly well preserved remains of a single masted Viking boat known as a longship. The constant freezing temperatures and relatively cool dry air in the cavern had preserved the wood in remarkably good shape. Professor Scott, who had done some research on the Vikings, lurched into one of his customary instructional lectures. "Gentlemen, what we see here is an amazing discovery of a true Viking boat or "longship" as the Vikings called them. Before the trip, I did some studying of the Vikings and this ship was built to carry their warriors and settlers from Scandinavia to the new world. It is living proof that the Vikings were the first Europeans to discover the North American continent. In Norse, this vessel was called a Knarr that was designed for ocean going. The average ship of this type would have been around fifty-five feet long and a beam of around fifteen feet. They were not big ships but very well constructed. For example, the keel was cut from a tall oak tree. They would cut long planks of wood for the sides and shorter pieces for supporting ribs and cross-beams and they would use wooden pegs and iron rivets to fasten the wooden pieces together. By overlapping the side planks and riveting them together, the ship was incredibly strong. This was called 'clinker-building.' As you can see, this ship had an elongated plain bowsprit but many were adorned with a dragon's head or some other type of decorative figureheads."

Steele injected a question. "Professor Scott, how did they waterproof these ships to withstand the constant battering of waves and rough water?"

"I read they used animal wool and sticky pine tar to stuff into every joint and crack. They were amazingly waterproof and strong vessels to be able to handle the rigors of a trans-Atlantic crossing."

"When do you think the Vikings visited this cavern?" Elijah questioned.

"The Vikings arrived in Greenland from 980 AD to 1000 AD and their settlements there lasted about 400 years, so I would guess they most likely discovered this place early in the 11th century, easily 500 years before Columbus came to America in 1492 AD."

"That's great information, Professor Scott," Simon conceded, "but I suggest we light a couple of torches and see where that corridor leads us. We'll save the oil lanterns for the interior of the cave."

As they reached the far side of the cavern, they noticed there was no place to dock the rowboat as an opening appeared that narrowed down to a large canal leading well into the interior. "What do you make of this, Jonah?" Simon asked the young archeologist.

"Because of its large size, this water borne passageway looks like it once may have been carved out by a large river. There doesn't appear to be a significant current or water flow from the interior so it must now be fed by the sea."

"The channel must be at least twenty-five feet wide and twenty-five feet high, large enough for that Viking longboat to pass through," Elijah remarked.

Scott added, "Since an average longboat had a fifteen-foot beam, by dismantling their mast the boat could easily have passed through this canal. We'll find out more as we travel through the passageway."

One of the seamen picked up on this and remarked, "Our orders were to carry you from the ship where you could disembark and continue on foot. We had no orders to row up a canal deep into the interior of this cave."

First Mate Stinson replied, "That is why Captain Swift sent me along...to make those decisions. There is no shore for us to disembark on so we will continue through this canal and see where and how far it takes us."

The matter was settled as the rowboat entered the canal entrance. The walls and ceiling in the tunnel appeared to be relatively smooth, indicating that the cavern was carved out by flowing water. Steele's theory appeared to be true. As they progressed through the canal, several stone struts extended from the walls that contained the remnants of torches placed there to light the way for the original occupants.

Another change was noticed as they moved deeper through the passage. The current seemed to be getting a bit stronger, indicating a water flow was coming from the interior through the canal and flowing toward the sea and not the opposite, as Steele had thought. The other noticeable change was the water temperature seemed to be getting warmer as confirmed by sticking a hand in the water.

Steele, seemed a bit confused as he made these observations. "There are some very interesting changes going on with the flow of water," he said. "I am most curious to see where this passage leads us. The mere presence of those torch holders along the walls pretty well confirms that humans once used this passage extensively...most likely the Vikings."

Even though the current had increased slightly, the two sailors continued to row easily with enough space on either side of the boat to allow the oars to pass freely through the water.

Elijah, who was sitting on the second seat next to Stinson and facing toward the bow, was the first to notice it. "Gentlemen, unless my eyes are playing tricks, I think I see a faint light up ahead."

"No tricks, Elijah, I see it, too," Stinson confirmed. In front of them there was a faint glow of light reflecting off the walls, and in the far distance a pinpoint of brighter light appeared.

"Daylight," Steele shouted. "It looks like we are coming to the end of the passageway."

As the boat moved forward, the light became stronger and the pinpoint became brighter and larger, indicating a distinct opening into daylight. Little did they know that the discovery they were about to make would be earthshaking and change history.

33

The Lost Viking Settlement

As the rowboat eased through the opening, they were amazed at what they saw. They had entered into a small lake with a shoreline filled with sparse green vegetation and a scattering of trees along the banks. Stretched out before them were a series of gentle rolling hills and some distant sheer surrounding rock cliffs protecting what appeared to be a pristine valley. It reminded Scott of what it would look like to find the fabled wonderland of Shangri La. The air temperature was warm, a very odd thing in this frigid land of ice and snow relatively near the Arctic Circle.

The rising bubbles in the lake were observed by Jonah Steele and confirmed his suspicions as he picked up on this quickly. "I think I can explain the warm temperature. This valley appears to be sitting over a hot spot where the earth's center of molten rock has been thrust up close to the crust's surface. Those bubbles you see rising in the water are released by what geologists call hydrothermal vents. I suspect there are several more thermal vents scattered around the landscape."

Steele's explanation seemed plausible enough so there were no questions.

= = = = = =

Elijah was the first to notice it as they approached the shoreline. It was a large stone statue of a humanlike figure with his
arm held high and with something held in his clinched hand.
The horned helmet, body armor, and heavy long beard identified
the figure as a Viking warrior. Professor Scott was mesmerized.
"Who do you think that figure could be?" Elijah asked.

Scott, who had done some extensive research of the Viking
history and culture prior to the journey, was quick to answer.
"He has to be one of the Viking gods. Old Norse mythology
identified the gods as the Aesir and there were several principal
gods representing several different things. Oden was the chief
divinity of the Old Norse pantheon and was the god of war and
death. He was also revered as god of poetry and wisdom. The
other principal gods were Thor, Balder, and Tyr."

"That figure over there must be Oden if he was the main
one," Simon injected. "I remember hearing his name mentioned
in one of my college history classes."

"No," Scott corrected. "That is not Oden. It has to be a statue
of Thor, son of Oden, and the god of thunder and protector from
the forces of evil. The giveaway is the object he's holding in his
hand waiting to be hurled at something. That represents Thor's
hammer that was called *Mjolnir*. Norse mythology tells us that
every time Thor hurled his hammer, a bolt of lightning would
flash across the sky. That statue was most likely put there by the
Vikings who settled here to protect their settlement from the
forces of evil."

"Very interesting, Professor, but where did you learn all of that stuff?" Elijah asked abruptly.

"History books, my boy, history books."

Elijah just rolled his eyes and shrugged, extracting an annoying stare back from the professor.

The air temperature was surprisingly mild as they beached the rowboat near the statue. A close examination of the effigy showed that the intricate features of the god, Thor, were carved into the stone by expert craftsmen, even down to the strands of hair in his long beard. The professor's immediate thoughts were how to get the statue back to the Washington museum, but realistically he knew there was no way to move this priceless heavy effigy weighing several tons.

As the group moved inland, remnants of low stone buildings appeared, neatly lined up along the roadway. The stone walls remained, however the beams that formed the roofs had long decayed and collapsed. The mounds of dirt and grass covering the remains were signs that these structures had been constructed as Norse turf houses. Some of the interiors of the buildings had been dug down to depths of three to four feet, which were common to many of the Viking houses found in Greenland. Among these ruins, they observed remnants of a few longhouses that either housed several Viking families or were used for group gatherings and ceremonial events. These structures confirmed the presence of a Viking settlement constructed long before the arrival of Columbus to the North American continent.

Scott was elated as he and Steele poked through the ruins in search of any relic that would have been left by a Viking settler. Poking through the ruins, the only thing they could find were a few scattered shards of pottery left by the former occupants.

Simon was the first to bring up the objective of their mission. "Professor, what about all of that treasure that was supposed to be here? You said the Scandinavian historian guy, Johansen, interpreted from the runestone you found in Iceland that this lost city had a huge treasure hidden here somewhere."

"Yes, that's what he told us. Any treasure left by the Vikings certainly would not have been left in any of the ruins. I would imagine they would have cached it somewhere to protect it from the elements...probably in a cave. The sheer rock walls protecting this valley are most likely loaded with caves and hidden caverns. We'll just have to search for it."

The group split up into two teams to search for the entrance to caves or other possible places where the Vikings might have stored their artifacts and treasures. Simon, Elijah, and Stinson moved out toward the southern portion of the valley while Professor Scott and Steele moved to the northern end. The two seamen were assigned to stay and watch the boat, knowing that was the only means of escape if they had to get out of the valley and back to the ship.

A couple of small cave openings were spotted by Elijah in a rock wall but proved to be too small to store a sizable cache of artifacts. As Scott and Steele topped a small hill, they spotted a copse of trees in the distance that might prove promising. At the edge of the wooded area they discovered a series of elongated mounds laid out in an orderly pattern that signified a possible group of ancient dwellings.

Scott and Steele were a bit puzzled because they appeared much different than the Viking ruins seen near the lake. Scott remarked, "Jonah, I don't think these are Viking ruins but look much like some of the ruins we saw in the Yucatan and in Peru, which turned out to be remains of dwellings built by the Toltecs and Mayan Indians. Let's take a closer look in that thicket to see if we can find any more of these mounds."

A small path through the trees led them into a large clearing and looming before them was the most unlikely spectacle they could hardly imagine. A very prominent and well defined pyramid towered above to a height of almost fifty feet. "Are you kidding me?" Steele stammered. "This is impossible this far north."

Scott was mesmerized and speechless. "This pyramid looks much like a smaller version of the Mayan pyramid we saw in Mexico a few years ago—very much like the one we saw near Tula."

"What could this mean, Professor?" Steele asked.

"I doubt if the Mayans or Toltecs could have possibly ventured this far north so it means that another unknown ancient Pre-Columbian civilization was here several thousand years ago and found this valley with the warm springs and heated vents to make it suitable to build a small settlement."

"But how could they have moved all these blocks of stone in here to build that pyramid?"

"I would imagine they mined and cut the blocks from the rock walls that surround this valley. Let's go find the others and bring them here. I have a feeling that the pyramid has some hidden rooms deep inside, a perfect place to hide a sizable treasure."

Scott and Steele found Simon and the others probing along

the cliffs along the western side of the valley enclosure. As soon as he explained his findings, the three men followed him quickly to the site of the pyramid.

Simon remarked, "In a million years I would never have expected to find a pyramid like this on Baffin Island and this close to the Arctic Circle. This structure looks just like some of the pre-Columbian pyramids we saw in Mexico. Those earthen mounds back there look like they could be the remains of man-made structures, maybe dwellings where the Indians lived. You know the Mayans could not have traveled this far north."

Scott had the logical answer. "I believe this site was once a settlement by members of an ancient civilization predating the Toltecs and Mayans."

"Where do you think they might have come from?" First Mate Stinson asked curiously.

"My guess is that they most likely migrated from northeast Asia, probably Siberia, Mongolia, or Manchuria, and across the Bering Sea into what is now the Alaskan territories and Western Canada. I've heard theories from some archeologists who believe that there was a large Bering land bridge that joined Asia and North America about fifteen to twenty thousand years ago. It certainly makes sense because it is highly unlikely these migrating tribes of people had the knowledge or means to build large boats to transport them across the sea."

"I doubt if they could have traveled across the Arctic ice cap through all the glaciers and heavy ice and snow," Elijah suggested.

Scott again offered an answer. "I read several scientific journals that suggested in the last few thousand years the earth has undergone several periods of climate warming and cooling. It would seem logical that these people traveled across northern Canada during a warmer period and were able to reach the northeastern section of the country which is now northern Quebec. From there they could have traveled by small boats across the Hudson Straight to Baffin Island and perhaps even across the Labrador Sea to Greenland. Many of these groups migrated further north and became the indigenous tribes of Eskimos and Aleuts we know of today.

"The most mysterious thing of all is how they could possibly possess the same knowledge and skills of the Pre-Columbian Indians of Mexico and Central and South America to be able to build a similar pyramid like we saw in the Yucatan. For them to build this structure in a remote place like this valley was an incredible and unbelievable feat."

The others stood there in silence, pondering over Scott's words until Simon offered his suggestion. "Well, let's don't just stand here speculating. We need to find a doorway and a passageway that will let us explore the inside of this pyramid."

34

The search for an opening proved to me more difficult than they expected as the group separated and explored all four sides of the pyramid. Much like a similar one in Chechen Itza, the structure had a single row of stone steps leading to the top where a small rectangular building had been constructed to overlook the former dwellings and parts of the valley below. Like the other pyramids in the Mayan world, the edifice was most likely used as a temple dedicated to one of the ancient gods worshiped by the original Indian settlers who built the structure.

Jonah Steele, whose trained eye was used to looking for imperfections in rock walls, was the first to spot the tiny cracks along the base several feet from where the steps started their steep incline. A closer examination revealed additional vertical cracks outlining a space where a former passageway had been placed probably during the construction. The crude mortar used to conceal the cracks disclosed the probability that the opening had been reopened at a later date…perhaps by the Vikings who had settled there a few centuries later.

Steele summoned the others to the spot and then, using a small tool he had taken from his pack, began to chip away at the mortar joints. The brittle grout fell away easily, revealing distinct uniform cracks that outlined a definite doorway.

"You found it, Jonah," Elijah shouted excitedly. "Now, how do we open it? That slab must weigh a ton."

"By using this," Steele replied, pointing to a small handle connected to a thin bar embedded within the crack. He grasped the handle and was pleasantly surprised as he was able to pivot the rod easily toward him. He began to crank the handle back and forth until distinct sounds emitted from within the wall and a large stone slab began to slowly swing outward and toward them…like a large door opening on hinges. The movement finally stopped, revealing a large dark doorway leading into the pyramid. The group was impressed with Steele's intuition as Simon said, "Well done, Jonah. Now, let's go inside and see if we can find a Viking treasure."

With the use of Professor Scott's oil fueled lamps, the men filed through the opening, with Steele leading the way. The passageway was surprisingly large as it permitted the men to walk normally without having to stoop over. There was no doubt that the corridor had been placed there to allow the ancient builders to move men and materials in and out during the construction of the pyramid's interior chambers.

The first thing Jonah noticed just inside the passage was a carved slab of stone placed on the wall, depicting an impression of what appeared to be an image of the sun with a serpent head carved within the circle. It stared down at them with sinister eyes, suggesting a warning not to enter this sacred place.

"Good grief!" Elijah commented, "What is that horrible looking thing?"

Scott replied with a slight laugh. "Like the pre-Columbia Indians to the south, it appears the ancient settlers here also worshiped a sun god like the Mayans worshipped Tonatiuh and Quetzalcoatl."

Simon added, "If this symbol is like the several carvings we saw in Mexico and Peru, we learned it could be a warning to keep us from entering this place. In a few of the caverns we walked through in the Yucatan, the snake head we saw with the exposed fangs meant certain death awaits those who enter this place. I suggest we be very alert for hidden traps and other deadly obstacles that could kill a person. The ancients had very clever ways of constructing hidden traps that could trap and kill you in a second. We saw some really bad ones during our expeditions in Mexico and Peru."

"I knew I shouldn't have walked into this pyramid," Elijah grumbled. "You know how much I hate snakes."

He well remembered the time during their expedition into the Amazon when he woke up one morning in his bedroll with a western green mamba curled up on his chest for warmth. The guide told him that species of snake was one of the deadliest pit vipers in the world. Luckily, the guide was able to sweep the reptile off Elijah's stomach and just before he wet his pants. That experience would be etched in his brain forever. He quietly maneuvered himself to the rear of the line.

First Mate William Stinson, who was a bit apprehensive about the dark passageway, strolled up next to Simon and asked, "You've been in these pyramids before. What can we expect to find inside this thing and what should be looking for? This place looks pretty sinister and dangerous to me."

Simon quietly responded. "You're right, Mr. Stinson, these pyramids can be very dangerous and snuff out a man's life in a split second. The ancient builders had some very ingenious ways of devising traps inside the passages and chambers within these structures."

"How can we spot any traps…what do we look for?" Stinson asked.

"Look for anything unusual or out of place. For example, any cracks in the floor might mean a trap door, or a threshold resembling a stone panel might spring loose under a man's weight and hurl him into a hidden cavern below. We recently encountered a trap like that in a cave in Venezuela. It cost one of our men his life. Also, look for any protrusions, carvings, or unusual objects that might initiate a trap door opening in the walls or ceilings. In other words, be very careful where you step or what you touch along the way. We have seen these traps spring out from all directions and they can hit you at any time."

"Okay, I get the picture," Stinson replied warily. As a naval officer used to leading his men, he instinctively moved to the head of the column. The group moved easily through the passage as Stinson maintained his vigil for signs of any device or irregularity that might trigger a hidden trap. They had progressed well into the pyramid when suddenly Simon grabbed the first mate's arm and forcefully pulled him backward. Both men tumbled to the floor, landing heavily on their backsides. Stinson turned to Simon and uttered, "What the hell!"

"One more step and you would have disappeared into oblivion."

Stinson's face showed total confusion as Elijah and Steele helped both men to their feet. Pointing to the floor to their immediate front, Simon explained his quick reaction to Stinson. "Look closely at the floor just in front of you. Do you see those hairline cracks outlining the stone slab you were about to step on?"

The first mate knelt and traced his fingers along the barely noticeable cracks. "Yes, I do see them now."

"Watch this," Simon said as he took a walking stick from Steele and pressed heavily on the floor slab. Suddenly there was a discernable swoosh of air and a distinct click as the panel pivoted downward, revealing a pitch-black void. "That, Mr. Stinson, was what I was talking about," Simon reminded him. "In seconds, you would have been hurled through that opening to a certain death."

A closer look into the pit revealed a small bright orange ribbon deep inside the void. "Do you see that tiny orange streak deep down in the pit?" Simon asked.

Stinson acknowledged.

"As you recall, this whole valley is situated on top of what they refer to as a hot spot and this hole you see is most likely a large thermal vent. That faint orange line at the bottom is a small river of molten lava that would have incinerated you in seconds. It's a good thing that I noticed those hairline cracks or there would have been no more First Mate Stinson."

After a few seconds of trying to compose himself, he replied, "Oh my goodness! Thank you, Simon…you saved my life. How can I ever repay you?"

Simon chuckled. "Well, for one thing you can keep your eyes open, be more observant, and step to the rear of the line to calm your nerves down a bit."

With a nod of his head and without hesitation, Stinson moved to the rear, content to follow the others in the group.

"How do we close the panel so we can proceed?" Steele asked.

"If this is like all the other corridor traps we've seen, there has to be a reset knob somewhere located on the wall." Simon's keen eye spotted the tiny stone protrusion at shoulder height on the wall to the right. He pressed the knob and the slab pivoted slowly back into place in the floor. Steel said, "What happens if we step on the panel? Won't it break loose again when a foot hits it?"

Remembering their experiences in their previous expeditions, Simon recalled what their former Mexican guide, Santos, had done to reset and lock the slabs. He reached over and pressed the stone projection again twice and was pleased to hear a double click beneath the floor and a stone locking bar slam into a recess. "This thing should now be locked in place," he said as he held his breath and took a step forward. The slab held tight as he passed over the repositioned panel with the group following. They continued through the corridor.

"That was a pretty gutsy thing you did," Elijah whispered to his cousin. "How did you know for sure that damn thing was locked?"

"I didn't," he chuckled. "I just held my breath and took a step of faith."

35

Unlike the pyramids they had encountered in the Yucatan and Peru, there were no adjoining rooms present along the passageway, only smooth bare walls. Soon they emerged into a large open space that was identified as the center interior of the structure. The chamber was bare except for a few discarded Viking spear points and abandoned swords lying about. On one side of the chamber was a small space constructed of stone blocks that was filled with skeletons and piles of bones. Professor Scott commented, "These skeletons and bones seem to be much smaller than those of the Vikings. There is no doubt it's an ossuary the Vikings used to stack the bones and remains they uncovered of the earlier natives who once occupied this valley…or maybe this was a sacred burial site and these are bones of the departed the ancient Indians placed here."

"To heck with the bones," Elijah shouted annoyingly, "where is all of the treasure? This room is practically bare except for these old bones and pieces of decaying weapons."

Simon and Professor Scott were as perplexed as Elijah as they had also expected to walk into a large cache of priceless artifacts made of gold and precious gemstones. Jonah Steele, who had skirted around the perimeter inspecting the walls, came back to the group holding a thin rectangular shaped stone.

"Look what I found," he said holding the object up with both hands.

Scott recognized the tablet immediately by the inscriptions and symbols carved into the surface. "Where did you find that?" he asked.

"It was lying against the wall," Steele answered, pointing to his rear.

"This tablet is a Viking runestone, just like the ones we found in Iceland and the cave in Venezuela.

"I wonder what the inscriptions say," Simon asked curiously. "Maybe they hold the key to the treasure's location."

"We'll most likely never know," Elijah reminded the group. "That Scandinavian translator guy, Professor Aavik Johansen, is not here to help us and probably went down with the pirate ship."

"Maybe we can translate the tablet ourselves," Scott suggested.

"How do we do that?" Simon questioned.

Scott answered with a reassuring grin. "Do you remember that meeting at the museum we had with Johansen when he translated the runestone tablets we found in Iceland and Venezuela? You will recall he gave me a copy of the notebook he used to make the translations. It was filled with Viking written characters, glyphs, and symbols. Well, I happen to have that notebook in my pack and I think we might be able to translate this tablet right here."

He turned to retrieve the book from his kit. With Simon and Steele peering over his shoulder, Scott began to search for corresponding inscriptions in the book to match the five inscriptions on the runestone. Steele spotted the first symbol comparison and came up with the first Norse word translation…*auðr*. It interpreted as *treasure*.

This created a stir in the room as they knew this tablet held the key to the treasure cache. Slowly the next inscriptions began to fall into place. The second symbol was a Nordic word for the number twelve…*tólf.* It was rare that the Vikings recorded numbers in their runestone tablets, but on occasion they did, using the actual Nordic words corresponding to numbers. The third was represented by a unique vertical symbol.

"What is that? Elijah questioned. It looks like some type of sword."

A quick scan through the book revealed the same symbol that meant sword. "That's exactly what it means," Scott assured him.

The notebook revealed that the fourth rune was found to be the symbol for the North Star. Steele expressed his interpretation. "The Vikings were great seafarers and navigators and relied on the North Star and constellations for directions. In this case, I'll bet they are referring to a specific direction and perhaps north as the North Star would indicate."

"Maybe it means the north side of this room," Simon added pointing to the adjacent wall.

The last inscription was a bit more confusing as the symbol was a circle with a spot carved in the center. Several suggestions were offered, but none made any sense.

First Mate Stinson came up with an idea. "This circle could represent the four walls surrounding this room and the spot in the middle would represent the word 'center' or 'middle' so if you put it all together I would think the starting point would be from the center of the north wall to the center of this room."

"A logical point, Mr. Stinson," Scott acknowledged.

Simon came up with another observation and directed his question toward Scott. "How long was a Viking sword?" he asked.

Thinking back to some of the museum displays of Viking artifacts Scott answered. "As I recall a typical Viking sword was from 70-80 centimeters. That would be about 2 ½ feet in length. Why do you ask?"

"Because the first rune inscriptions on the tablet refer to the number twelve and I think the word sword which would refer to a specific distance like the length of twelve swords lined up end to end. If a typical Viking sword is 2½ feet long, then twelve swords would be 30 feet in length."

Scott was starting to see the connection and now thought he could put the meaning of the inscriptions together. "So, if I put all of these runes together, it could read like this. The treasure is hidden starting from the center of the north wall and 30 feet to-ward the center of the room. If we pace off the distance of twelve swords, or thirty feet, then we should hit the spot that will lead us to the treasure cache."

The nods of approval around him indicated that the group concurred with Scott's interpretation of the tablet.

"Well, let's get started," Elijah said with a tone of anticipation.

Simon walked over to the corner of the north wall and stopped, placing his right heel against the base. "I know this is the north wall because it's at the opposite side from the entrance. I'm going to pace the distance to the far wall then reverse my steps by half of the paces. This should give us a fairly accurate distance across the room and mark the exact center of the wall. A normal step should be about 2½ feet."

He began his stride along the wall and across the width of the room. When Simon reached the opposite wall, he called out the number of paces placing him at the center of the wall. "Twenty-six paces," he shouted. This room is about sixty-five feet across."

He then reversed his direction and counted off thirteen paces. Turning toward the center of the room he walked off thirteen more paces and stopped. "If our assessment of the tablet is correct, the opening to the treasure chamber should be about here."

The others rushed to the spot where Simon was standing and gazed down at the floor. It was covered by centuries of dust and debris. Scott said, "Lets sweep off some of this dirt and see if we can find a slab or something covering an entrance to a lower room."

With the help of a spare shirt and knife blade, the floor was swept clean and scraped enough to reveal the cracks around a four-foot square slab of stone. The mortar was soft and crumbling from age. Steele took a small climbing axe and started to scrape around the seams with the sharp point. The cement broke loose easily. He then inserted the point of the axe into one of the cracks and pried the slab upward. The heavy panel was nearly four inches thick and appeared to be tightly stuck in place, but with continuous pressure, Steel finally felt some slight movement.

The stone was finally raised high enough for Elijah and Simon to get their hands under the slab and help pull it up. The cover finally broke loose, enabling the men to slide it to one side. The first thing they noticed was a narrow flight of stone steps leading down to a dark ominous looking cavity below. Professor Scott already had his oil lantern out and extended through the opening. The dazzling reflections and rays of light that bounced back shocked them into a sudden state of utter silence. Lying dormant for several centuries, the Viking treasure had been found.

36

Professor Scott carefully led the group down the steps into the chamber below. The brilliance of the reflections from the lantern confirmed that they had found something big and more valuable than they could have ever imagined. Boxes of gold coins were scattered around the room and stacks of artifacts of every description were displayed from the many Viking raids that took place throughout Northern Europe in the 10th and 11th centuries. On one side of the room there were boxes filled with jeweled rings, bracelets, pendants, plates, and heavily decorated crowns, obviously taken from the many castles and royal estates that housed members of royal families.

Also, they found chests full of intricately carved sculptures and busts. As the five men stood there in awe gazing at the fabulous display around them, Scott made the first comment, "Wow! Would you just look at this? This is the best of dreams for every museum and art collector in the world."

"And every treasure hunter in the world," Elijah added as he scooped up handfuls of gold coins and watched them slip through his open fingers.

"This is incredible," Simon shouted, picking a heavily jeweled gold crown adorned with diamonds and rubies and slipping it over his head. "Makes you wonder what European king wore this beauty."

Even Jonah Steele was mesmerized by the fabulous assortment of items stacked throughout the room. He was just as enthralled with the construction of the room itself and commented, "This pyramid was built by the early natives who lived here and predates the Vikings by at least a thousand years. It's amazing how they were able to construct this vault directly under the pyramid and, if you'll notice, they lined the walls and floor with heavy stone blocks and sealed it with sap or pitch to keep it watertight."

Scott acknowledged the remarks with an approving nod and then added, "This room was probably constructed as an ossuary to bury their dead, but by the time the Vikings discovered it, the human bones and other remains had long been dissolved. They found this room to be a perfect place to cache their looted treasures."

Simon totally changed the subject when he said, "All of this speculation is very interesting, but I think it's time to consider what brought us here in the first place and start thinking how we're going to move all of this stuff out of here and back to the ship. It's going to take more men and boats to move this treasure so I suggest that we make some plans and get started."

He turned to First Mate Stinson. "William, the first thing we need is more boats and men to carry this treasure and artifacts to the lake and transport it through the tunnel and back to the ship. Why don't you return to the lake and get the two men we left as guards to take you back through the tunnel to the USS Shannon? You can explain what we found to Captain Swift and help organize a team of seamen to assist us and complete the job."

Simon retrieved a small jeweled pendant and a hand full of gold coins and handed it to Stinson. "Give this to the captain to show him an example of some of the things we found here. This will convince him. Meanwhile the four of us will start moving items up the steps and into the main area of the pyramid."

Stinson acknowledged the assignment and made his way back to the upper level and to the lake. Simon, Elijah, Scott, and Steele began to gather various artifacts and carry them up the flight of steps. The boxes of coins were the heaviest and required two men to move them. Simon and Elijah had just manhandled a box to the upper level and set it on the floor when a noise was heard coming from the wall to their left. Scott and Steele were still in the lower chamber sorting through different items to move. "What's that weird sound?" Elijah shouted. "I think it's coming from your pack."

Simon rushed over to the wall where he had stored his bag and carefully opened it. He retrieved the small device and held it high in the air. "It's the Zenox," he said. "This thing is vibrating like crazy."

After a few seconds, the vibrations stopped and started emitting a static like sound with intermittent beeps. "I think this thing is trying to tell us something," Elijah suggested.

Simon turned toward the entrance and shouted, "Follow me outside and see if it will clear up some of this static."

No sooner than they reached the open air, the static stopped and erratic vocal sounds started transmitting through the Zenox. The sounds became more distinct, the words more discernable, and finally a familiar voice broke through the speaker. "Calling Simon Murphy... calling Simon Murphy... come in Mr. Murphy. This is Commander Ahular calling from the command ship SREX562."

The two men were totally stunned and couldn't speak for a few seconds. Simon quickly recovered and answered back. "Commander Ahular, this is Simon Murphy talking. I cannot believe it's really you speaking."

"Yes, Mr. Murphy. Our sensors picked up signals from the Zenox and we were able to track you to the valley of warm springs located on what you humans call Baffin Island. I thought you might have the Zenox with you."

"You know about this place, Commander?" Simon asked curiously.

"Yes, quite well. Nezar and I visited the valley a few years ago. It is a historical site once occupied by your earlier civilizations. We also know about the Viking settlement that was later built there."

"Is Commander Nezar still with you?

"Yes, he is and most anxious to see you again. Where is your close companion, Elijah Walker?"

"He is standing right here with me."

"That is good. It will be great to see both of you again."

"Where are you now, Commander?" Simon asked.

"Our ship is hovering over the warm lake as we speak and preparing for our immediate descent and landing at the south end of the valley where the terrain is level. I would like for you to meet us there. We have a lot to discuss."

"We will be there, sir," Simon anxiously responded.

The men rushed back into the pyramid to get Scott and Steele and tell them the news. The professor had previously flown on the ship during the two expeditions to Peru and would be hardily welcomed by Commanders Ahular and Nezar.

While Scott was elated by the possibility of riding on a spaceship again, young Jonah Steele was astounded and for a few moments speechless. He was trying to process this surprising information but soon recovered and turned to the professor. "I didn't believe that wild story you told me about outer space, aliens from other planets, and spaceships, but I guess all of that stuff actually happened if what Simon is saying is true."

"Yes, it is true, Jonah," Simon assured him. "I just talked to the alien commander and they are landing the ship right now at the other end of the valley. He asked Elijah and me to meet them so you and Scott will join us. There appears to be something very important going on for them to track us down with the Zenox."

The four men hastily left the pyramid and began their trek along the lake shore toward the southern end of the valley. When they reached the Viking statue, Simon spotted several rowboats exiting the tunnel passageway into the lake. Stinson was in the lead rowboat when he spotted and waved to them as the dinghies made their way toward the shore. The first mate was a bit surprised to see all four of them walking along the shoreline.

Stinson was the first out of the boat as he approached Simon and the others. "Ahoy, mates, I thought you would be bringing treasure and artifacts up to the main floor of the pyramid. I brought enough boats and men to transport it back to the Shannon."

Simon wondered how he was going to explain this bizarre turn of events to Stinson without him thinking they had all lost their minds. As fate would play its hand, a huge oval shaped object appeared over the rim of the valley, hovered for a few moments in the air, and then began a slow descent toward the far end of the valley. A total look of shock and apprehension appeared on the faces of the first mate and his seamen as a state of panic started to set in. Simon saw their confusion and shouted out across the water, "Everything is okay. The flying ship is our friend and will not harm you. We are on our way to meet them."

Simon turned to Stinson, "William, everything is fine. We have friends aboard that flying machine that want to talk to Elijah and me. Do you remember about five years ago a huge story the newspapers reported about the alien flying ship that saved our planet by destroying the huge asteroid that was hurling toward our sun?"

With a perplexed look, he thought for a second and nodded. "Yes, I think I remember reading it in the Washington Sentinel. It was in one of the first issues the sentinel released soon after it first started up in '73. That was one of the most incredible stories I have ever read…how could anyone forget that?"

"Elijah, Professor Scott, and I were aboard that ship when the event took place. The commander contacted me about thirty minutes ago on a communication device he gave me back then and said he was landing the ship and wanted to see us. I'm not sure what this is all about but we have to meet him as soon as we can get to the landing site."

"What do you want me to do?" Stinson asked, still in a state of bewilderment.

"Take the men to the pyramid and finish carrying all of the

treasure up to the main floor then carry it back to the boats and through the tunnel to the ship. Explain the situation to Captain Swift… he'll understand. You and the boats might have to make more than one trip to secure all the items, but when you have finished and the ship has loaded all the treasure and artifacts, tell the captain to set sail and take all the items back to the Washington museum. Have someone tell the curator, Robert Drake, what you saw here. He was also on our first expedition in Mexico and rode aboard one of the ships. He will know exactly what you are talking about. I have a gut feeling the commander of this ship will want us to accompany him somewhere. William, tell Captain Swift to instruct the men to keep all of this information confidential. This should be classified as top secret for now because we don't want word of an alien ship returning back to our Earth and causing a general panic among the population."

"I understand," Stinson acknowledged.

Simon then turned to Jonah Steele. "Jonah, why don't you go with Mr. Stinson and help him move the treasure back to Washington. I'm not sure where we might be going or what kind of dangers we might be facing."

Steele looked him sternly in the eye and answered, "I don't care where that flying ship takes us or what dangers we might encounter. I wouldn't miss this for anything—I'm going with you three and that's final."

Simon was hoping he would respond with that answer. He liked Steele and admired his geological knowledge and common sense. He chuckled and responded, "Okay, Jonah, it's your neck, so you can go with us."

As First Mate Stinson motioned for the boats to continue

on to shore, Simon and his three companions turned and headed toward the southern end of the valley.

37

Into Another World

As the men topped the second hill, they spotted the ship moored on the familiar four sturdy pods that extended to the ground. It was truly an evocative scene as memories flooded Simon's mind, reflecting of his prior adventures in the command cabins of the alien designated spaceships referred to as the SREX 235, and the SREX 282 or shortened to X235 and X282. For their own reference, Simon and Elijah had fittingly renamed the two ships *Toltec* and *Cuzco*. The spacecraft in the distance appeared to be huge, much larger than the two ships they had been on previously.

Jonah Steele couldn't believe his eyes. All the doubts he had harbored about Scott's wild story disappeared in a flash. Elijah's memory recalled the dangerous situation that happened with their last ride on the *Cuzco*. Elijah and Professor Scott had been assigned to place an explosive rod into a bore hole on the huge tumbling asteroid in an effort to destroy it. After he had set the charges and began his return to the shuttle craft, the magnetic devices in his boots that held him securely to the metallic face of the asteroid had been accidently shut off. The absence of gravity propelled him from the surface and pushed him high up into the airless void of space. Having floated miles away from the ship, he thought of how he could use the pressure and beam from his laser rod to propel himself back toward the asteroid to be miraculously rescued by Commander Ahular and the circling spaceship.

= = = = = =

As the four men approached the craft, a hatch opened and a set of metallic steps slowly descended to the ground. A strange looking figure stood at the doorway and motioned the group to come aboard. Simon, Elijah, and Scott immediately recognized him as Vice-Commander Nezar. Steele, not knowing what to expect, was slightly amused at the alien's appearance. He noticed the elongated head and large upper body as compared to the extremely slender lower extremities. His chest cavity appeared to be way out of proportion to the abdomen and waist. The thing that really caught his attention was the absence of ears. On either side of his head were small oval holes that served as ear channels. He surmised that this thing, or whatever it was, had to be from another world.

The one reassuring thing Steele noticed was the upturned slit of his mouth that portrayed the fact that the vice-commander was smiling and glad to see his human friends again. He greeted them with a right fist against his left upper chest, which related to Steele that this was a salutation or customary salute. The gesticulation did relieve the young geologist of any apprehension he might have had. He was further helped by a very comforting sensation he felt from the soft green light emitting from the ship's doorway and radiating throughout the interior of the ship. Simon returned the gesture to his own chest, acknowledging and responding to the greeting.

"Welcome my Earth friends," Nezar boomed out. "It is good to see you again. You have permission to enter the ship. Commander Ahular is up in the command center communicating with another of our ship's commanders and will be with us shortly, so please take a seat here in our assembly lounge."

Simon answered back, "Vice-Commander Nezar, it is good to see you again. I know you remember Elijah Walker and Professor George Scott from our last visit on the X326 a few years ago."

Nezar nodded his acknowledgment.

"We have a new member to our group," Simon said, turning to the young man standing beside him. "This is Jonah Steele. He is what we call a geologist who studies the history of our earth by examining minerals, rock formations, and strata in the layers of our rocks and soil."

"Pleased to meet you sir," Steele replied. "I must say, I am quite impressed how well you have command of our language."

Nezar let out a deep grunting sound that Steele interpreted as a chuckle or laugh. "Welcome aboard, Mr. Steele. We have been studying your planet for some time and now have command of most of the earth's languages."

The four guests climbed the steps and entered what appeared to be an assembly room. The greetings were interrupted by the presence of another figure entering the room. As soon as Commander Ahular saw the men, he repeated the salutation of the fist to the chest gesture. Simon responded with the same greeting response.

"Gentlemen, I am glad we were able to contact you through your Zenox. I was a bit surprised to find you in the valley and I am sure you were equally surprised to hear my voice."

"Yes, Commander," Simon acknowledged. "We had no idea that you had returned to our planet."

"Yes, we have been circling your planet for about four earth weeks and are still engaged in extensive studies of your two polar regions, and especially the magnetic effects of your North Pole on weather patterns and ocean currents. We have visited this valley of the warm springs before and carefully examined the ruins of the ancient Indians and the more current ruins of the Vikings who settled here much later."

"When do you suppose the Indians arrived here and built their settlement?" Scott asked.

"Our studies of the North American continent reveal that the first Indians migrated from Siberia across a Bering land bridge about 10,000 Earth years ago. About 30,000 years ago the seas around the Bering Straits began to drop and created a narrow land mass that connected Siberia and Alaska. Our analysis shows that, during all that period of time, the bridge went through several cycles of submerging under water and then exposed again due to the drop and rise of water levels, most likely caused by the freezing and melting of glaciers. When the Indians crossed over the land bridge, it had been elevated enough, allowing the migration to take place. Our instruments and an examination of the native ruins determine the site to be about 8,500 years old. The Viking ruins we examined were constructed about 975 AD based on your Earth measurement of time. We estimate these ruins to be about 900 years old. This far north, you would expect the valley to be covered with deep ice most of the year, but as you noticed, it has been kept warm by heat from numerous thermal vents covering the area. The history of this valley is quite interesting, but this is not the reason why I contacted and summoned you here to our ship."

By the tone of Ahular's voice, Simon and the other three men felt a sudden rush of apprehension. Elijah's gut feeling told him *this does not sound good*. Simon asked, "Why did you contact us, Commander? Is there something wrong?"

"As you know, we and our earlier explorers have been here studying your planet for a long time. You were with us when we saved your planet from destruction by stopping the massive underwater earthquake that would have split your planet apart, and when we destroyed the giant asteroid hurling toward your sun. The massive eruption of the sun would have incinerated all the planets in your solar system. We also helped you escape from some very dangerous situations during your expeditions to Mexico and Peru."

"That is true," Simon acknowledged. "You saved our lives on several occasions, so how can we be of service to you?"

"I have been informed that we have a very grave situation developing in our own galaxy, Scoros. We need your help and want you to accompany us back to Xeres, our home planet, so please follow me up to our command center and I will explain."

38

On the way up to the control cabin, Simon noticed the interior of the ship was somewhat similar to the layout in the prior two spaceships, except the rooms seemed to be larger and positioned differently. Other unfamiliar features were also noticed along the corridor that appeared to be various control and communication equipment bays. It was different than the Toltec and Cuzco.

"Commander Ahular," he asked, "this ship appears to be larger and different than your other two ships. Is this a different ship?"

"Yes, it is," Ahular responded. "The SLRX562 is our newest battle cruiser that replaced the others. It is larger, much faster, a much more powerful weapons system, and has many newer modernized communications and analytical detection features. It was assigned to us on our recent return to our planet Xeres. We will provide you with a detailed tour of the ship when we conclude our meeting."

They soon came to a flight of steps that took them up to the command and control room located at the forward upper level of the ship. Ahular motioned the Americans to a cluster of comfortable looking seats. A glance over the room was enthralling with its series of monitor panels and various navigation and communication instruments, but their attention was redirected to the commander when he began to speak again.

"Earth friends, I am sure you are very confused when I mentioned we critically need your help back at our home planet. Let me try to explain in earth terms so that you might understand. Much of what I am explaining is well into your future and will no doubt be confusing. Two years ago, our planet was visited by a species of intelligent aliens from another galaxy. We referred to them as Andoids as they identified their home planet as Andirite. Unfortunately, they brought unfamiliar microbes and deadly strains of viruses with them and infected our civilization with several unknown diseases. Our people are dying by the thousands each cycle of our sun and we have been unable to stop it."

Simon interrupted, "But Commander Ahular, we know nothing about things like that, so how can we help?"

"There are certain infection-fighting organs and functions in your human bodies than can help."

"I don't understand," Simon answered, totally confused, as were his other three companions.

Ahular continued, "Over the past few years of observing your planet and your species, we were able to determine that you humans have developed one of the strongest immune systems of any other species we have observed throughout our travels. We obtained some human corpses which we transported back to our planet for intensive medical studies. Our medical scientists conducted extensive research on the bodies and discovered many incredible things about the human species that we have not found elsewhere in our interstellar travels. You humans have some extraordinary organs and features that fight bad microbes and germs and create strong self-immune systems to the human body... protective features that we don't have. For example, your bodies have an organ called a spleen that produces white blood cells and controls the amount of red blood cells in your bodies. Also, your bodies have a unique lymphatic system with small organs called lymph nodes that carry white blood cells throughout your bodies that fight and destroy these dangerous microbes and germs. You have a unique bone marrow that produces an extraordinary amount of white blood cells. We desperately need cell samples of these organs to help us fight off these diseases. You can provide our scientists with the necessary tissue and cell samples so they can clone and reproduce these organs to transplant into our own bodies. It involves a simple painless procedure involving extracting tissue samples and dissociating the cells to create cell cultures. This will allow our researchers to use these cultures to clone and reproduce new organs for our populations and replicate your immune systems."

"Can't you get these things from human corpses?" Scott asked.

"They have tried that and failed. The cell specimens have to come from live human bodies and get processed very quickly, right after harvest."

The disconcerted look on Elijah's face was comical but conveyed his skepticism about the whole affair. "Good Grief!" he exclaimed. "That sounds like something worse than a snake bite from one of those slimy creatures we saw in the Amazon."

Both Ahular and Nezar emitted a deep guttural sound the Americans knew was the way they laughed.

"No, my friend," Ahular assured him. "The procedure is quite simple and fast and you will suffer no ill effects whatsoever."

"Commander Ahular, will you please allow us a few moments to confer with one another," Simon asked.

"Of course," he replied, as he nodded to Nezar to move over to the navigation console to allow their guests some privacy.

"What do you think?" Simon asked.

Elijah was the first to respond. "I think the whole damn idea is crazy. That planet is millions and millions of miles from here and we'll probably never get back home."

Scott said excitedly, "I for one will gladly go. Can you imagine the excitement we'll create when we get back home? We'll be the first humans to visit an alien planet inhabited by intelligent people…or whatever that call themselves. When we get back, I'll be in huge demand for speaking tours to describe our experience."

"How about you, Jonah?" Simon asked.

"I agree with Professor Scott. This is a chance of a lifetime and I wouldn't miss a trip like this for anything. Perhaps I might have a chance to examine some of their rock formations and other geological oddities on their planet."

Simon thought for a few moments before offering his thoughts. "As you know, I am married to a wonderful girl and we have a young son named Thomas. The thought of not seeing them again would be devastating. I have already been away from home way too much and if I don't return soon, Maggie might think I'm dead or even worse, she might give up and run off with another man."

Elijah chuckled. "You know damn well that woman isn't going to leave you for another man. Besides you have too much treasure stashed away from our former expeditions in Mexico and Peru."

"Well," Simon confessed, "like Jonah said, a journey like this to another galaxy and planet is a once in a lifetime experience. If we can help save the lives of millions of their people, then it will be worth it... I'm in."

Elijah spoke up. "Well, if you are going, I guess I'm in as well, because I surely can't let you go to that place without me along to look out for you."

"Thanks, Elijah. It wouldn't be the same without you along, and besides, I'll bet that planet has no snakes there." The laughs from Scott and Steele relieved the tensions as Simon motioned for Ahular and Nezar to join them.

"Commander Ahular, we are very grateful that you did save our planet Earth from destruction on two occasions and prevented the annihilation of our human race. If we can help you save your people from destruction, then we all agree to accompany you to your planet."

"Thank you, gentlemen," the commander said appreciatively.

"When do we leave?" Elijah asked.

"Vice-Commander Nezar will brief you on the preparations and inflight procedures so once we prepare the ship and our navigation data and sensors for the journey, we should be on our way very shortly."

39

Nezar led the four Americans into a small situation room to give them instructions for the flight to his home planet, Xeres. He turned to them and said, "To properly prepare you for the journey ahead, I wanted to provide each of you with information as to what to expect. This ship is much more advanced than the two former ships the three of you were exposed to both in Mexico and Peru when we traveled into space to destroy the asteroid." Nodding at Steele he added, "Since this is your first flight, this will all be new information to you."

Jonah was on the edge of his seat, eager to learn all he could about the ship and this new adventure.

"The X562 has many of the same features as the older ships you were familiar with, but far more advanced features with our propulsion engines, thrusters, weapons, and navigation system. For fuel, the ship still uses a combination of Trax and hydrogen gas. Properly mixed together, the new Trax fuel gives us an incredibly inexhaustible source of fuel for our engines, weapons, and the cell rejuvenation green light you see around you."

"How far is it to your planet, and how long will it take us to get there?" Steele asked.

"From your earth, our planet is nearly two billion earth miles away. Our new thrusters use a system called Vartz speed that can bend light bands and actually travel the speed of light. Our previous trips took us from twenty-eight to thirty of your days, but with our new Vartz propulsion components and other technical advancements, we can exceed that time by about nine or ten of your days. The overall trip will take us about twenty earth days, or almost three of your weeks."

This information was far above the men's level of understanding, but they were content to accept what Nezar was saying and not embarrass themselves by asking too many questions.

The Vice-commander continued, "We are equipped with incubator pods similar with those you used on your previous trip we took into space to confront the asteroid. The pods will allow you to enjoy a pleasant sleep while we are in flight."

Steele couldn't hold back any longer, "Mr. Nezar, how will we eat and use the bathroom?"

"The incubator pods are equipped with tubes that will feed you very nourishing food intravenously and easily remove your waste. When we arrive at our destination, you will awaken from your sleep and feel quite refreshed." Ending the instructions, he added, "Now I will escort you back to the command center where Commander Ahular would like a final word with you."

On the way back to the command room, Steele whispered to Simon, "I'm a little nervous about this whole affair, especially spending three weeks in that coffin he called an incubator pod. What do you think, Simon?"

"Five years ago, we spent several days in one of those incubators during our trip into outer space to destroy a huge asteroid hurling toward the sun. Ahular and Nezar and another one of their ships were able to destroy it and save our earth from being incinerated and completely destroyed. These alien people saved the human race from being totally wiped out. Elijah, Scott, and I were also with them eight years ago when they saved our planet from being split apart by a huge earthquake that occurred under the Atlantic Ocean. They also saved us from some very bad people when we were trapped in a cave in North Carolina, trying to secure a Confederate treasure hidden there. I trust these aliens completely and if we can help them save their race, then I will do anything I can for them... we certainly owe them that much. Besides, that long snooze in the pod is very peaceful and you won't know a thing until you wake up."

This seemed to calm young Steele's nerves as he nodded his approval and said, "Count me in, but I have another question. How did Commanders Ahular and Nezar learn to speak such fluent English?"

"They actually learned it from the computers on the first ship we discovered in Mexico. The ship had been dormant for hundreds of years in a cavern under the pyramid, but the onboard computers were still active, apparently fueled by that Trax stuff they had. When we first boarded the ship, I think the computers learned it from our casual conversation. Don't ask me how, but in a short period of time those computer things started talking to us. They told us their information storage banks had many languages in storage, including many early forms of the European language derivatives that predated English. I distinctly remember them telling us that our English language was an offshoot of Latin, Saxon, Sanskrit, and German."

Steele just shook his head in amazement. "Those machines had to be pretty darn smart to know all of that stuff."

Simon nodded an acknowledgement. "It is incredible how much information and knowledge those artificial machines have stored up in their memory banks."

= = = = = =

Ahular was anxiously waiting for them as Nezar ushered their four guests into the command center. He said, "I want to thank each of you for agreeing to accompany us back to our home planet. I just received urgent news that our people are dying at an unprecedented rate from some unknown microorganisms, and our scientists desperately need your tissue and blood samples. They need to clone these samples quickly so our bodies can produce your white blood cells. Once they obtain the samples, we have the means to clone, reproduce, and accelerate growth of these new organs very quickly to implant into our people."

Simon responded, "Commander Ahular, you saved our planet from total destruction on two occasions and also saved our lives several times as well. If we can in some way help save your people, we are most happy to do so."

The wide lipless smiles and accompanying nods from Ahular and Nezar conveyed their appreciation.

Ahular continued, "The Vice-commander will now escort you back to our incubation chambers where some of our crew members will help secure you into the pods and prepare each of you for the long journey."

On command, the thrusters were ignited, the landing pods were retracted, and the large spacecraft lifted upward toward outer space and worlds unknown to the Americans.

40

Each of the guests was directed to a horizontally positioned incubator capsule by a crew member and helped into the bed-like compartment. Jonah Steele was surprised at how comfortable and relaxed he felt as the alien attached several tubes and wires to his body and closed the clear glass-like cover. His last recollection of being awake was the sight of a light colored green gas surrounding his head as he slipped into a state of peaceful unconsciousness and a deep sleep.

In the command center, Ahular noticed that the X 562 was pulling away from the earth's gravitational field and entering the airless vacuum of space. He briefly glanced at some coordinates on a monitor and then motioned to the head navigator to accelerate the Trax thruster systems. As the ship picked up speed, the commander noticed the blue and white sphere of Earth growing smaller and smaller and then into a speck. They were fast approaching the outer bands of the earth's solar system and into the vast space of the Milky Way galaxy. In a few more moments, he would again direct his attention to the monitor screen as the ship initiated the protective invisible ion shield around it and, upon command, commence the Vartz speed that would accelerate the X562 to the speed of light and hopefully even a bit beyond. He knew there would be no sensation with the sudden acceleration when Vartz kicked in. The navigator watched carefully, waiting for the command signal from Ahular to begin the speed transfer. Satisfied that the correct navigation coordinates were set, the commander turned toward his navigator and nodded his approval to ignite the Trax turbines and propulsion thrusters. One push of a control switch initiated the process and, in an instant, the X562 burst forward to an unimaginable velocity.

It took two days to clear the Milky Way galaxy and enter into another endless void and another group of stars they had aptly named the Antholous galaxy. It was larger than the Milky Way and contained a million different solar systems consisting of active suns and revolving planets. Ahular and his explorers had visited several of the planets and found a few to be located within a temperate zone, meaning they were positioned an adequate distance from their suns to create an atmosphere, climate, and temperatures that allowed water to be produced that spawned an abundance of life-like forms in various stages of evolution and development. None they had seen had reached the levels of their own intelligent or for that matter the advanced state of Earth's humanoid species.

Ahular, Nezar, and the small number of crew members rotated rest periods in the incubator capsules to allow them to get adequate sleep and nourishment from the food pumped into their bodies. The X562 was well into their journey when the navigator, a crewman named Quapuac, noticed something very strange occurring on the monitor...something quite alarming.

The speed of the ship was being reduced rapidly, even though the Trax thrusters were indicating full power. Quickly he rushed to the commander's quarters to awaken Ahular. He opened the pod cover and turned on a valve to revive the commander who awoke with a surprised look on his elongated face. "What is it Navigator?" he asked.

"Sir, something strange is happening to the ship. My monitors indicate a drastic drop in speed even though our Trax thrusters are showing full power. I desperately need you in the control room."

Loosening the tubes, electrodes, and straps, Quapuac helped the commander exit the capsule and quickly return to the command center where the navigator drew his attention to the monitor. "Sir, the speed of the ship has dropped even more since I came to get you. We are now well out of our Vartz speed mode and our velocity still is dropping fast."

Ahular moved to the front starboard porthole only to see a totally blank space empty of any visual stars or other celestial bodies. "What do you think might be causing this?" he asked, with a concerned expression on his face.

Quapuac hesitated for a moment as he scanned another monitor on the control console. "Sir, it appears that our exterior sensors are registering a huge and most unusual gravitational pull on the ship. I'm afraid we have been drawn into a large black hole."

Turning to another crew member, Ahular ordered, "Bring Nezar and our four American guests to the command center immediately! There is no time for any further hibernation and sleep during this crisis."

= = = = = =

Simon and his companions, now fully awakened, were led back to the Control room where Ahular and Nezar were poring over some navigation charts and computer generated sheets with assorted symbols and figures. The serious looks of concern on their faces conveyed some serious problems that gave the men some apprehension. It was evident there was something happening that gave Ahular and the navigator some serious concerns.

Elijah leaned over and whispered to Simon, "I sure don't like the looks of this. By their expressions, it looks like we might be in a real pickle."

"Let's find out," Simon whispered back.

"Commander Ahular, there seems to be a problem. What's going on?"

Ahular turned to the four men and replied, "Yes, we seem to have run into a problem. Somehow the X562 has been pulled into a large black hole where we are free falling into the center. Our Trax thrusters seem to have no effect in reversing our course."

"What is a black hole?" Jonah Steele asked.

"Mr. Nezar will explain all of this to you as I am rather occupied at the moment."

The Vice-commander took over. "Black holes occur when a very large star implodes and falls in on itself. The star literally collapses and in many cases results in a supernova that blasts part of the star into space."

"Why are they called black holes?" Elijah questioned. "From

the forward port window, I don't see anything unusually dark or anything floating around out there."

Nezar continued, "You can't see anything because black holes are invisible. The intense gravity within a black hole draws all the light into the middle and will not let it escape back into space. Once we are trapped within the black hole and drawn deeper into the captured light, we should be able to see remains of shattered planets… huge chunks and pieces of broken rock and metal debris. It's hard to say because we have never been trapped within a black hole before."

"How long will we be trapped inside this hole?" Scott asked.

"Who knows," Nezar replied. "Perhaps this ship could be trapped here for a thousand of your earth years or until it possibly might be hurled back out into space by a supernova. In order to break the bond with the dense gravity, we would have to figure out a way to neutralize the force of gravity in order for the ship to accelerate out of it, and that might be very difficult to do."

Simon was devastated when he realized he might never see Maggie and his son Thomas again. "There has to be something we can do," he said.

"The key here," Nezar added, "is to create a force around the ship that is stronger than gravity. A possible electromagnetic field might do this and allow us to accelerate our ship faster than the speed of light. Our scientists have said that a powerful electromagnetic force is stronger than the forces generated by gravity, but I know of no instances where this has actually been tried except in laboratories."

Suddenly the voice of the navigator, Quapuac boomed out.

"We have an incoming large object hurling toward us. It looks like a huge asteroid broken off from a shattered planet."

Ahular shouted back, "Activate the forward laser guns and break it apart!"

A simple movement of a control lever and a quick adjustment in the power level brought the three forward laser weapons to bear. The target was acquired as Ahular gave the command to fire. Three concentrated and maximum powered laser beams shot across the empty space and hit the tumbling chunk of rock with its full force. The mass shattered in an explosive flash of light, hurling pieces of stone and tempered metal fragments away from the ship. Some smaller pieces harmlessly bounced off the impermeable hull. They had narrowly missed a horrific collision.

A thought popped into Elijah's mind. He tried to remember all the details of his experience five years ago when his feet were stuck firmly to the metallic surface of an asteroid hurling toward the sun. He, Simon, and Scott had accompanied Ahular and the alien ship into outer space with the purpose of destroying the huge asteroid comprised of rock and tempered metal. He thought about the magnetic boots he wore and how he was able to adhere to the surface and walk freely about to set the explosive device onto the asteroid. The process had been explained to him by one of the alien engineers. He remembered something about the cobalt rich surface emitted a negative magnetic polar field and the calibration on the boots had been adjusted to a positive setting to attract the boots to the surface. He thought about the instructions given. *What was that the alien said? Opposite magnetic polar fields attract and similar fields repel.*

Elijah remembered that the controls on the magnetic boot inserts had somehow been pushed to the maximum positive setting, which caused a tight magnetic bond that held him firmly to the negative metal surface. It most likely happened when he accidently brushed the control knob on a rock outcropping. In order to free him, Professor Scott had come back to help and in his haste, he had unknowingly turned the settings to the maximum negative position. The similar negative polar fields had a repelling effect and hurled Elijah off the asteroid and into space. He recalled the panic when he realized he was lost in space and rapidly drifting away from the asteroid and ship.

He turned to Vice-commander Nezar. "Mr. Nezar, do you remember the incident I had five years ago when your ship destroyed that asteroid that was hurling toward our sun?"

The alien nodded. "Yes, I remember that well. You were firmly stuck to the asteroid's surface until Mr. Scott adjusted your magnetic boots to the full negative setting which propelled you into space. I remember that you ingeniously used your laser rod to propel yourself back toward the ship where we were able to miraculously rescue you."

"Well, I was thinking," Elijah responded. "Are you able to magnetize the outside surface of this ship?"

"I believe we can," Nezar answered. "The hull is made of a very strong metal alloy found on one of our planets. It is the same planet where we get our Trax fuel ore. It is named Terchez Zen. The metal does, in fact, generate an inherent magnetic field...mostly positive I believe."

"Do the strong gravity forces holding us have any magnetic polar fields present?"

"Let me ask our navigator," Nezar replied, as he moved over toward the command console.

The question was repeated to Quapuac who reached for some control knobs. "Let me check with our milometer," he said. "It is one of our external sensors that can measure magnetic polarity. This is what we use to measure the magnetic effects of the earth's North and South poles."

A picture appeared on an overhead monitor filled with a series of graphic figures and symbols.

Quapuac examined it closely and then spoke. "Our milometer does indicate a strong negative magnetic polar field around us, most likely caused by the fast rotation of the black hole perimeters."

Elijah picked up on this. "Navigator, if the gravity polar field measures negative and the skin of the ship registers positive, won't that cause the two fields to attract and bind us together?"

"That's true, Elijah, but we do have a way of reversing the polarity of our hull from positive to negative. This might allow us enough of a repelling force that could help us break the bond."

Although much of this was like Greek to the Americans, Professor Scott picked up on the conversation. "From what I understand you are saying, the ship and the gravity forces in the black hole have opposite magnetic fields…is that correct?"

"That is correct."

"And you can reverse this to similar magnetic fields?"

"Correct, Mr. Scott. That is what I am going to do."

Commander Ahular joined the conversation and commented, "It sounds like we might be onto something that might lead to a solution." Noticing that Elijah had something further to say he stopped to let him speak.

Directing his comment to Nezar, Elijah commented, "I heard you say that an electromagnetic field is stronger than a gravity field. I'm not sure what all that means, but if this is true, couldn't you put a positive electromagnetic force field around the ship to repel the force of the gravity? Perhaps with this and the power of your Trax thrusters, the ship could gain enough speed to overcome the gravity and break out of the black hole."

Quapuac had an answer for this. "Mr. Walker's suggestion sounds logical. If we increase the strength of our ion shield, this should turn our shield into a strong positive electromagnetic field around the ship. This would give us a deterring force against the gravity and with the full power surge from our thrusters, the ship might break free and escape from this black hole. It's certainly worth a try."

Ahular was satisfied with the analysis and issued the command. "Navigator, you may commence the sequence of events you described and proceed with the breakout."

41

As Quapuac and his assistant prepared the X562 for the breakout launch, Commander Ahular advised Simon and his three
companions to strap themselves securely into some padded
chairs on the far side of the room. The commander and Americans silently watched as the navigator viewed an overhead read-
out on the monitor and moved some control levers and knobs to
begin the sequence for re-ignition of the thrusters. Ahular and
Nezar also strapped themselves securely into some chairs. The
first function was to reverse the magnetic field from positive to
negative on the bonded metallic and ceramic hull. This was easily done with an internal mechanism called a Trionex fillibrator
that aligns positive and negative electrons in the same direction.

He further remarked, "Like the iron ore found on your earth,
our metal alloy hull produces very strong electrons that will create a strong magnetic field and by adding a strong electronic
surge to our hull, this should give us the repelling energy to
initiate a breakout from the gravity that has entrapped us."

Quapuac activated the Trionex and then triggered the ion
shield. With a quick adjustment, he increased the strength of
the shield by a factor of three. The third step was to ignite the
Trax thrusters and slowly increase the power feed. He knew it

would take a maximum thrust to acquire the speed they needed to break out of the dense gravity of the black hole. All the occupants of the command center sat silently, watching out of the port and starboard windows as the sequence of events unfolded.

There was a feeling of apprehension throughout the room waiting for signs that the ship was actually moving. Steele leaned over and whispered to Scott, "I don't think we're moving. I can't see anything passing by outside the window."

"Just be patient, Jonah. These guys know what they're doing."

Simon looked up at the overhead monitor and also saw groups of figures and symbols changing rapidly...numbers perhaps. Quapuac looked at the same figures and confidently remarked, "Commander, I am pleased to report the ship is rapidly accelerating and picking up speed. The X562 is breaking the black hole's gravitational bond and continuing to move faster each second. I believe we have done it, sir. At this speed, we should exit from the rear of the black hole's structure within six hours."

There was a show of shouting and clapping in the control room as the ship continued to accelerate. The upturned slit in Ahular's face conveyed that he was smiling and very pleased with the initial success. Turning to Elijah he said, "I believe we should all thank Mr. Walker for planting the idea for initiating the electromagnetic energy surrounding the ship and changing the magnetic field from a positive to a negative. It appears that this was the key factor for breaking the gravitational bond that had us trapped."

Elijah's blushing didn't hide the fact he was proud to have thought of it.

Simon leaned over and whispered to his cousin, "How in the hell did you manage to come up with all those crazy ideas? Before meeting these aliens, we had never heard of electromagnetic fields and all that other scientific stuff."

Elijah gave him a silly looking grin. "It was only a wild guess. I remembered those magnetic boots I wore on that asteroid a few years ago. When Scott twisted the control knob to the full negative setting on the boots, it blew my ass off that stinking rock and way out into orbit like I had been shot up in the air from a giant slingshot. It sounded reasonable if those magnets would do that to me, then maybe the same principal might work on this spaceship. I guess it must be all that good gravy I eat that makes my brain so smart. Maybe you should eat more gravy."

Simon laughed and then rolled his eyes and shrugged, "I give up," he said. "Even though you came up with that brilliant idea, you are still hopeless."

= = = = = =

The X562 continued to accelerate until Quapuac announced that they had acquired the necessary speed and were moving toward the back side of the system's outer boundaries. Ahular approached the four Americans and said, "You have been a witness to a most unusual event. None of our ships have ever experienced a black hole before and the data we have collected will be most helpful in the unlikely event this ever happens again. But it now appears that the ship is safe and our journey back to our

Scoros galaxy and our home planet is now safely underway. I will have two of my crew escort you back to the incubator chambers where you can resume your rest for the next few days. And you, Mr. Walker, for your useful idea, I will have a special nutrient added to your feeding tube as a special reward. All of you will be awakened when we enter the boundaries of Scoros." He turned to join Nezar and Quapuac at the console table.

"Wonder what he means by a special nutrient, Simon?"

Simon laughed. "I'll bet they are going to feed some gravy and ground up biscuits into that tube."

Elijah gave him a funny look, "Yeah, I should be so lucky. Maybe he'll even shoot me a good ole shot of bourbon."

On the way back to the incubation room, Steele turned to Simon and remarked, "How on earth can we possibly go back to sleep after watching all that black hole stuff and the near asteroid collision experience we just went through?"

"Don't worry, Jonah, that green looking gas they pump into those cocoon incubators will knock you out like a swatted fly."

= = = = = =

With the ship's delay stranded in the black hole, it took fourteen days from the breakout to reach the outer limits of the Scoros galaxy and it would take them four more days to reach their home planet Xeres. The rest of the journey had gone relatively smooth with no more disruptions. Within two days from reaching their destination, Ahular decided to awake the American guests from their hibernation capsules so they could witness other planets in their galaxy as they passed by. He knew they wouldn't want to miss the experience of the ship's landing on Xeres.

Simon and the others were awakened by a crew member and led toward the command center where Ahular and Nezar were waiting. Surprisingly, the four men felt fully refreshed, nourished, and totally alert from the long sleep. On the way, they were able to stop by the mess area for some breakfast. "I don't see any cooks or kitchen, so how are we supposed to get anything for breakfast?" Jonah Steele asked. "I sure could use a cup of coffee with my eggs, bacon, and biscuits."

The other three couldn't refrain from a big laugh. Simon pointed to one side of the room. "You see those silver tanks lined up against the wall and do you see the long table and chairs just under the tanks?"

"Yes. What's that got to do with my breakfast?"

"Well, that is your breakfast," Simon responded, "inside those metal tanks hanging on the wall."

"You've got to be kidding me," young Steele responded with confusion.

Amused with Steele's comments, Simon, Elijah, and Scott remembered their own shocked reactions when they first saw the aliens eating from the tanks.

"No, that is the food the aliens eat…let me show you," as Simon escorted Steele over to the table. He released one of the hoses connected to a large metal cylinder and pressed a small lever to discharge some light-colored paste into his hand.

"What is that slop?" Steele asked.

"It's a variety of seafood and seaweed blended together…and quite nourishing. They told us the seafood is a blend of various species of fish, lobster, crab, and shrimp."

"Actually, it tastes pretty good," Elijah added.

Simon held out his hand. "Here, try a taste. You'll be quite surprised."

Steele was appalled. "You expect me to eat that goop?"

Elijah answered, "Well, Jonah, you only have two choices. You can either eat that goop or starve to death."

Steele hesitated for a moment and then scooped a sample with his finger. He stuck it in his mouth and rolled it around on his tongue, expecting that he would throw up any minute. His expression conveyed total surprise as he fingered another sample into his mouth. "Not bad," he admitted. "I'm starving…let's eat. But how do you eat this stuff?" he added, glancing up at the tanks.

His companions laughed again as Simon pointed out, "You have to take those hoses and stick the nozzle in your mouth. Press the little lever and the paste will flow into your mouth."

"Good grief!" he shouted. "As advanced as these aliens seem to be, you would think someone could have invented a spoon by now."

Steele was finally contented and he pumped and ate several helpings of the nourishing paste and was amazed at how quickly his hunger was satisfied. "Actually, this stuff tastes decent enough, but I need to teach these aliens how to make biscuits and fry an egg."

"And you also need to teach them how to make gravy," Elijah added with a big grin. "There is no doubt Fanny Whittington could kick their ass in a cooking contest."

This brought a big chuckle from the others.

Both commanders greeted them warmly as Ahular said, "You appear to have endured your long sleep quite well. We are three days from arriving on Xeres but I wanted you to be awake so you could observe several of our planets as we pass by them."

"Thank you, Commander Ahular," Simon responded. "This will be a great experience for us."

Ahular explained, "Our solar system is very much like yours, except instead of your seven planets, we have ten revolving around our sun, which is about one and a half times larger than your sun. If you will look out the starboard windows, you will see the planet Terchez Zen in the distance. This is where we mine and obtain our Trax ore that is refined into our fuel and numerous other uses. As we approach our planet, you will be able to see Aarnon, the other planet where we extract the Trax fuel ore."

Nodding at Simon, Elijah, and Scott, he added, "I believe you men have observed the photosynthesis generator tube with the bright beam of light that healed the wounds of two of your prior companions. That beam is composed of a refined and concentrated Trax compound that bathed the wounds and rapidly regenerated new cell growth."

Elijah vividly remembered the miracle and answered him. "Yes, I recall that. It was Robert Drake on the *Toltec* and Sam Roper on the *Cuzco* who were healed from a broken leg and severe knife wound."

Professor Scott offered his comment, "I work for Mr. Drake and his broken leg was completely healed and he has no limp at all."

"That is correct. The healing beam was a concentrated Trax generated ray that creates a healing procedure from an oxidation process called chemosynthesis. Also, the soft green light you see inside the ship and the gas surrounding you in the incubator capsule is also a Trax generated light that has basically the same effects, except on a much smaller scale. Now, I must return to my work and help guide us safely home. Vice-commander Nezar will be glad to show you around the ship if you wish."

"Yes, we would like that very much," Scott responded eagerly.

Steele leaned over and whispered to Elijah, "Do you understand all of that oxidation and light ray healing stuff he was talking about?"

"Good grief, not a word of it. All I know is I've seen that light ray work and it really does heal broken bones and wounds."

The four guests were very eager to explore the rest of the ship and compare it to the prior two ships they had experienced. Of special interest was the laboratory area. Simon and Elijah remembered the retaining tanks they had observed on both the Toltec and Cuzco that contained specimens of human bodies the aliens had collected while visiting Earth. They were told some of the specimens were very old. Simon also remembered the preserved remains of one man who the aliens had gathered from the ancient city of Lythe on the sunken continent of Atlantis. He remembered the man was a dying slave the aliens had taken in for the purpose of experiments to attempt to restore his life. He was later told the experiment had failed and the body was discarded into space.

The first stop was the aft section where the propulsion systems were located. This area housed the various complicated looking machines that controlled the boosters and antigravity devices. Most of the rear sections contained storage rooms that held supplies, spare parts, and various pieces of equipment.

Moving forward they soon entered the laboratory section where the research and experiments were conducted. The walls were filled with sophisticated looking equipment and several monitors to review the tests results. The main thing that caught Simon's eye was the six large tubular looking containers at one end of the room filled with a light green liquid. The most strik ing were the two humanoid bodies suspended in the translucent cylinders. He turned to Nezar. "Who did those bodies belong to?" he asked.

"The remains in the left tank are those of a well-preserved man of Asian descent found in a cave in your northern Alaska territory. It was interesting to note we found very similar genetic cell compositions as some other species we had examined from northeast Asia, specifically Siberia. The other specimen is an Eskimo we found on an island in your Arctic Circle. Both specimens were quite old and buried in solid ice. We believe the Asian humanoid was one of the early migrants that traveled across the Bering Strait into North America. The Eskimo was probably stranded and frozen on an iceberg and over time entombed in the ice. We thought a study of these early humans would be most informative about their origins and genetic characteristics."

"Have you ever been able to bring any of your specimens back to life?" Professor Scott asked, thinking that the word *specimen* was a bit odd as a reference term for a fellow human.

"Only once," Nezar responded. "The corpse had only been dead for a day so the vital organs were still functional and had not begun decomposition. Our Trax generator ray was able to regenerate cell growth and restore the man to a relatively good state of health. He was an Indian from the Algonquin tribe and we were able to release him back to his tribe in southern Quebec."

"What an incredible feat to bring someone back to life," Steele acknowledged.

The conversation was interrupted by Ahular's voice coming from a speaker. "Vice-Commander Nezar, we are approaching the outer gravity bands of Xeres, therefore, you may return our guests to the command center so that they may observe our planet and make preparations for landing."

42

Ahular directed the Americans to the forward ports so they would have a good view of the approaching planet and their impending arrival. The colorful sphere loomed in the distance and the first thing they noticed were the two moons orbiting Xeres and positioned on opposite sides of the planet. Having seen their planet Earth from space during the prior trip to destroy the asteroid, it was an amazing sight to see that this planet was very similar in general appearance. Distinguishable were several huge land masses with scattered bands of clouds, and further noticeable were large expanses of blue areas surrounding obvious continents of land. These were most likely oceans that proved Xeres had plenty of water contributing to a distinct atmosphere and climate, all capable of producing and sustaining many different forms of life. When the ship got closer, they could distinguish familiar looking patches of green located on the land. It had to be forms of plant life. Based on their prior observations of Earth from space, it appeared that this planet had more land mass and smaller oceans. Soon the ship began to reduce speed and rate of descent as the navigator, Quapuac, made a change in trajectory to assume a descending horizontal rotation around the globe as they began reentry into the planet's gravitational field.

The ship's destination was a city on the coast of one of their twelve continents pronounced Zin-Daragon. Unlike the earth, to the aliens, their continents were comprised of only one country, inhabited by a single race of people. The city named Zir-Auron was the capital of Zin-Daragon and home to 215 million aliens referred to as Auronians. Nezar also explained to the Americans, that his planet, Xeres, was about one and a third times larger than Earth and their sun was nearly one and a half the size of earth's sun. He also informed them that while our earth and its sun was nearly 93 million miles apart, their sun was positioned nearly 118 million miles from Xeres, which provided satisfactory temperatures and climate conditions to produce water and sustain life.

= = = = = =

As the ship descended closer to its destination, Commander Ahular told the men to strap themselves into the command center chairs for the final preparations for landing. Soon the SERX562 began its final glide toward the ground. Across the horizon, Scott noticed the long shore line connecting the ocean with the endless expanse of beaches. It reminded him of America's east coast and the sandy beaches stretching from Miami to New Jersey.

The ship slowed its rate of descent and hovered over a field surrounded by some squatty looking buildings. The landing pods were extended as the ship landed softly on a tarmac. Simon noticed a small group of aliens standing near one of the buildings, obviously a collection of officials and perhaps medical specialists waiting to greet Ahular and their anticipated visitors from Earth. The door finally opened as the commander and Nezar led the Americans down the steps to the ground. Scott noted with a great sense of satisfaction, for the first time in history a human from planet Earth planted his feet on the soil of another planet located in another far-off galaxy. He was filled with thoughts of what it would be like when he returned home and their story was revealed to the people of Earth. He would be in very high demand for speeches and lectures to countless academic and scientific organizations throughout the world. He would be famous and his notoriety would make him rich beyond his wildest dreams.

Elijah, on the other hand, could only think of his stomach. *Wow! I sure hope these aliens will serve something better to eat than that glop out of the tubes. I sure am starving for some good home cooking.*

Young Jonah Steele could only hope they would get out of this place in one piece and home alive.

When Ahular, Nezar, and the Americans exited the ship, they noticed several distinguished looking individuals dressed in a variety of colorful looking suits walking toward them. Simon figured the greeting party was made up of political leaders, military personal, and most likely an assortment of medical specialists. After all, he figured he and his three companions had been frisked off to this planet to contribute cell and tissue samples from their specific defense fighting organs…those that provided immunity properties to fight harmful microorganisms and germs invading the body.

It was no surprise that the greetings, interpreted into English by Nezar, were brief. The funny grunts and strange sounds of the alien's language were as confusing to the Americans as English was to them. The four guests were hastily ushered into a strange transport machine called a dacidron that lifted off the ground and moved swiftly to the city. Commander Ahular had stayed behind to meet with his superiors for a debriefing while Nezar was assigned the task of accompanying and transporting the Americans as their personal guide and interpreter.

Before entering the dacidron, the Americans noted how easy it was to breathe the air…it seemed to be no different than the air they breathed on earth.

Jonah Steele leaned over to Simon and asked curiously, "What the devil is this contraption we're riding on? I didn't notice any wheels and I would swear we were riding above the ground."

"We are cruising on a cushion of air," Simon answered. "We first saw one of these in Peru just before we discovered the lost city of El Dorado. Ahular and his crew were using a large cavern under a pyramid to conceal their ship, the *Cuzco*, as we later named it, and conduct some research. We got to ride on it before we boarded the X326 on our trip to outer space to destroy the asteroid. It's an amazing machine and Nezar told us it was fueled by a gaseous compound called hydrogen."

Steele was totally amazed how a gas like substance could possibly power a machine that could skim across the land on a cushion of air while at home his species still relied on horses and buggies to move them around. He was amazed at all the new technology possessed by this alien species, things that humans had never even thought of yet.

The dacidron carried them on a circuitous trip around the city to a large complex of one and two story buildings. Nezar explained this was a medical research center used for experiments and all types of medical studies. This was where the medical researchers would perform the procedures to extract the tissue and cell samples they needed from the Americans. The facility also housed the laboratories that would clone and accelerate the growth of the various organs for implantation into their own species. The experiments and research on prior human cadavers previously transported back to Xeres gave some direction to the researchers as to the locations of the specific organ tissue and cell samples that they would need to harvest—samples from organs like the spleen, lymphoid organs, lymph nodes, tonsils, thymus, and most importantly, human bone marrow that produces white blood cells. All the tissue samples were to be extracted from Simon and his three companions and then cloned and reproduced into similar organs to be transplanted.

The Americans had great difficulty understanding how anyone could have the knowledge and advanced technology to accelerate the process of reproducing organs needed to fight the deadly microorganisms that were infecting and killing off the Xerenoids at a rapid rate.

The realization of all this finally registered with the American guests as they were quickly ushered off to four separate operating rooms for immediate surgery. Elijah would have to wait on his biscuits and gravy because human cell harvest time had finally arrived.

43

The last thing Elijah remembered was the intense green light that surrounded him and one of the alien doctors placing a mask over his face, just before he was out like a light. Professor Scott glanced around the operating room and marveled at the sophisticated looking equipment lining the room...then he was asleep. Simon and Steele had the same observations about the green light and wondered if they would ever wake up again. The procedures took about an hour and a half before the anesthesiologists induced a chemical to awaken them. Each of the four men were amazed how refreshed they felt, with no noticeable after effects. Also, the alien surgeons appeared satisfied the procedures were a great success as vials of tissue samples were hurried off to waiting laboratories and technicians who were preparing for the cell cloning process.

The four patients were taken to a recovery room where Nezar was anxiously waiting for them. "I am told the procedures were highly successful," he said. "And it appears that each of you survived the operations very well. Now we shall board the dacidron where I will take you into the city and to your suitable accommodations we have prepared for you."

Turning to Nezar, Steele had a question "Can I ask you a question, sir?"

"Certainly, Mr. Steele."

"Why is it I feel refreshed and seem to have plenty of energy after an operation like that? I don't feel anything hurting or uncomfortable at all."

Nezar let out a funny guttural sound, interpreted to be a chuckle. "Before going to sleep, do you remember the green light that surrounded you?"

Each of the four men nodded an acknowledgement, stating they distinctly remembered the green light.

"That green light is the same Trax generated light we use throughout our ships and especially the concentrated beam we use in the Trax photosynthesis generator tube that quickly heals wounds and injuries to the body. As I mentioned earlier, your human bodies respond very well to the Trax light. The concentrated light that bathed you during the procedure quickly regenerated new cell growth that replaced those of the tissue samples that were removed from your organs…your organs are now responding as if the cells were never removed."

"That is incredible," Steele responded.

Nezar chuckled again. "Yes, it is quite remarkable what our medical technologies have achieved."

The dacidron sped along, passing a long group of one and two story buildings. Anything higher than that was rarely seen. Professor Scott was most curious. "Mr. Nezar, why aren't the buildings built any higher than two stories? It would seem that it would more practical and economical to build them at least three or four stories high."

Nezar had the answer. "Actually, Mr. Scott, the buildings do range from four to six stories high, except more than half of what you don't see is built underground. Our sun is considerably larger than yours and omits more radiation waves than your sun. The underground facilities help reduce the amount of ultraviolet radiation absorbed by our bodies. In your language, you call it sunburn, which occurs on our skin as well."

The dacidron reached the heart of Zir-Auron and descended to the ground. Nezar wanted to show his guests what normal life was like on another planet. To the Auronians, the earthlings were oddities that commanded a great deal of stares. Their physical features were totally different and it was the funny protrusions of the human ears and noses that brought deep guttural sounds that were their way of laughing. Of special interest were the funny puffy lines around the human mouth slits that caught gazes…lips of course. It was equally amusing to Simon and his companions that the Auronians had no lips, ears, and noses, only slits for the mouth and holes representing noses and ears. They had large upper chests that narrowed down to very thin hips and lower torsos, but their upper skulls were bigger, which could only mean to the Americans that they must have larger brains.

Elijah leaned over and whispered to Simon. "As intelligent and more advanced as these aliens are, compared to us, you would think that their bodies would catch up to their brains. Makes you wonder if they evolved from lizards and snakes."

This brought a big laugh from Simon who replied, "It also makes you wonder if they have any monkeys and apes on this planet."

With his usual instructional assessment of the topic, Professor Scott jumped into the conversation. "Actually, like on earth, there are many things that affect the way living things evolve and change into a stronger species. Most of it involves environment, weather, atmospheric conditions, food supply, and the body's ability to adapt to these conditions. All living things go through this evolutionary process for long term survival of their species."

Jonah Steele had a chance to glance around at the surrounding landscape and pick up a few rocks to examine. "Very interesting," he muttered.

"What is very interesting?" Elijah asked.

"The surrounding landscape and these rocks are igneous. I don't see any signs of sedimentary rock anywhere."

"What does that mean?"

"It means this landscape was formed by magma or lava flows and not by rocks formed by fine particles dissolved in water, such as limestone. These two samples appear to be basalt. This whole area appears to have had a very violent geological past."

This conversation was getting too deep for Elijah who changed the subject with a question to Nezar, "How do your people eat? Do you have any public cafes or restaurants and if so, what kind of food do they serve?"

"Yes, we do have public eateries that serve a variety of food. In your language, they would be pronounced with a word that sounds like *teorium*. If you wish, I will take you to one of my favorites for some nourishment. I am sure you must be hungry after your surgeries."

"That would be great," Elijah responded enthusiastically. "We are all starving."

They all reentered the dacidron and Nezar lifted off the ground and turned the machine toward a group of buildings in the distance. Elijah whispered to his companions, "Wonder how the patrons pay for their food. We don't have any of their money."

Scott threw out an answer. "Well, we may just have to wash dishes."

= = = = = =

The teorium was a simple looking place with very plain décor. On the walls were a few paintings that looked like the artist took swipes and splashes with a paint brush and splattered them on the wall. The Americans had no idea what they meant until Nezar explained they were underwater ocean scenes. He ushered the four men to a table with very simple looking stools. Once seated, in his strange language Nezar ordered a few dishes from an attendant.

It did not take long for two servers to bring a platter filled with a weird looking fish-like thing, unlike any of them had ever seen before. "What on earth is this horrible creature?" Elijah asked. "It looks like a sea monster."

"That's probably what it is," Steele responded with a chuckle.

The oddity appeared to be encased in a large shell and had six legs with claws on each. The weirdest thing was the two large eyeballs that protruded from stems coming out of both sides of the head.

Nezar was amused at their reaction and explained, "This creature, as you call it, is a species of our Zanopitus shellfish and it comes from deep in our ocean. On your planet, you might call it a member of the cuttlefish family related to your squid, octopuses, and nautiluses. But I can assure you it is quite tasty."

Nezar nodded to one of the attendants who promptly produced a slender looking tool with a hook on one end. He inserted the hook into the shell and began to peel it from the crustacean's body. The meat appeared pink with a few red streaks noticeable. Nezar took a thin knife and began to cut slices off the body and pass them around to his guests. The dish was accompanied by an assortment of little square looking delicacies piled around the platter. Nezar explained these little blocks of food was comprised of an assortment of very nutritious sea vegetables made from kelp, algae, seaweed, and other underwater delicacies.

Steele took a small nibble and then a larger bite and glanced at his companions. He smiled and then commented as he took another mouthful, "This stuff is really good."

The others nodded in agreement as their portions were consumed ravenously. Elijah leaned over and whispered in Simon's ear. "Do these aliens ever eat anything but seafood? That goop in the tanks is seafood paste and what we are eating now is seafood stuff. Don't they ever eat any meat?"

"That's a good question. I don't recall seeing any animals since we've been here."

"I should have told Ahular to stop and grab a couple of cows and stick them on the ship before they took off."

The meal was finished and everyone seemed satisfied, with full stomachs. Nezar then escorted them from the teorium and back to the dacidron where the next stop was to their quarters.

44

Their housing was located in a drab one story building with their accommodations on the second basement level, or three levels from the top. The building was a six-story structure with five of the stories underground. Simon and Elijah were assigned one room and Scott and Steele another separate room. Each accommodation was adequately equipped with two separate bedrooms and a comfortable lounge area separating the bedrooms. A large bath was to be shared by each of the two men in each billet. The Americans, not used to flushable, running water type toilets, were totally captivated by the bowl-shaped device that would serve as their latrine. The United States and other countries on earth had not evolved to this type of modern convenience. They were amazed at the commode and concluded that the aliens most likely had somewhat similar waste elimination functions as humans.

Simon and Elijah's thoughts were interrupted by a sudden knock on the door. Elijah opened it to find Commander Ahular, Vice-Commander Nezar, and another uniformed individual with them. His appearance signified that he was of substantial ranking and someone of significant importance. Standing behind the three aliens were Professor Scott and Jonah Steele, with expressions of total confusion.

Ahular was the first to speak. "We need to come in and talk to you about an urgent matter that has come to our attention."

"Please do, Commander," Simon replied, leading them into the lounge area.

"Let me first introduce our senior leader, Supreme Commander Malquazar. He is leader of all the combined martial service commands of Zin-Daragon. This matter is of extreme importance and he felt it essential that he meet you in person and thank you for your contributions to our populations. The supreme commander does not speak your language so Mr. Nezar will interpret for him." Ahular motioned the men to be seated.

Malquazar began to speak in their strange language as Nezar repeated his words in English.

"On behalf of all Daragonions throughout our continent, Supreme Commander Malquazar wishes to thank you for your valuable donation of cell samples from your organs that contribute to your unique human immunity systems that help you fight diseases. We are hoping your cells will help save millions of Daragonions' lives and also many lives from our other continents."

Simon nodded his understanding and acknowledgement for the group.

Malquazar continued, "A very disturbing situation has developed that might put your lives in great danger. On the other side of our ocean, Murk, there is a continent named Zin-Terazine occupied by a civilization called Scarbalites. We refer to them as Scarbs. They are a very warlike group that would like to eliminate us and occupy our lands. They, too, have been infected with unknown pathogens and dangerous microorganisms that are killing their people. Like us, they do not have strong enough immune systems to combat these diseases."

Nezar paused for a moment to let this sink in. "We just uncovered a Scarb spy in our medical group that passed along the information of you humans helping us by donating your vital cell samples from your strong immunity producing organs. Unfortunately, we also received information that the Scarbs are in the process of mounting a mission to capture the four of you and transport you back to Zin-Terazine to gather samples to clone organs for their own people."

Scott directed a question to Nezar, "Ask the supreme commander if you would agree to sell them some of the cloned organs you produce from our tissue and cell samples. It might help formulate a peace and some mutual cooperation between your two countries."

His reply was most disturbing. "Unfortunately, we are told they do not want our cloned samples but instead they want to completely strip you of all your internal organs that would leave each of you dead. We are positive that they are making plans to kidnap you very soon, before we have a chance to return you to your planet Earth."

"This is not good," Simon remarked. "What can we do to prevent this?"

Ahular opened a bag and removed four unusual looking items and answered Simon's question. "These are hand held laser weapons that will hopefully protect you in the event of an attempt from the Scarbs to capture you. You have observed how our laser guns worked on the X235 and X 326. The effects from these laser handheld weapons are very similar, but of course much less powerful. They are very simple to operate," he said as he handed a weapon to each of the Americans and visually took them through the steps on how to operate them.

Ahular continued, "As a precaution, we will have food delivered to your rooms and we will maintain two armed guards stationed outside your doors. Our word for food or meals is pronounced as *torp*, so when you hear that word from the opposite side of the door, you will know an attendant is delivering you your meals. We must leave you for now, so please try to stay confined to your quarters."

The three aliens then turned and left the four men to think about their situation.

= = = = = =

The Scarbalite ship lifted off the tarmac from Zin-Terazine late in the afternoon, scheduled to land in Zir-Auron just after midnight. The elite commando group, led by a ruthless Scarb commander named Zurkin, planned to land the ship close to the hanger that housed the X562. They had a transport dacidron on board that would carry the unit to the building where the Americans were housed. The Scarbalite spy had done a thorough job in obtaining information as to the location where the Americans were billeted and passed the information to his contact in Zin-Terazine.

A plan was formulated to overpower the guards and grab the Americans. The trip back to the docking area would be relatively quick if they could avoid being spotted. Zurkin had firm instructions that the human specimens had to be brought back to Zin-Terazine unharmed. Their medical specialists had to have the earthlings alive and in good shape so they could harvest their healthy organs. Once the organs were removed, the lifeless outer body shells would be discarded.

It was relatively dark when their dacidron pulled up behind the building housing their targets. The Scarbs knew the earthlings were housed in an accommodation two floors underground and would most likely have guards positioned close by. Their laser guns were prepared for a quick confrontation if necessary. Zurkin and seven commandos filed off the vehicle, leaving two behind to guard the craft and prepare it for immediate departure once their captives were aboard. Silently, the group entered the building through a back entrance and moved quickly to the atrium where an open well dropped down to the bottom level. Two elevators were positioned at opposite corners of the cavity.

Glancing two floors down, Zurkin spotted slight movement along the railings and the muzzle of a laser gun resting over the top. This confirmed the presence of guards. He instructed two of his troopers to take the elevator down while he and the other five would sneak down by the stairs. The element of surprise was essential to take out the guards to prevent alerting the earthlings in their rooms. The Scarbs knew the only noise that might be heard is a possible muted yelp from a guard being vaporized by the lasers…the weapons were silent killers.

Zurkin and his Scarb troopers exited the stairwell at the same time the two Scarbs on the elevator reached the third floor. The guards recognized the threat and answered by firing at the two armed intruders as they passed through the elevator door. The laser rays tore through their bodies with ease, completely burning their upper torsos in half. At the same time, the Scarbs exiting the stairwell opened up on the guards and vaporized their bodies to a blackened crisp. The whole elimination process only took seconds. There was no noise except for the faint distant clatter of one of the guard's weapons smashing into the bottom floor. The blast had thrown the gun over the railing and into the open well to the floor below.

The intruders had rehearsed their mission well. Zurkin knew that it was probable that food for the earthlings would be delivered to the door by attendants. With weapons ready, one of the soldiers knocked and announced the word *"torp."*

A voice from the other side said, "Who is it?" The trooper shrugged, having no idea what that meant.

Zurkin whispered for him to repeat the word.

"Torp," he shouted again.

A few moments passed and then a click was heard coming from inside. Elijah opened the door, expecting to see an attendant holding a big tray of food. Instead, five fierce looking aliens burst through the door with a brutal looking fellow behind them that seemed to be directing the operation. Three of the laser weapons given to the Americans by Commander Ahular were lying on the table and quickly confiscated, leaving the earthlings defenseless.

Looking down the barrels of five laser guns, the gestures from the intruders were obvious. The Americans meekly raised their hands, signifying surrender.

45

Simon and his companions were ushered from the room and prodded up the stairs to the top floor. They were then led out of the building and loaded into the waiting hovercraft. Since Zurkin couldn't communicate with his prisoners, he had to rely on hand and body gestures to direct the captives—his forceful signals were understood. They were placed in the last four seats at the rear of the transport when the dacidron's pilot started the turbine and begin skimming along the ground toward the airstrip where their ship was parked.

The Scarbs had not bothered to restrain their captives, knowing they were unarmed and powerless to attempt any escape. The transport was approaching the tarmac when Jonah Steele casually leaned over and whispered into Simon's ear.

"I still have my laser gun tucked in the waistband against my back," he said. "They forgot to search me."

Very quietly, Simon whispered back. "Slip it out of your pants and hand it to me behind your back."

Steele's soundless motions went unnoticed as he eased the laser gun from his belt and moved it slowly over to Simon's waiting hand that grasped it and unlocked the safety lever with his thumb. The dacidron was hovering barely off the ground and approaching the hanger where the X562 was parked when Simon swung his arm around and fired the laser into the back of the vehicle's driver. The center of his body was vaporized to a crisp as the dacidron skidded along the tarmac and came to an abrupt stop, slamming three of the aliens to the floor.

Two commandos arose from their seats, swinging their guns around, when Simon calmly fired again, blowing the smoking and blackened heads from their shoulders. The remaining Scarbs froze. Elijah, Scott, and Steele had quickly moved to the front and opened the hatch, with Simon close behind. Commander Zurkin was furious as his facial contortions and guttural screams conveyed his rage. Simon pointed his laser in a motion that told him to hit the deck, and quick.

Once outside the dacidron, Elijah slammed the hatch door and Simon pulled the trigger and moved the laser ray along the edge to weld the door shut. Quickly, the four Americans ran into the hanger where the X562 was waiting.

Luckily, the hatchway was still open as the four men scurried up the steps through the door. Service attendants had been loading provisions aboard the ship and were not quite finished. This allowed the Americans easy access and saved them the hassle of trying to access passwords or codes which might have been difficult, or more likely impossible. It was only a matter of time before Zurkin and his Scarbs broke out of the dacidron and found out that Simon and the others had sought refuge in the Zin-Daragon spaceship.

Once inside the reception area, Elijah tripped a familiar lever allowing the door to shut and another twist locked the hatch. He then turned to Simon and asked. "Now that we're inside this thing what are we going to do with it? I know the Scarbs will soon figure out where we are."

Simon's expression was serious when he announced, "We're going to fly this big bird out of here and back home to our Earth."

With a look of disbelief, Elijah asked, "Well, how in the hell are we going to do that? We're a billion miles from home."

"If you remember, I commanded and flew both the *Toltec* and *Cuzco* ships in Mexico and Peru so why can't I fly this one, too? Besides, these smart ships fly themselves…at least the computers fly them. I'll just tell it what to do."

"Yeah," Elijah retorted, "You'll probably get the computer so confused that it will dump us into another black hole somewhere out in space."

Simon was getting annoyed as he glared at his cousin. "Do you just want to sit here and get recaptured by those space savages and get us carved up into little pieces?"

Professor Scott and Jonah Steele were taking all of this in when Scott asked, "How do you plan to get this big thing off the ground? We need Ahular and Nezar here to do this."

Simon didn't answer but turned toward the navigation console and shouted, "SERX562, this is Commander Murphy and I command you to start your engines and lift us off the ground."

There was a slight sound of static as a voice erupted from an overhead speaker, "Sorry, but we do not have proper authorization to initiate your command."

"I am Commander Simon Murphy, former commander of your *Toltec* and *Cuzco* spaceships and I demand you lift this ship off the ground."

The overhead speaker blared back, "Those names are not registered. You are not authorized."

Professor Scott, who had been glancing out of one of the portholes, shouted to Simon, "You better do something quick because I see that Scarb devil and his soldiers pouring through the hanger door."

Elijah looked up at the speaker and shouted, "Let me handle this. Computer, this is Vice-Commander Elijah Walker. You are commanded to authorize Commander Murphy, former commander of the X235 and X536 to operate this ship and you must do it now! Both of us are registered in your memory banks."

There were a few moments of silence and then suddenly the overhead metallic voice spoke back. "Yes, we do have Commander Murphy and Vice-Commander Walker registered in our data banks as a former commander of the X235 and X536. We now have authorization for you to take command. Welcome aboard, Commander Murphy. We are initiating liftoff as requested."

As the landing pods were retracting, the battle cruiser accelerated the vertical thrusters and anti-gravity turbine and slowly lifted from the ground. Simon issued a further command. "Computer, you may take the ship through the open hanger door and up into the sky. Once airborne I will issue a command for our final destination."

Jonah Steele glanced over and asked Elijah, "How in the world did you get that computer machine to follow your instructions when they rejected Simon?"

Elijah laughed. "Well, this happened once before. I learned in the army that when you throw enough commands at someone they will eventually get confused and follow your orders. I guess we just confused that machine enough to find our names hidden somewhere in their information storage vaults. Looks like I jogged their memory and it worked. Besides, I don't think the names *Toltec* or *Cuzco* were registered with them, but apparently, they did recognize the proper designations for the two ships associated with our names."

Inside the hanger, Zurkin saw what was happening and raised his laser pistol and fired. The laser ray, adjusted to a lesser setting to vaporize flesh, bounced harmlessly off the impenetrable hull of the X562. Two other Scarbs also fired with similar effect as the huge ship drifted out of the door and began its rapid ascent into the air. Zurkin was livid as he ordered his troopers back to their own ship. He raised his fist and screamed toward the sky, "You earthlings cannot escape me. We will catch you and I will surely watch you die!"

46

An aide quickly walked into a debriefing meeting with Ahular, Nezar, and the supreme commander. He had an urgent message. "I hate to interrupt the meeting, Commander, but we have just received word that the American earthlings have just been captured by some Scarb raiders. They were last seen taking our guests aboard their dacidron and heading toward the air field where our SERX 562 is parked. Their ship has been spotted there so we think they are going to be transporting the earthlings back to Zin-Terazine."

The supreme commander jumped up from the table, furious. "This is devastating news."

The aide added, "Sir, two of our guards were found dead at the American's billets, along with two dead Scarbs."

Turning to his officers he said, "Commanders Ahular and Nezar, you need to rush to the air field immediately and intercept them."

"Yes sir," Ahular responded as he and Nezar jumped up from their seats and rushed out the door.

= = = = = =

Back at the hanger, Zurkin was enraged as he and his three remaining commandos rushed aboard their own ship. He turned to the pilot and navigator. "I order you power up immediately and follow that Draconian ship that just took off from the hanger."

"Yes, sir!" The pilot responded as he turned to the console and began to press buttons and move levers.

"Prepare the ship's target acquisition screen and forward laser guns for immediate firing."

In a matter of moments, the Zin-Terazine ship was powered up and ascending rapidly into the sky.

= = = = = =

Aboard the Zin-Daragonion ship, Simon was watching the navigation screen as the craft sped upward toward open space. Suddenly a familiar voice boomed through the overhead speaker. "Simon Murphy, come in Mr. Murphy. This is Commander Ahular calling Simon Murphy."

Simon answered, "Hello, Commander, this is Simon Murphy."

Ahular responded, "We see you were able to successfully commandeer the X562 and escape from the Scarb raiders."

"That is correct, Commander. We were able to overpower them on their dacidron and escape on the ship."

"We are not sure how you obtained authorization, but it appears the computers are responding to your commands. Our sensors indicate the Scarb ship has been launched and on a direct intercept course behind you. The Scarb leader knows he cannot return to Zin-Terazine without you and your companions alive. If he fails to capture you, he would be disgraced and most likely executed for failing to fulfill his mission. He knows your capture from the X562 in flight would be impossible so he has no intention of letting you escape alive. I am afraid your ships will have to fight until one or both are destroyed. We have some options and we think we can assist you. I will launch another ship and together we should be able to maneuver to a suitable position to destroy their craft."

Simon spoke back into the speaker. "What would you have me do, Commander?"

"You and the other Americans take a seat and we will instruct the computer to adjust your course to a 38-degree west trajectory back toward Xeres. We want you to go into an orbital course so I can put our ship in a position to intercept you and the Scarb's ship. We will initiate most of the commands, so if you feel any unusual and sudden maneuvers, do not be alarmed."

Simon's three companions heard the message from Ahular which prompted Elijah to say, "Well, I guess we can all sit back and relax while we watch those Scarb devils blow our ass out of the sky."

Simon barked back. "No, Ahular knows how to fly and maneuver this ship much better than we do and we know nothing. The computers do it all."

At that instant, a transmitted command from the navigator Quapuac, in the Zir-Auron headquarters, instructed the X562 to make a sharp vertical climb and a sudden half loop to reverse its trajectory back toward the planet. The thrusters accelerated their speed and in the far distance Scott spotted the enemy ship zooming toward their direction. The X562 had been spotted as well. "I see the Scarb ship. It's heading this way," he yelled.

The others rushed to the ports and also saw the enemy alien ship streaking toward them.

"Tell the computer to speed it up," Elijah shouted. "That damn ship is headed right toward us."

At that instant, the Vartz boosters kicked in and the ship shot forward with an incredible burst of speed, allowing the X562 to zip past the opposing ship. They also caught a glimpse of the laser ray that zoomed past and barely missed their underbelly.

"Good grief!" Steele screamed. "Those Scarb devils are shooting at us."

Commander Ahular's voice boomed back over the speaker. "Commander Murphy, we will guide the X562 to an orbit altitude of 50 earth miles above the Xeres's surface where we will intercept you at our coordinates 356.2-416.5. Our combined lasers should be able to bring down the Scarb ship. At that point, we will reduce your speed to 2,000 miles per hour to allow us easier contact with the X562 and the enemy."

"I hear you loud and clear, Commander Ahular," Simon shouted back.

Elijah looked at his cousin and then said. "Did you hear that, Simon? Ahular addressed you as 'commander.' It looks like they finally recognized the ranking the *Toltec* assigned to you on our first flight in Mexico."

"Yes, it sure seems that way," Simon mumbled, with a concerned expression, with his thoughts concentrating on the Scarb ship closely on his tail.

It did not take long for the X562 to reach the designated altitude and level out to begin a steady trajectory around the planet. The men were a little more relaxed knowing Ahular would be along shortly to help them, but their confidence was short lived when an alarm bell suddenly sounded.

As the four Americans crowded the ports trying to identify any impending threats, the speaker blasted a metallic computerized sounding voice. "Attention X562 personnel. Our internal transponders have picked up signals from an inbound space cruiser. The signatures confirm the imminent treat is that of a Zin-Terazine battle cruiser of the Casmot 24 class. It is armed with two 75 raydon forward laser guns and two 55 raydon aft guns."

Simon rushed over to the console and spoke to the computer. "Are our laser guns armed and ready to fire?"

"That is an affirmative," the voice replied.

"What is the strength of our weapons?" Simon asked.

"Our three forward guns and two aft guns are all registered at 75 raydons."

"What difference does that make and what the hell is a raydon?" Elijah shouted anxiously.

"How should I know? I just wanted to make sure we're on equal terms with the Scarbs."

"We have an incoming attack closing in!" Steele screamed from one of the starboard ports.

A quick glance showed the Scarb Casmot ship fast approaching from the Starboard side and most likely setting up their sights and locking the target for a probable kill. The Americans were their target.

Simon yelled out an order. "Computer, take the X562 to an immediate vertical climb and maneuver to a position to the rear of the enemy Casmot ship."

Due to the absence of air in the outside void of space, there was no sensation to the four occupants as the X562 suddenly shot upward and well above the enemy ship. Another glance through the ports saw two bright bursts of pure laser energy streaking by just below their hull…another close call. The ship then performed a roll and looping maneuver to position itself well behind the Scarbs.

"Prepare our forward lasers to fire," Simon shouted as he looked at the screen just above and maneuvered a lever to acquire the enemy ship. "Fire lasers," he yelled at the speaker.

Three bright streaks of light shot forward toward the Casmot, but missed as they zoomed past the rear of the ship. At the same time, Zurkin performed a similar vertical roll and turned to maneuver behind the X562. Simon anticipated this and managed a similar maneuver but downward and to his rear. Once again, two laser streaks from the Casmot flashed by the upper hull, only missing a hit by a mere few feet.

"This is getting too close for comfort!" Elijah bellowed. "Where is Commander Ahular when we need him?"

"Those Scarbs mean business," Simon shouted back. "We're on our own and can't count on him to help us."

Luckily, the X563 had maneuvered to a flight position where the enemy's ship could be seen cruising in the distance on their

port side. Professor Scott had had enough of the rapid maneu-
vering and futile waste of laser shots. "Let me have those bloody
guns," Scott shouted to Simon. "When we were in training at
the Washington Armory, I didn't hit all of the bull's-eyes for
nothing."

Simon gave him a questioning look but didn't resist as he
moved aside to allow Scott to move over to the console and the
firing and aiming instruments.

"The way I see it," Scott said, "The computer's automated
aiming device is not allowing the guns enough lead for that
ship's speed and degree of angle. Locking on the target directly
to the center of the ship is not the answer. I need to adjust for
the variation of their trajectory."

"How do you do that?" Elijah asked.

"Watch me. We're going manual."

Scott pressed a couple of buttons and took hold of the weapon's control lever. The target was acquired on the aiming screen
and Scott maneuvered the lever slightly to the front and right
of the enemy ship. "Four clicks to the vertical and six clicks to
the right should do it," he mumbled to himself. His three companions watched the professor in fascination as he manipulated
the controls.

"I sure hope you know what you're doing," Elijah remarked
sarcastically.

Scott's sharp glance was enough to tell Elijah to shut up and
stop interrupting the gunner's concentration.

"I've got it," Scott shouted as he initiated the trigger mechanism.

Three bolts of burning hot lightning energy flashed across

the sky toward the enemy ship whose high velocity drove it directly into the path of the laser beams. The ensuing explosion was spectacular as the Casmot Class battle cruiser disintegrated in an enormous ball of fire, hurling millions of pieces of blackened debris into orbit. Mercifully, the Scarbs didn't know what hit them as they were all instantly incinerated.

"Wow, you did it!" Elijah yelled. "You made an incredible shot that the computer wasn't able to do."

Scott responded with a slight shrug of his shoulders and modestly said, "Ah, nothing to it, fellows. It was like shooting sitting ducks in a pond."

The spontaneous laughter from his companions released their tension and conveyed jubilant relief that they were still alive and in one piece. Their reverie was suddenly broken by a voice blaring from the speaker. "Commander Murphy…Commander Murphy come in…This is Commander Ahular calling."

47

Ahular's voice continued. "Our sensors detected a large explosion and lost all electronic signals coming from the Scarb ship. What happened?"

Simon answered, "We were able to maneuver the X562 around the Scarbs and Professor Scott shot it down with the laser guns. The Scarbs are now nothing but little pieces of cinders floating around in orbit."

"Quite amazing," Ahular retorted. "We convey our compliments to you and your crew."

Elijah looked with a questioned look. "Does he know we're the only crew?"

"I'm sure he does," Simon replied.

"Where are you located, Commander Ahular?"

"We are positioned 1,250 nautical earth miles directly behind you and closing. I want to board the X562 ship with Vice-commander Nezar, navigator Quapuac, and seven other crew members. We want to transport you back to your home planet, Earth."

"That sounds great, Commander, but how do you plan to come aboard out here in space?"

"In exactly fourteen minutes, I want you to order the ship to

304 | ALEX WALKER

come to a complete stop and we will maneuver our ship close to you. You are to then order the ship to de-pressurize the lower bay compartment and direct it to open the lower hatch doors. We will transfer to the X562 with our dacidron. You can direct the computer on the control panel and it will initiate your commands."

"I understand, Commander Ahular. I will comply with your wishes immediately."

After the communication disconnect, Elijah asked, "Does anyone have a stopwatch?"

"Of course we don't," Scott answered. "But I have already begun counting the seconds...21, 22, 23, 24..."

After what seemed like an hour, Scott announced, "Fourteen minutes, time's up."

"Close enough," Simon quipped, as he looked at the speaker. "Computer, I command you to stop the ship and bring it to a standstill. And then I want you to depressurize the lower storage bay and open the lower hatch doors."

The metallic voice answered back, "Orders confirmed. Shutting down forward turbines and thrusters and depressurizing. Doors will open after storage bay depressurized."

= = = = = =

After the doors were opened, it took Ahular, Nezar, and the seven crewmen about fifteen minutes to make the transfer on the dacidron. Once inside the lower hatch, the doors shut tight and the chamber was pressurized. The dacidron was stowed safely inside and would remain there for the duration of the trip. The air and oxygen levels were quickly stabilized and the aliens disembarked the hovercraft and moved to the upper decks and command compartment. Ahular and Nezar found the four Americans in the control room awaiting their arrival.

= = = = = =

The commander seemed to be pleased to find his human guests unharmed and in relatively good condition. Ahular had to ask, "Commander Murphy, tell me how did you manage to outmaneuver that Scarb battle cruiser and bring it down with your lasers? They are some of the best navigators in our world and certainly have very competent gunners."

"Commander, you really don't have to address me at my old rank of Commander Murphy since you now have control of the ship and that temporary ranking was only given to me by the computer on the X235, *Toltec,* in Mexico, when we were the only ones aboard.

"You are correct, Mr. Murphy. Your commander title is now suspended."

"Actually, our sensors picked up the Scarb ship before it reached us, so we had an early warning of their approach. Their first attempt to hit us with their lasers failed, so I ordered the computer to put the X562 in a roll and loop maneuver that positioned us well behind them. We both fired several laser beams at each other but missed."

"Apparently, your target acquisition and aiming sensors functioned properly for you to lock on the target and bring it down."

"Actually, Commander Ahular, it was Professor Scott who brought the enemy ship down with a perfect strike."

"Please explain. That seems highly unlikely he could have done it without our weapon sensors to acquire the target."

Simon turned to Scott. "George, you tell him how you did it."

"Well, the solution was quite simple," Scott explained. "The laser shots we missed were caused by the aiming device being locked on to the target and most likely that was the reason the Scarbs missed us as well. The aiming sensors failed to take into account the high rate of speed factor of both ships. I just removed the device from automatic and switched it over to manual where I could compensate for their speed and direction changes by visual reckoning. I gave the rays enough lead whereby their ship simply caught up with our laser steams that blasted them into pieces."

"That is quite ingenious," Ahular admitted. "I will have to mention this to our armaments experts when I return to Xeres."

Scott had one more comment. "At home, when we go deer hunting with a rifle, we call that adjusting for windage. But up here, there isn't any wind so I adjusted the beams for speed."

Ahular had no idea what the earthling meant, but let it pass. Turning to the group he said, "I am sure you would like to know the results of your tissue and cell contributions. The experiments were a huge success as our medical professionals were able to clone and multiply your cells and are now growing thousands of organs that will contribute to our population's immunity systems. By subjecting the cloned cells to our Trax photosynthesis generator rays, the process has been accelerated greatly and new organs such as spleens, lymph modes, and thyroid glands are being produced in quantity. Also, new bone marrow that produces white blood cells is now being produced and being injected into our people's skeletal systems. Our scientists feel certain that your tissue and cell contributions will have a huge effect in creating strong immune systems for us to fight off destructive microbes, germs, and deadly diseases. In other words, your generous contribution has probably saved our species from eventual extinction and for that we are eternally grateful."

"That is great news," Simon responded. "You saved our planet Earth from destruction on two occasions, so we are glad we could help in some way to help save your people."

Ahular nodded his appreciation and said, "And now my friends, I think it is time to prepare the ship for another long journey to take you back to your own Milky Way galaxy and home to your planet Earth."

There were certainly no objections from their earthling guests.

48

Comfortably tucked into their incubation chambers, the four Americans were hooked up to the various monitoring and feeding tubes and mildly sedated by the green gas into a peaceful sleep. They would be awakened when the X562 reached the boundaries of the Earth's solar system. When asked by Ahular where they wanted to disembark the ship, Simon promptly asked to set down in a vacant field he knew of in Bladensburg, Maryland. It was within walking distance to Simon's home and his wife, Maggie, and young son, Thomas. The spot was also near Washington, DC, and a short buggy ride to the National Museum.

At the control console, Commander Ahular switched the X562 to Vartz speed and the ship accelerated into an invisible flash.

During the eighteen days of flight time, the Americans had been awakened twice to stretch their legs and relieve themselves without the use of tubes. They had been put back in the incubators and would stay there until they reached the outer boundaries of the Milky Way galaxy. Three days out from planet Earth, they were awakened for the last time and unhooked from the support tubes. Ahular wanted them awake for the flight through their own solar system and the final approach for landing. The four men were in the command center when Nezar called them over to the starboard ports. "If you notice, the large sphere passing by is one of your outermost planets, Neptune. It is considered an ice planet, along with Uranus, that is composed mostly of a large amount of ammonia and methane."

The men were not exactly sure what all of that meant but they gave nods of understanding, not wanting to convey ignorance. They did get the picture that Neptune was covered with ice. Of interest was the large number of smaller objects floating just outside the planet's orbit that Nezar identified as populations of trans-Neptunian objects or dwarf planets that had separated from Neptune millions of years ago.

The next day, it was hard to miss watching the largest planet, Jupiter, passing by. As Nezar explained again, Jupiter was a gas giant composed mainly of hydrogen and helium, unlike the terrestrial planets, Earth, Venus, Mercury, and Mars, composed mostly of rock and metal.

All of this was extremely fascinating to Jonah Steele who had to pose the question that the four earthlings had all wondered about. "Mr. Nezar," he asked, "how did our solar system form?"

The vice-commander paused a few seconds to collect his thoughts so he could provide an answer in a manner he hoped they could understand. "It is estimated your solar system, like so many in our universe, formed about 4.6 billion years ago from the gravitational collapse of a giant interstellar molecular cloud leaving your sun as the largest body of the system's mass."

Simon glanced at the others with an expression of total bewilderment.

Professor Scott had a nebulous idea and offered his thought. "If I understand you correctly, this huge mass of matter exploded and flung thousands of stray pieces into space that eventually turned into our planets and other objects like asteroids."

Nezar let out a funny guttural sound, obviously a chuckle. "You might say something like that." He thought to himself, *these primitive earthlings are so far behind in their knowledge of such scientific things.*

"The universe is full of many different objects and systems such as galaxies, planets, dwarf planets, comets, asteroids, meteorites, suns or stars, and a variety of other floating pieces of rock and metal that resulted by the collisions and explosions of numerous planets."

= = = = = =

Like Professor Scott, Jonah Steele had a very inquiring mind. The difference was that Scott, with his training in anthropology and archeology, specialized in the study of past civilizations and ancient cultures. Steele, on the other hand, had been educated in the new science of geology which directed his attention more to the studies of the earth's physical structures and features like rock types, formations, strata, and the effects of erosion. This also stirred his interest in the history of the earth and the surrounding planets. The comments made by Vice-Commander Nezar only stirred this interest further.

Turning to Nezar, he asked, "You and your ancestors are so

far ahead of us in your technology and studies of the universe, so can you tell us something about your travels and knowledge of far off planets. At night when I look into the sky I see thousands of bright stars up there. They seem to be limitless."

The vice-commander gave him an approving nod and said, "The question you ask is very complex and far more complicated than the human mind can comprehend. Let me try to explain it in terms that you might understand. The universe is an incredible miracle and basically a limitless vacuum of space filled with billions of objects floating within this huge void. What you see up there at night with your eyes is an infinitesimal number of the celestial bodies that are out there. Our scientists have estimated that there are at least 800 billion stars in the universe and perhaps many more.

"Within those stars there are billions of galaxies and billions of solar systems within their respective galaxies. Of course, your solar system lies within your Milky Way galaxy and includes your sun, Earth, and six other planets revolving around the sun. There are billions of other systems just like yours throughout the universe. Our explorers have traveled to several hundred of these systems and have found many planets much like your planet Earth that revolves around their suns in a very organized and timely manner. Like your earth, we have found many planets that are located within a comparable or relative distance to their suns that positions them into what is known as a temperate zone.

"This means over a period of millions of years the planets have developed the conditions that sustain moderate temperatures, climates, and an atmosphere that supports a combination of gases like oxygen and hydrogen that produces water. Your oceans and frequent rainfalls are a good example of that. Water is an element that produces life forms from tiny microorganisms to large species of fish and mammals that can evolve into advanced genres like you and I."

"You mean over the years they can turn into living forms like us humans and your species," Steele injected.

"Our genetic species are some of the most advanced forms we have found. Over the years, our explorers have discovered many life forms similar to you and me and in various stages of evolutionary development. All of these species have many different looking body forms and have evolved through many different stages that are all influenced by climate, temperature, environment, terrain, food sources, and many other influencing factors. The intelligence levels of these species have also developed through many evolutionary stages. As a matter of fact, the intelligence levels you humans have achieved is quite advanced as compared to most of the other species we have encountered, and like our species, some are even more intellectually advanced than you."

Scott injected a thought. "So, you are saying there are other intelligent life forms out there in space."

"Yes," Nezar confirmed, "there are many more similar varieties of intelligent mammals out there. The amazing thing is that throughout the universe there seems to be a very organized and uniform pattern, natural order, and sense of structured organization of how everything works. This is true with everything, including the tight orbits our planets follow around their sun down to the seasons experienced by those planets within the temperate zones.

"It is also interesting to note that all living things have a way of rejuvenating their species to replace those segments that die away. Just look at the leaves on your trees that grow back each year to replace those that wither and fall from the limbs during your fall weather. Also look at the birth and death cycles of your own species as an example. You see, everything in our universe follows a very organized structure and uniform pattern that continues year after year through very constant and stable cycles.

"You humans attribute all of this to a divine presence that controls everything. Our species also have similar feelings that there is something out there that has a central control of the universe, mainly because of the uniformity and consistent pattern of how all things happen and work together. This is true throughout the whole universe. Now gentlemen, if you will excuse me, I believe we have a ship to land on planet Earth."

Nezar turned to return to the control center while his four human guests were left speechless in an effort to wade through all of this new information.

Turning to his companions, Simon asked, "Did all of you understand any of this?"

"It sounds like we are not the only living creatures in this universe walking around and talking to each other," Scott conceded.

Elijah quipped, "I wonder if any of those other things out there know how to cook biscuits and gravy."

Commander Ahular commanded his navigator to alter the flight path slightly so that the ship would avoid the asteroid belt that existed between the orbits of Jupiter and Mars. A mid-space collision with a large hunk of drifting rock would totally obliterate the X562 and all of the occupants.

= = = = = =

Deciding to have lunch, Simon led his companions to the mess compartment where they would dine for the last time on the gooey paste from the wall tanks and feeder tubes. They were all hungry and this was all that was available. Once alone, they were able to talk.

Simon turned to Scott. "Professor, did you happen to stick that metal tablet in your pack...the one you found in the cave under that Seljalandsfoss waterfall in Iceland?"

Scott was not surprised at the question. "As a matter of fact, I did. For some reason, I thought we might run into Ahular and Nezar again. I knew you had the Zenox with you so I brought the metallic tablet along, thinking it was something their predecessors might have left in that ice cave. I'm hoping they can translate the symbols and inscriptions for us."

"Why don't you go grab that tablet really quick so we can show it to the alien commanders?"

Scott stood up and hurried to his cabin.

The professor had just returned with the tablet when, ironically, Nezar entered the room to inform the group that the ship was approaching the earth's outer bands of the gravitational field. He was certain they wanted to observe their planet from space. It was a perfect time to show the tablet to the vice-commander.

Nezar was quite surprised to see the tablet and recognized it to be something most likely left on earth by his predecessors. He carefully studied the glyphs and inscriptions on the sheet before speaking. "This tablet was inscribed by our early explorers who visited your planet hundreds of years ago. It is written in one of our ancient dialects and appears to be inscribed in your early eleventh century…somewhere around 1015 AD."

"What does it say?" Scott asked.

"The tablet tells us that our earlier explorers visited Greenland and Iceland and encountered several Viking settlements. Of particular interest, it mentions that they visited an isolated Viking village in a hidden valley on Baffin Island. They refer to this as the *heated valley*. They also encountered a large statue of the Viking god, Thor, sitting next to a warm lake and the remains of an ancient settlement constructed by a much earlier civilization of settlers. This has to be the valley warmed by the hydrothermal vents and the place where we contacted and met you."

"I guess that confirms what we thought about the Vikings and the pre-Columbian Indians who settled there," Scott acknowledged.

"There is one other thing the inscriptions reveal," Nezar affirmed uneasily. "Just north of the warm valley they found traces of an unusual ore on the island that could eventually be dangerous to your species…something strangely akin to our energy ore, Trax."

"How could that be?" Steele asked. "From what I saw, your

Trax not only provides powerful energy to fuel your spaceships but incredible healthful healing rays that helps cure wounds and accelerate new cell growth."

"That's true but this new ore is much different. The tablet explains the explorer's ship sensors detected strong traces of radioactivity that has the potential to release deadly explosive and deadly radiation effects to any living organism around it. Our Trax ore does have immense energy capabilities, but it is non-radioactive and harmless to live organisms and species such as ourselves. Potentially, I can see this new ore they discovered as producing sufficient energy to power your future machines, but it can also be very harmful if used improperly."

"Do you mean humans could use this radioactive stuff to produce weapons in warfare?" Elijah asked.

"Quite possible," Nezar suggested.

"What is radiation?" Steele wanted to know.

The vice-commander pondered the question for a second. "A simple answer would be the emission of energy as electromagnetic waves from subatomic particles that cause ionization, or in other words, the process that causes atoms and molecules to acquire positive or negative charges."

The dumbfounded expressions on the four faces in front of him conveyed total confusion and bewilderment, so he thought it best not to continue the conversation.

As Nezar stood up to leave, Simon said, "We'll be along shortly. We have something to discuss about your comments and the tablet."

They were alone again when Steele commented, "I'm a geologist and have studied rocks, metallic ore, and minerals for several years. I've never heard of such a thing. What do you suppose he meant by their early explorers detecting a potentially dangerous ore with radioactivity? Nezar used words I've never heard of...subatomic particles and ionization."

"Scott had some thoughts. "I've never heard of such a thing either, but it sounds like the ore might transmit some dangerously hot energy waves strong enough to pose a danger to humans and other living things."

Simon concluded, "This information is all new to me as well, but I think it's something we should mention to President Hayes and our top military brass when we get back to Washington."

49

From the forward ports in the command center, Simon, Elijah, and the other two Americans got an incredible view of planet Earth looming in the distance. The immediate view clearly showed the continents of North and South America surrounded by large blue areas indicating the Atlantic and Pacific Oceans, spotted with white clouds. Although Simon, Elijah, and Scott had seen this view of Earth when they accompanied the aliens into space three years preciously to destroy the asteroid, it was a view that the rest of mankind had never seen before.

The X562 ascended on a deliberate glide path, carrying it one more complete orbit before it was to land in Bladensburg, Maryland. At the reduced speed, the ship had sailed over Asia and then Europe before making the final descent across the Atlantic. The horizontal thrusters were engaged and the ship hovered over the destination that Simon had described—a large vacant field just north of the city limits of Bladensburg and within walking distance of Simon's house.

It was dusk when the ship extended its landing pods and settled gently to the ground. Simon led his three companions down the steps and back to the ground of mother Earth. They were followed by Commander Ahular and Vice-Commander Nezar.

Ahular was the first to speak. "Again, I wish to thank you for your cell and tissue contributions to our civilization. Please take comfort in knowing there will be a little of each of you in the organs we produce and implant into our populations that will greatly strengthen our immune systems and save millions of lives."

"Commander, we were happy to do it," Simon acknowledged, noting the affirmative nods from Elijah, Scott, and Steele to signify their accord. He reached into his bag and retrieved the Zenox and handed it to Ahular. "We probably won't need this anymore."

"No, my friend, you keep the Zenox. Unpredictable events happen in our universe and you might need it again sometime. I intend to do a bit more exploration of your planet before we depart, so we will be here for a few more days before we return to Xeres. Your magnetic poles have a particular fascination and interest for us and we would like to take a few more readings and gather some more information. Who knows, we may see you again. However, if we do not meet again, just remember the lasting friendship we have formed between our two worlds will last a very long time."

"We will never forget," Simon assured him.

Ahular and Nezar placed their fists against their chests in their customary gesture of salutation. All four of the Americans followed suit with a clinched fist as well. With this, the two alien commanders turned and returned to the X562. In moments, the pods were retracted and the ship gently lifted, accelerating upward into the air until it was a speck and then disappeared.

Elijah turned to his cousin. "What now?" he asked.

"The first thing we'll do is to walk over to my house and see if I still have a wife and son. If so, we'll drink some good Kentucky bourbon and cook an old fashion American dinner and then tomorrow we can take a buggy ride down to Washington and pay our respects to President Rutherford Hayes and our old friend, Robert Drake, at the Washington museum."

Scott remarked, "You and Elijah can go see the president, but first you can drop Jonah and I off at the museum. I can't wait to hear Drake's reaction to the Viking treasure we discovered and sent him from Baffin Island. Jonah and I are going to really enjoy examining the runestones and all of those old artifacts the Vikings looted from Northern Europe."

= = = = = =

The first knock on the door got no response but the second knock resulted in a slight rustle behind the door. The door handle turned and the door opened to reveal a little boy standing there smiling. Simon knelt down. "Thomas," he said.

The boy hesitated for a moment and then answered, "Daddy?"

All of Simon's emotions spilled out with the tears building in his eyes as he swept the little boy into his arms. "Yes, Thomas, this is your daddy."

Elijah, Scott, and Steele were also caught up in the emotion of the moment as they watched the reunion of their friend and his little son.

Maggie, who was in the process of fixing dinner in the

kitchen, heard the voices and hurried to the front door. "Oh, my goodness, Simon! It's really you…you're alive," she cried as she rushed into her husband's arms. "I thought you were dead. Where in the world have you been?"

"It's okay, Maggie, I am very much alive. I have an incredible story to tell you."

She led the four men into the parlor where Simon walked over to a cupboard and pulled out his favorite bourbon, a bottle of Buckhorn Creek, distilled in Kentucky. "This is really good stuff," he said as he grabbed four small sniffers and handed one to each of his friends.

"What about me?" Maggie shouted. "I could use a couple of swigs as much as you fellows."

The men chuckled as Simon handed his wife a glass and poured her a shot.

"Where have you been?" she pressed. "I haven't heard a word from you in weeks and I had almost given you up for dead."

"You'd better brace yourself, Maggie. We have been on a distant planet located in a far-off galaxy millions of miles away."

She stared at him for a moment with an incredulous expression and then downed the shot of bourbon in one quick gulp. "You've been where?"

In the next few minutes, Simon and the others told Maggie about the Viking discoveries on Baffin Island, the ride on the space ship with Ahular and Nezar to their planet, the medical procedures to donate tissue and cells, the capture and escape from the Scarbs, and finally, the trip home.

"Do you really expect me to believe all of that fairy tale?" she snapped.

Elijah reaffirmed the story. "It's all true, Maggie. Just think, tomorrow Simon and I have to slip down to Washington and tell President Hayes the same story. I just hope he doesn't think we have gone totally insane and lock us up, especially when we tell him about that strange radioactive ore the ancient alien ship discovered."

Maggie looked at her husband with an incredulous expression and then snapped, "Give me another shot of that whiskey."

= = = = = =

The next morning it was a seven-mile buggy ride to Washington D.C. En route, Professor Scott reminded Simon to drop him and Steele off at the museum. He had no interest in seeing the president, but couldn't wait to get started on the Viking artifacts. The reminder was not necessary because it was Simon's intent to stop by the museum with them to see the curator first before visiting the president.

Their old friend Robert Drake was surprised but very eager to see them as the four filed into his office. "Where on earth have you fellows been?" he asked. "I was certain you were all dead."

"It's a long story," Simon answered. "It involves a long trip on one of those alien space ships like the *Toltec* we all rode on in Mexico... the one where your leg was healed by that strange light ray."

"I'll never forget that experience," Drake answered. "But first I want to know about the Viking treasure."

"What do you mean," Robert. "It was delivered to the museum, wasn't it?"

"No, we never got it. I was told by Secretary of the Treasury, John Sherman, the USS Shannon and the Viking treasure were hijacked by some of the officers and crew."

"WHAT!" Simon shouted. "That's impossible."

Drake continued. "I guess you wouldn't have known if you were joyriding around in a spaceship somewhere. It seems that a couple of the officers and some of the crew got greedy and decided to keep the treasure for themselves. Captain Swift and First Mate Stinson, along with three crew members, were left for dead, stranded on a small barren island just off the coast of Newfoundland. They were suffering from starvation and thirst when a local fisherman found them and took them back to his village along the coast. They all survived, thanks to the villagers who fed them and nursed them back to health."

"If that's the case, I assume President Hayes and Secretary Sherman know all about the Viking treasure," Simon surmised.

"Yes, they do. Swift and Stinson told them all the details of the discovery, recovery from the pyramid, and the hijacking."

"Where did they go?" Scott asked.

"It was reported that Stinson heard one of the crew mention the name *Faroe* when they were rowing them to the island."

"What or where is that?"

"The only thing we can conclude is that Faroe is the name of an archipelago located between the Norwegian Sea and North Atlantic. It's a group of islands about halfway between Iceland and Norway."

"Why would the hijackers take the USS Shannon and the treasure to a remote place like that?" Elijah questioned.

"It's a logical answer," Drake answered. "The Faroe Islands

are remote and the last place they think we would look for them. Remember, the Vikings were pagans primarily from the Scandinavian countries of Norway, Sweden, and Denmark. They invaded and occupied all the surrounding countries around them, including England, Scotland, Ireland, and some of the Baltic countries. All the treasure and artifacts were most likely looted from the nobles and their castles located in those countries. The officers and crew who hijacked the Shannon and the treasure figured that the best place to dispose of the treasure and get money from it would be those countries where it originated, mainly England, Norway, and Sweden.

"The Faroe Islands have several secluded fjords to dock their ship and the weather usually stays above freezing because of the Gulf Stream. It would give them a quick and easy access to those collectors and museums that would want the priceless items and pay top money for them. You fellows saw the treasure. What did it consist of?"

Simon answered, "There were several chests of gold coins, some Roman. We saw lots of golden artifacts like cups, plates, statues, plaques, vases, and other assorted items. Many of them were encrusted with gemstones…diamonds, rubies, emeralds, and other colored stones. Collectively, it represented a very large fortune."

Drake's sense of excitement was evident as he imagined such a priceless display of these items at the museum.

"What is the government's stake in recovering the treasure since you sponsored the expedition and we discovered it for the museum?" Simon asked.

"President Hayes and Secretary Sherman want the gold

coins to shore up the treasury to support the gold standard, but they said we could keep all of the artifacts for the museum. Remember, the museum is owned and financed by the government, so actually they would legally own all the treasure."

"How do they plan to recover it and the ship?" Elijah asked.

"The president told me they would commit a naval warship to sail to the Faroe Islands to intercept the Shannon and recover the treasure. The hijackers and brigands would most likely be hanged or spend the rest of their lives in prison. However, I'm sure they know this and would fight to the death."

Simon glanced around at the others, assessing Drake's explanation.

"There is one other stipulation," Drake added, looking directly at Simon and Elijah. "Since you two were the first to discover the treasure, I was told the president said you treasure hunters will have to accompany the Navy on the recovery mission."

50

The White House, Washington D.C.

After Simon and Elijah left the museum, they guided the buggy down Pennsylvania Avenue to the White House. The carriage was secured and the men went to the front gate and announced their identity and urgent need to have an audience with the president. After a few minutes, an aide met them at the door and ushered them into the president's office where he was thumbing through an assortment of papers spread across his desk. Hayes, recognizing his two visitors, motioned them to take a seat and then told the aide to fetch three of his cabinet members, Secretary of the Treasury, John Sherman, Secretary of War, George McCary, and Secretary of the Navy, Richard Thompson.

Within a few minutes, the three secretaries filed into the room and took their seats. The president turned to Simon and Elijah and said, "I assume you have talked to our museum curator, Robert Drake, and he filled you in on the hijacking of the USS Shannon and our plan to recover the treasure."

"Yes, sir," Simon replied, "He did."

"Before we get into the details of the mission, I would like an explanation from you as to why you and your compatriots disappeared from Baffin Island and why you were not present with Captain Swift and the other three men that were stranded by the mutineers on that barren rock off the coast of Newfoundland?"

Simon glanced at his cousin and then took a deep breath. "Mr. President, I am sure you heard from your predecessors about the prior contacts we had with the aliens from a far-off planet that saved our planet Earth from destruction from the massive underwater earthquake in the Atlantic. Perhaps you will also recall those same aliens who saved us from a huge asteroid hurling toward the sun that would have incinerated our solar system five years ago."

Hayes raised his eyebrows as he pondered Simon's statements. "Well, yes I did hear bits and pieces of those fantasy stories, but I had my reservations about them."

"They were not fantasies," Simon assured him. "These things really happened and we were with them."

Simon spent the next hour relating how Commanders Ahular and Nezar contacted them on Baffin and the incredible space trip the four Americans took to their planet in the Soros Galaxy millions of miles away. Simon lost the president and the secretaries when he explained how they donated tissue and cell samples to the alien medical experts to help save their population by helping them to strengthen their immune systems against deadly microorganisms.

Simon got to the part about being captured by the Scarbs, their narrow escape, and how they commandeered the X562 spaceship. His explanation of how they destroyed the Scarb's ship with laser guns really left four heads in the room scratching.

Secretary Sherman's incredulous expression disclosed his

complete skepticism as he responded, "Mr. Murphy, are you sure you're okay? Would you like me to call in some medical assistance?"

Elijah had to chuckle as he said to his cousin, "Simon, show them the Zenox. Maybe you can raise Ahular, since he said they would be exploring our magnetic poles for a few more days. Maybe his voice will convince these men that our story is true."

Simon nodded and reached for his satchel. He withdrew a flat oval looking object and held it high enough so the four officials could see it. He then flipped a tiny switch and the blinking red light came on, indicating the device was powered up. This left the four politicians squirming in their seats, not knowing whether to trust Simon or quickly exit the room.

Simon held the device to his mouth and spoke. "This is Simon Murphy calling Commander Ahular in the X562. Please come in Commander."

Only silence ensued, causing the politicians' skepticism to soar. *This conversation is getting out of hand,* President Hayes thought.

"Calling Commander Ahular, this is Simon Murphy. Come in please."

Hayes and the three secretaries were sensing a deceptive ruse until a burst of static flooded across the room. "Commander Murphy, this is Commander Ahular. We hear you loud and clear."

"Thank you for responding, Commander. I am glad I caught you before you departed for home. I am sitting here with our country's leader, President Hayes, and three of his cabinet members, explaining to them about our journey to your planet. I'm afraid they don't believe my story so I was hoping you would talk to them."

"Yes, we will be circling planet Earth for a few more days so can we can record more data about your remarkable magnetic poles."

"Would you speak directly to President Hayes and support our story?"

"I would be happy to talk to your leader."

President Hayes hesitated for a second, trying to understand what was happening and then, with a sense of uncertainty, took the Zenox Simon handed him.

"Hello, President Hayes. I am Commander Ahular of the space command battle cruiser X562. The facts presented by Mr. Murphy are absolutely true. He and his three companions accompanied us to our galaxy, Soros, and our home planet called Xeres. Their thoughtful contributions of tissue and cell samples will help us duplicate your remarkable immunity systems and save millions of our people by allowing them to build up their immunity against deadly diseases."

The expression on the president's face was a mixture of bewilderment and amusement when he spoke back. "Hello, Commander. This is President Rutherford Hayes. I had heard some of the stories, but is it true you that your command saved our planet from destruction on two different occasions?"

"Yes, Mr. President. The first incident occurred eight years ago when our sensors picked up a huge pressure buildup of the Eurasia and African tectonic plates along your Mid-Atlantic ridge. The plates were splitting apart and would have destroyed your planet had it not been for the fast thinking of Elijah Walker. He suggested that we combine the full force from our three forward laser guns to weld the plates together. The process was successful and the plates were stabilized.

The second incident happened three of your Earth years ago when we were able to destroy a huge asteroid that was hurling toward your sun. The catastrophic explosion would have incinerated all the planets in your solar system. Again, Elijah Walker helped by landing on the asteroid and setting the explosive charges that blasted it apart into small pieces of rock and metal."

Ahular hesitated for a moment to let the politicians absorb all of this. "There is one other matter Mr. Murphy needs to discuss with you, involving a potential dangerous ore that our earlier explorers detected near Baffin Island. It is something that could have disastrous effects for your future populations."

President Hayes was speechless as he handed the Zenox back to Simon. He couldn't think of anything else to say to an alien from another planet.

Secretary Sherman leaned over and whispered to McCary, "This is the first time I can remember seeing the president at a loss for something to say."

Ahular ended the conversation with a final abrupt transmission. "Goodbye, Simon Murphy and Elijah Walker. I hope we can meet again in the near future. Commander Ahular, out."

The president stared at his two guests and then finally said, "Gentlemen, I can't believe I actually talked to an alien from another planet who speaks our language. I'm starting to believe your story is true and it seems, Mr. Walker, you are quite the hero in helping save our planet from destruction. Now, what is this about a dangerous ore these alien things found?"

Simon spent the next few minutes telling them about the radioactive metal discovered by the early ship's sensors. "We were told it produces strong energy waves that could someday power our future machines, but also could be used to make explosive devices that could destroy large masses of people. I am sure this is well into the future and well after we are gone. It's something our future scientists will have to deal with. Now, Mr. President, Robert Drake told us you were making plans to send a military team to recover the treasure."

"That is true. Secretary Thompson of the Navy has selected one of our ships to sail across the Atlantic to the Faroe Islands to search for the treasure and the traitors who commandeered the USS Shannon. We intend to recover the treasure and our ship and bring the mutineers to justice…and I want both of you to accompany them."

After Simon and Elijah had left his office, President Hayes turned to his three cabinet members and said, "I don't know about you three, but I think I need a stiff shot of brandy."

51

"You are going where?" Maggie screamed when Simon and Elijah told her about the president ordering them to accompany the naval ship going to the Faroe Islands. "Where are the Faroe Islands anyway? Ever since we got married you have been trekking off to some godforsaken place for days and weeks, leaving me to raise our son by myself and fend for myself. You told me you were through with all this treasure hunting nonsense. I can't take it any longer. If you leave me again, Thomas and I won't be here when you return, that is, if you even come back alive."

Simon noted that this is the first time she had reacted this way. Maggie was hot.

"Maggie," he tried to reason, "President Hayes has ordered Elijah and me to accompany the men who are going to recover the Viking treasure and capture the mutineers who commandeered the USS Shannon and stole the treasure. We are the ones who discovered the treasure on Baffin Island and they want us to be there to account for the contents when the sailors retrieve it. The Faroe Islands are located just off the coast of Northern Scotland and it won't take but a few days to complete the mission and return home."

Maggie had cooled off a bit, but Simon could tell she was

still angry when she said, "Simon, for once in my married life I want a husband to be here with me to help in raising our son."

"I promise you, Maggie, this will be my very last assignment and final mission because I am officially retiring from the treasure hunting business. Besides, I'm getting tired of the uncertainty of taking chances in dangerous places. I'm ready to stay at home and grow old with you and Thomas."

"And no more traveling around the universe on spaceships or whatever those silly things are," she added.

"No more riding around in spaceships," he promised.

Maggie threw herself into Simon's arms and gave him a passionate kiss. "You had better come home soon in one piece, you crazy man, or I'll shoot you myself!"

Elijah, who was with them in the same room, said to Maggie, "I will personally see that nothing happens to him and bring him back home safely."

"What are your plans, Elijah, when you return?" she asked.

"I'm going to hop on the quickest train back to California and marry a beautiful girl waiting there for me. I've decided that running a ranch is not so bad after all. Besides, I want a son just like Thomas so I can take him hunting and fishing with me."

Maggie smiled and asked. "When do both of you have to leave?"

"Secretary Thompson told us to be at the naval docks by noon tomorrow, so I'll get Sam Harmon next door to take Elijah and me in his buggy. I'm sure he won't mind."

= = = = = =

That evening, Maggie prepared a big meal for them consisting of fried chicken, roast potatoes, field peas, and biscuits with plenty of gravy. She knew how much Elijah loved gravy. She was not surprised or disappointed when Elijah devoured five biscuits smothered in chicken gravy.

The next morning, Sam was waiting outside ready for the nine-mile ride to the naval docks. Simon gave Maggie one last hug with another assurance from him that this was his very last assignment. They climbed aboard the buggy and were off. Maggie watched the buggy disappear in the distance and, like the previous trips before, she thought, *Will I ever see him again?"*

Harmon arrived at the specified dock at exactly 11:15 AM and watched as his two passengers reported to the duty officer, climbed up the gangplank, and boarded the USS Manassas. The captain, a seasoned navy officer named James Patton, greeted the new passengers by the railing on the main deck. As was customary, and as their prior military training took over, Simon and Elijah snapped to attention. "Permission to come aboard, sir."

Captain Patton responded, "Permission granted. Welcome aboard, Gentlemen. We have been expecting you. Ensign Turner will escort you to your quarters."

The Manassas was built in 1873 by Cramp Shipbuilders of Philadelphia and was an iron hulled, double ended, side-wheel Mohongo class gunboat. Its main armaments consisted of one 200 mm smoothbore Dahlgren gun, two 60 pound Parrott rifles, two 20 pounder Parrott rifles, and four 24 pounder howitzers. The ship was well equipped to defend herself.

Ensign Turner led the men down a flight of stairs to the second deck and through a passageway with cabins designated as officer and guest's quarters. Their bunk compartment was surprisingly spacious, considering they were quartered in the center of a Navy warship. It was equipped with two bunks separated by a small desk and two wooden straight back chairs.

Once settled, the two men laid out their packs and stuffed a few items into some pullout drawers. Elijah asked Simon, "I know we heard Commander Ahular say they would be departing in a few days, but did you bring the Zenox along?"

Simon reached into his pack and pulled out the small oval shaped object. "I would never leave home without it. You never know when we might need it again."

The two men were sitting there chatting when a loud knock was heard at the door.

Elijah walked over and opened the door. He was totally bowled over when a loud voice boomed out, "Surprise!"

Standing in the doorway with a big grin on his face was Professor George Scott.

"What in the hell are you doing here?" Elijah shouted. "We thought Robert Drake wanted you to stay with the museum."

"I talked him out of it and told him I needed to be here with you fellows to help with analyzing the contents of the treasure cache. He called the president to get me included on the ship. Besides, I needed to recover those other two Viking runestones we found inside the pyramid on Baffin Island…those we left with the treasure."

"Where is Jonah Steele?" Simon asked.

"He wanted to come along but Drake wouldn't let him. He said he needed someone at the museum to help him."

The men talked further for a few minutes when an unexpected figure appeared at the open doorway. "Can I come in?" a familiar voice rang out.

"It's Jonah Steele," Scott shouted. "We were just talking about you. How on earth did you get here?"

Steele stepped into the compartment. "Early this morning I slipped out of the museum and made my way to the dock. I was lucky to find a seaman's shirt and hat and slip aboard, disguised as a member of the crew. You didn't think I would miss out on another exciting journey with my adventure and treasure seeking friends, did you?"

Suddenly, they felt a slight movement of the ship. The deck hands had released the mooring lines from the pier's bollards and the USS Manassas was departing.

Elijah with his usual uneasiness with ships said, "It's getting crowded in this cabin, so let's go topside and watch as she sails down the Potomac." There were no objections.

The four men filed up the flight of steps to the main deck where they walked over to the port railing to observe the shores of the Potomac River slipping by. They were engaged in casual conversation when they heard two familiar voices approaching. Simon was the first to turn when one of the voices said, "Do you mind if we join you?"

It was none other than Captain Barnaby Swift and First Mate William Stinson from the USS Shannon standing there.

"Well, Captain Swift," Simon remarked, "For being hijacked and stranded on a barren island for several days, you and Mr. Stinson look remarkably fit."

"That's what good food and plenty of rest will do. The kind

folks in the little fishing village took very good care of us before the Navy picked us up," Swift replied.

"Can you tell us what happened?"

"Yes. We recovered all the treasure from the pyramid and got it loaded aboard the Shannon. When we left Baffin Island and entered the Labrador Sea, two of my officers and most of the crew got greedy and decided to steal the treasure for themselves. I suppose they decided they could make more money disposing of the artifacts in Europe, so we heard they headed across the North Atlantic to the Faroe Islands, which gives them easy access to England and the Scandinavian countries where the Vikings once lived."

"It's a good thing they let you live and dropped you on an island."

"Yes, we were lucky we were found by a fisherman. That so called island was nothing but a big hunk of barren rock. One of the officers was our gunnery officer, Richard Frantz and, and, the other was in charge of navigation, James Finley. We saw the murdering swine shoot two of my officers and four seamen and dump their bodies overboard. I can't wait to hang those mutinous traitors from the bowsprit or even over the side from one of the deck railings and then feed them to the sharks."

"Captain, I hope you have the opportunity," Scott remarked. "They deserve no better."

"How many men are opposing us on the Shannon?" Elijah asked.

Swift thought for a moment. "Considering the five of us who were rescued and the six other men who resisted the hijackers and were murdered, I would say there are two officers and fourteen or fifteen seamen still aboard the Shannon."

Simon commented, "From what I have observed, with the additional crew members we have on board to help you navigate the Shannon home, I would think we have enough men to handle the situation."

From the aft deck, Captain Patton saw the group of men talking on the deck below. He walked down the short flight of steps to join them. "Well, gentlemen, I see you have had a chance to rejoin and catch up on things."

"Yes," Simon said, "It's great to see that Captain Swift and Mr. Stinson have recovered from their ordeal and looking fit again."

Patton glanced at Jonah Steele. "Well, I see we have an unfamiliar face with your group. Young man, I don't recall seeing you when you came aboard."

Professor Scott picked up on this and interceded, "Mr. Steele is my assistant at the Washington museum and he accompanied us on the Baffin Island expedition to help us recover the treasure. He came aboard with me."

"I see. In that case, welcome aboard Mr. Steele. We'll make sure you are properly recorded on our passenger roster."

Simon asked, "We were all wondering about our plan of action. Can you advise us what the next step is?"

"Of course," Patton replied. "We plan to sail on a northeasterly course toward Iceland and when we reach the 60-degree latitude position, we will veer 68 degrees to the northeast which should place us just to the north end of the Faroe Islands. From there we will search for the mutineers and execute a plan of attack to recapture the USS Shannon and arrest them."

That seemed to answer the question as Captain Patton

nodded his parting and then returned to the bridge. The group glanced over at the disappearing shoreline as the USS Manassas exited the Potomac River into the Chesapeake Bay for the continuing journey around the southern tip of New Jersey and into the Atlantic.

52

Aboard the USS Shannon

Gunnery Officer Richard Frantz called his navigation officer, James Finley, into his stateroom to discuss the disposition of the treasure's artifacts. They had decided they would keep the eight chests of gold coins and distribute enough coins to the remaining crew members to satisfy their immediate needs. Their plan was to keep the rest of the coins. The chests were safely stored in a shallow cave at the southeast edge of the Slaettaratindur mountain range in the Faroe Islands. The USS Shannon was docked in a fjord and near the tiny village of Funningqur in the northern section of the main island. Frantz was satisfied the American Navy would never find them there. Once the crew members had been paid their meager share, Frantz and Finley would take the fortune in gold coins and settle somewhere in Europe with a lavish lifestyle, knowing the girls would flock to them like the seagulls that usually circled the ship.

"What about all the rest of the treasure? The gold cups, vases, trays, and all that other stuff we stored in the ship's holds?" Finley asked. "Those things have to be worth a fortune."

"I sent messengers to Oslo and Copenhagen to find us some

buyers. They each took a couple of samples with them to show the buyers the quality of the artifacts. Remember, most of these items was stolen by the Vikings in those countries and I already know some of the museums and private collectors will pay us a tidy sum for them."

"Any response yet?"

"We have a museum and an independent collector in Oslo, a German fellow I believe, who will buy the whole lot and pay us in gold kroners. We also found a museum in Copenhagen who will take some selected pieces and pay us with their gold kroners. There's no telling what the Norwegian and Danish governments would pay to get their stolen artifacts back, and I'm sure the English would also pay a handsome price for this stuff since the Vikings also occupied parts of England and looted everything valuable they could find from the nobles."

"What's our next move?" Finley asked.

"Tomorrow, we'll take the ship over to Oslo and talk to the buyers. I'm sure they'll want to come on board to look at the artifacts for themselves. We'll have them drooling over the items with several chests full of their money."

Aboard the USS Manassas

The USS Manassas was well into the North Atlantic when Captain Patton called a meeting to discuss a strategy and plan of attack. Attending was Simon, Elijah, Scott, Steele, Captain Swift, Stinson, and three of Patton's officers. They had three priorities: recover the treasure, get the navy's ship back, and capture the mutineers and their two leaders. Patton and Swift had two options with the two ringleaders of the hijackers, take them back to the states for trial or serve justice aboard the USS Shannon or Manassas. Their preference was the latter.

Addressing the group, Patton held up a map showing Scotland, and a lower portion of the Scandinavian countries, Norway, Denmark, and Sweden. The Faroe Islands were visible just above the northern tip of Scotland, just east of Norway.

"What is that group of islands just to the west of the Faroe Islands?" Elijah asked. "They look much closer to the countries where they would want to dispose of the treasure."

"Those are the Shetland Islands," Patton answered. "They are a part of Scotland and more inhabited than the Faroes. I'm sure Frantz and Finley wanted a more remote location to operate from and wanted less attention from the British Navy. It's got to be the Faroe Islands since Stinson overheard Frantz mention it."

It took the Manassas three more days to reach the Faroe archipelago and the entrance to the deep fjord slicing through the main island. The map showed the fjord provided a channel connecting the North Atlantic with the North Sea. Patton decided to take his ship through this passage, knowing Frantz would have most likely taken this route. Most of the shoreline was barren until they reached a tiny fishing village located off their starboard side. As the Manassas steered nearer to the coastline, a sizable pier was observed extending from the shore—one suitable for a larger ship.

From the bridge, the captain scanned the dock through his spyglass and noticed two men sitting on the dock with fishing poles. They were staring at his ship. The appearance of a dark blue unkempt shirt on their backs looked suspiciously out of place. They resembled part of a uniform. He handed his glass to Captain Swift standing next to him. "Do you recognize these men?" he asked.

"Yes," Swift replied angrily, "one of them was one of my gunners and the other looks familiar."

Patton shouted into the wheelhouse. "Steer the ship to that pier to our starboard and prepare for immediate landing and debarkation."

The two men, observing the large ship turning toward them, suddenly dropped the poles and then turned and took off for the shore. They recognized the ship's markings as U. S. Navy.

The navigator eased the Manassas into the dock and the gangplank was lowered. Four seamen hurried to the pier to secure the lines to the pilings. A complement of eight armed Marines disembarked with Captains Patton and Swift just behind. Simon, Elijah, Scott, and Steele trailed a short distance to the rear. "Find those two men," Patton barked. "Start with that shed up on the hill."

The little village of Funningqur sat in a shallow depression next to the fjord. The gentle rise of two small mountains sloped up on either side of the town and gave the village a degree of protection from the wind. The surrounding terrain was void of trees and heavy vegetation, but the ground was covered with lush green grass. There was little or no cover for the two renegades to hide. The shed that sat to one side of the village was a small building most likely used to store a boat and other fishing supplies. The Marines surrounded the building and Patton shouted, "We know you men are hiding in the shed so come out with your hands in the air and we won't harm you. We need some information."

There was no response.

Patton shouted again. "Come out now or our Marines will storm the shed and come in firing."

After a few tense moments, the door slowly pushed open and two heads peered out. One of the men recognized Captain Swift who was the closest to him and charged the captain. "You will not capture and hang me!" he screamed, grasping a large knife tightly in his fist. "I'll see you in hell first."

Swift was not prepared for the onslaught and would have been fatally stabbed had it not been for the quick reaction of Jonah Steele who was standing close behind him. In a flash, Steel jumped in front of Swift and dropped to one knee. He met the attacker with a shoulder slam to his midsection and then performed a quick pivot and upward body thrust. The man did a complete summersault in midair and the knife flew from his hand and fell harmlessly to the ground. He landed heavily on his back but reacted by thrusting his boot toward Jonah's groin.

The young geologist jumped to one side, missing the impact. Professor Scott, who was standing just behind the attacker, flung his arm around his neck. With his free hand clutching his chin, he gave the man's head a quick jerk to the left. The loud distinct snap was heard by everyone as his neck was cleanly broken and the man flopped lifelessly to the ground.

Steele picked up the knife and handed it to Captain Swift and said, "Here, sir, why don't you keep this as a souvenir."

Swift, a bit shaken, took the knife and then grasped Jonah

Steele's hand. "You saved my life, young man. Thank you. I don't know how I can ever repay you."

"No repayment necessary. You would have done the same for me."

Steele dropped back next to his companions and Elijah leaned over and whispered, "That was a pretty neat move you made on that guy. Was that another of those slick maneuvers you learned from that Japanese instructor?"

"Yeah, that was a defense maneuver I learned in jujutsu. You use the movement of your body to gain unexpected leverage against your opponent."

"You'll have to teach me some of those moves sometime."

The group then turned their attention to the second mutineer who was cowering against the wall of the shed. Patton shouted out, "You there, what's your name?"

"Jeb Hawkins," a frightened voice called back.

"Do you want the same treatment as your friend? We can hang you right now unless you're ready to cooperate."

"Please, don't do that to me, sir. I'll tell you what you want to know. Besides, I know where some of the treasure is hidden and it's not far from here."

Captain Swift assessed the young sailor and then said, "You know you are in very serious trouble with me and the navy. Munity and hijacking an American ship is a very serious offence and punishable by hanging. What do you have to say for yourself?"

"Sir, I did not want to be a part of this mutiny, but when I saw the two officers shoot the other officers and men I was scared for my life. I had to pretend I was going along with the other mutineers or I would be shot and tossed overboard like the others.

"What is the name of the officer in charge of this plot?" Patton asked.

"There were two of them," Hawkins answered willingly. "One was a gunnery officer named Frantz and the other was a man named Finley, James Finley I think. I believe he had something to do with navigation and steering the ship."

"Where are these men now and where is the ship they hijacked?"

"I overheard some of the men say they were heading for Oslo, Norway to meet with some buyers who have an interest in the treasure."

"You said you knew where much of the treasure was hidden on the island."

Hawkins replied, pointing toward the hill behind them, "Yes, they left the eight chests of gold coins in a cave atop that mountain. We overheard them talking how they were going to pay the crew some of the coins and keep the rest for themselves."

"Can you take us to this cave?" Captain Swift questioned.

"Yes, I can take you to the exact spot it was hidden."

Patton directed one more comment to the frightened sailor. "Hawkins, if you will lead us to the gold coins and agree to fully corporate with us, then we might consider some leniency for you."

"Thank you, sir," the hapless sailor replied. "I am definitely on your side."

53

Slaettaratindu Mountain, Faroe Island

The climb was relatively easy as Jeb Hawkins led the party up the narrow path toward the summit. Patton had his men rig a series of heavy hand poles and makeshift rope harnesses to use for carrying the heavy chests down the mountain. Simon and his three companions followed close behind with Patton and Swift next in line. A contingency of sixteen sailors and Marines were assembled to the rear of the column to carry the heavy chests down the mountain and into the holds of the Manassas.

Hawkins led them across a rarely used path and through a narrow plateau where some outcroppings abruptly rose to a higher peak. They stopped under one of the cliffs where two large boulders had been placed against the embankment.

"We need to move these rocks," Hawkins informed them. "Frantz had the men roll these in place to hide the entrance to the cave."

Four Marines surrounded the first boulder and begin to tug and pull. It slowly began to move. The rock was relatively rounded so, as it began to rotate, it started picking up speed on the downward slope. It rolled over the path and careened over the ledge. The heavy boulder plummeted down the mountain and with a huge splash plunged into the fjord. The second boulder was a bit heavier and took an extra pair of hands, but it also began to roll toward the ledge and plummet into the water below.

The opening that appeared before them was large enough for a man to pass through, so with two lanterns illuminating the way, the men filed into the cavern.

The first thing Patton and Swift noticed as they entered the shallow cave were the eight wooden chests stacked against the wall. Professor Scott's curiosity couldn't restrain him as he rushed over to the first chest and pulled open the latch to the lid. The light from the lanterns released a bright brilliance that dominated the grotto with the radiance of thousands of bright dazzling gold coins. Scott knelt and scooped up a double handful of the coins.

He examined them for a few moments and then shouted, "This is incredible! These coins are definitely Roman. I recognize the faces of the emperors Augustus, Domitian, and Antonius Pius. The Vikings must have looted these coins from the nobles and royalty of Britain when they conquered the country. Julius Caesar invaded Great Britain in 54 BC as a part of the Gallic War and the Roman Empire occupied and ruled Britain from 54 to 410 BC."

"I am impressed with your knowledge of Roman history," Patton said to Scott. "Where did you learn all of that information?"

"History books, my dear captain…history books."

Elijah couldn't resist a brief chuckle as he turned to Simon. "Captain Patton had better end this conversation now before

Professor Scott spends the next hour and a half giving the group a lecture on the history of the Roman Empire."

Apparently, Patton picked up on this possibility as he turned and instructed his men to prepare the poles and harnesses to load and carry the chests down the mountain and on to his ship.

Aboard the USS Manassas

As the chests of coins were being loaded aboard the Manassas, Patton asked Simon and Elijah to accompany him and Captain Swift to a stateroom where they wanted to question Jeb Hawkins further about the hijackers aboard the Shannon.

"When did Frantz and the ship leave for Oslo?" he asked the apprehensive seaman.

"The day before yesterday," Hawkins answered respectfully. "Based on what I heard from other crewmen, I believe they were to meet with officials from the Oslo Museum and later with an artifacts collector. I heard one of the petty officers say that once they sold and collected the money for all the artifacts, they would return and pick us up and get the chests of gold coins. Since they couldn't return to the States, he thought Frantz would take the ship into the Mediterranean Sea and try to sell the ship to France or maybe find a buyer in Rome. From there we would all be on our own to find a place to live somewhere in Europe."

"How much was he going to give you for being a part of the scheme?"

"They didn't say but they implied it would be a substantial amount for us to start a new comfortable life."

Swift remarked, "Greedy men like Frantz and Finley don't share their wealth. They might have given each of you a small handful of coins to make you think it was a handsome payoff, but I'm sure their plan was to keep most of the treasure for themselves. You sailors were fools for believing them."

"I understand, sir. I was a fool and perhaps should have taken my chances to escape from the ship, but we were at sea and there was no way off the ship or anywhere to go."

Patton asked, "Were there any more sailors who were forced into this mutiny…any who were frightened like you and wouldn't have joined the ranks had it not been for Frantz and Finley killing those officers and men?"

"I know of four others who were too frightened to resist."

"Okay, Hawkins, I believe you, so we won't press any charges for now. You are free to move about the ship but keep yourself available in case we need any more information."

"Yes, sir, I will. And thank you, sir."

As the others filed out of the room, Captain Patton walked back to the wheelhouse to see his navigator.

Chief Petty Officer Roberts looked up from the wheel at his captain who had entered the compartment. "What are your orders, sir?"

"First, I want you to contact Petty Officer Raines in the boiler room and tell him to rev up the steam for the engines. I want him to bring the ship up to full speed. And you, Helmsman, I want you to set our course for Oslo, Norway."

"Aye, Aye, sir."

Oslo, Norway

The Manassas slipped into the fjord and cruised its way through the entrance of the Oslo Bay where the USS Shannon was spotted moored to a slip on the far side of the anchorage. On Patton's instructions, the navigator eased the USS Manassas into another slip behind two large cargo ships where she would be concealed from view by the mutineers. Captains Patton and Swift held a conference with Simon and his three companions to develop a plan of action.

Swift remarked, "James, I want my ship back undamaged if possible. A direct confrontation with our big guns blazing would get the whole Norwegian Navy and Army on our ass and cause a big problem between our two governments. I would suggest we try to recapture my ship by slipping some Marines on board to round up the mutineers aboard the Shannon without drawing too much attention."

"Good idea," Patton agreed. "We can dress them in an assortment of civilian clothes and uniforms so they'll look like dock hands and some of their mutineer cohorts. Our men can carry concealed side arms so they won't arouse suspicion. Once the Shannon is secured, you and your new crew can follow them aboard to take command of the ship and sail her back home."

Simon added his comment, "We would like to accompany Captain Swift aboard the USS Shannon to inspect the treasure we found on Baffin Island…that is if those two renegade officers haven't unloaded and sold all of it. We can sail back to Washington with him."

"That's agreeable to me," Patton said.

Remembering what Jeb Hawkins told them, the mutineers

consisted of fourteen sailors led by two officers, Frantz and Finley. Patton assumed that some of the hijackers were having a good time ashore drinking in the bars located near the docks and would never suspect another American warship was in the area and enter the bay. He figured a group of twelve Marines followed by Swift's crew members should be sufficient to take command of the Shannon and capture the insurgents. The Marines would be led by 1st Lieutenant John Mason. Each man would be equipped with new Colt 1878 Frontier six shot revolvers that would be concealed until aboard the Shannon.

Adequately dressed in a disheveled assortment of clothes, they left the Manassas and in pairs made their way along the pier toward the Shannon. Led by Lt. Mason, the Marines arrived in individual small groups and made their way up the gangplank to the main deck where they spread out along the railings. The first observation indicated there were only a handful of men tending the ship who paid little attention to the boarders, thinking they were mates returning from the bars. One by one, the Marines were able to disarm three hijackers and tie and gag them in a small room beneath the bridge. Lt. Mason and two Marines entered the wheelhouse to find two more mutineers sipping on rum bottles and playing a two-handed game of poker. Looking down the barrels of three Colt Frontiers loaded with .40-44 bullets, the two men easily surrendered.

"Where are the two officers?" Mason demanded sharply. "Frantz and Finley!"

"They went into town," one of the sailors, a man named Staunton, replied meekly.

"And where is the treasure?" Mason pressed.

"Some of it is stored in a hold on the second deck, but Mr. Frantz sold some of the choice pieces to the Oslo Museum. I also overheard him telling Finley that he had a private buyer he was meeting on the ship later this afternoon. The collector was going to purchase the rest of the artifacts with gold coins."

Mason turned to one of his Marines. "Tie and gag that other man and take him down with the others…and Corporal, be sure and guard them well. We'll catch the other mutineers as they board the ship." Pointing to Staunton he said, "You are going to lead us down to the treasure, or I'll be the first one to hang you from the nearest mast."

The young seaman was terrified as he submissively replied, "Yes sir, I will show you where it is."

As Mason and the prisoners returned to the main deck, Captain Swift, First Mate Stinson, and his crew had already boarded and dispersed to their assigned stations to take control of the USS Shannon. Simon, Elijah, Scott, and Steele had also boarded with their packs. Lt. Mason advised Swift and the others about his conversation with the captive sailor and motioned for them to follow the defeated man down to the second deck and to the room that held the remaining artifacts.

As the young sailor had told them, they were pleased to find that there was still a sizeable number of artifacts still remaining.

Professor Scott was particularly interested in the two Viking runestones that they had discovered on Baffin Island and scrambled around the room in an effort to find them. He was distraught when there was no sign of the stone tablets. He turned to the young captive, Staunton. "Where are the two stone tablets that were included with the treasure?" he demanded.

"Sir, I don't know. The two officers had them but I don't remember the tablets being included with the other items the museum people hauled away. I think Frantz or Finley most likely hid them on the ship somewhere."

"I've got to find those runestones," Scott mumbled to Simon. "They might hold the key to finding more Viking treasures and artifacts."

= = = = = =

Back on the main deck, Staunton was secured and confined with the other captives. Five of the hijackers were now accounted for, and based on the count Jeb Hawkins had provided, Frantz, Finley, and seven more insurgent sailors were left to be captured. Captain Swift ordered the men to position themselves in strategic concealed positions to apprehend the mutineers as they re-boarded the ship. He was certain the wait would be short.

It was only twenty minutes when a group of three mutineers stumbled up the gangplank and onto the deck, obviously unsteadied from too much rum. They were immediately subdued, tied, and gagged and then placed with the others who had been moved to a secure converted holding cell on the third deck. The remaining sailors returned to the ship in pairs where they met the same fate as their companions. One man however, in a drunken stupor, bolted for the side and dove over the railing into the frigid water below. He never surfaced, indicating his water soaked weighted clothes dragged him down to his watery grave. There was still no sign of Frantz and Finley.

In a few more moments, a buggy drove up to the side of the ship where a dignified looking man climbed down and strolled up the gangplank. Reaching the main deck, he announced to Swift, "I am looking for Captain Frantz. He is expecting me."

The first thought that came to Swift's mind was, *looks like that traitor Frantz is trying to pass himself off as the captain of my ship.*

"Mr. Frantz is not here at the present. Can I help you, sir?" Swift replied discreetly.

"Yes, my name is Karl Bachmann and I am a private collector of ancient Viking artifacts. I am here to purchase a collection of artifacts from Captain Frantz."

"We are expecting him shortly, but if you will wait a few minutes over near the railing, he should be arriving in a few minutes."

"I will be happy to do that. I do not want to miss out on that incredible collection," Bachmann replied.

Captain Swift did not want to reveal the truth to the collector in fear that he might see Frantz on the wharf and warn him of the situation aboard ship. Swift would also stay back from the railing so Frantz or Finley wouldn't spot him. Two Marines were assigned to the side of the deck to watch for the approach of the two men. It was nearly a 30-minute wait but soon one of the Marines approached Swift and said, "Sir, there are two men approaching the ship from the direction of town."

Frantz and Finley turned toward the gangplank and made their way up to the main deck where they were confronted by ten Marines and ten Colt Frontier .40-44 caliber revolvers.

Captain Swift quickly moved out from his concealed position under the bridge. He faced the two mutinous officers and shouted, "Frantz and Finley, you are hereby under arrest for thievery, munity, murder, and treason to your country and the United States Navy."

Frantz, with a look of distress, turned to bolt down the gangplank but was blocked by four Marines who had moved around them to prevent such an escape. He tried to shove one Marine aside but was met by a clinched fist that drove into his solar plexus, knocking him to the deck. Finley, on the other hand, stood meekly to the side, realizing the ship was now in control of Captain Swift and his crew. Like the other mutineers, both men were tied and gagged and then taken to a separate holding cell on the third deck.

Artifacts collector, Karl Bachmann was horrified, not knowing what had just happened. "Why are you arresting the captain of this ship?" he shouted to Swift. "I came here to pick up the collection I purchased."

"Have you paid for it yet?" Swift asked.

"No, but I have a chest full of gold coins in the buggy."

"The deal is off," Swift informed him forcefully. "I am Captain Barnaby Swift, the real captain of the USS Shannon and these men are traitors and mutineers who stole the treasure and commandeered this ship from the United States Government. So now, Mr. Bachmann, I suggest you take your leave and return to your buggy."

The defeated man silently turned to the gangplank and departed.

While the substitute crew took over control of the ship, 1st Lieutenant Mason ordered his Marine detachment back to the USS Manassas. Captain Swift, Simon, and Elijah followed them for the purpose of thanking Captain Patton for his help in re-capturing the Viking treasure and USS Shannon and putting an end to the rebellious affair.

= = = = = =

Within the hour, the USS Manassas left the Oslo Bay for the return voyage home and Captain Swift and the two treasure hunters returned to the deck of the USS Shannon. From the bridge, Swift ordered all hands to pull the gangplank and prepare to make sail. The destination was the naval docks in Washington D.C.

The ship sailed from the entrance of the Oslo Fjord and well into the North Sea when Captain Swift called Simon, Elijah, Steele, and Professor Scott to his stateroom. "It's time we interrogate Mr. Frantz and Finley. I would like for you to come along. We'll be accompanied by my first mate, William Stinson, and some guards."

In a separate room on the first deck, the two mutineers were brought before Captain Swift and the others in the room. Four

armed seamen were standing behind the two prisoners to en-
sure security. Directing the first question to Frantz, Swift asked,
"Why did you decide to steal the Viking treasure and seize my
ship? You murdered six of my men in the process."

There was no answer from Frantz.

Swift was getting angry. "Why the hell did you leave me and
First Mate Stinson on that deserted rock without food or water
and left to die?"

There was still no response from Frantz as he stared at the
captain with a cruel looking smirk.

"What did you do with the money you received from the
Oslo Museum for the artifacts you sold and where are the two
runestone tablets that were with the treasure?" Still no answer.

The captain was reaching the limit of his patience. "Damn
you, you murdering traitor, answer my questions or else?" he
yelled.

Frantz roared back, "Go to hell, Swift!" Then he spat toward
the captain.

Swift sat back down, trying to regain his composure. He
then stood back up and announced, "I hereby declare this inquiry is now terminated and we shall immediately begin the trial of
Gunnery Officer Richard Frantz who is accused of theft of government property, mutiny by hijacking a first line warship from
the U.S. Navy, abandoning his ranking officer and first mate on a
deserted island to die, the murder of two of my officers and four
innocent seamen, and gross insubordination to a ranking officer.
What have you to say for yourself, Officer Frantz?"

"I'll repeat it again," he screeched. "Go to hell, Swift."

Captain Swift replied as calmly as possible. "Officer Frantz, your actions today confirm your admission of guilt, therefore you give me no choice but to find you guilty of all charges. As captain of the USS Shannon and commander in charge of a U.S. Navy warship at sea, I hereby sentence you to immediately be taken to the main deck where you will be hanged from a yardarm on the main mast."

He then turned to his first mate. "Mr. Stinson, you and the guards may now escort Mr. Frantz to the main deck to prepare for the execution…we will join you on deck shortly."

After the men had departed with the prisoner, Swift turned to James Finley and said, "Now, Mr. Finley, will you tell us what we want to know or would you prefer the same fate as Mr. Frantz?"

After witnessing what had happened to his accomplice, Finley was totally defeated and scared out of his wits. He meekly announced, "Yes, sir, Captain Swift, I will tell you everything you want to know. The chests of gold Norwegian kroners paid by the Oslo museum and the two stone tablets are hidden in a secret compartment on the bottom deck near the bow of the ship. I will take you there, but I beg of you, please spare my life."

Looking at Finley with a cold glare, Swift replied, "When we have possession of the gold coins and stone tablets I will make that decision."

54

Captain Swift led Simon and his companions to the center of the main deck where two sailors were attaching a rope and noose to a yardarm connected to the main mast. Frantz, who was being restrained by three sailors, saw the captain on deck and screamed at the top of his voice, "I should have killed you when I dumped you and Stinson on that rock. It's a shame you didn't die like you were supposed to."

This hit a raw nerve in Swift, who shouted to the officer in charge of the execution, "Hold up on the hanging of the prisoner. I have a better idea. I have changed the method of punishment. My new sentence will be the same punishment that was used by pirate captains on the old sailing ships. My new sentence for traitor Frantz is death by keelhauling."

"You can't do that," Frantz screamed. "Keelhauling was outlawed by the navy years ago."

"Watch me, you murdering swine," Swift shouted back.

On First Mate Stinson's command, two sailors carried a long rope to the bow and attached a weight to the center to allow the rope to sink beneath the keel. It was then passed under the bowsprit and lowered below the bow and then dragged along both the port and starboard rails to the center of the ship where it looped over the railings on each side of the main deck. Frantz was pushed to his knees where one end of the rope was securely fastened to his wrists and the other end to his ankles.

The man was defiant to the end as he continued to toss and heave and yell obscenities at Swift and the crew members. Two sailors picked up the screaming mutineer and slung him over the side where he hung by the rope attached to his wrists. Then on command, three seamen on the opposite side of the ship began to pull on the rope, causing Frantz to be lowered down the side and toward the frigid water below. Soon he was submerged and disappeared from view.

As the men on deck continued to pull the rope, Frantz was dragged along the keel and under the ship to the port side. They then reversed the direction of the rope and pulled his body back to the starboard side of the ship. The crusted barnacles attached to the hull ripped through his clothing and tore strips of flesh from his back, buttocks, and legs. With his body torn apart, the murderer quickly drowned and was dead on the second pass. The ropes were cut from his limbs and the shattered body of Richard Frantz settled toward the bottom.

Justice had been served as Captain Swift peered over the side into the blood-stained water below and whispered, "I commence you to the deep."

Jonah Steele leaned over and whispered to Elijah, "It looks like the poor bastard got himself overhydrated."

"What's that supposed to mean?"

Steel replied with a devilish grin. "It means the bloody fool drank more water than he could handle."

Another idea came to Swift as he turned to First Mate Stinson. "What was the name of that young sailor we met on the Faroe Islands, the one who led us to the gold coins hidden in that cave?"

"I believe his name was Hawkins...Jeb Hawkins."

"Bring him to me," Swift ordered.

Young Hawkins, who had witnessed the execution, was shaking with fear that his fate would be the same as Frantz when he faced the captain.

"Oh, please spare me, sir," he pleaded.

Swift noticed his fright and chuckled a bit as he said, "Don't worry about that Mr. Hawkins. You convinced me that Frantz forced you into the mutiny and you did freely provide us with valuable information and helped us recover the chests of coins on Faroe Island. I do believe you were a victim caught up in the devious plot so I hereby exonerate you of your participation in the mutiny and grant you your freedom. You will rejoin my crew in your prior duty capacity."

"Oh, thank you, sir," a greatly relieved Jeb Hawkins replied. "I promise to be a loyal member of your crew."

"And Mr. Hawkins," Swift added as an afterthought. "If you will identify the four seamen being held who were forced into the mutiny against their will, I would like to talk to each one of them so I can make proper judgment of their degree of guilt."

"Yes, sir, I will be very happy to do that."

Captain Swift and Stinson then turned to James Finley, who had also witnessed the execution event. The officers ordered him to take them to the hidden cache of gold coins and runestones. Simon, Elijah, Steele, and Professor Scott were asked to join them. Finley led the group down three flights of steps until they got to the boiler room level, then he turned toward the bow. He stopped in front of a reinforcing strut that covered a hidden compartment next to the bow's inner plates. Finley reached behind the strut and opened a small door leading into a compartment just big enough to accommodate one man.

A lantern provided just enough light to clearly see three small chests and the two runestones stacked close together. Professor Scott couldn't stand the suspense as he inched forward and stooped down to grab the handle of a chest. He was able to slide it toward the door where Stinson and Elijah picked it up and moved it to one side. With the other two chests removed, Scott grabbed the two stone tablets and held them gently, like they were newborn babes. With help from sailors in the boiler room, the chests were carried up the three flights of steps where they were taken to Swift's stateroom and deposited in a large safe. With the two tablets in hand, Professor Scott and Jonah Steele retired to their cabin while Simon and Elijah went to their quarters to get some much-needed sleep.

Scott was dead tired but determined to begin translation on the runestones. Steele climbed into his bunk and was asleep in minutes, but Scott reached into his pack and retrieved the Nordic translation booklet given to him by the Scandinavian professor, Asbjørn Ulvestad.

It was a tedious and very difficult task matching the runes on the tablet to a corresponding inscription in the book. Many of the symbols looked similar and many had more than one translation. He worked on the first tablet for the next two hours before sleep finally overtook him.

Early the next morning, Scott was up early. Dressed, he followed Steele to the mess hall where Simon and Elijah had started eating breakfast. "Did you start on the translations yet," Simon asked, already knowing the answer.

"Yes, I got started on one tablet, but only got four or five runes interpreted before I fell asleep. I'll get back on it right after breakfast."

Back in his room, Scott went back to the mind-numbing task of translating. It took him four hours to get half way through the tablet, but the results so far were discouraging, with no reference to gold or treasure. The initial translation appeared to describe one of the Viking's longboat voyages to the new world with a Viking chief named Valdemar. That evening Scott returned to the task and by midnight he had completed translating the first runestone. As he viewed his notes, the completed translation confirmed the account of a Viking longboat landing on the shores of Greenland where a settlement had begun to be built.

The next morning, the USS Shannon was well into the North Atlantic when Scott began translation on the second runestone. The number of inscriptions appeared to be shorter, giving him a bit of encouragement that he could complete the interpretation by evening. He spent most of the day working on the tablet and, after a brief dinner, he was back to the chore of translating the ancient Nordic runes. It was midnight when he finished the translation. Looking at the piece of paper he was using to record the interpreted symbols, he shook his head in disbelief, "This can't be...I'd better recheck this. I'm dead tired, so I'll do it in the morning."

= = = = = =

The next morning, the ship's navigator estimated the USS Shannon had three more days of sailing before reaching their Washington D.C. destination. Captain Swift called his first mate Stinson, Simon, and Elijah into his stateroom for a brief meeting. He wanted to make sure that everyone understood how the treasure was to be distributed. His first priority was to make sure the mutineer prisoners were turned over to the proper naval security officials. He was certain a court martial would ensue and proper punishment would be handed out, depending on the degree of each man's involvement in the mutiny.

After a personal interview with each of the four sailors Hawkins had identified, Captain Swift decided that in fear for their lives they had been forced against their will into the mutiny by Frantz and Finley. The captain exonerated each man and returned him to duty.

Those who encouraged the theft and hijacking would be dealt with more severely. Finley, who was one of the ringleaders, would probably receive a long prison sentence unless the navy decided to hang him as a traitor to his country. Frantz was lying at the bottom of the North Sea, so he was no longer a concern.

= = = = = =

In his stateroom, Swift begin the conversation. "When we went to pay our respects to Captain Patton just before they disembarked, he and I discussed the disposition of the treasure. The chests of gold coins we captured in the Faroe Islands are still in the hold of the Manassas. Mr. Patton plans to turn these chests over to President Hayes and the U.S. Treasury Department. The three chests of gold coins we retrieved that Frantz received for payment from the Oslo Museum will also go to the treasury department. Since many of the artifact items were originally stolen by the Vikings and most likely came from many Norwegian estates, the Oslo Museum is entitled to them and can keep the pieces they bought from Frantz. This will spare us any international incident with Norway and I'm sure their citizens will enjoy viewing the treasures in the museum."

"What about the rest of the artifacts that we have in the hold of the USS Shannon?" Elijah asked.

Swift answered, "I'm sure your Professor Scott and Curator Robert Drake will be pleased to know we received authority to turn them over to the Washington museum for our citizens to enjoy for generations."

= = = = = =

Back in Scott's cabin, Jonah Steele had returned to the room. He had been topside, not wanting to disturb the professor's concentration in translating the tablets. Steele was intrigued to find Scott with a huge smile on his face and a piece of paper with some words scribbled on it.

"Where are Simon and Elijah?" he asked anxiously.

"I believe they are having a conference with Captain Swift in his stateroom," Steele replied.

Waving the piece of paper over his head, Scott shouted, "Let's go find them immediately. I finished the translation of the runestones and they have got to see this," he said as he handed the young geologist the piece of paper. Steele glanced down and read the words and then he gasped.

55

A sudden knock on the captain's cabin door stopped the conversation. "Come in," Swift shouted with a hint of annoyance.

An ensign entered the room with Professor Scott and Steele following behind. The young officer announced, "Sir, I'm sorry to interrupt you, but these two gentlemen said it is most urgent that they see you and your guests immediately."

"That's okay, Ensign. That will be all." he replied as he motioned for Scott and Steele to come in. "Mr. Scott, what is so important that you interrupt our meeting?"

"Captain, I have translated both runestones. The first tablet gives a brief narrative of a Viking chieftain named Valdemar and his voyage to Greenland, but the second tablet is the one that is most intriguing. Apparently, the scribe who carved the symbols onto the runestone was most poetic, highly unusual for the Vikings. I had to interpolate a few of the runes into English, but I'm sure the translation is accurate."

He laid the piece of paper on the table for all of them to read.

Through the wall of rock our treasures lie,
Through the wall of fire our warriors die.

"Wonder what it means?" Elijah asked curiously.

"Can't you see it?" Scott replied. "Those are definite clues to a large cache of more hidden Viking treasures. I suspect this may be their main cache. Now all we have to do is figure out what they mean and the location the clues are referring to. Any suggestions?"

Jonah Steele, who had seen the paper a few minutes earlier, had a little time to think about it and offered a theory. "The first clue is 'through the rock.' To me this means the treasure is hidden behind a rock barrier and we would have to somehow pass through the barrier to find it. More logically, it would refer to something underground like a cave or cavern which is surrounded by solid rock."

"That makes the most sense to me," Simon agreed.

Swift and Stinson concurred by nodding their heads.

"What about the 'wall of fire?' Elijah questioned. "If it is anything like that river of lava we encountered underneath the Toltec pyramid in the Yucatan, then you would think they would have used the term 'river' or 'stream' instead of 'wall' of fire.' This tells me it might not be a continuous flow of lava but something entirely different."

"What else would constitute the use of fire?" Stinson asked. "It would have to be something more permanent, certainly not like a forest fire that doesn't burn very long."

Steele had another thought. "If the first clue involves an underground cave or cavern, then the only thing that would constitute the presence of fire would have to be molten lava. If it's not a river of lava, it has to be molten lava coming from another source that created a wall of fire the Vikings refer to on the runestone. If their warriors tried to pass through molten lava they would die."

Simon spoke up. "I think the first thing we need to do is concentrate on the location. Where would we look for a place that had a cavern with the presence of molten lava?"

The answer came to Professor Scott and Jonah Steele at the same time as they both blurted out, "The hidden valley on Baffin Island."

"That's the place where you found the Viking city and hidden treasure," Captain Swift emphasized.

"Yes, Simon agreed. "It has to be Baffin Island. When we were on the space ship, Commander Ahular told us that particular valley is one of the locations of hot spots. Those are places where the molten magma from the center of the earth pushes up close enough to the earth's surface to create unusual heat anomalies. That's why the air temperature and water is so warm in that valley, even though the place is located fairly close the Arctic Circle. He called it thermal vents and the water was warmed by what he referred to as hydrothermal vents. He also told us there are other hot spots in different locations on earth and he made particular reference to a hot spot in our Wyoming territory that shoots plumes of hot water into the air. He said that they had visited the place a couple of times."

Scott recalled, "I remember he called them water spouts and even referred to one as a geyser. That valley on Baffin Island is honeycombed with caves, so all we have to do is find the right one. I guess we'll find out what the wall of fire is when we find the cave and hopefully the treasure," he concluded.

Captain Swift, who had mostly listened through the conversation, finally intervened. "Well, Gentlemen, that settles it. Once we unload our prisoners and deliver the gold to the treasury and the artifacts to the museum, we'll re-provision the ship and set sail for Baffin Island. You will have a couple of days to get your supplies and personal affairs together. As bad as President Hayes wants more gold for the treasury, we'll have no problem getting the navy to reassign this ship for the mission."

= = = = = =

It took the USS Shannon exactly two more days to enter the Chesapeake Bay, sail up the Potomac River, and maneuver into a pier at the Washington Docks. Captain Swift had the mutineer prisoners brought on deck where they were turned over to a special navy provost guard detachment. They were taken to a naval confinement facility where they would be held until a general court martial could be convened.

Swift dismissed the crew for two days of shore leave. Young Jeb Hawkins and his four exonerated sailor friends who Swift assigned back to normal duty, would have a lot to celebrate.

This would also give Swift time to replenish the vacant positions in the crew to give the USS Shannon a full complement of men. This also gave Simon time to go to Bladensburg, Maryland to see his wife Maggie and young son Thomas. His cousin, Elijah, went with him.

"What do you mean you have to go on one more voyage up to Baffin Island? You've been gone for three weeks and you still want to go on another adventure. I feel like I don't have a husband anymore."

"Maggie, I promise this is my last assignment because I am officially retiring from the treasure seeking business after this."

"That is what you said last time."

"I mean it this time. Cousin Elijah is also finished with this adventure business. He told me he is going back to the ranch in California and marry his girlfriend, Rosita."

"Simon, I need a husband and Thomas needs his father. What is so important about this trip?" she asked.

"Professor Scott has translated a runestone that has clues to another vast Viking treasure hidden on Baffin Island. President Hayes wants us to recover that treasure to help reinforce the gold standard he has been so passionately trying to stabilize. He thinks the gold from this treasure will do the trick."

"When do you have to leave?" she asked.

"The USS Shannon departs day after tomorrow and we have to be aboard ship by noon."

"Will this trip be dangerous?" she asked."

"No," he said." It will only be a quick recovery operation that shouldn't take over a week or so. I'll be home very soon and promise I will be a good faithful husband to help you raise our son. I also promise this is the last expedition. It's time I settle down as a good family man."

"Well, okay," she said with some reservations as she threw herself into Simon's arms. She then added, "The last time? Promise?"

"Yes, the very last expedition. I promise."

Elijah, who was sitting in the parlor sipping on a tumbler of Simon's Buckhorn Creek bourbon, overheard the conversation in the kitchen and murmured to himself, "Good Grief! I sure hope he can live up to that promise or Maggie is going to have his head."

= = = = = =

Departure day came quickly and, again with the help of neighbor Sam Harmon, Simon and Elijah got back to the docks and boarded the ship forty minutes early. Professor Scott and Jonah Steele arrived fifteen minutes later. After stowing their gear in their same assigned cabins, the four men met on the main deck to watch the ship depart. Simon was anxious to hear how the Viking artifacts were received by curator Robert Drake and the Washington museum.

As Simon and Elijah stood by the starboard railing, the short voyage down the Potomac River brought back vivid memories of their past expeditions, especially their departure for their Amazon River adventure five years earlier. As they sailed by Mt. Vernon, Simon made a mental note that when Thomas got older he would take him and Maggie to visit the magnificent home of George Washington.

He turned to Professor Scott. "What did Robert Drake think of the Viking artifacts?"

"The curator was ecstatic," the professor replied. "There were enough artifacts turned over to the museum to keep us busy for the next two years, especially the research that will be needed to identify each item and tag them for display. Drake suggested that a special section would be needed to explain the Viking connection and the history of the pieces."

= = = = = =

It didn't take long for the ship to enter the Chesapeake Bay where a view of the 1864 St. Charles Lighthouse stood proudly in the distance. The short trip south brought the USS Shannon warship around the tip of the Virginia's Eastern Shore peninsula and into the Atlantic Ocean where it turned due north, bound for the Labrador Sea and Baffin Island. Little did they suspect that another harrowing adventure was about to begin.

56

The Hidden Valley on Baffin Island

Once again entering the Cumberland Sound, the ship slowly made its way to the fjord and cavern entrance that led to the hidden valley and lost Viking settlement. Two longboats were lowered and occupied by Simon, Elijah, Scott, and Steele, accompanied by two armed sailors and two rowers in one boat and First Mate Stinson and seven sailors in the second. As before, Captain Swift elected to stay with his ship.

Entering the large chamber just beyond the entrance, Scott was the first to spot the hull of the Viking ship sitting on a dry strip of land at the edge of the water. "We have got to figure a way to get the remains of that Viking longboat back to the museum," he said. "It would be a sensational addition to the Viking collection."

"Let's concentrate on finding the treasure first," Simon reminded him, "and then we can worry about the boat."

Luckily, their timing was good because the high tide allowed the seamen to paddle the boats easily up the underground stream and into the lake where the statue of the Viking god Thor stared down on them like a menacing demon ready to hurl his battle axe. Both boats were pulled ashore and the men assembled near the statue to discuss their strategy. Aside from Simon, his three companions, and First Mate Stinson, there were eleven armed sailors ready to help them search for an entrance to a cave that would lead them to the cache. Simon pulled out the piece of paper listing the clues and read them to the group.

Through the wall of rock our treasures lie,
Through the wall of fire our warriors die

There was a stirring among the seamen, especially hearing the line that referenced to the wall of fire where warriors die. It suggested something very sinister and dangerous, most likely blocking a passage where the treasure lay... something very deadly that could easily kill a man.

This part of the clue was the most mystifying, but to the young geologist, Steele, he reasoned that since the valley was located within a geological "hot spot" the source of the fire had to be molten lava. Perhaps the lava had subsided over the years... hopefully if they could find the right cave they would know if the threat was real.

Simon assured the men that the Vikings had to have found a route around the wall of fire in order to be able to store the treasures on the other side. If the Vikings found out how to get around this obstacle, then Simon and his party could certainly find the passage to the other side.

= = = = = =

The first order of business was to break the group up into search teams that would have to explore the entire perimeter of cliffs surrounding the valley. Assigning two men to a team, Simon and Scott broke the group into eight units and instructed them to a specific section of cliffs to examine. The cliffs overlooking the lake were mostly inaccessible and Simon reasoned that the Vikings would not have had the ability to transfer and cache the heavy loads of treasure from the water. Scanning the bluffs from across the lake showed no signs of any entrance to a cave anyway. This section was eliminated.

Simon and Elijah comprised one team, Scott and Steele, another, Stinson and young Jeb Hawkins a third and the rest of the sailors were broken into five more teams. Since the precipices around the valley were lined with numerous caves, it was assumed the entrance they were looking for would be close to ground level due to the heavy weight of the containers of gold. The Vikings would not have been able to lift the chests very high in the air.

Each team was advised to check out each entrance carefully, and if accessible, enter the cave to determine if a passageway extended beyond the entry where the height of a man could have hauled heavy chests through the passageway. Steele suggested that most of the caves would most likely be a dead-end and could be eliminated. Each team knew their assignment, so they dispersed to their designated areas. The search was on.

= = = = = =

By late afternoon, it was apparent that the searchers were finding it more difficult than they had expected. Of all the cave openings explored, not one of them had a passageway large enough for men or heavy chests to pass through. The caves they examined were dead ends surrounding nothing more than a hollow cavity. Of the four possibilities that were found, the passageway only extended for no more than a few yards until they stopped at solid rock walls. It was early evening when Simon called for a halt to allow the men to cook some dinner. The search would continue in the morning.

That evening around the campfire, Simon asked Steele, "You are the geologist and expert on caves, what do you think?"

"This valley has to be the location," he answered. "The *wall of fire* clue confirms it because according to what Commander Ahular told us, this valley is the only hotspot the Vikings could have encountered during their period of occupation. I'm thinking that the reason we found that treasure stowed in the pyramid was that it was probably used as a storage facility to stockpile the gold and artifacts that was to be moved into the cache deep within the rock cliffs. For some reason, the Vikings never got the chance to move it. Tomorrow, I think we should concentrate our search to the northern part of the valley." The others agreed.

= = = = = =

As Steele suggested, the next morning the plan was to concentrate the search toward the north end of the valley, closer to the pre-Columbian pyramid. With eight teams scanning the cliffs, Simon and Stinson felt their chances were fairly good that an entrance would be found to the treasure cache referred to on the runestone. The teams spread out to their designated sections, but by noon nothing promising was located. A few small openings led to small caves but again, all ended with enclosed spaces confined by solid rock. Simon and Stinson's frustration were mounting as they met with Elijah, Scott, and Steele at the base of the pyramid to discuss their options.

Simon turned to the young geologist, Jonah Steele. "Any suggestions Mr. Geologist? We keep running into dead ends."

"Somewhere in this valley there has to be an entrance to a cave that will lead us to that treasure cache. I'm thinking that the Vikings did a pretty good job of sealing and disguising the entrance. All we have to do is find the right one."

"Do you think the entrance could be somewhere other than the side of a cliff?" Elijah asked. "We've searched every stinking square inch of the rock walls that surrounds this valley."

The thought hit Professor Scott like a lightning bolt. "Of course," he shouted excitedly. "The pyramid is where we found treasure and runestones. A hidden entrance in the walls of that lower room in the pyramid would be the closest spot from where the Vikings could move the heavy chests of treasure. The chests we found were probably stored there to later move to a more secure place inside the cliffs."

"Worth a try," Simon concurred. "Let's go check it out."

After gathering the search teams together, the group walked over to the pyramid and entered through the doorway into the large center chamber. The panel stone in the center of the room that they had discovered and lifted during their previous visit was still set aside like they had left it. The steps leading down to the lower room allowed them an easy access to ascend to the lower level where the previous Viking treasure and artifacts had been stored. The chamber was located below ground level so the search would begin at the north end, facing the cliffs.

Two of the seamen were left on the upper level to provide security and make sure the mission was not compromised by possible intruders. The search would be conducted by Simon, his three companions, Stinson, and the remaining five sailors.

The ancient Indians who had constructed the pyramid had dug out the lower level and lined the walls with heavy stone blocks measuring about 2' x 3'. The blocks had been set into place in a remarkably uniform pattern, attributing to the amazing skills of the ancient builders. The challenge was to find a spot where they could be removed to expose an entrance to a passageway that would lead them into the cliffs and hopefully to a large cavern beyond. The clue about the wall of fire was still the biggest mystery, one that would not be solved until they encountered it… that is, if it still existed.

Starting at each end of the wall, Jonah Steele and Professor Scott, followed by Simon and Elijah, began their search along the stacked courses of stone.

"Pay attention to the seams," Steele instructed. "Look for any irregularities or anything out of place like an open crack or stone block slightly ajar. It would most likely be at eye level or lower."

The room remained deathly quiet and the suspense mounted for several minutes as the four men probed along the wall.

Elijah was the first to spot it as he blurted out, "I think I found something."

The others rushed over to the center of the wall and noticed a slight unevenness in one of the blocks. Steele ran his fingers along the seam and felt the slight protrusion at one edge as the block was pushed out ever so slightly. There was a thin vertical crack noticeable with a distinct line of darkness discernible behind the stone.

"We need something like a thin crowbar to squeeze into that crack so we can try to move the stone. Is there anything like that handy? Perhaps a heavy knife would do."

"How about using one of those discarded Viking sword blades lying around upstairs?" Scott suggested. "They forged their swords into pretty strong steel."

"Yes," Steele replied as he turned toward the steps.

In a few minutes, he returned with two blades in his hands. One was broken off at the hilt, but the other still remarkably intact. Since there was no mortar to contend with, he rammed the point of the first blade into the crack and with some steady pressure, started to lever it toward the adjoining block. The block was tight and wouldn't budge. One of the seamen looking on, a stout young man, said, "Sir, let me try it."

Steele moved aside as the sailor grabbed the upper part of the blade and began to push. "Push harder, Sam," one of his ship mates yelled from the crowd looking on. The young man put his weight into the blade and suddenly the stone nudged forward a bit. He increased the pressure and the stone block moved even more. With continued pressure, the stone pivoted out far enough to where he could stick his hands in the hole and grasp the back edge. He continued to pull and suddenly it broke loose and fell to the floor.

A pitch-black rectangle of darkness appeared behind the breach, indicating a cavity behind the wall. Three more sailors joined their shipmate and began to pull on the adjoining blocks. More stone blocks broke loose and fell to the floor. Soon a large opening appeared, adequate enough to allow Steele and Scott to squeeze through. A lantern was passed through the hole and the illumination indicated they were standing in a large cavern with another sizable entrance at the far end that appeared to lead to another dark passageway disappearing into the wall.

"Wow!" Elijah commented loudly, "Those Vikings sure forged good steel."

Simon was ecstatic as he shouted, "Congratulations, Mr. Steele. Your theory was correct...you did it! Now, let's go find that Viking treasure."

57

With two armed sailors assigned to stay back and guard the entrance to the cave, the other thirteen men filed through the opening and into the cavern where the passageway began its curving route into the cliffs. Steele wanted to take the lead so he could study the strata of the rock walls to determine the type and changes in the layers as they proceeded. As he figured, the rock composition was plutonic igneous indicating the source was of a volcanic origin, cooled and solidified underground. As they proceeded, he noticed the rock became lighter in color and the texture identified the strata as granite, confirming to him the cave had led them well into the cliff face.

The temperature was unusually warm for a cave of this type, indicating the presence of hot lava flows nearby. "What do you think, Jonah?" Simon asked. "I think it's getting hotter down in this hole."

"I think we're getting close to a hot magma deposit, so we had better be vigil and keep our eyes open."

After a brief rest break, the procession moved deeper and deeper underground until they came to a narrow fissure in the wall. Hot foul smelling air was being expelled from the hole. "We have some hot lava nearby," Steele warned. "This whole place reeks of the smell of sulfur."

As they came to a slight bend, the corridor began to gradually widen and a dull flickering light was seen flashing erratically along the walls. Steele led the men cautiously around the bend where the passage abruptly halted next to a deep crevice spreading across the path. A constant radiance of bright light was coming from deep within the hole and brightening up the whole space around them.

Just beyond the fissure, the passageway continued to widen, turning the narrow cavity into a large deep cavern. A seaman edged his way to the front and confidently said, "That fissure only looks to be about five feet wide and I can easily jump over that."

Before Steele had a chance to voice a warning, the man lurched forward and took a high leap into the air. Suddenly, there was a loud hissing and rumbling noise as three heavy streams of hot lava came shooting out of the wall through some blowholes. The streams struck the man broadside. The molten lava engulfed his entire body, igniting it like a torch and the ill-fated seaman dropped through the fissure in the floor. He was nothing but a burning cinder when he splashed into the white-hot lava flow below.

As the lava streams subsided, the passage appeared clear for several moments, but soon another hissing noise sounded and three more blasts of hot molten lava were hurled from the wall and splashed against the opposite wall, allowing the lava to stream back down into the fissure.

Steele counted between the bursts and found them to erupt in five to seven second intervals. He reasoned that for the lava to be expelled that quickly through the holes meant the flow had to build up a tremendous force within the tube and with a very fast rate of pressure.

Simon turned to the sailors and shouted. "Does anyone else want to be a hero and turn themselves into flaming ball of fire?"

The men were silent for a few seconds while they absorbed the horror they had just witnessed.

"I thought not," Simon said. "This place is a very different and dangerous unknown mystery to us, so you don't want to try anything heroic or you might end up like your shipmate who turned himself into ashes."

"Good grief!" a man in the rear shouted frantically. "Weldon shouldn't have tried to jump over that crevasse. He didn't have a chance. This has to be the *Wall of Fire* described on the stone tablet you told us about."

"Jonah, what's causing those streams of lava to launch across the passageway with such terrific force?" Simon asked. "It's like they're being blown out of a cannon."

Steele replied, "Apparently, the molten magma is being forced up inside the wall through a hollow column and it builds up enough pressure to be hurled out of those blowholes and across the shaft to the other wall. I've never seen anything like it before. It shoots out in strong spurts when the pressure gets strong enough to blow it out through the holes about every five seconds. No wonder the Vikings described it as the *wall of fire where warriors die*. We've just witnessed a geological anomaly. This thing is a real death trap."

Professor Scott was getting impatient. "How are we going to get past this fire trap?" he asked, pointing across to the other side of the crevasse. "I have a feeling that there is a huge cache of treasure waiting for us over there…and maybe some more runestones."

"Remember the clues on the tablet," Steele reminded him. *"Through the wall of rock our treasures lie."*

Scott's perplexed expression indicated he was still unsure of how to interpret the meaning. It seemed the others didn't either.

Steele tried to explain his thoughts. "If we can't cross the wall of fire, then we have to find another way around the crevasse. The first clue tells us there is a way through the wall of rock to the other side and that can only mean there has to be another tunnel or shaft around the fire pit…one that was large enough to allow the Vikings to carry the heavy chests of gold."

"So how do we find it?" Elijah questioned.

"We'll have to search every square inch of the walls, ceiling, and floor of the passageway and see if we can find some sort of a trigger to open a doorway. Let's fan out and see if we can find it."

Elijah leaned toward Simon. "Where is Santos when we need him? He could spot those switches anywhere, just like he did in that pyramid in Mexico and the ones he spotted in Peru."

The group began their search along the walls for anything that could trigger the opening of a doorway. Steele told the men to look for anything that looked out of place, like a projection, indentation, cavity, button, lever, or anything that could be moved or pressed.

It took about twenty minutes when the voice of Jeb Hawkins boomed out. "Over here! I think I've found something."

The men quickly assembled around Hawkins where he was pointing to a small indentation in the wall. In the center was a tiny flat stone, definitely not part of the smooth rock surface surrounding it.

"Let me take a look," Simon said as he positioned himself for a closer look. "This looks like a similar device we saw in a shaft in Mexico. Stand back and let's see if I can activate something."

He pressed the stone with his thumb. Nothing happened. He pressed it a little harder…still nothing.

"It's definitely not a part of the rock around it," Scott observed. "Let me try it."

He pulled out a hunting knife from his pack and tapped the stone with the metal butt tab in an attempt to break any seal that had been formed over several hundred years of disuse. With both hands, Scott then placed his thumb over the stone and pushed hard. He felt a slight movement. He pushed again and suddenly the stone compressed deep into the surface with a dull clunk.

The men stood there in anticipation of seeing something dramatic happen, but there was only silence.

"Nothing is happening," a voice shouted out from the rear.

Simon answered, "If this device is like the ones we saw in Mexico and Peru, it takes time for the sequence of events to take place to move objects like a heavy stone panel."

It seemed like an hour but within a few seconds a deep rumble and scraping noise was heard coming from deep within the wall. A thick door panel began to move outward, revealing another dark shaft extending beyond the wall. "This is ingenious," First Mate Stinson shouted. "How on earth did a bunch of Vikings figure out how to do this?"

"They didn't," Simon answered. "This door panel device was

built by the ancient Indians long before the Vikings came to North America. It is similar to the devices we saw in Mexico built by the Mayans and Toltecs. They learned the use of weights and balances to move stones and levers to use in their pyramids and other secret caverns used for burial sites and storage rooms. There must have been some sort of communication between the pre-Columbian Indians in Mexico and their northern Inuit counterparts in the north to be able to create this device on Baffin Island."

"I have to agree," Scott remarked. "All of these similar building techniques had to come from some sort of common intelligence. When you look at the ancient Egyptian pyramids and the pre-Columbian pyramids in Central and South America, you see some astonishing similarities. This is especially interesting when you consider the Egyptian pyramids were built about 2,500 years earlier and 7,500 miles apart from those by the early Indian civilizations in Mexico. It sure makes you wonder, doesn't it?"

All Stinson could do was shake his head and mumble, "Amazing, simply amazing."

= = = = = =

With lantern in hand, Simon was the first to enter the doorway to discover a small alcove area that led to steps ascending upward. Steele was close behind him. Glancing at the inclined shaft above him the geologist remarked, "I guess this solves the first clue on the runestone, through the wall of rock our treasures lie."

Simon then turned to the men milling around the opening and said, "Now, Gentlemen, if you'll follow me in single file up these steps, we shall proceed beyond the wall of fire and see if we can find that treasure."

58

The climb up the steps was not too bad, considering the alternative of jumping through a blast of hot lava. After seeing their shipmate disintegrate in a ball of fire, the sailors knew better than to try anything foolish. They gladly fell into line and followed Simon and Steele up the steps where the shaft leveled out and crossed over the spot where the lava jets were blasted from the wall. Steele, continuing to take the lead, noticed a change in the floor. Instead of the rock surface they had been walking on, the ground turned into a uniform pattern of stone panels set tightly together. How odd, he thought. Perhaps the builders constructed this section as a bridge over the fiery crevasse.

After several more steps, he heard an ominous click and suddenly the ground opened up beneath him, hurling him down through the opening. His spontaneous yell alerted Simon who looked up in time to see the young geologist disappear through the floor.

"Jonah!" he shouted in shock as he stopped to peer down into the hole. The first thing Simon saw was the ribbon of molten lava flowing through the deep cavern well below him.

"What happened?" Elijah yelled as he moved up beside Simon and peered down into the cavity.

"Jonah Steele fell through the floor into the river of lava below. The floor panel fell out from under him and dropped him into the fire pit. It was another one of those deadly traps the Indians built."

"Damn those murdering Indians," Elijah yelled. "They were no better than their predecessors in Mexico and Peru. They sure enjoyed killing people with their horrible traps."

All of a sudden, a faint groan rose out of the opening. "Help me...I can't hold on much longer."

"It's Steele," Elijah shouted. "I can see him hanging on the edge of the floor panel with one hand."

"Jonah," Simon shouted, "Hang on, we'll get you up from there."

Turning, he said, "Someone hand me a rope."

Within seconds a rope was passed forward from one of the sailors. Simon peered back down into the hole and yelled, "Hold on Jonah, I'm passing a rope down to you. Grab it with your free hand and then let go of the panel and then grab the rope with both hands. We'll pull you up."

"I'll try," Steele yelled back.

Simon dangled one end of the rope over the hole and lowered it down to Steele. He had to swing it back and forth until it touched the floor panel Steele was holding on to. One hand reached out for the rope but missed. "I'm losing my grip," he shouted.

"Try again," Simon yelled back. "I'll swing it back toward you."

The rope swung back and forth again, finally brushing across Steele's arm. With his free hand, he reached again for the rope and luckily managed to grab it. With all his willpower, he reluctantly released his grip on the floor panel and clasped his other hand on to the rope. With both hands now holding on to the rope, he swung freely in midair. Elijah and three of the seamen grabbed the rope and began to walk it backwards as Steele was slowly pulled upward toward the opening. With his shoulders level to the edge, Stinson and another sailor grabbed under his arms and hauled him over the ledge and onto the floor. He lay there gasping for breath for a few seconds and then finally managed a forced grin. "Thanks fellows, I thought I was a goner for sure. What happened?"

"That was a trap door you stepped on," Simon informed him. The floor panel was rigged to break loose with your weight. We encountered the same type of traps inside the pyramid in the Yucatan and saw a couple of men die from it. It was lucky you were able to react in time to grab the panel as you fell. Your strength and quick reaction saved you from falling into a river of molten lava."

"How can we close the panel and lock it?" Stinson asked. "We sure can't jump over that hole. It must be six feet wide."

Simon answered, "If this trap is similar to the others we saw in Mexico, there should be a reset and locking trigger somewhere on the wall. The Indians who built this thing would have to have had a way to lock it in order to pass back and forth from the cavern up ahead. Let's look for a reset device on the walls."

It was easy to spot. On the wall to their right and just above the height of an average man was a small stone lever that projected from a shallow depression in the rock. Simon remembered the sequence their guide Santos had showed him in Mexico. He pulled the lever down and a process began to move some stone levers and bars that retracted the panel back into place. He then pushed the lever inward and heard a distinct thud that indicated a locking bar had engaged into a hole in the ledge that locked the panel firmly in place.

From his prior experience, he knew the panel was now safe to walk over. He knew the others would be skeptical so he took the first step and walked safely to the other side. Simon took the lead with Elijah, Scott, and Steele right behind him, but noticed the hesitation from Stinson and the sailors. "Come on," he shouted. "The panel is now safe to walk on."

Stinson took the first step and motioned for the others to follow, which they did.

Jonah Steele was curious and asked Simon, "Why would the Indians build a trap like that at the top of this passageway? It doesn't make sense to me."

"It does seem a bit odd, but I would think it was put there to keep their enemies away from whatever lies ahead. The Indians most likely used the chamber as a burial site and wanted to keep their departed tribe member's spirits safe from outsiders."

"Yes, and protect a huge treasure if there is one ahead," Scott added.

= = = = = =

Several yards further, they came to another flight of steps that descended back down to the ground level. Simon carefully scanned the steps and walls to assure there were no more traps, and satisfied the passage was safe, led the column down and through another doorway that led into a large cavern. The chamber was an eerie looking place cast in shadows and bizarre looking apparitions dancing on the walls accentuated by the light from the lanterns.

To Elijah, the place appeared to be occupied by ghosts from long dead Indian's departed souls. The first thing that was noticed was the figures and symbols inscribed on a wall. The largest was an image of a polar bear and her two cubs. It was an amazingly accurate rendition. Another drawing depicted an image of a seal, one of the primary food sources for the Eskimo. A few other strange symbols were shown on the wall, but the meanings were unknown to the American intruders.

To one side of the pictorial display was the crude drawing of a Viking helmet with a horn jutting out from either side. It was totally out of place from the other drawings.

Professor Scott, who was examining the display, commented in his normally scholarly manner, "There is absolutely no way an ancient Eskimo could have drawn that helmet. We know the Vikings arrived here much later. It had to be inscribed by one of the Vikings who thought he had artistic abilities. This only proves the Vikings found their way past the fire wall into this cavern."

"I wonder how many of their warriors fell through the nasty trap I fell into," Steele questioned.

"No telling," Simon responded, "but that trap door is so well concealed that you can bet it claimed a few. Jonah, you can be very thankful you are not dissolved into a tiny blob of lava you see in that lava stream flowing below."

Steele's expression conveyed his awareness of the close call.

A few of the sailors with claustrophobic feelings were huddled near the walls, wondering why they had been picked for this dangerous mission. The fear of the unknown was creeping into their minds and the apparitions dancing along the walls only heightened their fear of this ungodly place. Simon spotted this reaction and mentioned it to Stinson who turned and approached the seamen.

"I know you guys are nervous about being here, but this should be the last leg of the journey, so all we need to do is find the Viking treasure, then we're out of here." That seemed to relax them a bit.

A sudden shout from Steele across the cavern attracted everyone's attention. "Over here! I found something."

He was standing in front of several mounds of rocks piled up in several rectangular shapes. Scott offered his assessment. "Simon was correct when he mentioned Indian burial sites. These mounds have to be Eskimo burial mounds. This was the normal way they buried their dead. I read they just folded the bodies and covered them with rocks. I also read that in Greenland some of the Eskimos disposed of their dead by dissecting them and throwing the body parts into the sea."

Scott heard one of the sailors whisper to a mate, "That would sure be the easiest way. Just toss them to the sharks."

Simon shouted out to attract their attention. "Okay, you men, we're here to find the Viking treasure, so let's all fan out and search every square inch of this cavern."

The men dispersed and began examining along the walls for signs of a possible doorway. Nothing was found. Simon, Scott, and Steele were getting quite frustrated. The clue of the rune-stone clearly stated *beyond the wall of rock our treasures lie.* They had passed the *wall of fire* and the *wall of rock* and here they stood in a huge empty cavern with no signs of treasure chests. Simon drew Stinson aside. "Mr. Stinson, tell your men to closely examine every square inch of the walls again. There has to be a secret doorway somewhere leading to another chamber. I can just feel the treasure is nearby."

The first mate huddled his sailors together and conveyed Simon's request.

Simon and his three companions were discussing their options when there was a tap on his shoulder.

A young sailor was standing behind him with his hand extended holding two small shiny objects. "Sir, I found these over against the back wall," he said handing them to Simon.

They were two gold coins. Scott took one and held it up to examine it. "This is a very old Roman gold coin," he said.

"How do you know?" Simon asked.

Scott wondered why Simon would question his historical knowledge. With one of his annoying looks he glanced at his friend and replied, "Because I know something about Roman coins. The head on the front is a bust of Emperor Augustus and the date on the reverse side shows it to be minted in 48 BC. Many Roman coins were brought to England by the Anglo-Saxons."

"What is this other coin?" Simon asked.

"I'm not too sure about this one, but it looks like it might be a very early minted Anglo-Saxon gold sovereign."

"Show us exactly where you found these," Simon said to the seaman.

The man led them next to the back wall where he pointed to a spot on the floor.

Scott remarked, "These coins further confirm the Vikings were here and the treasure should be close by."

There were a few more etchings along the back wall, mostly comprised of unrecognizable glyphs and symbols most likely drawn by early Inuit natives…a few even looked like Viking runes. A careful examination indicated there was no lever or visible switch that would activate a doorway.

Professor Scott was particularly interested in the etchings on the wall. He noticed a few of them were similar to some of the runes he had seen in his Nordic translation book. One particular symbol caught his attention. He reached into his back pack and pulled out the booklet. Scanning through the pages he found the identical rune.

Scott turned to his companions and showed them the symbol in the book. Pointing to the wall he said, "The rune in this book is the same as that etching you see on the wall."

"What does it mean," Simon asked.

"In Nordic it is called a *Mjolnir*. It is the symbol for Thor's hammer."

Steele recalled the statue overlooking the lake they had crossed. "I'll admit it does look like that object the statue is holding in his hand."

"That's right," Scott confirmed. "This rune symbolizing the hammer has to be the key to the treasure. Let's check it out."

On the bottom of the rune, the base flared out to represent the striking stubs of the hammer and the upper extension of the handle. There were snake-like features that curved inside each of the base extensions. The holes in the center of each curve were represented by two flat stones carefully affixed to the rune.

"Those look suspicious," Scott said as he reached up to touch the symbol. He pressed the stone on the left and nothing happened. It was solid. He then reached for the second stone and pressed it with his thumb. He felt slight movement. He pressed harder. Surprisingly, the stone pushed deep into the wall, emitting a distinct clicking noise. In silence, they waited.

Suddenly, a dull grating noise was heard as a heavy rock door panel began to pivot outward from the wall. The men were greeted by a pitch-black void, indicating another room on the other side. Their hopes soared as Simon led the group cautiously through the opening and perhaps into another unknown area of danger.

59

With the lanterns radiating light throughout the cavity, they could tell the room was much smaller than the large cavern behind them. Suddenly, as if on cue, reflected rays of dazzling brilliance splashed across the room, displaying sparkling bursts of light. Before their eyes, the men observed several rows of wooden chests, many with lids open that allowed the contents to reflect a fiery effervescence of different brilliant colors throughout the room. They had finally found the main Viking treasure. Professor Scott was the first to reach the cache, but instead of stopping at a chest, he continued to the opposite wall where another five Viking runestones were stacked. To the curious professor, the discovery of these new tablets was more exciting than the entire lot of the chests full of gold coins, ingots, and gemstones.

Simon, Elijah, and Steele each knelt in front of separate chests and ran their fingers through the piles of coins which were comprised of every type and denomination one could imagine. They were all old...very old. Many of the coins were of Roman origin and many were undefinable. They had one thing in common; they were all made of solid gold.

Simon assembled the group and announced, "Now that we've found the treasure, we have the difficult task of transporting these chests out of here and back to the ship. It will not be easy, especially with the steps we have to climb that bypasses the fire wall. We lost one man in that burst of lava so we now have thirteen of us left to move the chests…and as you know, they are very heavy."

Turning to the first mate, he said, "Mr. Stinson, please separate your men into teams of…

He never finished the sentence as he heard a shout from the back of the cave.

"Mr. Murphy…over here…we've found something." It was the voice of Jeb Hawkins.

Simon and Stinson walked toward the voice and found young Hawkins and another seaman standing next to an opening in the wall. It led into a small alcove. Professor Scott, with lantern in hand, was right behind them. Simon took the lamp and turned to enter through the doorway. The scene before him took his breath away.

Stacked neatly throughout the small room was an assortment of artifacts that reflected sparkles of luminosity from an abundance of silver, gold, and inlaid gemstones. Stacks of plates, cups, platters, vases, plaques, sculptures, and numerous other items revealed a huge display of wealth gathered by the Vikings during their rampage of the nobles and aristocrats across medieval Europe. Professor Scott was ecstatic with the discovery.

He shouted, "This will be the greatest display of the Viking conquest the world has ever seen. Wait until Mr. Drake and the others at the museum see this assortment of artifacts and the runestones we found."

As exciting as this was, the discovery of all this new treasure complicated the situation. Simon didn't have enough men to haul all the chests out of the cavern and back to the ship without more men. This task of moving the artifacts would triple the effort. He called Stinson and his three companions together for a conference.

"We don't have the manpower to move all of this stuff without more men and several trips. First, I suggest we divide our men into teams of two assigned to one chest. With the men we have, it will allow us to move six chests in one trip. With two men to each chest, the extra man can carry as many of the artifacts as he can handle. Once we get the chests to the ship, we'll get Captain Swift to give us more of his crew to help move the rest. I think with the additional help we can move it all in two more trips."

Stinson confirmed he could arrange that.

With a man grasping a handle at each end, they began the gruesome task of carrying the chests of coins and ingots up the steps, across the cavern, and through the tunnel to the pyramid where they had more steps to climb. Simon and Elijah grabbed one chest, Scott and Steele another, and Stinson and his seamen another four chests. Jeb Hawkins was assigned the task of carrying a load of artifacts consisting of some gold goblets and trays.

It took the rest of the day to manhandle the first load from the pyramid and another three hours the next morning to get the chests loaded on the longboats. Unfortunately, they would have to wait another two hours alongside the lake for the high tide in order to get the boats back through the water passage and to the USS Shannon.

= = = = = =

Captain Barnaby Swift was making his rounds when he spotted the first boat floating out of the cavern entrance into the fjord. Noticing the low profile of the vessel in the water, he could tell that it was loaded with something very heavy. Simon was sitting in the bow and with a big grin shouted. "Ahoy, Captain Swift, permission to bring some treasure aboard."

"Permission granted," Swift replied back with an equally big smile.

With the use of a boom and heavy straps, the chests were lifted from the longboats and slung onto the deck of the Shannon. Simon and the rest of the men made their way up the ladders and fell exhausted to the deck where they were served beer and sandwiches from the galley. That evening, Captain Swift invited Simon, Elijah, Scott, Steele, and Stinson to his stateroom where they enjoyed a special meal prepared by the ship's chef. Simon explained all about the journey through the pyramid and tunnel and how they discovered the treasure cache. Especially tough was the description of how one of his crew members had been incinerated in the wall of fire.

"The man should have known better than to try and jump over a flaming crevasse," Swift acknowledged, shaking his head. "He should have known better."

With additional crew members assigned to the task, it took two more days to recover all the chests and artifacts, but finally all the treasure was loaded aboard and safely stored into the USS Shannon's holds. Swift called Stinson and his helmsman together with instructions to set sail for the docks of Washington. It appeared the mission had been a huge success until the unexpected happened.

As the ship exited the fjord and was making her turn into the Cumberland Sound, the metal hull swiped an underwater rock outcropping at the north end of the Kikastan Islands, resulting in a jagged gash in the hull plates.

Two seamen in the boiler room felt the collision and heard the sound of metal tearing. They rushed to the bow to find sea water pouring through the split. One of them hurried topside to inform Captain Swift.

Simon and Elijah were on the main deck conversing when they felt the ship lurch from the impact. In a few moments, they saw a seaman hurrying out of a hatch and toward the bridge. They knew something very serious had happened.

Chief Petty Officer Warren also rushed to the bridge to give Captain Swift a report of the damage. Simon and Elijah followed him.

"Sir," he reported, "the collision has caused damage to our starboard hull. Apparently, we have damage to our outer plates that have created a gash, leaking seawater into the bow."

"How about the bilge pumps?" Kirby asked.

"They are running at top capacity and so far, we are maintaining neutral buoyancy, but the ship has lost a two-degree list in the bow."

"Can we make it to Newfoundland, Mr. Warren?"

"I don't believe so, Sir. The forward motion of the ship will only force more water through the hole and overwhelm our pump capacity. I'm sure the Shannon would sink before we could get to their nearest port of St. Johns. Also, the added weight of our new cargo is compounding the problem."

"I see," Swift responded. "I would hate to have to dump all of the Viking treasure overboard and compromise our mission."

"Perhaps we could beach her, Captain."

"I'm afraid that's impossible. The islands around here are nothing but sheer rock and would tear up more bow plates if we ran her aground. It appears that we have a very serious problem, Mr. Warren. We can't run those pumps indefinitely. Sooner or later we will run out of fuel to operate the pumps."

Simon and Elijah entered the bridge as Swift was winding up his conversation with his petty officer. "Captain, we felt the ship lurch when she apparently collided with something. Is there anything serious?" Simon asked.

Captain Swift explained the whole situation and emphasized the hopeless outcome that could possibly happen. "Simon, I'm afraid there is nothing you and your companions can do. We could toss the treasure overboard but that won't help repair the damage to the hull. I also have another concern. If we have to abandon ship, we don't have enough boats to handle all of the crew, and if anyone tried to jump overboard in this frigid water they would never be able to swim to any of the islands before freezing to death."

Simon turned and whispered a few words to Elijah then turned to Swift. "Captain, it's a long shot but maybe there is something we can do. It's certainly worth a try. I'll need to return to my cabin and get something, but I'll be back shortly."

Simon and Elijah left the bridge, leaving Captain Swift in a quandary. He thought, *I wonder what on earth those two could possibly be up to. It will take a miracle to save this ship.*

= = = = = =

Back in their cabin, Simon went to his pack and retrieved the Zenox. The two men returned to the main deck to eliminate any interference for a transmission. Elijah remarked, "You'll be lucky if you can even reach Commander Ahular with the Zenox. I'm sure they left for their own galaxy days ago. Remember he told us they had a few more days of research of our magnetic poles and then they would be returning to their own planet."

"I know that, but we have to try and reach him," Simon replied as he flipped on the activation switch to the communications device. "He also told us the transmission from this thing will reach a very long distance."

"He's not going to turn around and help us if he's a million miles from here."

"I know that but we have to try or this ship will surely sink with all of the treasure aboard and us with it. He might be able to help us. We really have no other options."

Professor Scott and Jonah Steele entered the room. "What's all the commotion topside?" Scott asked. "Sailors are running about everywhere."

Simon explained the situation and then rushed out of the cabin with his three companions following close behind. They found a secluded spot on the stern deck and approached the railing. Simon pressed the activation button on the Zenox and spoke into the speaker. "Commander Ahular, this is Simon Murphy calling…Commander Ahular…please come in. Commander Ahular, please answer."

There was only the sound of splashing waves hitting the hull…the Zenox was silent. Simon repeated his transmission… still silence."

"You see," Elijah reminded him, "I knew they have already departed for their own galaxy and probably are millions of miles from us."

The despair on Simon's face revealed the hopelessness of the situation as each of the men began to think of the ship and priceless Viking treasure sinking to the bottom. After all their prior harrowing experiences, they couldn't bear the thoughts of drowning, or at best, being stranded on a barren rock in the Labrador Sea to die of starvation and thirst. Scott was distraught knowing the runestones would be lost forever and he would never have a chance to translate them.

"It's no use," Simon admitted as he turned to return to the bridge.

Suddenly, the sound of static erupted from the Zenox, followed by the distinct sound of a voice. "Mr. Murphy, our transponder just received your transmission." It was the familiar voice of Commander Ahular.

"Commander, I am so glad to hear your voice. Where are you, sir?"

"We are currently directly over your North Pole. Our research is concluded and we are preparing for our journey back to our own galaxy. We have been ordered home by our superiors. Our sensors show your location just to the south of Baffin Island and close to the Labrador Sea."

"That is correct, Commander. We were returning from the hidden valley where you met us a few weeks ago and are on a ship that has hit an underwater rock, ripping a gash into our hull. The ship is sinking and we desperately need your help."

Simon could hear some conversation in the background and then the voice returned. "Our celestial navigation instruments indicate your exact coordinates. We can arrive at your location in thirteen minutes and twelve seconds."

"Thank you, Commander. We'll be looking for you."

= = = = = =

The men hurried back to the bridge to tell the captain of the help on the way. "You mean to tell me there is an alien spaceship en route to help us?" Swift said suspiciously. "Mr. Stinson told me about you guys disappearing on some spaceship that landed in the valley before we were hijacked. I thought he was going nuts."

"It's true, Captain. It should be arriving any minute now," Simon assured him.

"What can a flying ship do to help us?"

"You would be surprised at the instruments on that ship," Scott remarked. "Those things can even operate underwater like a submarine. That's how we got to the lost continent of Atlantis back in 1870."

Captain Swift just shook his head thinking, *I'll have to see this to believe it.*

= = = = = =

It didn't take long for a tiny spot to appear in the distant sky. Quickly, it got bigger and bigger as the X562 spaceship approached the floundering USS Shannon. Captain Swift was enthralled as he watched the approaching craft ease down and hover over the water just fifty yards away. A hatch opened and a small dacidron hovercraft exited the ship and headed across the water toward the Shannon. The sailors stared in awe as the small transport momentarily hovered over the ship and then descended to the main deck. Two unusual looking figures emerged from the hatch and walked over to where Simon, Swift, and the others were standing. As customary, the two aliens placed their doubled fist to their chest as a salutation gesture to the Americans. Simon, Elijah, and Scott returned the salutation. Swift didn't know what to do.

Simon turned to Swift and said, "Captain, I would like you to meet our two friends from a far-off galaxy and a planet named Xeres. This is Commander Ahular and Vice-commander Nezar."

"My pleasure, Commanders," Swift responded with a stiff military salute of his own. "I have heard about you. Thank you for responding to Mr. Murphy's call."

"What seems to be the problem, Captain," Ahular asked. "Mr. Murphy told us your ship has sustained damage to your hull and is taking on water."

"Yes, sir," Swift answered. "We collided with an underwater rock outcropping that ripped a gash in out hull plates. We are taking on seawater into our bow section."

"We can see your ship is listing at the bow. Perhaps we can help. I notice your hull is comprised of metal plating which will help the situation considerably. We might be able to give you a temporary repair to enable you to get to your destination, which I assume would be to one of your naval docks."

"That would be the navy yard in Washington D.C."

Ahular continued. "Direct your crew members toward the stern and away from the bow while we assess the damage and initiate necessary repairs to the metal plates."

"Yes, sir," Swift replied as the two aliens turned and boarded the dacidron to return to their craft.

"What can they possibly do to repair our hull?" Swift asked Simon.

"You just wait, Captain; you will be amazed at what the machines aboard that ship can do."

Officers began to round up the crew members and move them to the rear of the main deck while Swift, Simon, and the others climbed the steps up to the stern deck. They watched in astonishment as the SERX562 dipped toward the water and slipped beneath the surface.

Swift turned to Simon with a perplexed expression. "What are they going to do?"

"I'm not too sure but I would imagine they are going to attempt to weld the plates back together and close up the gash in the hull."

Captain Swift was even more confused. "How can they possibly do that underwater?" he asked. "It takes a very hot flame to weld metal together and we all know fire doesn't burn under water."

"Just watch closely, Captain. "I'll explain it to you in a few minutes."

= = = = = =

Aboard the spacecraft, Ahular had his weapons control officer adjust two of the forward lasers to a fifteen percent power level and combine the two lasers and aim them toward the tear in the plates. The alien officer adjusted a couple of more controls and pressed the fire button. A stream of bright light tore through the water and hit the forward edge of the gash, causing the metal to begin to melt and fuse together. The cold water accelerated the hardening process as the energy beam traversed across the ruptured seam.

On board the Shannon, the men gasped when they observed a steady display of bubbles and steam rising to the surface and dissipate into the air. Swift's first thought was that the rent in the hull was widening and bubbles were escaping from the inside of the bow. Simon assured him that was not the case. He explained, "The spaceship is using its laser guns to melt the metal and weld the tear in the plates back together. We were with them a few years ago when they prevented a catastrophic earthquake in the Atlantic Ocean from splitting our planet apart by using their laser guns to weld the two rock plates together. They saved our planet from total destruction."

Swift could only shake his head in total awe and amazement.

The spacecraft slowly rose from the water and hovered close by as the hatch opened and the dacidron came back over to land on the main deck. As the hovercraft was approaching, a seaman from the boiler room walked up and addressed Swift. "Sir, the water has stopped flowing into the ship and the bilge pumps are now discharging water from the lower level back into the sea. The lower deck should be cleared within a couple of hours." He turned and disappeared back through a hatch leading to the lower decks.

Commander Ahular exited the dacidron and walked over to Simon and Swift who were waiting for him on the main deck. After another fisted salute to his chest he spoke, "Captain, we have managed to weld together the tear to your hull and you are safe to continue your voyage to your destination."

"Thank you, Commander," Swift responded appreciatively. "You have saved our ship and my crew and I can't thank you enough."

Motioning toward Simon with his hand, Ahular continued. "This man and his companions most likely saved our species through the donation of their tissue and cells to strengthen our immune systems from harmful germs and microorganisms. The reports I am getting from our planet confirm the results from their gifts have been very successful."

"I am most gratified to hear that good news, Commander."

Turning back to Simon and Elijah, Commander Ahular had some final words to say. "My friends, Vice-commander Nezar and I have been recalled from Earth to conduct further research in another galaxy very far from here. It appears this is our final parting as we will not be seeing you again. The Zenox you have will not be in contact with us anymore, but you are free to keep the device as a memento and reminder of our experiences together and perhaps it can be used to contact another one of our exploration ships in the future. I bid you farewell."

With this he turned and boarded the dacidron and returned to the X562 spacecraft.

As the ship lifted into the air, Simon and his companions could not help but remember the harrowing trips they had experienced with the aliens and the incredible trip they had back to their home planet. It was a story that would rewrite the history books and be retold thousands of times by countless future generations.

Far into the sky above, they watched the spacecraft as it quickly turned into a tiny speck and then disappeared.

60

Washington D.C.

Captain Swift had new duties to attend to as he turned to Stin-son and commanded him to get the ship underway for their final voyage to Washington. He had a ship to repair and refit, a new crew to be assembled, a huge Viking treasure to distribute to the Treasury Department and Washington National Museum. Most likely, he would have a lot of reports to write explaining the traitorous activities of the mutineers who sat in the federal prison near Washington awaiting judgments from a Navy Trial Judiciary Board.

He pondered whether or not he should include the rescue by the alien spaceship but had some reservations when he thought a naval board of inquiry might think he had lost his senses. He also knew the story would get out anyway from the crew mem-bers, so in reconsidering the issue he reasoned... *Well, why not.*

The trip home was uneventful as the USS Shannon sailed past the coast of Newfoundland and the port of St. Johns, past the city of Halifax, Nova Scotia, and along the New England coasts of Maine, Massachusetts, Connecticut, and finally New York City, which was seen in the distance. As the Shannon rounded the extreme southern tip of the Eastern Shore of Virginia and into the Chesapeake Bay, the crew lined the starboard railings and cheered. The final swing to portside and through the mouth of the Potomac River brought more cheers…the men knew they were finally going home.

The cruise up the Potomac gave Simon and Elijah time to reflect on the adventure and talk about the future. Simon looked at his cousin and said, "We have been gone a lot longer than I told Maggie we would be. I wouldn't be surprised if she has moved out of the house with little Thomas. I even told her this would be my last expedition, but I don't think she really believed me."

Elijah laughed, "Are you kidding me? That sweet woman loves you more than you think. Especially with all those gold coins you have stashed away somewhere. I know she wouldn't leave you for anything."

"Well, we shall see," Simon responded with reservations. "How about you?" he asked. "What are your plans, Elijah?"

"I don't know for sure. I think I'm getting too damn old for these treasure hunting trips and besides, I do have a beautiful girl waiting for me on a ranch in California. If I had any sense I'd catch the next train back there and marry her. The problem is, I'm not sure I want to be a rancher and have to chase cattle all over the place. Maybe you and Maggie would like to move out there with me and you and I can become Wild West cowboys."

"Not a chance, Cousin Elijah…not a chance. I think I'll just retire to being a good husband and father. You say you are getting too old for this business. Considering you and I were 22 years old when we left the war for Mexico, you realize now we are only 35 years old. Actually, we have plenty more years left to hunt for treasures."

"You have got to be kidding me, Simon, you just told me you were going to settle down and be a good husband and father. Do you really want to search for more treasures?"

Simon laughed and answered, "I'm just kidding, cousin. Maggie would never forgive me if I took off on another treasure hunting expedition."

= = = = = =

The ship pulled into the Washington Docks late afternoon and was eased into a waiting slip by a tugboat. A group of distinguished looking men were waiting on the dock...three dressed in naval officer's uniforms. When the gangplank was lowered, they casually walked up the plank and on to the main deck where Captain Swift was waiting to greet them.

One individual specifically asked where he could find Simon, Elijah, and Professor Scott. Swift pointed to four men standing by the railing and said, "They're right over there."

The man approached Simon and his three companions and introduced himself. "Gentlemen, my name is John Irwin and I am an emissary sent here by President Hayes. He would like to see you men right away. If you'll gather your belongings, I have a buggy that will carry us directly to the White House."

Simon glanced at his three accomplices and replied, "Mr. Irwin, if you'll give us a few minutes we'll go to our cabins and gather up our baggage. We'll meet you shortly at the bottom of the gangplank."

Irwin nodded and returned to the dock.

"Wonder what this is all about," Elijah questioned.

"I don't know but it sounds important if he wants to see us right after we docked."

As the men approached the gangplank, they stopped to bid Captain Swift farewell. "Well Captain," Simon said, "it has been quite an adventure, hasn't it?"

"That it has, Mr. Murphy. I will always remember how you, Captain Patton, and your friends helped save Mr. Stinson and me and my ship. You also helped recover all the treasures we found for our government and the museum. It has been quite an experience. Perhaps our paths will cross again...who knows what fate has in store for all of us."

The four men shook hands with Swift and walked down the gangplank where Irwin was spotted standing next to a large buggy.

Irwin saw Jonah Swift as a fourth man and asked, "Mr. Murphy, I see you have another accomplice with you. The president specifically spelled out for me to fetch you, Mr. Walker, and Professor Scott. Who is your other companion?"

"This is Jonah Smith, a geologist who works with Mr. Scott and the museum. He was with us during the entire journey and played a major role in helping us find the Viking treasure. He was a part of our team and needs to be with us."

"Very well, sir. I'm sure the president will be pleased to see him as well."

= = = = = =

The ride from the dock to 1600 Pennsylvania Avenue took nearly 35 minutes when the buggy pulled through the gate and up to the front entrance to the White House. An aide met them at the door and ushered them into a well decorated room displaying portraits of several past presidents. The aide politely said, "Make yourself comfortable gentlemen, the president will see you shortly."

John Irwin also dismissed himself as well.

It was about a ten-minute wait, but President Hayes walked into the room with Treasury Secretary John Sherman and Secretary of War George McCrary following close behind. Simon and the others had met Sherman, and were introduced to McCrary. Hayes motioned for everyone to take a seat. He looked at his guests and said, "Well, gentlemen, it appears our treasure hunters have returned from a most perilous journey and fulfilled their mission in a grand fashion. The chests of gold coins and ingots were delivered to our secure treasury vaults a short while ago and the initial assessments of value are far greater than expected. We believe that with the combined gold that was delivered to us from your first visit to Baffin Island and the chests we just received from the USS Shannon, our total supply of gold will now be able to solidify and back up our country's monetary system, returning to the gold standard. This will allow the value of silver to fluctuate to its own value through the forces of normal supply and demand. Your country owes you a great amount of gratitude."

"Sir, how about all the artifacts and the Viking runestones we discovered?" Professor Scott asked with apprehension. "I personally found the last five tablets in a hidden underground room not far from the pyramid."

Secretary Sherman answered his question. "Mr. Scott, you will be happy to know that all of the artifacts, including those five stone tablets you found, have been delivered to the Washington museum and are now under the protection of our curator, Robert Drake and the museum security team."

"Thank you, Mr. Sherman. This is great news. I can't wait to get back to the museum and start translations on those runestones."

Secretary of War McCrary brought up a subject that Simon and his associates were not prepared for. "Mr. Murphy, I have heard stories about your prior encounters with a flying ship from some place very far away. Although I have reservations about of some of the tales, I also heard the ship has some incredibly powerful weapons on board. One of the officers aboard the USS Shannon just told one of our staff members that the ship picked you and your companions up in that valley on Baffin Island and carted you away somewhere for several days. This was just before Captain Swift and the USS Shannon got highjacked by the mutineers.

"Also, we were told that upon your return, the ship mysteriously showed up at the site in the Labrador Sea about the time the ship hit an underwater reef that caused a split in the hull. Those who observed the incident said the flying ship dove beneath the surface and somehow managed to weld the plates together that allowed her to become seaworthy enough to continue to your destination to Washington. Is all of this true?"

Simon hesitated for a moment, trying to decide how much

to divulge. "Yes, Mr. Secretary, most of what you heard is true. The ship is from another planet very far away and the individuals are much like us humans, but somewhat different in appearance. We first met them several years ago on an expedition to Peru and later in the Amazon when we found the fabled city of El Dorado. President Grant walked aboard one of their ships and met their commander to thank him for saving our planet and solar system from a catastrophic impact with a huge asteroid."

This was getting too much for McCrary who just stood there shaking his head.

Simon continued, "The weapons you speak of are called laser guns that shoot very powerful rays of energy that are capable of destroying most any object. They have a means of varying the strength of the beams depending on the size and strength of the target. In order to weld the metal hull plates together, I suspect they lowered the strength to a bare minimum or the ship would have been vaporized into nothing."

"How about those weapons?" the secretary asked. "We could certainly use something like that in our arsenal. They would make us the most powerful nation in the world and protect us from any threats from any rogue country. Is there any way you could arrange for these space travelers to provide us with the technology for these energy guns?"

"No, sir, that would be impossible to do. These laser weapons were developed by a race of aliens that are so much more advanced than us and they are much too technical and powerful for any of us humans to possess. They would never let us have them. Besides, they are en route back to their own planet, located millions of miles away. We could never reach them."

President Hayes had heard enough of this questionable conversation as he reached under the table and pulled out four small boxes. He then turned to Steele. "Young man, I was told you were a vital part of this team that helped find the treasure on visits to Baffin Island occasions. Also, I was informed that you are engaged in the new scientific field of geology."

"Yes, sir, that is true. I'm now working with Professor Scott and the Washington museum. I hope my new field can benefit the museum in some manner."

"I believe you have already done that, Mr. Steele," the president acknowledged. He reached for the boxes and distributed one of them to each of his guests. "For your success, we felt each of you should share in some reward for your services. You will find enough gold coins in the chests to hopefully provide you with some monetary comfort."

Hayes stood up. "Now gentlemen, if you'll excuse us we have duties to attend to so you are free to leave."

An aide escorted Simon and the others to the front door where Irwin was waiting with the buggy to transport them to the destination of their choice. While Scott and Steele wished to be dropped off at the museum, Simon and Elijah chose to be taken to Simon's house in nearby Maryland.

Bladensburg, Maryland

Simon invited Elijah to spend a few days with him to allow him some leisure time to decide what he wanted to do. As they walked up the stone paved sidewalk, Simon wondered if Maggie would still be there or whether she had decided to leave him after all. She was pretty hot about him traveling back to Baffin Island. When he knocked on the front door, his hopes sunk when there was no answer. He knocked again. His hopes sunk even more when there was still no answer, but suddenly he heard some rustling behind the door. Finally, the door slowly opened and there was his son Thomas standing there.

His innocent little face looked up at Simon as he spoke, "Daddy... Daddy, is that you?"

"Yes, Thomas, it's me," Simon said as he swept his son up into his arms. "It's really me."

Maggie heard the noise and rushed out of the kitchen, only to see her husband tenderly holding his son in his arms.

"Oh my, it's you!" she cried. "It's really you. I didn't know whether you were dead or alive."

Maggie rushed into his arms, tears streaming down her face. "I haven't heard from you in weeks and didn't even know if you were still alive." She buried her face into his chest, holding on to him tightly as if he might turn and run across the lawn.

"Maggie, I promised you I would come home and, like I said, I am here to stay."

"Oh, you crazy man," she cried, "this time you'd better mean that."

Maggie then gave Elijah a cursory hug and ushered the two men into the parlor.

"Oh, my goodness," she said. "I need to get more chicken from the box now that I have two more mouths to feed. I was getting ready to prepare supper for Thomas and me." She turned and hustled back into the kitchen.

Elijah nodded to Simon with a bantering look. "Mighty fine woman you've got there, cousin. I think she's really glad to see you. I need someone just like her in my life."

Simon responded with a big grin. "Well, I'm mighty glad to see her and Thomas. Don't you have Rosita waiting for you back in California?"

"Yes, but like I said earlier, I don't know if I'm cut out for cattle ranching."

Simon stood up and walked over to the cupboard where he retrieved his familiar bottle of Buckhorn Creek bourbon and two glasses. He poured a healthy shot into each glass and handed one to Elijah. "Well," he said holding the glass into the air, "here's to our treasure hunting days and coming home alive."

"I'll drink to that."

Elijah took a big swig and said, "Speaking of treasure, I read somewhere that back in 1848 some guy named Marshall discovered gold at a place called Sutter's Mill. That's what kicked off the big California gold rush that lasted for about seven or eight years. I'll bet there are plenty of gold nuggets still left in those streams up in Northern California. Just think, if you, Maggie, and Thomas were to move with me to California, we could go panning for gold and probably find us a mother lode somewhere."

A shrill voice boomed from the kitchen as Maggie stuck her head through the doorway. "I heard that, Elijah Walker. That is never gonna happen… and you'd better stop talking such nonsense to my husband or you won't get any fried chicken and I'll usher you straight out the front door. Simon Murphy is here to stay and if I even hear a hint of him agreeing to another wild goose chase, I'm going to tie him up with chains and lock him in a closet."

Both of the men laughed as Simon assured her, "Don't worry, my dear wife, I'm home to stay."

Maggie flashed them a surreptitious smile as she returned to the kitchen.

Elijah leaned over to his cousin and whispered, "I guess so much for treasure hunting."

The dinner consisted of southern style fried chicken, potatoes, chicken gravy, an assortment of greens, and biscuits. As usual, Elijah managed to create heaping islands of mashed potatoes and biscuits surrounded in a sea of gravy. Maggie, who was familiar with Elijah's eating habits, chuckled out loud, while Simon just shook his head in amazement. Elijah was in food heaven and offered his compliments to Maggie by filling his plate with three helpings. She acknowledged his appreciation by serving a slice of pecan pie topped with whipped cream. As Elijah devoured the last bite of pie he thought, no doubt that this woman could kick anyone's ass in a cooking contest. We should fly her back to that planet and let her teach those aliens how to eat properly.

= = = = = =

The next two days were relaxing as Simon and Elijah spent time visiting with Maggie and playing with little Thomas. Elijah became very fond of the boy and was especially touched when Thomas tagged him as "Uncle Eli."

He witnessed the joy and fun of having a child like Thomas around who was totally dependent on the parents, but as a toddler, determined to go his own way. This connection reinforced his conviction that he should go back to California, marry Rosita, and start having kids of his own. He vowed to go to the nearest train station tomorrow, send a telegram to his old companion, Santos, at the Rio del Viejo ranch, and then check out the train schedule to San Diego.

With the use of Simon's buggy, he did just that. Elijah was delighted to learn that a track had been completed from San Diego to Capistrano which would save him time and the trouble of having to rent a horse for the final leg. At the telegraph office, he pondered a few minutes over the correct words to use in the telegram. He finally completed the wording and handed the slip to the telegraph operator. Elijah knew Santos would check the designated arrival times and be there to meet him at the station when he arrived.

He finished writing out his message. SANTOS. STOP. TELL ROSITA I AM CATCHING A TRAIN FROM WASHINGTON TO CAPISTRANO THIS THURSDAY. STOP. I AM RETURNING TO THE RANCH. STOP. ALSO TELL HER I LOVE HER. STOP. ELIJAH

61

Washington National Museum

Professor Scott had spent the last four days translating runes on the last five tablets he had discovered in the hidden room on Baffin Island. With the help of the Nordic translation booklet Professor Aavik Johansen had provided him, he had so far managed to translate four of the runestone tablets. They turned out to be routine accounts for the locations of Viking settlements in the new world. Of interest was one settlement located near the current town of Gander, Newfoundland. The Viking settlers were led by a warrior chief named Dalgaard who sailed his longboat over from Norway in 1021 AD.

The second tablet was very similar as it described another small settlement established in Nova Scotia by another Viking named Rolvsson in 1023 AD.

The third was the most intriguing as it documented an account of a Viking settlement on the coast of northern Maine established in 1025 AD. The Viking leader was a chief named Erikson and the location pointed to a short voyage up Machias Bay and the current township of Machhiasport. Through further research, Scott found that the site was the spot where a trading post had been established by the Plymouth Company in 1632 AD to serve the Indian tribes located in the vicinity.

The fourth tablet was a description of a brief skirmish the Viking warriors had with a band of Indians just off the southern coast of southern Quebec. A small exploration party led by a Viking chief named Olofsson had encountered a group of hostiles who outnumbered the Vikings three to one. The battle was fierce, costing the Vikings seven warriors, but the Indians were no match for the Viking battle axes and broadswords who won the skirmish and drove the Indians inland. The natives were not identified, but some research led Scott to believe they were possibly early predecessors to the Algonquins.

On the fifth day, Scott turned to the fifth tablet and two of the translated runes aroused some definite interest. One rune was translated as the word 'gold' and another rune the word 'ice'. To Scott these runes pointed to one thing. *The Vikings had hidden another cache of gold near a place covered with ice.* This meant the treasure could be buried under an ice cap which pointed the location northward again and toward the Arctic Circle. As he continued his translation, his excitement soared. The completion of the translation took Scott the rest of the day.

= = = = = =

Early the next morning, the professor called for Jonah Steele to join him. The message was labeled urgent. To Steele the summons from Scott, who had secluded himself into isolation for the past five days, meant the professor had most likely found something very promising. He made his way to Scott's private study where he found the professor beaming with excitement. He handed Steele the piece of paper and said, "Take a look at this, Jonah. I've translated most of the last runestone and it contains definite clues to more Viking treasure buried somewhere well north of the Baffin Sea."

Steele read the paper carefully, trying to visualize a map of the Arctic Circle and especially the water routes that might allow the Vikings to negotiate a possible passage with their wooden long-boats. These ancient mariners had few options with sea routes that far north. Scott excused himself to the map room where he pulled out a map of the Arctic Circle and returned with map in hand. He knew beforehand that the Arctic had not been fully explored, so several conclusions would be guestimates at best.

"Jonah, the rest of the clues specifically includes a translation that means *narrowest passage to the north of Vinland*."

"What is that supposed to mean?" Steele asked.

"The word Vinland is an old Norse word meaning the north coastal region of North America. If you look closely at the map, and follow the Labrador Sea northward, you'll see where the Baffin Sea constricts down to a narrow passage that separates Greenland and the Ellesmere Islands."

Scott pointed at a specific spot on the map. "You can see this piece of land that juts out from Greenland bordering this thin strip of water called Smith Sound that separates Green-land from Ellesmere Island. That whole section of Greenland is called Knudrasmussen Land. During a warm summer, I think the Vikings could have sailed a longboat as far north as the

Smith Sound and found a place to hide their treasure along the shores of Greenland."

Steele drew in a deep breath. "Good grief, George. You're talking about the absolute middle of nowhere and probably covered with ice."

"The weather is still warm, so I'm sure we could get a small ship up there."

"You really think there is a huge Viking treasure in Greenland?" Steele asked

Scott put one of his big conspiratorial smiles on his face. "Yes, I do and that's what makes another expedition up to the far north so interesting, doesn't it, Jonah?"

"I guess so," the young geologist answered.

"Let's go show this to Robert Drake and see if he will allow the museum to finance another trip to the Arctic Circle."

Bladensburg, Virginia

The knock on the door brought Simon to his feet as he moved toward the front hallway to answer it. A young courier was standing there with a slip of paper in his hand. "I have a message for Mr. Simon Murphy from the Washington National Museum." The envelope was marked urgent.

He carried it into the parlor where Elijah was reading Thomas a children's short story. "I have an urgent message from the museum. Wonder what they want?" He opened it.

"What could be so important that the museum would have that message hand delivered and marked urgent?" Elijah asked.

"It's from Professor Scott," Simon said as read the message. "He said he has made a startling discovery and both he and Robert Drake would like both of us to come to the museum immediately."

Maggie heard the conversation and walked into the room. "What is it?" she asked suspiciously.

"The Washington museum's curator, Robert Drake, wants Elijah and me to come to the museum. Says it's very important."

"I hope you two aren't planning something crazy like another trip somewhere," she fired back.

"No, it's nothing like that. It says they have made an important discovery and want us to see it. It shouldn't take too long. Besides, Elijah wants to stop by the telegraph office to see if he got a response to the wire he sent to California a couple a days ago."

"Okay," she replied. "Supper should be ready when you get back."

It only took a few minutes for Simon to harness the horse to his buggy and head for Washington. The plan was to stop by the telegraph office first, which was located conveniently on the way. Elijah was anxious to see if Santos had sent him a reply to his earlier wire. He had to know if he was still welcome at the Rio del Viejo ranch. Ironically, there was a telegram waiting for him. He took the wire and rushed back to the buggy.

He began to read it. ELIJAH. SEND ME YOUR TRAIN SCHEDULE. STOP. I WILL MEET YOU UPON ARRIVAL AT CAPISTRANO STATION. STOP. ROSITO

LOVES YOU VERY MUCH AND WANTS YOU TO COME HOME. STOP. SANTOS.

"Wow! You see that Simon. She still loves me and wants me to come home."

Simon nodded, "You see. I always knew there was a big spark between you two."

Elijah added, "Well, it also looks like the Central Pacific Railroad finally finished the span of track into Capistrano and it looks like I'll probably be riding on it in a few days."

They arrived at the museum where an attendant led them straight to Robert Drake's office. They were not surprised to see Professor Scott and Jonah Steele sitting there. The curator stood up to greet them. Simon noticed the big grin on the professor's face and concluded he had found something on the runestones that had him really excited.

"Great to see you two again," Drake said. "Glad you could get here on such short notice."

Simon nodded, "Good to see you again, Robert. Your message was marked *urgent*. What on earth have you found that has you guys so excited?"

"I'll let Professor Scott explain it to you," he replied.

With that surreptitious grin, Scott began his explanation of the runestone translations. "I completed the interpretation of the five runestones. Three of them gave us a brief description of Viking settlements in Greenland and along the northeast Atlantic coast. The most intriguing translation was about a settlement that the Vikings established in 1025 AD along the coast of northern Maine. The fourth runestone described a battle be-tween the Vikings and a band of Indians in Montreal. It is the fifth tablet that has our attention. It contains clues about a huge Viking treasure hidden somewhere along the western coast of Greenland where the Baffin Sea narrows down to a thin passage between Greenland and Ellesmere Island."

"Another Viking treasure?" Elijah exclaimed. "You would think the Vikings stole every single gold coin and valuable arti-fact throughout all of Europe."

"They were quite the band of thieves," Scott quipped.

Drake continued, "The museum and I want to finance an ex-pedition to travel up to Greenland and find that treasure. This venture would be a clandestine operation and independent of the government, of course. With the artifacts we have now, the treasure would fund our museum for many years and we will be able to offer the greatest displays of Viking artifacts in the world. And while you are up there, you can recover the remains of the Viking longboat you discovered in that cavern on Baffin Island."

Simon looked at Drake suspiciously. "Robert, did I hear you say the word 'you'?"

"Unquestionably! You and Elijah are some of the best trea-sure hunters in the world and with Professor Scott and Mr. Steele to assist you, there is no way that treasure would not be found."

Elijah looked at Simon to see the disapproving expression on his face. "Not a chance, Robert. I told my wife that my trea-sure hunting days are over and I am now committed to stay home and be a good husband and father to my son. Besides we want to have a couple of more kids."

Elijah threw in his comments. "I agree with Simon. I have train tickets for this Thursday to return to California and marry a beautiful young lady I left behind. Looks like I'll be running a large cattle ranch after all."

Drake countered. "Both of you will be handsomely paid for your services."

"We both have plenty of money saved from all of our prior discoveries and besides, you cannot offer us enough money for me to give up my wonderful wife and son and Elijah his bride to be. Thanks for your offer, Robert, but we will have to decline."

"Is there anything I can say to change your mind?" The curator asked hopefully.

"Sorry, Robert, there is absolutely nothing you can say."

Simon shook hands with Drake and turned to Scott and Steele. "Well, my friends, we have shared some amazing and harrowing times together. Those memories will always be with us."

They all concurred as the four men embraced and said their goodbyes. On the way out of the door, Simon remarked. "George, if you and Jonah proceed with that mission and find the Viking treasure, we'll dub you two as the world's greatest new treasure hunters."

Scott and Steele laughed as Simon and Elijah turned and left the museum to return to Bladensburg and home to Maggie and Thomas.

EPILOGUE

Early the next morning, Simon and Elijah were preparing to leave for the Chesapeake & Ohio railway station right after Maggie had prepared them a good breakfast when young Thomas jumped into Elijah's arms. "You are not leaving Uncle Eli… are you?"

"Yes, Thomas, it's time that I have to go home."

"Who's going to read me stories?" he asked.

With tears in Elijah's eyes, he answered," Your daddy will be here to read to you. I'm going to really miss you, little buddy. Always remember that Uncle Eli loves you very much."

He handed the boy over to Simon who hugged him. "I'll read you a story tonight, Thomas."

It was a very touching scene that even brought tears into Maggie's eyes.

Elijah gave Maggie a big hug and said, "I am going back to marry Rosita and I hope we can have a little boy just like Thomas." Then he added, "A beautiful little daughter would also be great. And we'll expect the three of you to catch a train and come to visit us soon. I'm going to make a cowboy out of Simon yet."

The three of them laughed as Simon replied, "We'll be there with Thomas…I promise. I know he is going to miss his Uncle

Eli. I'm not sure when, but we will come out there sometime soon for a visit. Keep us posted."

The two men turned and left the house.

The B&O train station was a short ride which gave the two men a chance to rehash some of the incredible experiences they had shared. Elijah, remarked, "You know it was fate that brought us together during that brief skirmish over in west Tennessee during the war. If we had not called that brief overnight truce, we would have never found out we were blood cousins and never embarked on our adventures."

"That's true. I'll never forget the name of that place… Cockelberry Creek, wasn't it?"

"That's it." Elijah acknowledged.

"Do you remember that Union payroll we buried in Mississippi while we were on the run to Mexico?"

"Yes, I do. You know, we never went back to that spot, so I imagine it's still sitting there in the ground."

"I had forgotten all about that. Wonder if we could ever find it again?"

"Perhaps, that is if we're not old men in wheelchairs by then."

Simon chuckled. "I'll also never forget that little town in Louisiana where you accidently set off the tent full of gunpowder and nearly blew the town off the map."

"Yeah, I remember that, too. It's a wonder I wasn't blown up with it."

"It's lucky we even made it to Mexico with the whole Union Army chasing us."

"And it's even luckier we're even still here to talk about it."

= = = = = =

The carriage pulled up to the station entrance where both men dismounted to say their last goodbyes.

After a brief embrace, Elijah said, "Are you sure you don't want to come out to California and go panning for gold?"

"Not a chance, cousin, not a chance." Simon and Elijah laughed. "Maggie wouldn't have it. I'm sure she would turn into a mountain lion and rip my head off with her claws."

"Well, Cousin Simon, I have a train to catch, so I guess this is goodbye for now. You promise to bring Maggie and Thomas out to visit us? We may have a little playmate for Thomas by then."

"That's a promise," Simon answered.

As he watched Elijah disappear through the station door, a few final thoughts popped into his head as he quickly reminisced on some of the highlights from their previous expeditions. He smiled as he whispered to himself, "Well, I guess our treasure hunting days are finally over."

He hesitated for a moment with a few reflective memories and perhaps some slight reservations, and then he added, "I really wonder...are they?"

CPSIA information can be obtained
at www.ICGtesting.com
Printed in the USA
FFOW04n0857200218
45092030-45496FF